A

Bronwyn Scott is

2018 novella, *Dan*

RITA® finalist. She

forward to the ne

with other writers and readers about books they like

and the writing process. Readers can visit her at her

Facebook page at Bronwynwrites and at her blog at

bronwynswriting.blogspot.com

Regency Secrets

Regency Secrets:

The Cornish Dukes

BRONWYN SCOTT

MILLS & BOON

First Published in Great Britain 2022
By Mills & Boon, an imprint of HarperCollins*Publishers*
1 London Bridge Street, London, SE1 9GF

www.harpercollins.co.uk

HarperCollins*Publishers*
1st Floor, Watermarque Building,
Ringsend Road, Dublin 4, Ireland

REGENCY SECRETS: THE CORNISH DUKES © 2022
Harlequin Enterprises ULC.

The Secrets of Lord Lynford © 2019 Nikki Poppen
The Passions of Lord Trevethow © 2020 Nikki Poppen

ISBN: 978-0-263-31799-2

MIX
Paper | Supporting
responsible forestry
FSC™ C007454

THE SECRETS OF
LORD LYNFORD

For Jeff, who is very much the embodiment of the legacy of Richard Penlerick in this story and this series. Throughout his life Jeff loved others unconditionally and gave generously of himself for the betterment of this world. He left this earth the week I finished this story, and it is safe to say, our world is vastly improved because of him and the lives he touched.

Prologue

London—June 18th, 1823

Death had officially come to Mayfair. Richard Penlerick, Duke of Newlyn, and his Duchess were buried, and the funeral witnessed by the *ton*'s finest that morning in the hopes of bringing closure to the tragedy that had stunned their exalted world a week earlier: a peer— a *duke*, no less—and his wife, stabbed to death in an alley after an evening theatre performance.

Eaton Falmage, Marquess of Lynford, closed the front door behind the last of the funeral guests, wishing he could just as easily shut the door on the week's horror for the sake of those who remained within the Newlyn town house on Portland Square. But for them the journey into grief was only just beginning. Now that the pageantry of death was over, the real mourning could commence, as he and those closest to the Penlericks could give free rein to their emotions.

Eaton found that inner circle, a collection of friends

he'd known and loved since childhood, gathered in the library, a male conclave of power and strength, both of which had been lent unreservedly this week to Vennor Penlerick, the heir.

Vennor stood by the sideboard, pouring brandies, a rare blond in a room full of dark-haired men. He glanced in Eaton's direction, his eyes asking the question.

'Yes, they are all gone,' Eaton offered in low tones. 'I had the servants sweep the halls for stragglers.' He gripped Vennor's arm in a gesture of assurance. 'We are entirely alone. At last.'

The week had been nightmarish for all of them, but none so much as Vennor, and it showed. Despite his immaculate grooming, Vennor bore the unmistakable signs of strain and grief. To lose one's parents without warning, even at twenty-eight, was devastating. Vennor had been strong all week, the ideal heir, the consummate host to those who'd imposed their company and their own grief. Eaton took both the glasses. 'Come, sit, you needn't be on display with us.'

The group had gathered around the cold hearth. Someone, Inigo perhaps, had culled chairs from about the room and arranged them in one central place to accommodate the group known throughout the *ton* as 'the Cornish Dukes': heirs from four long-standing ducal families whose patriarchs had grown up together in the wilds of Cornwall and in turn so had their four sons. The bond between those fathers and their sons was legendary, as was their loyalty to one another.

That impressive connection had been on view

throughout the week for all of London to see, as if to say 'let no one doubt there are no lengths to which we would not go for one another'. The fathers had taken their leave discreetly a half an hour ago to give the four friends privacy to grieve together, as they would no doubt be doing themselves at another undisclosed location. They had lost their dear friend just as Eaton and the others had lost a man they'd looked upon as an uncle and mentor but Vennor had lost a father and a mother all in one blow.

'Thank you, Eaton. I'm glad the guests are gone.' Vennor took the brandy and slumped into the chair beside Inigo. He favoured them with a tired smile. 'I had no idea my father's friends possessed so many daughters of a certain age. I knew it would happen, of course. I just thought people might have the decency to queue up *after* a period of mourning. I don't think I can tolerate one more offer of marriage wrapped in a condolence. I can't bear to hear one more time that my father was a good man who'd want me to look to the future as soon as possible. Dear lord, some of them weren't even subtle about the fact that I'm an only child and the Penlerick nursery is a veritable ghost town in *immediate* want of infants.' There was none of the usual humour underlying Vennor's words. There was only anger today, as well there should be. The deaths of Richard Penlerick and his wife were violent, senseless crimes.

Eaton's chest tightened at the thought. *Thank God it hadn't been his own father in that alley.* The guilt of such a sentiment gripped him, as did the reality. It

hadn't been his father *yet*. One day, though, it would
be; an accident, old age, God willing *not* a crime, but
the terrible moment *would* come. Not just for him, but
for all of them. Eaton looked about his circle of friends:
dark-haired, strong-jawed Cassian, heir to the Duke
of Hayle, enigmatic Inigo, Boscastle's scion with the
pale blue Boscastle eyes handed down from generations of Boscastle Dukes. Were they thinking the same?
That this scene would be re-enacted in variation three
more times as each of them assumed the titles to which
they'd been raised? They would all lose their fathers. It
was an inherently deadly business being a duke's son.

The morbid aspect of that 'business' had Eaton stag-
gering emotionally as much as the visceral quality of
the murder had him reeling, along with the rest of the
haut ton. If a duke could be murdered in cold blood at
the theatre, no one was safe. People did not like reminders of their mortality. Rich people especially. It was a
brutal prompt that not even piles of money could stop
death. It was never a question of 'if', but merely 'when'.
Just as long as it was not yet. He wasn't ready to lose
his father. But this week had proven age was no barrier
to death, to the ending of an existence. Life was finite.

Penlerick's death had been a wake-up call to the
difficult knowledge that a man's legacies were all that
would remain of him to remind others he'd been here
on this earth. Eaton recognised that perhaps he felt
the hard truth more keenly than the others. With the
smallest amount of luck, his friends would eventually
leave behind children, heirs to their legacies, while he
would not. Ever. No amount of luck, large or small,

would change that for him. His legacies would be of the inanimate sort: schools, hospitals, places that would continue to do good long after he'd left this life. But there would be no sons or daughters to tend them. It was a truth Eaton didn't enjoy facing. There'd always been time to delay facing it, but Richard Penlerick's death proved his logic had been faulty. Not even time was on his side.

Vennor raised his glass. 'A toast, to all of you and your support this week. I could not have borne up without it.' He nodded to each of his friends. 'Here's to friendship in good times and bad.'

They all drank and Eaton fetched the decanter to refill glasses. He poured another brandy for Vennor. It was better to stay busy in order to keep his thoughts from straying too darkly. This was what he did best—taking care of the others. It was what he'd always done. How ironic that that particular talent would not be lavished on a family of his own. 'You've done your duty splendidly this week, Ven. You can get tap-hackled to the gills now if you want. There's no one to see, no one to judge.' It would do Vennor good to get shamelessly drunk and let loose the emotions he'd kept on a tight rein since the news had come, but Eaton feared Vennor had other ideas.

Vennor shook his head. 'There's too much to do. Father had important legislation in the House of Lords. It would be a shame to see it falter now. I will take up his seat as soon as it's allowed. Until then, I mean to direct things from here so we don't miss a step. It will be my tribute to him.'

Eaton exchanged a worried look with Cassian. Going to work would only suppress the grief, ignoring it instead of dealing with it. Cassian leaned forward. 'Why don't you come to Cornwall with me and rusticate a bit in Truro? It's what everyone expects and it will get those matchmaking mamas off your back for a while. As you said, there is a period of mourning to observe—it would be entirely natural if you didn't take up the seat until next year.'

'*I* expect it of me,' Vennor cut in sharply. 'Besides, there's more than legislation to look after. If I am here, I can see justice done.'

'Justice or revenge?' Eaton questioned. In his opinion, Vennor needed distance from the crime if he was going to come to terms with his loss, not to immerse himself in it. 'You needn't interfere. The Watch will handle everything.'

'And I will handle the Watch,' Vennor answered firmly. 'I will find my parents' killers and bring them to justice.'

Eaton's gaze slipped unobtrusively around the circle gauging the group's reaction. He wasn't the only one concerned about Vennor's course of action. The thugs who had mindlessly murdered Newlyn and the Duchess had left behind no clue. They might never be caught. He didn't want Vennor disappointed. At what point did serving justice become an obsession? Would Vennor recognise that point when it arrived? How could he leave his friend alone to manage his grief, knowing that Vennor would obsess? Yet how could he stay away from Cornwall much longer? He had plans, too; his school, the musical conservatory, was set to open this autumn. His *legacy* was waiting. He'd not intended to stay in London long this year. He'd come up to town with the intention of supporting Marianne Treleven's debut as a family friend, and then returning to Porth Karrek immediately. But it only took one look at Vennor's face to make the decision to stay. His friend couldn't be left on his own or he'd work himself into oblivion.

'If that's what you're going to do, we'll stay with you.' Eaton scanned the group to see heads nodding in agreement. They would all put their plans on hold for their friend.

'No, that's not necessary,' Vennor argued. 'Eaton, your conservatory needs you. You cannot spare any more time away from home. I know what a sacrifice it would be for you, don't tell me otherwise. My father would not approve. He supported your school and he'd not want it delayed on his account. You've devoted the last five months to preparing—you even cancelled your trip to Italy and I know how much that meant to you.' Vennor shook his head. 'I won't have you throw it all over just to play nursemaid.' He fixed Cassian with a stern look. 'I won't have you staying either. You can't build your Cornish pleasure garden from London. Besides, your fathers will be here. I'll hardly be alone.'

It wasn't the same, though, Eaton thought. When grief closed in, Vennor would want a friend his own age, not his father's compatriots. Yet how like Vennor to think of others first. They all had their gifts and that was Vennor's. He understood people the way Inigo understood money: intuitively. But Vennor could not be allowed to win this argument.

Eaton was about to launch his rebuttal when Inigo settled it. 'We'll be here. Father and I have banking business. We would be staying regardless to see how Parliament handles some new investment legislation.'

'Inigo can stay. I will allow that. Are you satisfied, Eaton?' Vennor smiled his gratitude and the knot of worry in Eaton's gut eased. Inigo would look after their friend with the same dedication with which he did everything else.

In the wake of the decision, silence claimed the group. Brandy glasses were nearly empty again and the business of helping Vennor take on his ducal responsibilities was settled. Eaton was aware of the mantel clock ticking, loud and insistent, a reminder that it was time to move on, that there was nothing more that could be done now. It was time for the four friends to say goodbye and go their separate ways. He and Cassian would leave early tomorrow for their journey home to Cornwall. Inigo would settle back into his London habits. Vennor would establish new routines.

Nothing would be the same.

Vennor would be invested as a duke the next time they met, with the accompanying ducal responsibilities. Vennor would marry soon and that would change the equation entirely. This was a last moment, the ending of a chapter. Part of the adventure of living, Eaton supposed, although it didn't seem very adventurous at the moment. On the contrary, it seemed sad. Something was being mourned in this very room as they took another step deeper into adulthood, another step further away from their childhood. A piece of Eaton's soul rebelled at the notion. Hadn't he lost enough already? Need he lose that, too? But it was inevitable that he would. It was the way of life for dukes. His friends would marry in time, not only Vennor. Would they all still be close even when their affections were shared with another beyond their circle? When a wife and family claimed their attentions? Their fathers had managed it. But perhaps that was because they all had wives and family in common. Eaton would likely never marry. Would that decision make him an outsider? They would never intentionally exclude him, but it might happen accidentally.

Cassian shifted in his chair, casting a quizzing glance at Eaton. *What next?* They were all looking to him. He would have to be the one to do it. Among the four of them, he was the ringleader, the adventure master. A swift bolt of memory took him, of blue skies and rolling surf, of four boys who'd spent summers combing the Cornish beaches, playing at being smugglers, or pirates, sometimes soldiers fighting the French fleet, or treasure hunting. He remembered the summer he'd found the map, the last great summer before the trajectory and expectations of his life had subtly veered. Of course, the four of them had not known it would be their last, any more than Richard Penlerick had known when he'd sat down for breakfast a week ago that he'd not see his bed that night. It had been a good summer, full of real adventure, even if they'd never found the treasure. He must have led them through every tidal cave along the Porth Karrek beaches. There'd been bonfires and camp outs, nights of star gazing and the whispered secrets of newly minted adolescence. They had all looked to him then and they were looking to him now to take the next step, to help them say good-bye.

Eaton raised his glass, searching for words against the emotion crowding his throat. They needed hope right now, they needed to know that as much as things were about to change, the things that mattered would stay the same, a piece of constancy they could cling to in a world that only promised uncertainty. He was suddenly hungry to be home at Falmage Hill, home in Porth Karrek surrounded by the familiar: his new school, his orangery, his favourite paths in the Trevaylor Woods, his science experiments, his hound, Baldor. He'd been gone too long. 'It's time, gentlemen. A last drink for the road. If there's one lesson this week has taught us, it's that life is surprising and short. We are guaranteed nothing. We already drank to the past, let us now drink to the future. Here's to our pursuits. May all of them be served through the best of our efforts in the time that we have. My friends, here's to making every minute count.' Especially when every minute was all one had.

Chapter One

Porth Karrek, Cornwall—September 1823

Every minute mattered now that the school's opening was upon them. Eaton pushed up his sleeves and gripped the oak table. At the other end, his headmaster, the renowned composer Cador Kitto, gave a nod and, with a mutual grunt, they lifted the heavy table. Around them, workmen painted and swept with feverish urgency. School began in three days and some students would arrive early to be on hand for the open house in two. The past few days it had been all hands on deck, even his—*especially* his. Eaton didn't believe in leading idly. He refused to stand back, shouting orders to others, without lending his own efforts to the project. Besides, staying busy made it possible to forget other unpleasant realisations, albeit temporarily; that Richard Penlerick was dead, life was short and there was nothing he could do about either.

They manoeuvred the table into place at the front of

the room and set it down with a relieved thud. Damn, but good oak was heavy. Eaton swiped at his brow and Cador laughed. Eaton groaned. 'Did I just smear dirt across my forehead?'

'Yes, but no matter. There are no ladies about to see you.' Cador winked.

'Just for that, you can unpack the books.' Eaton chuckled.

'Oh, no, I've got instruments to oversee.' Cador wiped his hands and nodded towards the door at the arrival of Eaton's secretary. 'Looks like you've got business to attend to.'

Eaton turned, stifling a sigh. He far preferred physical labour to the never-ending tedium of paperwork, especially when there was so much to get done, so much to forget. It was too easy for his mind to wander into difficult territory when he was doing paperwork. He found a smile; it wasn't the secretary's fault. 'What is it, Johns?'

'There's someone asking to see you, my lord.' Johns was young, hired to help with the record-keeping and correspondence at the school, and today he looked every inch of his mere twenty years. Johns shifted from foot to foot, his cheeks tinged a fading pink which Eaton didn't think was due to the exertion of the stairs. Whoever was waiting had been quite insistent.

'Do they have an appointment?' Eaton looked about for a rag to wipe his hands on. Johns would have to learn how to be a better gatekeeper.

'No, my lord.'

'Has one of the boys arrived early?' Eaton gave up

on a rag. His mind was already working through options. There were rooms ready on the third floor if needed and the cook could be called in to prepare food a day earlier than planned, although provisions weren't expected to arrive until tomorrow...

Johns cleared his throat. 'It's one of the patrons, my lord. One of the widows.' Johns's tone was urgent now. Some of the insistence that had been pressed upon him by the unexpected visitor was now being relayed.

Eaton relaxed, although he did wonder what had upset his secretary. Two of the school's patrons were wealthy widows and he couldn't imagine either of them being the source of such angst. 'Is it Mrs Penhaligon? Has she come to see that her piano is properly installed?' Austol Penhaligon's widow had donated her expensive Sébastien Érard double action keyboard piano, much to Cador's delight. The other, a Mrs Blaxland, was an extraordinarily rich woman from Truro, whom Eaton had never met. He'd assumed her age, which must be considerable, had brought about an inability to travel. Her husband, Huntingdon Blaxland, had been sixty-five when he died and that had been five years ago. She likely let her money do the travelling for her these days. Thanks to her generous donations, the boys would have the finest music instructors Cador Kitto had been able to find, acquired from the Continent on his summer honeymoon.

Soft fabric rustled behind Johns, giving Eaton his only warning before no-nonsense female tones announced, 'No, not Mrs Penhaligon, I'm afraid.' Apple-green skirts and shiny chestnut hair swept past Johns

with an imperious air that smelled of peach orchards
and vanilla, the very best and last of summer. 'I'm
Eliza Blaxland.' She ran a gloved hand along the surface of the oak table, collecting dust on the pristine
tip of one finger. 'And you, Lord Lynford, have some
accounting to do.'

Eaton gave her an assessing stare. *This* haughty vi-
rago was Eliza Blaxland? What had the elderly mining
magnate been doing with a woman like her? She was
no frail grey-haired widow, practising philanthropy
from her armchair. This was an elegant, sophisticated
woman in her early thirties with decades of life and fire
still left to her, a woman who valued being in control.
If so, she'd have to adjust. He was more than happy to
take her money for the school, but not her orders. He
was the Marquess of Lynford and his deference was
given sparingly. He could not be bought, nor could he
be intimidated. 'Accounting, Mrs Blaxland? In what
way? I was unaware we had an appointment, let alone
any accounting to do.' He was usually the one who did
the intimidating. How interesting that she thought the
interaction might go differently. She needed to learn
that her cheques did not allow her carte blanche in the
school and that included showing up two days early
for the open house.

She was not daunted by his cool reception. Instead,
she returned his assessing stare with one of her own,
making him acutely aware that she was entirely his
antithesis. While he stood before her sans waistcoat,
jacket and cravat, shirtsleeves wrinkled and rolled with
a belatedly remembered smudge of dirt on his forehead,

she was all elegant summer perfection in her apple-green walking ensemble of India muslin, matched head to toe from the brim of her green-crepe chapeau Lyonnaise to the peeping toes of her green half-boots. 'I disagree. You are two days from opening and this place is a madhouse.' She held up the dusty finger of her glove in reminder. 'My money did not pay for chaos.'

Eaton summoned up a smile from his repertoire, the one known for successfully impressing older, more conservative women who occasionally found his love of adventure a tad too liberal—until they tried it for themselves. 'I assure you, all will be in order for the open house.' She was not convinced. Her gaze roved about the room, taking in the painters, the movers, the sweepers, casting doubt and disappointment wherever her eyes landed. Eaton grimaced. He needed to get her out of this room. There were plenty of spaces that were finished. It was too bad she hadn't found him in one of those. 'Might I offer you a tour, Mrs Blaxland?' The woman was likely to poke her nose into all the rooms on her own—at least this way he could keep an eye on her. He could control a tour, although it would cost him an hour of work to squire her around. Still, better an hour of work lost than a lucrative patron. Disappointed patrons often bred other disappointed patrons. 'On our tour, we can discuss whatever it is you're doing here.' It was a subtle reminder that she was the one in the wrong, the one who'd shown up uninvited.

He gestured to Cade, giving her no chance to refuse. 'Let's start with an introduction to our headmas-

ter, Cador Kitto, lately from Vienna. He's composed
at the Hapsburg court.'

Cade, with his wavy blond locks and Continen-
tal élan, bowed over her gloved hand with a courtly
aplomb that made Eaton envious of the man's slender
elegance. 'A pleasure to meet you at last, Mrs Blaxland.
Our students will benefit greatly from your patronage.'
A little dose of Cade could go a long way in smoothing ruffled feathers—at least that was what Eaton was
hoping for, particularly when he didn't know what had
ruffled her feathers in the first place.

'What you describe as chaos, Mrs Blaxland, I consider progress. Allow me to show you.' They left Cade
and the busyness of the classroom behind. He toured
her through the students' rooms on the third floor,
showing her chambers with neatly made beds, braided
rugs, dust-free wardrobes and bright white curtains
hanging at the windows. The rooms smelled of lemon
polish and linseed oil. 'Mr Kitto's wife designed the
dorms,' Eaton explained, making no effort to hide his
pride. 'She believes the homelier the place feels, the
more comfortable the boys will be here.'

'And the less likely they will be to leave,' Mrs Blaxland translated in more blunt terms. 'Tell me, how is
enrolment? Do we have enough boys to fill these chambers?'

Eaton shut the last door behind them and directed
her back towards the staircase. 'We have two-thirds of
the rooms accounted for, which I think is excellent for
a first semester.' Twenty-one boys ranging in age from
seven to fourteen would be arriving the day after the

open house. 'Once word spreads regarding the quality of student and the superiority of musical education we offer at the Cornish Academy, we will reach capacity soon enough,' he assured her, but her sharp green eyes met his assurances with questions.

'Do you have quality students?' she asked pointedly. 'I think the challenge of such a school is not the idea of it, but the location, as I've mentioned before in correspondence. Why would a person of any talent want to travel to the wilds of Cornwall for a musical education when one could be in London? Or go abroad? I fear those who have choices will not choose the academy at Porth Karrek.'

She was bold-tongued, her comments blunt and bordering on rude. Perhaps that was simply how it was in business circles where money mattered more than manners. Eaton chose to be impressed with her analysis rather than offended by the implication that the academy would only be capable of drawing mediocre students.

'The talent you seek will come if you and the other patrons tell them to. Quality enrolment is all of our obligation.' Richard Penlerick had been adamant on that issue. He'd been promoting the academy in London just days before the murder. 'One cannot simply throw money at a project and expect that to be enough to ensure success.' The words came out harshly against the sudden tightness of Eaton's throat, but he wouldn't apologise for them. If Eliza Blaxland took his response as a scolding, then so be it. He wasn't entirely sure he didn't mean it as one. He was the son and heir of a wealthy family. If it had only been about money, he could easily have bankrolled the school entirely by himself. He didn't need patrons' funds the way a struggling orphanage in St Giles did. He needed the names and reputations behind the funds.

Eaton cleared his throat and offered Richard Penlerick's often-voiced sentiment. 'The quality of our students will depend on the quality of our patrons. That is why I sought you out in particular. You are well known in Cornish circles for your appreciation of education.' Even if those circles had failed to convey how young she was.

At the bottom of the stairs he showed her into the drawing room where the Sébastien Érard piano stood in pride of place. 'This is where our recitals will be held. Mr Kitto will perform at the open house, of course.' He smiled, reminding her he'd done his part in securing a well-known musician for headmaster, one with a name that would draw talented students.

He allowed her to appraise the Sébastien Érard with her sharp eyes before he got to the heart of the matter. 'Surely all of this checking up could have been handled at the open house. Why have you really come, Mrs Blaxland?' Did she have a student she was hoping to get admitted? Did she have an instructor who needed to be hired? Whoever they were, they would have to earn their place here, no matter how much money she donated. Kitto wanted only the best. They wouldn't attract the best if they took in just anyone.

She gave him a polite smile he did not mistake for friendliness, although it did serve to warm him none the less. 'I have found in the years of running my late husband's mines that scheduled appointments can often result in misleading impressions. When one arrives unannounced, one sees a clearer representation of the truth.' She was already a fortress of perfection in her dress and in her speech, but in her directness she was nigh on impenetrable. Eaton felt the urge to penetrate that directness, to lay siege to its walls.

'You mean an ambush, Mrs Blaxland?' Sparring with her was quite a warming exercise indeed. A part of him that had been dormant since returning from London was waking up.

'An ambush assumes someone can be taken by surprise, that someone lets his guard down,' she countered smoothly. 'If one is always prepared, one cannot be caught unawares.'

When was the last time Eliza Blaxland had been taken unawares? From her cool façade, he would guess it had been a while, if ever. It was hard to imagine anyone got anything past her. Eaton would take that as a challenge—not that he wanted to take advantage, but he would like to surprise her, just to prove to her that it could be done. How would she react when things were out of her control?

He studied the flawless perfection of her face, its smooth contours with its elegantly set nose, green eyes and that mouth—that gorgeous pink mouth with its full, kissable lower lip. His gaze lingered there while his thoughts drifted. What would bring a crease to those perfect features? What might fluster her well-ordered world? Had old Huntingdon Blaxland ever flustered her, aside, perhaps, from dying? Would a kiss be enough to offset that world? She was a widow, after all. He could presume she'd been kissed before. Would she like to be kissed again? He found he would like to pursue that course of action. Between Richard Penlerick's death and the school, it had been a while since he'd felt a spark of interest.

They were hardly the thoughts one ought to have about a wealthy patroness, yet when the patroness was so aloofly, coolly attractive, it seemed a natural progression of thought to wonder, what if? They returned to the main hall, the front door just feet away, providing a less-than-subtle opportunity to bid Mrs Blaxland farewell and get on with his day. 'If there's nothing else, I'll leave you here. As you have already ascertained, there's much to be done.'

'There is one more thing.' She gave him another long perusing stare with those intelligent eyes. 'I thought you'd be older. I was unaware Bude's heir was so...young.' She was implying that perhaps he might not be up to the task of overseeing a school, that a man of his age and station was better suited to the frivolous pursuits of London.

'Twenty-eight is young?' he queried with a sardonic cock of a dark brow. It was an odd remark coming from a woman who couldn't be more than thirty-three, but time and age were different for females. 'It's been some time since anyone has thought of me as young. Good day, Mrs Blaxland. I will look forward to seeing you at the reception.' He gave her a small bow in farewell. 'I assure you that you needn't worry. I am in my prime.' He'd been unable to resist the final remark. Intuition suggested that no one teased Mrs Blaxland and someone ought to. People didn't build impregnable fortresses around themselves without reason. He was intrigued as to what her reason might be.

'You most certainly are,' she acknowledged with a slight, indifferent nod of her head, but beneath that cool exterior, something akin to interest sizzled and flared in her gaze before it was snuffed out by practice and perhaps practicality. But it was too late. Eaton smiled over his little victory. She'd already given herself away. Eliza Blaxland wasn't as unaffected or as distant as she appeared.

Chapter Two

It had been a long time since she'd been surprised—not since the day Huntingdon had left for the office and never returned. Five years, eight months and three weeks, to be precise. Eliza sat back against the leather squabs of her coach and let out a deep sigh. In the intervening years, she'd become used to being the one doing the surprising; she'd had to if she meant to keep the shareholders on their toes. But Eaton Falmage, Marquess of Lynford, heir to the ducal seat of Bude, had done all the surprising this afternoon. The ambush had been her idea, hers to control, but she'd not been prepared for *him*. Eliza reached for her fan. From the first glance of his dark eyes, his heat had nearly incinerated her glacial cool.

Years of practice had made her confident in the belief that her skills would rise to any challenge, that her icy façade could not be cracked, that she was impervious to the powers of men. Lynford had challenged her today, though, not only as a patron, but as a woman.

The former, she could deal with. Patronage was simply one of many business arrangements she conducted. The latter, however, well…that was different. She hadn't been a woman—a real woman with real feelings and affections—since the day her husband died. For her daughter's sake and her own sake, she couldn't afford to indulge such a fancy.

When men looked at her, they saw a female facsimile—one that dressed elegantly, spoke with cultured tones, and danced divinely; one they often sought to possess—but the illusion fell away when she sat across from them at the boardroom table and delivered her verdicts in those cultured tones. Some men called her a snake in the grass, a viper waiting to strike, others called her a Siren, luring men to smash themselves against the icy granite of her façade. But today, Lynford had been formidable, a veritable Odysseus, undaunted by her surprise visit and undaunted by her.

She wished she could say the same. Eliza plied the fan a little faster. He was not only younger than she'd anticipated, he was also younger than *her* by five years. He was taller, broader, endowed with dark eyes that looked into a person's gaze and long, powerful legs. Oh, how she loved a good pair of legs on a man and his had been on blatant display with no coats to hide them. In fact, his tight breeches and open-necked shirt had hidden nothing. He'd been in utter, unmistakable déshabillé, yet he'd not once apologised for his appearance or attempted to cover it up. The primal woman in her, so rarely unleashed, had rattled the bars of her cage, thrilling at the masculinity on show, a reminder that she wasn't dead after all. It was an uncomfortable revelation.

Eliza closed her eyes. It had been so long since she'd felt anything akin to desire, or its milder counterpart, attraction. What a shock to discover it after five years of sexless living where she didn't dare act either too much of a man or too much like a woman for fear she would be ridiculed for overstepping herself or taken advantage of for *being* herself. But what a most inopportune time for that discovery. She would have preferred Lynford to be a man nearing middle age, bearing a paunch at his stomach and silver at his temples with a conservative, tired air about him. She knew how to manage those men.

Her husband had been such a man, thirty-seven years older than she when they wed. Those men populated the Blaxland Mining Corporation board of shareholders, but Lynford exuded alertness, energy, a fresh boldness. He thought himself infallible and perhaps rightly so. He was a duke's son. He was used to asserting himself, used to ordering the world according to his desire. He was not a businessman, a man like her husband had been, who limited the scope of his world to balance sheets. And Lynford, unlike her husband, was most definitely in his prime.

She had no such experience with a man like that: a man who looked at women and openly admired their beauty, a man who didn't patronise, a man who matched her directness with his own. Nor could she allow herself to acquire such an experience.

The one flicker of attraction she'd felt today had

been nice in its own way, a reminder that she was more than a moneymaking automaton, but she could not fan it into anything resembling a flame. She had a daughter to raise and mines to run, her husband's legacy to preserve so that her daughter would never know want and penury as she had simply because she'd been born female. Such pursuits did not leave room for passion. Such a task required that she walk a tightrope. One false step and all she'd worked for and all she envisioned for the future could be so easily lost.

Neither did such a pursuit serve her as a patron for the school. She hoped by donating generously to his school, in return, Lynford would support her bid for establishing schools for children in the villages up and down the coast wherever there was a Blaxland mine. To mix business with fleeting pleasure could jeopardise that connection.

Hence the reason for her visit today—to see if Lynford was worth the investment. Could he get the job done, or was he another lazy dilettante? She wanted to see that everything was well in hand for the opening reception. She would do her part to make sure the conservatory succeeded. Her own plans depended on it, as did keeping her own reputation intact. The trust of her shareholders was essential now as the Porth Karrek mine prepared for expansion. She'd learned early on after taking the reins of her husband's business that one could never have too many friends, but a woman could have too many lovers—even just a single lover was often one lover too many. A misguided affair at this juncture could cost her everything, just as it had her mother, a widow left with a daughter and a fortune and no sense about how to manage the latter.

The outcome had been obvious: her mother and her money had been soon parted thanks to an affair that had blinded her to the incompetence of her lover. Eliza had been fourteen when that had happened and she'd vowed she would never put her heart above money. Nor would she put herself in a position where money wasn't readily available. She'd set out the next day to learn all she could about managing funds, starting with the bookkeeper for the family's mine. Knowledge was power. She believed that education could keep the wolf from the door and it could buy her independence so that she needn't rely singularly on a marriage to save her. There were too many women like her mother who hadn't a clue how to manage their own freedom, who needed men. Eliza was determined to avoid her mother's mistakes. This time, for this woman, Eliza vowed it would be different. She was far too astute to fall prey to the charms of a handsome lord.

Two days later, the Academy Open House

This time, it would be different. Eliza entered the conservatory's drawing room with that mantra firmly entrenched in her mind. Tonight, she would be ready for the oh-so-attractive Eaton Falmage. His good looks and confident manner would not catch her by surprise. She knew what to expect now and this time they wouldn't be alone—a point emphasised as soon as she arrived. The room was practically a crush and a very well-dressed one at that, with men in dark evening clothes and women in silks populating every corner of the grand salon. It was a far more robust turnout for the academy's opening than she'd anticipated. This was no mere gathering of a board of directors and a few patrons. But then, perhaps the outstanding attendance stood to reason. When a duke's heir gave a party, everyone wanted an invitation.

Eliza unfurled her fan and began to stroll about the room, looking purposeful. No one need pity her aloneness. She'd made an art of it. Over the years, she'd become accustomed to attending events on her own and others had become accustomed to it, too. She arrived alone, she left alone. She'd learned not to be afraid of her own company. She actually rather enjoyed it. There was no conversation to worry over, no egos to flatter or polite compliments to muster. She could survey her surroundings at leisure, study her options and make her own choices as to how she spent her time and who she spent it with. At the moment she wanted to spend that time with Lynford. Congratulations were in order. A private smile skimmed her lips in satisfaction as she assessed her surroundings. Lynford had succeeded against what had looked like overwhelming odds. One would never guess that two days ago the place had been in varying states of chaos.

Eliza scanned the room, her gaze glancing over the masculine decor done to perfection in shades of muted teal and beige against a backdrop of walnut panelling and chair rail that ran the perimeter, interrupted only by a bank of French doors opening to the gardens beyond where paper lanterns winked. She made a mental note of the gardens—those gardens might provide a convenient escape from the crowd should she need it.

Her gaze hurried on, still seeking as it brushed over the multi-armed brass chandelier at the ceiling, the coveted Sébastien Érard, lid raised, at the front of the room—neither item enough to halt her rampant gaze. These were not the things she was looking for. She'd nearly completed her visual circuit of the room when she found him at last, standing at the fireplace, just feet from the Sébastien Érard. It was time to test her hypothesis.

The fan in her hand halted its oscillation, her mind flooding with a certain sense of satisfaction. *He* was what she'd been looking for. Lynford stood in profile, talking with a group of men, all dressed alike in dark evening clothes, yet he was no more like them than the sun was like the moon. She knew instantly her mantra was wrong. This time was *not* going to be different after all, unless one counted the fact that Lynford was fully clothed. He was no less handsome for the more formal attire. Eliza began to ply her fan in earnest.

His dark, tangled curls were tamed tonight, carefully styled into compliance, perhaps painstakingly so given the extent of their unruliness the other day. His jaw was smooth-shaven, setting off the strong planes of his face, the wide, almost simian flare of his nose, the broad, high sweep of his cheekbones beneath his dark eyes; in his face, the elegant classical construction was unabashedly at war with the harsh masculinity of his primeval ancestors. In evening clothes, the result was devastating. He stood out, a powerful stallion among the herd, a man born to lead no matter what his age.

Tonight, authority's mantle sat comfortably on his broad shoulders, not an ounce of that breadth fabricated, even if the rest of his body gave the impression of wanting to be out of doors tramping the moors and cliffs of Porth Karrek. His was not an indoor physique. Not that she should be assessing such things. Her attendance at the conservatory's opening reception tonight was all business and business did not mix with pleasure. *Ever*. Hadn't her experience with Miles Detford taught her that much? She had too much to keep her busy between the mines and the school. She could not allow herself to be distracted with useless speculation about the Marquess of Lynford. She certainly could not allow herself to be caught staring. He might interpret a stare as interest.

Too late. She didn't look away soon enough. Lynford caught her gaze and returned it with a wide smile, broad like his shoulders and just as genuine, the kind one gives when one is truly pleased to see someone. That worried her. After their last visit, why would he be pleased to see her? She watched in horrified fascination as he excused himself from the group gathered at the fireplace and moved towards her. There was no escaping; she was well and truly flushed out. What could he possibly want? She should be annoyed by the thought that he'd demand anything of her, but there was only intrigue where annoyance ought to be—another reminder that she was very much alive and very much a woman.

He snared two glasses of champagne from a passing tray as he approached. 'Mrs Blaxland, it's so good to see you.' He offered her a glass, his smile unwavering. 'I trust everything meets with your approval. No dust on the tables. Your gloves will be spared this evening.' She had the sensation that Lynford was laughing at her, that there was a private jest, some innuendo involved.

'I've only just arrived.' Her cool tone insinuated there was still time to be disappointed. Would he let her have the lie? Or would he make her accountable for the shameful truth: that she'd been there long enough to take notice of things and the only thing she'd noticed was him? Eliza sipped her champagne, thankful to have something to do other than admit he'd trapped all her attention, that for all her earlier concern about the state of the school, she'd given the issue only the smallest fraction of her attention, while her gaze had raced around the room, gliding over the details in its hurry to find him. Even in a room full of men, all clad similarly, he'd managed to stand out, managed to capture her eye *and* her thoughts to the exclusion of all else. That was a dangerous position to be in. It made her vulnerable. It was time to go on the offensive.

'Whatever you want from me, you must want it badly, given your champagne and your smiles, Lord Lynford. So, let's have it.' She gave him a smile of her own, one full of directness.

'Ah, you like champagne. Duly noted. I shall make a note.' He smiled wickedly. Lynford *liked* the edge. She'd not expected that. She'd meant for it to be off-putting, but instead a spark leapt in his dark eyes.

'What makes you think I want anything other than your approval?' he drawled.

She laughed at that. 'My approval or my acquiescence? You will not get the latter. If you are looking for it, then you misunderstood my concerns the other day. I was worried you might not finish your preparations in time, *not* that I wanted you to fail.' Eliza tapped his sleeve with her fan. 'I have every hope this school will succeed. I do not sign on to doomed ventures.' True, she had wondered if he could do it, if he could bring everything together in time. But she'd not wanted him to fail. Failure did not suit her purpose. 'This school may be the touchstone. Perhaps people will see the value in other types of schools. I've been contemplating opening grammar schools for my miners' children so that they might grow up with the opportunity to develop a broader range of skills than their parents.' She paused here, wondering briefly if she should go on. Not everyone shared her views, not even her own board. 'And with those skills, have more choices about how to make their living.'

Lynford's eyes were two thoughtful dark stars. For a moment, she feared she'd offended him. What would a ducal heir think about empowering miners with education? Would he even understand the necessity? Perhaps she'd overplayed her hand? But Lynford nodded and smiled, his dark gaze intent. 'I would enjoy speaking about the subject further, Mrs Blaxland.' He clinked his glass against hers. 'Here's to successful ventures in all their forms. Speaking of which, you might be able to aid our cause tonight.'

Ah, there it was. The real reason for his approach. Eliza stiffened in anticipation. Her instincts had not been wrong. He did want something, but she owed him. If he hadn't called her out on her lie, she couldn't call him out on his. 'I was hoping you would say a few words tonight as one of our most generous donors.'

A speech? She sipped her champagne, her mouth suddenly dry despite the cool liquid. He wanted *her* to make a speech? Of all the cruel and unusual punishments she could think of, this was by far the worst. 'A speech?' She choked on the idea.

'It's hardly Pericles' Funeral Oration, Mrs Blaxland, just a few words. Something like, welcome to the school, we are so excited to begin this venture, etcetera, and then lead in to an introduction of Mr Kitto, who will perform afterwards.' *And* he wanted her to introduce the famous Mr Kitto, a man she'd briefly met once? It was as if Lynford had looked into her soul and pulled out her worst fear. She could face down a boardroom full of stockholders, she could stand her ground against men who didn't think a woman could do successful business in their world, but speaking before a crowd without preparation was entirely different. There would be no heat of the moment guiding the interaction. A speech was a planned, formal affair. People would be staring at her—*a lot* of people—and they would be judging every word, every gesture. She'd spent years earning the right *not* to be judged.

'You *are* prepared for such a contingency, aren't you?' Lynford solicited. 'Surely, as our largest benefactor, you've anticipated such a request? I have it on good authority that preparation is the best protection against surprise.'

There was an echo of their previous interaction in his words and she knew: this was tit for tat.

This was an ambush.

good humour, the gentle question of the man you're
married to—
There was no copy of that presence in the
his world, and he knew he was wrong ….

Chapter Three

Eliza studied Lynford, seeing his gambit all too clearly
now. 'Is this revenge, Lord Lynford?'

He grinned, mischief lighting his eyes. 'This is just
business, Mrs Blaxland. Something akin to unplanned
visits, I am sure you understand.' He relieved her of her
empty glass and deposited it on a passing tray with his
before offering his arm. 'I would like to introduce you
to a few of the board members, some of our parents
whose sons will perform tonight and our other donors.'

'You need a hostess,' Eliza quickly deduced. It was
a large request that looked much smaller when compared to giving a speech. Perhaps he'd planned it that
way, knowing she'd be less likely to refuse. She'd often
used that same strategy with her shareholders when
asking for an approval of funds.

'Mr Kitto's wife, Rosenwyn, was to play hostess,
but she's indisposed,' Lynford explained with a melt-
ing smile. 'These events need a woman's presence to
smooth out conversations between strangers.' She'd

not meant to draw attention to herself tonight. Playing hostess and making a speech would put her at the centre of the festivities. Still, she could turn this to her benefit. His introductions would pave the way for other discussions she wanted to have later about schools for the miners' children. She caught sight of Cador Kitto's blond head, a trail of students behind him with instruments, and her pulse sped up. It was almost time for the programme, almost time for her speech.

She was going to make Lynford pay for this.

'Shall we?' Lynford steered her towards the front of the room where the new students and Kitto were settling into position.

'Are you sure there isn't someone else who should speak?' She tried to avoid it one last time. 'Perhaps Mr Burke?' He'd been a pleasant, well-spoken man in the last group they'd visited and another generous benefactor of the school.

Lynford shook his head and gave her one of his disarming smiles. He'd been using them liberally tonight with the guests, but that made them no less effective. 'No, I want *you* to do it.' She knew what that meant: an ambush for an ambush. He covered her gloved hand where it lay on his sleeve and gave it a conspiratorial squeeze. 'You will do wonderfully.' He leaned in, giving her a teasing whiff of clean, autumn male, the woodsy scent of English oak mixed with the sweeter note of hazelnut. Good lord, that scent was intoxicating. It reminded her of strength, of bonfires beneath starry skies when she was younger, when she didn't carry the world on her shoulders, when autumn was a time to laugh and dream. His voice was a husky whisper at her ear, a tone better reserved for the bedroom. 'I have every confidence in you. You are not a woman who knows how to fail, Mrs Blaxland.' Then he slipped away from her, his long strides taking him to the front of the room, the very presence of him compelling people to quiet their conversations, to find a seat and anticipate what came next.

She envied him his confidence, the ease with which it was assumed whereas hers was a hard-earned façade; once acquired, she had dared not lay it down for fear she might never be able to pick it up again. This was not the life Huntingdon had imagined for her, but this was the life she had, the life she'd chosen out of necessity.

At twenty-eight, she'd gone from running their home to running a mining empire, from sponsoring parties to sponsoring schools and other educational causes. If there was one thing the past five years had taught her, it was that education was everything. She'd transitioned into her husband's position only because she'd had the skills to do it. She could read, she could write, she could do sums, she could keep a ledger and myriad other things. She could think critically and she'd spent her marriage listening, learning and planning ahead against the inevitable: an eighteen-year-old bride would doubtless outlive her fifty-five-year-old husband. The majority of her life would be spent in widowhood. The only question was when it would happen and what she'd do about it.

That foresight had stood her in good stead. If this life was not the one imagined for her, it was a far better one than what she would have had. Without those skills, she would have been passed from relative to relative; her husband's legacy, his mines and her daughter Sophie's inheritance would have been taken out of her hands and put into the care of an apathetic male relative. She'd seen it happen to women around her, women like her mother, who lost everything when their husbands died, even the very control of their own lives. When Huntingdon had died, she'd reaffirmed her vow that would not happen to her. She would secure her freedom at all costs and her daughter's, too. Now that she had, she would see to it that others had the opportunity to develop the same skills.

Lynford finished speaking and gestured that she should come forward. She rose and smoothed her skirts, her head high. She wouldn't let anyone see how this unnerved her. Lynford was right. She didn't know how to fail. She knew how to fight. That gave them something in common. He no more wanted to see her fail in this speech than she'd wanted him to fail in having the school ready. It occurred to her, as she stood before the guests, that she and Lynford were compatriots whether they wanted to be or not. Philanthropy, like politics, made for strange bedfellows indeed.

She was magnificent. Eaton listened to Eliza Blaxland address the guests, her cultured tones confident and strong. He watched her, looking for little tells that hinted at her nerves and finding none. Still, he stood on guard, feeling protective, as if he had the right to defend her, to intervene if she faltered. But she didn't falter. He suspected she didn't know how. It was not in her nature. Eliza Blaxland was all cool competence in her dark blue silk and pearls, her shiny chestnut hair dressed simply, elegantly, in a braid that coiled at the nape of her neck. If he hadn't seen the initial flicker of uncertainty in her eyes when he'd asked her, he never would have known she didn't welcome such opportunities.

What else didn't he know about her? What he thought he knew of her up until two days ago had been entirely wrong. An *old* rich woman, she was not. He found the prospect of righting those misnomers intriguing. He'd known widows before—women with a sharp worldliness to them—but they'd not got under his skin so quickly. Or ever. Who was Eliza Blaxland? Was she truly all cool smiles and sharp eyes, or did something hotter burn beneath that smooth, uncrackable façade, waiting for a reason to come out?

She was introducing Cade now, taking the opportunity to cede the room's attention to the school's headmaster and his musicians. When the applause began, she attempted to slip away to the gardens. If Eaton hadn't been watching, he would have missed her. Seeing her go only made him impatient to follow her out. But it would be bad form to leave before Cade got the little concert underway. Was she counting on that? Was she hoping to slip away before he could find her? Did she think to hide from him, or was this an invitation to join her? Perhaps she wanted him to follow?

Eaton took the first chance he had to drift towards the French doors and then fade unnoticed into the gardens, aware he might be too late. An initial sweep of the garden suggested he was right, but a second survey revealed her, sitting on a stone bench, face tilted to the night sky in lovely profile. 'Are you avoiding me or waiting for me?' Eaton approached from behind, his voice low. 'I thought for a moment you might have played Cinderella and slipped away before I could follow. What are you doing out here?' It was a bold question, one that demanded a direct answer in return. But why not be bold? She was not afraid of him. Even now, alone in the garden, her widowhood protected her reputation and granted her the freedom to respond as she liked.

With that freedom, she might take a lover. Had she? Would she? Did she have a lover now? A man who knew the truth behind her façade, who was allowed the luxury of seeing her without her cool armour. Eaton found the prospect disappointing. He didn't want Mrs Blaxland to belong to someone else. He didn't want someone else to know what he did not. There was that sense of exigence again, the same urgency he'd felt in the drawing room while watching her slip away. Wanting to know her, to obtain information about her had escalated from merely acquiring facts to something bordering on obsession. He wanted to acquire her. She would be a delicious distraction from the darkness that had dogged his steps since Penlerick's funeral. Perhaps she would be someone who could bring him back to life, someone who could hold his grief at bay.

It would not be the first time he'd taken a lover for such a purpose. His own lovers were women of the world who enjoyed time with him until it suited them both to move on to new experiences, new adventures. But it was the first time he'd wanted to do so with such covetousness. It was not the usual reaction he generally had towards his lovers. The intensity of that emotion must have showed in his gaze for in the next moment, Eliza Blaxland suddenly rose and made excuses to leave with far less fluency than she'd delivered her speech. 'I ought to go, it's getting late.'

Was she looking for an invitation to stay? It didn't sound like a question. It sounded like a decision. He hadn't believed she'd be a runner, but she showed every sign of wanting to do just that. How interesting. If she wasn't running from him, that only left the option of running from herself. Was she running from her reaction to the attraction that simmered between them? Did this flame that sparked between them unnerve her? How intriguing that the unflappable Mrs Blaxland could be unnerved by the nascent overtures of a flirtation when barging in on a man unannounced hadn't flustered her at all. But she'd been in control then. She'd been the one to do the barging.

'Leave? Surely you don't mean to return to Truro tonight?' The protectiveness he'd felt in the grand salon surged again. He didn't like the thought of her out on the dark Cornish roads. It was three hours on the road in daylight between Truro and Porth Karrek. A man could do the trip in a day on horseback, but it was a long day and a lonely one. Cornwall was full of wide, empty spaces, especially when one's wheel or axle gave out. She'd be miles from any help if there was need.

'I have rooms at the inn by the harbour. I need to visit one of my mines early tomorrow and then return to Truro. I've been gone from home for three days already and I am eager to return. Thank you for the evening.' Such eagerness prompted the question of who or what was waiting for her? A lover? Was she already otherwise engaged? Was that the reason she was so fluttery now? Covetousness flared alongside his protectiveness.

'Perhaps I shall see you in Truro. I often have business there.' Eaton thought he might find a little more business in Truro. Cassian was in Truro, working on plans for his amusement gardens. Perhaps a visit was in order once the term started here and Cade no longer needed him. 'Or should I be expecting any more surprise inspections?'

Her fan tapped his sleeve. 'They wouldn't be surprises if you expected them, my lord.'

'Call me Eaton, please. There's no need to stand on ceremony.' He made the bold offer spontaneously, his earlier urgency surging to the fore once more. He did not want to be 'my lord' or 'Lord Lynford' with her; he wanted to be something more intimate, more personal, something that would separate him from any other who attempted to claim her attentions. It was the fanciful wish of a schoolboy with a crush. He reached for her hand, bending over it. 'You were a delightful hostess tonight, surely you've earned the right to address me more informally.' He could count on one hand the people who had that right: Cassian, Inigo, Vennor, their fathers, of course. He didn't need both hands for that count now. He pushed back the grief that managed to edge its way to the surface at the oddest times and in the oddest ways.

'I was pleased to be of service. I hope the term begins splendidly. I'll be looking forward to Mr Kitto's reports on the students' progress. If weather permits, I might make the journey for the Christmas concert.'

He doubted her on both accounts. 'Don't lie to me, Mrs Blaxland. You did not want to give that speech tonight and the weather in December is too questionable.'

'I was being polite.' She withdrew her hand in a deliberate gesture.

'I prefer you be honest.' Eaton felt disappointed at the prospect of her leaving. How could he unravel her mysteries if she was three hours away? Already he was devising reasons why he might call her back. He might need her counsel on the school, for instance; they might want to discuss her own schools in person rather than through correspondence and, when that was done, he might take her truffle hunting in the Trevaylor Woods. Eaton leaned close, breathing in the peach-and-vanilla summer scent of her, his mouth near her ear as if imparting a secret. 'And in the spirit of being honest, Eliza, I find you to be a complete revelation.'

'I assure you, I am quite ordinary.' But the words pleased her. He heard her breath catch despite her cool response and she hadn't corrected him on the use of her first name, proof that this encounter, this response, was not ordinary for her, that *he* was not ordinary to her.

'Then we must agree to disagree since I find nothing plain about you.' Eaton let his gaze hold her eyes, let her see the interest she raised in him. They were both experienced adults. They needn't play coy games. He would be honest, too. He did not want the conversation to end. 'I've been wrong about you from the start. I thought you'd be older.' He gave a low chuckle. 'It seems we have that mistake in common.'

'My husband was considerably older than I. It is a common assumption.'

'If you'd not come to the open house, I might never have known.'

'What difference did my age make when we corresponded about the school? What difference did my age make to my donations? My age is of no import.'

'Huntingdon Blaxland was sixty-five when he died.' Eaton remembered his father noting it one morning over breakfast and newspapers. His father had commented that Blaxland's death would leave a gap in the mining industry, a power vacuum. Eaton had assumed his widow was of a commensurate age. Never had he imagined Blaxland's widow was in her thirties.

'Yes, and he was fifty-five when we married. I was his second wife, of course, his first having died a few years before.' Perhaps that was why he'd thought Mrs Blaxland would be older. He'd not realised the first wife had passed; he would have been a child, after all. It was hardly the sort of news an adolescent paid attention to, even if he hadn't been recovering from the throes of his own illness. But now, it was like finding a pearl in an oyster and Eaton filed the precious knowledge away along with the champagne. It was the most personal piece of information she'd offered. His collection of facts was growing: she was a widow, a second wife; she was confident, strong, stubborn and direct; she was young, *attractive*; she liked to be in control.

She was asserting that desire now, perhaps sensing the conversation was fast slipping beyond her ability to command it. 'I fail to see what consequence any of this holds. It doesn't matter.' But it did. She wasn't as sure of herself as she wanted him to believe. Did she think he didn't see the flutter of her pulse in the lantern-lit darkness, or the way her eyes met his and then slid away? She wanted to know, as much as he did, what it would be like if they acted on the spark that jumped between them when they argued, when they challenged one another, when they were merely in the same room together. He'd been aware of her tonight long before he'd gone to her. He'd been aware, too, that she'd been looking for him the moment she'd arrived.

What could it hurt to find out? She lived miles away and was hardly in the habit of haring down to Porth Karrek.

'It *does* matter.' He slipped his hand behind her neck, drawing her close, letting his gaze linger, letting the proximity of his body signal his intentions as he murmured, 'I am not in the habit of kissing grand-mothers.'

'And I am not in the habit of—'

Eaton didn't let her finish. He captured her lips, sealing her rejoinder with his mouth. They could discuss her habits—or lack of them—later.

Chapter Four

Apparently, she was *not* in the habit of completing her sentences. She certainly wouldn't be capable of doing so now. All her mind could focus on was that *he was kissing her.* The realisation rocketed through Eliza, a bolt of white-hot awareness. There wasn't a single part of her that wasn't aware of him—the sweet, sharp autumn scent of him in her nostrils, the feel of his touch on the bare skin at her neck, the press of his mouth against hers—all combining to stir her to life, perhaps for the first time.

His tongue teased hers; a slow, languorous flirt confident of its reception. His hand adjusted its position at her neck, tilting her mouth, deepening his access to her until she gave a little moan. She had never been kissed like this, as if the kiss was a seduction within itself, as if every nuance of mouth and tongue and lips communicated a private message of desire designed just for her. She felt herself wanting to give over; there was no question of resistance, no desire for it. She wanted this kiss, wanted to fall into it, wanted to see where it led. Perhaps it led to other wicked desires, other wicked feelings. But only if she let it—and she wouldn't, she promised herself.

All the reasons why began to reassert themselves, slowly coming back to the fore of her defences after the initial onslaught of this new pleasure. She shouldn't be kissing a stranger, a man she'd only met once. She shouldn't be kissing a man with whom she meant to do business. She was a mother; she had to think of her reputation for her daughter's sake. She was a business owner; she also had to think of her reputation for the sake of the mines. Kisses were for women who could afford them.

The last thought brought her up short. She pushed against the hard wall of his chest. Did he think she could afford to give away kisses? That she'd come out to the garden on purpose to signal her intention—that she was willing to acknowledge *and* act on the flicker of attraction? Had he taken what she'd intended as an escape as an invitation instead?

The white-hot burn of pleasure turned to heated mortification. 'My lord…' She should have been more astute. Widows often had a reputation for discreet licentiousness. The widows the Marquess of Lynford knew most certainly did. But she could not be one of them. It was for that very reason she'd been so careful of her own reputation for five long years. 'I fear I have given you a most inaccurate impression of myself. I apologise, sincerely. I must go. Immediately.' Eliza tried to step around him, but all the height and

breadth she'd appreciated about him earlier worked to
her disadvantage. He was not a man easily evaded. She
should have left when she had the chance. She should
not have lingered in the garden, tempting fate. She'd
come out thinking to put some distance between herself and those dark eyes. But the garden hadn't been
far enough.

He moved, subtly positioning his body to block her
departure, a hand at her arm in gentle restraint, his
voice soft in the darkness. 'When will I see you again?'
It was 'will' with him, not 'may'. Lynford wasn't the
sort of man to beg for a woman's attention. He went
forward confidently, assuming the attention would be
given. *Will.* The potency of that one word sent a frisson of warm heat down her spine. His dark gaze held
hers, intent on an answer—*her* answer. Despite his
confident assumptions, he was allowing that decision
to be all hers.

'I don't think that would be wise. Business and pleasure should not mix.' She could not relent on this or
she would come to regret it. An affair could ruin her
and everything she'd worked for. The shareholders in
the mines would no doubt love to discover a sin to
hold against her.

'Not wise for whom, Mrs Blaxland?' The back of
his hand traced a gentle path along the curve of her
jaw. 'You are merely a patron of the school I sponsor.
I don't see any apparent conflict of interest.'

'Not wise for either of us.' If she stood here and argued with him, she would lose. Sometimes the best way
to win an argument was simply to leave. Eliza exer-

cised that option now in her firmest tones, the ones she reserved for announcing decisions in the boardroom. 'Goodnight, Lord Lynford.' She was counting on him being gentleman enough to recognise a refusal and let her go this time, now that any ambiguity between them had been resolved.

Eliza made it to the carriage without any interference. She shut the door behind her and waited for a sense of relief to take her. She'd guessed correctly. Lynford hadn't followed her and it was for the best. He was probably standing in the garden, realising it at this very minute, now that the heat of the moment had passed. The kiss had been an enjoyable adventure. It had added a certain spice to the evening, but it was not to be repeated. He didn't know her. He didn't know the depth of her responsibilities, or that she had a child— Sophie—the true love of her life.

If he did, he'd most certainly run. A man like Lynford, a man in his prime with wealth and a title to recommend him, was expected to wed a young woman capable of giving him his own heirs. She knew precisely the sort of bride who was worthy of a ducal heir: a sweet, young girl, who had no other interests than stocking her husband's nursery. Lynford would want, would *need*, a family of his own. All dukes did. The Marquess would never seriously consider a woman with another man's daughter clinging to her skirts and who spent her days running a mining empire, any more than she would consider him as a husband.

She would never marry again. She had no inclination to give up her hard-won control over her future and her daughter's. The risk was too great, even if the cost was also great. Sophie must come first, ahead of her own personal wishes for a family. Eliza had come to such a realisation early in her widowhood and it had been both a relief and a disappointment.

It was the only thing the doting and decent Blaxland hadn't been able to give her and the only thing she would not risk giving to herself. He'd given her security and a future, but he could not give her a family. Despite ten years of marriage, there was only to be her darling Sophie between them. Another husband, another man, younger, more virile, might provide her with those children, but she did not want to turn her responsibilities over to a husband in exchange, nor could she risk her reputation with the entanglement of a lover. The well-intentioned overture from Miles Detford years ago had shown her how even the smallest misstep could weaken her position.

On either front, she had no business kissing the Marquess of Lynford in the academy gardens. She was the daughter of a mine owner, the widow of a mine owner. Her family came from business. Cits on all sides, including her late husband's. Such a background wasn't for a marquess. Eliza knew how the world worked. She could be nothing for him but a brief dalliance until whatever mystery he saw in her was solved. Men could do as they liked. But *she* would never outrun the stain and neither would Sophie.

That was the lesson she told herself as her coach deposited her at the inn. But it didn't stop her from dreaming that night of a dark-eyed man who'd called her extraordinary and kissed her body into an acute awareness of itself, who'd made her feel alive in ways she hadn't felt for years, perhaps ever. There simply hadn't been time or place for such realisations. There still wasn't. Whatever that kiss had awakened had to be suppressed. That kiss could stay in her dreams, but it could go no further. In the morning she would wake up, visit the Porth Karrek mine and return to life as usual. As earth-shattering as tonight had been, it simply couldn't be any other way for her.

It simply couldn't be this way. The lumber order for the tunnel timbers was excessive. Eliza sat back from the ledgers, hazarding a glance at the clock on the wall of the mine office. It was eleven already. The morning had slipped away while she'd grappled with the receipt, trying to make sense of the overabundance of ordering. She'd meant to leave for home by now and she was nowhere close to making that self-imposed departure. If she left it any later, she'd miss tea with Sophie. She'd promised she'd be back in time and she never broke a promise. But ultimately, she was the one who had to answer to the shareholders in a few weeks at the annual meeting, the one who would be accountable for this over-ordering.

Eliza went to the window and looked down on the bustling scene below: carters pushing wheelbarrows of ore from the mine to the sorters; sorters separating the ore; her foreman, Gillie Cardy, shouting orders. The sight of her mines at work brought a certain thrill, a certain proof that she'd accomplished something. She caught Gillie's eye and gestured for him to come up. He would know why so much lumber had been ordered.

Gillie knocked on the door before entering, sweeping off his knit cap as he stepped inside. 'Mrs Blaxland, how can I be of service?' She liked Gillie. He'd been the site manager even before her husband died. He was competent and knew the mechanics of mining thoroughly, and he'd been a friendly face when she'd first taken over.

She motioned towards the ledgers. 'I have some questions about the lumber order.'

Gillie chuckled and shook his head. 'I'm no good at numbers, ma'am. I just do what I'm told. You want someone to find a lode in the mine, I'm your fella. But if you want someone to do the books, that's not me. I know mining and not much else.' Eliza nodded. This was yet another reason her schools were vital. People needed mathematics and reading skills no matter what their profession. Education was power and protection. Without it, people were waiting to be victims.

'I've done the sums,' she assured him. 'With the amount of timber ordered we could build a tunnel twice the length.'

He twisted the cap in his hand, looking worried. 'The tunnel *is* very long, ma'am. We are tunnelling out underneath the ocean.'

Eliza stared at him in disbelief. 'We are not! We opted not to take the risk at this time.' Her stomach began to turn. The board had decided at the last quarterly meeting not to go that far.

'Pardon me, ma'am, but Mr Detford said we were tunnelling under the ocean.'

Miles Detford? He ran the Wheal Karrek mine for her. She trusted Detford, counted him as friend. Miles would never go against the board's decision or her wishes. He knew how she felt about the dangers of tunnelling beneath the ocean. Surely, there must be some mistake, that Cardy had misunderstood or that Miles Detford had been pressured by someone, because if that wasn't the case, it meant she had misunderstood—not just the decision not to tunnel, but so much more. Her board was willing to override her decisions.

If it were true, it was a slap in the face. Someone thought she wouldn't notice, either because she wasn't diligent or because they thought she wasn't smart enough. The other answer was even less appealing. Maybe whoever ordered the timbers simply didn't care if she noticed. Her wishes were to be overridden. Not everyone on the board had agreed about the tunnel. It had been contentious and hotly debated. She'd rather put the money towards mining schools. Others had not felt that way. There was no money to be made from the schools.

Eliza pressed a hand to her stomach, trying to settle the roil that had started with the realisation. After years of proving herself, it seemed things still weren't beyond that first year. Hadn't she been the one who had insisted on steam engines to replace the horses? Hadn't she been the one to institute safety protocols? The worst of it was, *she'd* thought things were better.

But they weren't. Someone was laughing behind her back, playing her very publicly for a fool.

Already, her mind was running through options. Which shareholders had conspired against her? Was it Isley Thorp or Sir Gismond Brenley, the other chief shareholders? It must have been if they had enough leverage to force Miles Detford into ordering the timbers. Miles would never have ordered them on his own. He would have defended her decision.

She returned to her desk chair and drew out a piece of paper from the drawer, penning a note with instructions. There was no question of returning to Truro until this mess was resolved. She folded the note and handed it to Gillie. 'Have a messenger deliver this to the town house with all haste.' Sophie and her governess could be here tomorrow. That would give her time to find suitable living arrangements. The inn wasn't a decent place for a young girl. But where? Who did she know in town to whom she could turn? Did she dare ask Lynford? He was her only acquaintance likely to have any connections. The thought of Sophie at the inn, driving guests mad with her exuberance, settled it. As hesitant as she was about asking Lynford, she didn't have a choice. Wheal Karrek needed her and she needed Sophie.

Decision made, she took out a second sheet and penned another note. 'Take this up to the new conservatory.' She reread the note, making sure she'd struck just the right tone, short, concise, a very businesslike message, nothing that Lynford would misconstrue as an invitation to continue what they'd started *and* finished in the garden. Satisfied, she sent Gillie off. That only left sending a note to Detford. Her stomach surged once more at the thought. She settled it with a reminder that this was all a misunderstanding. Miles would come and explain all. She'd been on her guard for so long, it was too easy to see trouble where there was none.

Chapter Five

Eliza had barely finished the note when the commotion of an arrival sounded in the yard below. Perhaps another wagonload of supplies was expected today? But when she reached the window, there was no wagon in the yard, only a lone man on a chestnut horse— a tall, broad-shouldered man, dark hair unruly and windblown. He dismounted in a fluid motion and Eliza's breath caught. Lynford was here! He'd come and immediately. He couldn't have received her message more than an hour ago.

He looked up at the window, shielding his eyes against the sun, and Eliza reflexively stepped back even though there was little chance of being seen. She was both flattered and flustered by his attention. What to do? Allow him to come up or should she go down to meet him? She would go down. *Things* tended to happen when she was alone with him. Crowds were safer. She took up her hat and gloves and paused a moment to check her appearance in the small mirror behind the door before whispering, 'Breathe, Eliza. He's just a man.'

A man who had kissed her. A man who had not been intimidated by her when she'd surprised him at the school. A man who had come to her immediately even though she'd not specifically requested it. She stopped at the foot of the stairs to collect herself. She should not be excited. This was an entirely girlish reaction. She'd summoned him for business purposes because that was the nature of their acquaintance and she knew no one else in the area who might be positioned to help her. She'd *not* summoned him because of last night. She wanted to be clear with herself on that. In fact, that had been the singular reason she'd hesitated to send for him in the first place.

She stepped outside, striding forward with confidence, hand outstretched in a mannish greeting. 'My lord, how good of you to come and how surprising. I'd expected a list of recommendations in response, not an actual visit. I hope this isn't disrupting your day?'

He shook her hand and gave her one of his broad, winning smiles. If he was put off by the masculine gesture he gave no sign of it. 'Not at all. There's nothing left to do up at the school except get in the way while Kitto tries to settle the students.' Sweet heavens, he was just as devastating in daylight and plain clothes as he was by night. Perhaps more so. Without the elegance of evening clothes, it was too easy to forget he was a marquess, heir to a dukedom and entirely above her touch. Today, he looked the part of a country squire and eminently more attainable, dressed in riding boots, tight buckskins, and a long greatcoat suited for the autumn air that blew in off the sea.

Lynford did not relinquish her hand, but covered it with his other. 'Tell me, what sort of accommodations do you require for the longer term? A manse? A cottage? An estate? I have a place in mind if you think it would suit. There's a dower house at Falmage Hill. It's not far from here. It would be close to the mine and it's well situated between Porth Karrek and Penzance. I am in residence at the main house, or else I'd let the whole estate to you instead.'

'I don't need a whole estate.' Eliza laughed. 'The dower house will be ideal.' Did she sound as flustered as she felt? The offer was overwhelming, all the more so because she couldn't recall the last time someone had lifted the burden from her shoulders. Her world was full of wolves and vultures, but here was a stranger—an acquaintance at best—who'd shouldered the weight of this one task without hesitation. This was arguably the best news she'd heard all morning. But did it come at a cost? What guarantees was Lynford looking for? Why would a man she barely knew offer such largesse?

'Are you sure, Mrs Blaxland?' Eaton's gaze narrowed, matching her own speculation. 'If so, why are you looking at me as if I were a predator?' She should have been more deliberate with what she let show on her face. She'd become sloppy in the wake of the morning's tensions.

'Are you? A predator? A girl can't be too careful. When something sounds too good to be true, I've learned it usually is.' Eliza didn't back down from his challenge. 'Truthfully, Lord Lynford, I *am* wondering why a man who hardly knows me would volunteer such lavish accommodation. What could he want in exchange? I shall pay you rent in coins and in nothing else.' She needed to be clear on this point, especially based on last night in the garden. Did he think there were additional kisses to be had? Or perhaps something more than kisses?

'You will do no such thing. I am not asking for money…or for anything else,' Lynford answered with the swiftness of an insulted man. 'As for why I am doing this, it is because I can. I have an empty house and you need one.'

Did she dare believe him? She was not used to taking men at their word. But what choice did she have? Sophie and her governess would arrive tomorrow. Eaton swung up on his horse and for a moment she thought he'd retract his offer, offended by her scepticism. Then he leaned down and offered his hand. 'Come up, we'll ride out and look the property over. You can decide then if it will suit.'

'But my coach is here,' Eliza stammered, craning her neck to look up at him. Lynford appeared twice as large atop the big horse as he did on the ground and twice as commanding.

'Send it on ahead.' Lynford answered easily, dismissing the detail. 'Stop stalling and come up, Eliza. We've already established I'm not a predator. It's a beautiful autumn day, perfect for a ride, and I promise my horse will behave.' She noted he said nothing about himself. She also noted he'd used her first name.

She should be wary. She should refuse on grounds of impropriety. What would people think if they saw her with him? The argument had no teeth. *Who* would see them? Who would care? Miners on their way to their shifts? People who didn't even know who she was? She lived quietly and Truro was further than most of these people would ever go in their lifetime. But *she* would know. But when he looked at her with that smile and those dancing dark eyes, something deep inside her began to stir, as it had last night, as it had the first time she'd laid eyes on him—that reminder that she was alive, that she was something more than a book-keeper and an overseer. She took his hand and leapt.

He settled her before him on the saddle and clucked to the big chestnut with an enviable ease, apparently unbothered by the proximity of the female sitting in front of him. Eliza wished she could claim such sang-froid. She could not. The rhythm of the horse beneath her beat a tattoo of freedom as the cliffs and fields of the Cornish landscape sped past. But neither dominated her attentions like the presence of the man behind her. She'd not counted on the practical act of transportation, such a mundane task, feeling so intimate.

Huntingdon hadn't been a rider. They'd always gone everywhere by coach. To ride astride with a man was a very different thing. There were the thighs to contend with, muscular thighs that bracketed her legs, the chest she couldn't help but press against as they cantered along the cliff road to Falmage Hill, the arm that came around her, the leather-gloved hand that held the reins resting at her hip. She could smell the wind on him, could feel it in her face, the thrill of freedom humming in her blood. It was fanciful to ascribe such poetic feeling to the ride. Lynford would likely be stunned to know how a simple act had conjured up such fanciful connotations for her.

The newly awakened wildness in her was disappointed to see Falmage Hill come into view, disappointed to turn into the drive, disappointed to slow the horse to a trot, the wind settling to a light, arbitrary breeze in her face. Eaton turned the horse down a path, giving her a tour of the drive lined by tall, impressive oaks with a green lawn extending in all directions. 'The main house is straight ahead, but the dower house sits on the west corner of the property. It has a nice view of the sea.' She couldn't care less for the sea view at the moment. She was transfixed on the lawn. Sophie would love running here. There was precious little space for a girl to run in town. A twinge of guilt pricked at Eliza. Courtesy dictated she should tell him she wouldn't be his only guest. But privacy counselled caution. She was protective of Sophie and those who came into contact with her. A woman or a girl with a fortune couldn't be too careful.

The entrance to the dower house was dominated by two thick stone pillars and a wrought iron gate that stood open, ready for them. The house itself was a square, brick manse with ivy growing up its walls and five white-framed windows decorating the second storey. The entrance was set on the right side of the house and covered with an arched arcade. Eliza found the home immediately charming, a place where a family might take a holiday. Where children might frolic in the yard with a puppy. She pushed the sweet image away. There was no purpose in torturing herself with what she couldn't have. Besides, she never took a holiday. She was too afraid of what might transpire if she looked away from the mines for a moment. Apparently, it hadn't mattered. Things had transpired anyway.

Out of nowhere, a man in livery materialised to hold the horse. Lynford dismounted and reached for her, his hands easy and comfortable at her waist. Was she the only one who noticed how much they touched? Was she the only one moved by it? The only one whose pulse thundered with each contact? One would think she was fresh from the schoolroom, not a woman who'd had a husband and a child and who dealt with men every day. There should be no mystique in a man's touch. She was helped in and out of carriages, escorted into dinners on the occasions when she went out in Truro. Touch was no stranger to her, yet Lynford's touch managed to stand out.

Eaton set her down and gestured towards the house. 'Shall we go in? I sent word ahead to the staff to start cleaning once I received your note. The worst of the dust should be gone by now.' He slid her teasing look. 'I know how you are about dust.'

'You're very…efficient.' *And confident*, she added silently. He'd been sure she'd accept his offer…and he'd been right. Was she that predictable or was he that sure of himself?

Eaton ushered her through the front door, a hand resting at the small of her back. Another touch. Another reminder that he stirred her. 'There's a parlour, a dining room and a library space you can use as an office here on the first floor. The kitchen is below stairs. The bedrooms are upstairs. I will send down staff for cooking and cleaning. I have plenty to spare with only me to look after at the big house.'

He'd anticipated everything, Eliza thought as they climbed the stairs. 'There are five chambers up here and seven beds.' Eaton led her down the hall. 'You can have your pick, perhaps a bed for every night of the week.' He laughed, coming to stop at a room nearest the stairwell. 'This one is the largest.'

Eliza stepped into the airy room, impressed. Eaton's staff had already been here. The bed linens were fresh and the window was open to let in the crisp autumn air. A small bud vase with deep pink ginger lilies stood on the table beside the bed, lending the room a personal touch, an extra detail. She was aware of Eaton behind her, his words a quiet, masculine rumble. 'Will it suit?' At the enquiry, her eyes began to sting, tears welling. She was glad she was facing the window. How would she explain that a simple question had moved her to tears?

She cleared her throat, summoning a modicum of control. 'Yes, it will do splendidly.' But she did not turn from the window. The echo of her previous thought came again: How long had it been since someone had taken care of her? The jingle of harnesses sounded in the drive, announcing the arrival of her coach and saving her from any further awkwardness. At the sound of horses, Eaton was in motion. 'I'll go down and tell them to bring your things up.' His boots sounded on the stairs and, within moments, her trunk was deposited in her room. 'I'll have one of the maids unpack,' Lynford offered.

'No, I'd like to unpack on my own. Thank you.' Eliza turned from the window, finally the mistress of her emotions. 'You've done more than enough.' He'd done so much, in fact, that she was on the brink of tears, perhaps a sad commentary on her life that such acts would have this effect, especially when he clearly viewed the efforts as basic acts of politeness.

Lynford gave her a grin and a bow. 'Then I will leave you to it. I have business to complete, but before I go, I would like to ask for your company at dinner tonight. It gets lonely eating by myself. Meanwhile, if there's anything you need, send to the house for it.'

Eliza set to undoing the buckles on her trunk. She needed to stop being overwhelmed by him. It would be too easy to fall into the trap of relying on him, of laying her burdens down. This afternoon was proof enough she needed to be wary. Men bearing gifts always wanted something and Lynford's gift was far more than Detford's bonbons and roses had ever been. Perhaps she was being too cynical. Perhaps it was just as he'd said—he'd given it because he could.

Eliza shook out her dresses and hung them in the wardrobe. Today had been upsetting. Tomorrow would be better. Sophie would be here by teatime and she'd have a clear mind with which to think about the situation with the ledgers. Until then, however, there was dinner with Lord Lynford to keep her busy.

Chapter Six

The school was still busy with move-in-day excitement when Eaton returned. It had been a bustling hotbed of activity when he'd left and, if that hotbed wasn't precisely still boiling in the late afternoon, the chaos of housing the boys and reassuring their parents remained very definitely at an energetic simmer. Trunks from later arrivals were piled in the drive awaiting the attention of footmen. Parents milled in the wide hall while instructors, strategically placed about the hall, attempted to direct the last of the boys and pair up roommates. It was a good kind of chaos, reminiscent of his own days at school. The sight put a certain nostalgic warmth in his heart. His own father had made it a point to travel with him to school for the start of autumn term the first few years he'd gone instead of consigning him to a servant's or tutor's care for the journey. Not all the boys at Eton had been that fortunate and he looked back on those times fondly. He remembered their parting ritual, that last manful shaking of hands as his father said goodbye in the main hall and pressed a secret five-pound note into his palm with a wink.

There were still a few families saying farewell in the hall, but from the looks of it Cade had everything in hand, a realisation that was both satisfying and bittersweet as Eaton slipped into the headmaster's office unnoticed.

Eaton poured himself a drink from the sideboard and slouched into a tall wing-backed chair with a silent toast. His vision of a music school had come to fruition most magnificently. Richard Penlerick would be proud. That was something for which to be thankful. It had been a tremendous undertaking accomplished in a short period of time. Today, watching students arrive and move in was something to celebrate. But it also carried a tinge of sadness to it. His part in the school was done. Cade Kitto would take things from here, as had always been the intention. Eaton knew he wasn't relinquishing his association with the school. He'd always be in the background, raising funds, recruiting patrons and students, but the school wouldn't be *his*, not any more.

Eaton twirled the stem of his glass, indulging in a moment of whimsical melancholy. The school had absorbed him entirely since December when Rosenwyn Treleven had first put the idea to him. Since then, he'd embraced the project fully. He'd cancelled his long-anticipated trip to Italy in March. He'd foregone most of the Season, spending his summer here instead putting the finishing touches on the school. It had filled his days, but that was over now. It was time to get on to the next project, whatever that might be. Urgency surged. He didn't like being at a loose end. Life was short and unpredictable, Richard Penlerick's death had proved it, but even that ghastly reminder hadn't been enough to spark an interest in a new project.

The door opened and Cade slipped inside, all smiles despite spending a trying day of student arrivals. 'I thought I might find you here.' The sight of a satisfied Cade Kitto did much to alleviate Eaton's melancholy. In many ways, this school had been for Cade and Rosenwyn. If not for them, the school wouldn't exist. 'I don't know if I've answered a thousand questions or just the same question asked a thousand different ways.' Cade laughed good-naturedly as he poured a drink. 'I think everyone is settled now.' He took a seat across from Eaton and crossed a leg over one knee. 'Here's to you. Without you, today wouldn't have been possible. You saw the potential of Rosenwyn's idea and made it a reality. You provided the house, the funds and the prestige of a name that would draw worthy students. Rose and I can't thank you enough.' Cade saluted him with his glass. 'What will you do with yourself now that the school is up and running? You'll have time aplenty on your hands.'

'I was just thinking the same before you walked in.' Eaton smiled, determined not to lose the joy of the day. 'I will have time to work in my orangery, perfect my truffle oil recipe. I can plan my trip to Italy again.' But his tone lacked conviction. None of the ideas held any appeal.

'And Mrs Blaxland? Is she settled to your satisfaction?' Cade asked with keen eyes. 'I got your note that you'd ridden out to assist her. I hope all is well?'

'Yes, I put her up at the dower house at Falmage Hill,' Eaton replied neutrally, but not neutrally enough to escape Cade's attention.

'At your family estate?' Cade's brow creased in surprise and perhaps concern.

'Yes, is there a problem with that?' Eaton asked somewhat teasingly. He'd not expected Cade to react one way or the other.

'It's just the suddenness of it all,' Cade answered. 'You hardly know her and now she's entrenched on your family's property. I would have thought a cottage near Penzance or even rooms at the Trelevenses', where she'd have female company.'

'They'd be strangers to her,' Eaton dismissed the suggestion. 'She's been a generous donor to the school. It was the least I could do and I know plenty about her.' Did he? He knew only that he was attracted to her, that she stirred something in him that hadn't been stirred in a long while. How would he explain if Cade asked what that meant? 'She's alone, she knows no one else here she can turn to,' Eaton offered obliquely. 'I helped her because I could.'

Cade chuckled, but Eaton did not miss his warning. 'She runs a mining empire. She's not helpless or without resources. Do not, for a minute, my friend, think Eliza Blaxland is a damsel in distress.'

No, he would not make that mistake. 'She is definitely not that.' Eaton had seen the flustered look on Eliza's face today when he'd offered the house. There'd been relief in her eyes and disbelief, too. For a moment she'd been able to lay down her burden. 'Perhaps that's why I did it,' he mused. 'Sometimes even the strong need a hand.'

Cade offered a wry smile. 'Like helping court musicians establish a music school?'

Eaton shifted in his chair, uncomfortable with the praise. 'The estate was from my great-aunt. She'd be pleased to see it used as a school. Quite possibly, I should be the one thanking you. The house was standing empty before Rosenwyn suggested it. As for the funds, those came from patrons. It would be a mistake to think I singlehandedly funded the school and those patrons came because of you, because of the chance to study with Cornwall's very own home-grown genius, Cador Kitto, Porth Karrek's finest musician.'

Cade leaned forward in earnest, not distracted in the least by Eaton's rebuttal. 'You know what I mean. It's not only the school I thank you for. It's everything this school represents: a chance for me to work in one place, a chance to give up the risk of the itinerant lifestyle, moving from court to court with no assurances of commissions. It's relieved me of the shame of relying on my wife's dowry for funds. I will always be truly grateful for what you've done for me. Without your efforts behind this school, Rosenwyn and I would never have been able to marry. I would have left Porth Karrek in December and returned to a life of wandering. I would never have known what it was like to have a wife and a family.'

The last was said with all the passion of a newly-wed man only a month out from the bliss of his honeymoon, but there was something else in Cade's words that caused Eaton to think he wasn't talking about Rosenwyn's five sisters when he referred to family. 'Family, Cade? Do you have something to tell me?' Eaton smiled, a few other subtle hints from throughout the last weeks falling into place like Rosenwyn's indisposition rendering her unable to play hostess for the open house.

Cade's face broke into a beaming smile. 'I am going to be a father in March.'

'That's wonderful news, for you both,' Eaton congratulated him. He and Cade had grown close in the last months, bonding over the school. He knew how much having a family meant to Cade, who'd grown up in Porth Karrek as mining poor, and to Rosenwyn, whom Eaton had known since childhood. The Trelevens and Falmages were both part of the district's society. He'd saved Rosenwyn from a disastrous marriage a couple of years ago in London and the happiness she'd found with Cade was all he could wish for his old friend. Yet there was a stab of jealousy as they drank to Cade's good news. Cade had the dream: meaningful purpose, a wife who was a partner and companion, who challenged him, who loved him, and very soon Cade would have a child to dote on as well. Envy speared Eaton, driving deep. How was it that a poor miner's son should have all those things while a duke's son did not?

Cade clapped him on the knee and rose. 'I need to get back out there and make sure all the parents have left, then the masters and students will have our first supper together as a school in the dining hall. Reverend Maddern is coming to say the blessing.'

Eaton rose with him. 'I need to go as well. I asked Mrs Blaxland to dinner. I wouldn't want to be late for my own invitation.' He wanted fresh air in his face, the power of his horse beneath him. What he needed was a good hard canter to push away his jealousy and dilute his anger over the hand fate had dealt him.

Outside, he swung up on Titan and kicked him forward, letting his thoughts race with his horse's hooves. It wasn't the idea of a marriage that sparked his envy of Cade. He could marry anytime he wanted. Candidates were thick on the ground for a man of his attributes and expectations. It was the quality of that marriage he envied. Rosenwyn had fought for Cade. She had wanted him despite the limitations of his station. She loved Cade for who he was, not what he was. It was the one thing Eaton could never ask of a woman. He could marry whenever he wanted, that was true, but it came at a cost.

He could make a woman a duchess. He could never make her a mother, could never give her a family. A measles epidemic when he was fourteen had seen to that. But it was not him society would be unkind to. Society never believed it was the man's fault when there were no heirs. Debutantes were raised for titles and aristocratic motherhood much like heirs were raised to be aristocratic studs. He would not burden a wife with a foregone conclusion of failure she could do nothing about. What woman of his circle would care for *him*, live for *him* without the promise of a family? No one he knew, quite honestly. So, he remained unwed and would choose to remain unwed.

In terms of the ducal succession it did not worry him. He had his younger brother to see to the line. But in terms of his own personal journey, he minded very much. He would make the journey of life entirely alone. No wife. No children. No one even to confide in. Naturally, the family had kept this a secret. No one knew except their close circle of friends and they were sworn to secrecy. He would reach a certain age when society would begin to speculate about him. There would be questions: Why didn't he marry? A duke's heir was duty-bound to wed. His source of intimacy would be reduced to a collection of temporary relationships with temporary women to see him through. Who else would want the broken heir to the Duke of Bude?

Eaton let Titan's hooves eat up the ground, let the wind push against his thoughts. He did not want to wallow in his own misery. He was lucky in other ways. He would rejoice instead in the little thrills, the small joys that were available to him, like dinner with a beautiful woman whose pulse raced when he was near.

What was she doing, dressing up for dinner with a marquess? Staying in his home—well, on his property—spending time with him alone? All this, *after* she'd allowed him to kiss her. If he offered her an affair tonight, she'd have only herself to blame. She was sending all the wrong signals, quite possibly right down to the very gown she wore, yet she seemed unable to resist.

Eliza surveyed her image in the long mirror. She smoothed the silk of her blue skirts, debating yet again what to wear. Was the gown too sophisticated for the country? She eyed the other gown on the bed, a mignonette-green India muslin. It was far simpler, perhaps too simple for supper with a marquess regardless of where they dined. Eliza bit her lip in contemplation. Better to overdress than underdress. She would stay with the blue silk, but no jewels, just her pearls, and she'd wear her hair up in a modest style, devoid of curls and ornate braids.

No sooner had Eliza made her decision than the sound of carriage wheels crunched on the drive. She peered out of the window and froze in feminine panic. Lynford was here with an open carriage! Heavens, she wasn't quite ready. Eliza dabbed a quick spot of perfume on her wrists and snatched up her shawl from the bed. Was that everything? Oh, her bracelet! She took it from the vanity and headed down the stairs, trying to fasten it as she went, but the dratted clasp wouldn't catch.

'Let me help with that.' Eaton met her at the bottom of the stairs, grinning at her efforts, his fingers nimble at her wrist as they worked the stubborn catch, her pulse fluttering at the contact. He was once more turned out in evening attire, his unruly hair combed in stark contrast to the windblown man who'd ridden into the courtyard of her mine today. He smelled of his woodsy toilette and clean linen, a scent that was just as intoxicating tonight as the smell of the outdoors on him had been today. Maybe it was the duality he presented that was intoxicating—a man of elegance and refinement by evening, a country squire by day. Or perhaps it wasn't his looks that made him intoxicating, but his manner; his competence, his confidence, the way he took charge whether it was finding her a home or managing the tiny clasp of her bracelet. She had to be careful. That competence was something she could not indulge for long. She had her own competence to look after and exercise.

'There, now you're ready.' He released her hand and offered her his arm. 'Your carriage awaits, madame.'

'As does my escort, it appears. I wasn't expecting you or a carriage.' She was glad now that she'd chosen the blue silk. 'This is greatly appreciated, but I could have walked up. It's so much work to harness the horses just to go to the main house.' She didn't want him to think she had to be pampered.

He handed her into the carriage and took the rear-facing seat across from her. 'All true. However, we are not going to the house. We are going to the orangery and, with the weather being so fine, I thought we might enjoy a drive before supper.' He reached beneath his seat and pulled out a hamper. 'I have champagne, still chilled. I recall how much you enjoyed it at the reception. If you could help with the glasses, I might endeavour to pour.' He freed the cork with a loud pop, the sound and subsequent fountain of foam causing her to gasp and twitch her skirts out of the way with a laugh.

The first attempt at pouring was met with a spill of

champagne on the carriage floor and laughing instructions from Eaton. 'Hold the glass still.'

'I am!' she protested as the carriage hit a rut in the road and more champagne sloshed in sacrifice to his efforts.

'Steady now,' Eaton cautioned, this time managing to get enough champagne in each glass for drinking. He set the bottle aside. 'Now we can toast. Here's to a day that will end better than it started.'

She held his eyes as she drank, trying to divine what he meant. Did the toast hint at a forthcoming proposition? Or was he merely toasting the truth? Her need earlier today had been assuaged. She hoped for the latter, but felt compelled to mitigate cause for the former. She did not want to have to refuse him point-blank later tonight. Perhaps she could insinuate as much. She raised her glass for a toast of her own. 'Here's to a friend indeed.' It was well done. She was certain he heard her subtle message. If seduction was on his mind, he'd been warned not to pursue it.

His eyes glinted with their dark spark over the rim of his champagne flute, a knowing smile playing on those sensual lips as his low voice rumbled enticingly, 'I'm always glad to be of service, Eliza.'

Eliza. There it was again. She'd never thought of her name as sexy before. Eliza was a plain name, but not on his lips. On his lips, it might be the most beautiful name in the world. Damn him. With one word, he'd destroyed her efforts and ridden roughshod over her warning. If there was a proposition, he would make her refuse it bluntly at the critical moment.

'More champagne?' he offered, holding up the half-empty bottle. 'The road is smooth through here, I should be able to manage pouring another glass, if you can manage keeping it still,' he teased. They poured with more success this time, Eliza catching sight of the label.

'Veuve Clicquot?' It was French and expensive. No wonder it tasted divine.

'You know it?' Lynford smiled, pouring the remnants into his glass.

'Only by name,' Eliza admitted. 'My husband was wealthy, but he was also frugal.' They'd had luxuries aplenty, but not champagne unless they were hosting an important party.

'It's a special day and I thought it called for a special champagne. We are celebrating our students' arrival for the first term and your first night in the dower house.'

'Oh!' Eliza gasped regretfully as memory flooded her. 'You had students today and I called you away.' She felt awful that he'd spent so much time with her, as if he'd had nothing better to do. He must have gone back to the school after he'd left her.

Lynford laughed, setting her at ease. 'I was expendable, I assure you. Kitto had it all under control.' He gave her a mockingly serious look. 'You would not have liked it, too much chaos with all the boys running willy-nilly up and down the stairs.' But *he'd* liked it, Eliza thought. She saw it in his eyes and heard it in his tone. The day had pleased him, as well it should have.

'You've done a remarkable thing with that school,' she complimented. The sun was starting to set, turning the sky blossom pink. It was her favourite time of day, the magical hour between day and dusk when she liked to imagine the world was at peace, slowing down from whatever had caused it to race during the day. She felt that peace now in the carriage with Lynford, a comfortable silence settling between them as they drove through the grounds of Falmage Hill, sipping their champagne as the sun dipped.

Lynford offered to open a second bottle, but she declined with a smile. 'I chose the champagne for another reason, too,' he said, tucking the bottle back beneath the seat. 'Veuve Clicquot is named for the widow who ran the vineyard. You remind me of her. She was twenty-seven when she took over the family empire. And, like you, she was successful, too.' He held her gaze and a bolt of heat went through her at the intensity of his attention. 'You impress me, Eliza. I am so very glad you didn't turn out to be an old woman.'

A bolder woman might return the compliment and say she was glad he'd turned out not to be an older man. But that would invite an intimacy she did not want. She offered a tremulous smile instead, uncertain how to respond. Once again he had caught her off guard. No one had ever flirted with her using her own accomplishments as compliments. Goodness knew there were few men who approved of those accomplishments. Usually, they were seen as failings to be held against her. 'What I've done is nothing more than the tasks laid before me. It's a little like giving a stranger a home, isn't it? I did them because I could.'

'Touché.' He raised his glass in salute and drained

the last of it as the carriage rolled to a halt. 'Here we are, the orangery, my pride and joy.' He hopped down and offered her his hand. 'This way, Eliza, dinner is served.'

Chapter Seven

T̲hat was an understatement, Eliza thought, taking her seat at a crystal-and-candle-laden table in the orangery. Dinner wasn't served, it was *presented* on white china plates, arranged in elegant perfection with carefully drizzled sauces and an array of colours—pink salmon, orange carrots, green herbs—all set against a backdrop of exquisite beauty. The orangery itself was breathtaking with the remainder of the setting sunlight coming through the glass, turning the table crystal to diamonds. Potted palms lined a path through the building along with fruit trees sporting oranges and lemons that perfumed the air with citrusy scents. The sound of trickling water came from deeper in the room and somewhere birds chirped.

'This is like a tropical paradise.' Eliza looked about her, unwilling to hide her appreciation. 'It's a little world all of its own.'

'We can walk through it after dinner,' Lynford offered, popping the cork off a bottle of chilled white wine. He poured a small amount into her glass. 'This will bring out the flavour of the salmon.' They'd been served a single plate containing a little of each food item and the servants had withdrawn, leaving them alone in the candlelit paradise.

It was a different way to eat, Eliza recognised immediately. She approved. There were no courses, no stuffing of oneself, no drinking to excess. There was savouring and sipping. This meal was art and science all in one, pairing tastes with one another to maximise both the fish and the wine. Each bite was a revelation, as was the man across the table from her. 'This is the most delicious meal I think I've ever eaten.' Eliza took another slow, deliberate bite of her fish. 'I would not have guessed you to be a gourmet.' The Marquess of Lynford was a big man, the kind of man she associated with a hearty appetite, who preferred puddings and roasts in copious quantities and was more interested in quantity than quality. 'I've found Cornishmen tend to prefer the solid foods of the countryside,' she tried to put it delicately.

Lynford laughed at the comment. 'You're not incorrect. There is much diversity, however, to be found in the countryside. Some Cornishmen are just more inventive than others.' He gestured to the salmon. 'These are from Bodmin Moor. A smart man can fish the upland rivers until December. A smarter man knows fish is healthier, too, than a heavy beef diet. It keeps the gout away.' He poured her a little more wine. 'I am interested in the science of food—not only the different tastes and flavours we can create, but how we can use food to eat well and live well. I've worked with the cook at the school to design a diet for the boys in the hopes they will learn the value of healthy eating along with their studies.'

'Are orange trees part of that?' Eliza sipped her wine, finding the conversation fascinating. Or was it the conversationalist? It was heady, sitting with him, exchanging ideas. There were layers to this man, unsuspected depths and she was filled with the urge to peel each of them back, like one of his oranges, until she reached his core. What would she find at the heart of the Marquess of Lynford?

'Orange trees are essential. Citrus fruits are excellent for keeping scurvy away. They are also extremely difficult to grow in the wild given the English weather. So, I grow them here. The school will be well provided for.'

'That's ingenious,' Eliza complimented, truly impressed with his foresight and his creativity. 'Whatever gave you that idea?'

'Not a what, a who.' Lynford smiled, his gaze taking on a nostalgic cast. 'A mentor, a friend, suggested it. He has—*had*—spectacular greenhouses at his estate.'

'Had?' Eliza asked softly, picking up the past tense reference. She sensed a change in his mood. The nostalgia was tinged with sadness.

'He died this past summer. Richard Penlerick, the Duke of Newlyn. He was a strong supporter of the school and the things I want to do there.' Lynford's dark eyes were shadowed but frank. 'I miss him very much. He was like an uncle to me. His son and I are close friends.'

Newlyn. Of course. The newspaper in Truro had covered it. The Cornish Duke had died tragically, if she recalled. A sudden death, unexpected. She reached out a hand and covered Eaton's where it lay on the table. 'I am genuinely sorry.'

Lynford nodded slowly, accepting her sympathy. The candlelight played across his face, catching sorrow, resentment, lingering anger and something more: bone-deep grief. She knew a little something about that. She'd felt that way for months after Huntingdon had died. 'I don't know what is worse,' she offered. 'To have time to prepare and know the end is coming, or to face it suddenly without warning.' She paused. They did not know each well. Perhaps it was wrong to think she could offer counsel, but she forged ahead, preferring to err on the side of empathy. There'd been no one to grieve with her, to help ease her pain when she'd lost Huntingdon. She would not leave someone else to face that grief alone if she could help it.

There was a certain intimacy between them, the orangery having shrunk to the circle of light surrounding them as she spoke. 'The day Huntingdon died was a normal day, just like any other. He had breakfast. He reminded me we had guests coming for dinner that night. Then he walked out of the door and didn't come back. He had no idea and neither did I that it would all be over in a few hours.'

Eaton's eyes glittered like polished obsidian. 'You loved him? You had a good marriage?'

She smiled fondly. 'Yes, he was a decent man and I knew going into it it would not outlast me, that I would be the one left behind. I just didn't think it would be that day. I suppose one never does.'

Eaton picked up her hand and threaded his fingers through hers, watching the candlelight bathe the bracelet at her wrist. 'Left behind. You've captured it precisely. That is exactly how I feel. He left me. He left Vennor, his son. He left all of us and we didn't even get to say goodbye. It wasn't just goodbye that went unsaid. It was all the other things. The loving words, the gratitude, the acknowledgement of how much his kindnesses, his very life, mattered.' He shook his head. 'Does the hurt, the emptiness, ever go away?'

'No, but it does change.' Eliza's voice was just above a whisper. 'You start to carry them with you instead of your sorrow.'

They were both whispering now. 'And the anger? Does it change, too? I've been angry for months. I wanted his life to matter. I wanted his death to matter. He deserved better than a blade in the dark, killed by a common criminal for no reason.' She felt his fingers tighten on hers. 'I want there to be a reason,' he admitted before pulling back with a rueful smile. 'My apologies. I didn't mean for the evening to take such a turn. I don't normally invite people to dinner and then lay myself bare to them.' He gave a short laugh and wiped his palms on his breeches. 'Thank you for listening. I haven't talked about Richard Penlerick since I came home. Perhaps I needed to.'

'Perhaps there was no one to talk to. I think it matters who you tell. These things…' Eliza waved an ephemeral hand '…cannot be told to just anyone.' She was touched he'd chosen her.

'I'm glad it was you.' Lynford pushed back from the table with a burst of energy, wanting to leave the recent conversation and its emotions behind. 'Are you ready for the tour? I think the orangery is ready for us.'

Beyond him, the path through the orangery had been lit. Eliza had been so intent on him she'd not noticed the servants discreetly placing the lanterns to guide their way. 'This place must be a wondrous refuge in the winter.' Eliza took his arm, looking about her as they strolled.

'It is. I spend a lot of time here, though not in the summer. With all the glass, it gets too warm.' He pointed out the palms with coconuts hidden under their large, leafy fronds, the orange trees with their waxy leaves and citrus treasures, the potted lemon trees that had come all the way from Italy. There were flowers, too, poinsettias from the Caribbean and rare varieties of orchids from Asia.

'I hope to bring the boys from the school here for lessons.' Lynford stopped to study the leaves of a lemon tree. 'I want them to learn science by visiting the ocean, by fishing in the rivers, by tromping through the woods and respecting the natural science around them in their own region.'

He smiled at her and she was nearly undone. 'You've not only designed a diet for them, you've designed a curriculum as well.' Lynford hadn't just built a school, he'd built a world. An entire lifestyle had been subtly woven into the fabric of the conservatory. It shamed her little vision of miners' schools. She had not dreamed big enough.

'I didn't do it alone. Kitto and I worked on the curriculum together. I think it's rather novel. It's hands-on learning, much like music instruction is. We thought, why not extend that idea to other subjects like science and history? They can learn history by visiting old ruins and follies, by re-enacting key battles. They can't learn everything that way, but a good portion of what they need to know can be taught with far more activity than it traditionally is.' He warmed to the subject as they walked. 'When I was growing up, the lessons I liked best and remembered the most were the ones where my tutors set aside the books and showed me. In the summers, I grew a garden and, as I tended it, my tutor talked about soil and the importance of crop rotation, how to calculate crop yield.' He paused here and grinned at her and she could see the boy he'd been in that teasing smile. 'That lesson was a good one. It combined mathematics *and* science.'

'It certainly sounds more exciting than my lessons when I was young. I am already wondering if I can adapt these ideas for the miners' children.' They were accustomed to plenty of activity during the day and definitely not used to sitting for long periods of time. For them, traditional school would be a challenge. 'Is that why you wanted to establish a school? To try out your ideas?' It had intrigued her from the beginning, when she'd first been approached in January to support the conservatory. Why would a man of his stand-

ing want to found a school? Self-importance? Legacy?
But the urgency behind the school, the determination
to open it this autumn, didn't support that theory.

Lynford laughed. 'Oh, you don't want to know.'

'Now I *especially* want to know,' Eliza cajoled. He
almost seemed embarrassed and that was interesting
when he was usually the epitome of confidence.

'All right, but it has to be a secret.' He gave her a
conspiratorial wink, his eyes dancing. 'I had a friend
who suggested it in order to convince Cador Kitto to
stay in the area on a more permanent basis. I wanted
my friend to be happy, so I set up the school.' He looked
sheepish with the confession. 'You'll be disappointed
now, knowing that it wasn't entirely altruistic, not originally.'

'Just for the good of a friend. Must be a very good
friend,' Eliza pressed. Her curiosity wanted details.

'An old friend, down on their luck,' Lynford offered.

'A woman, perhaps?' He was being cryptic, a sure
sign a woman was involved and Eliza felt confident
she knew who, but perhaps not why. 'Rosenwyn Treleven, maybe?'

Lynford looked surprised. 'Why would you think
that?'

'You mentioned she and Mr Kitto were newly married.' She bit her lip, trying to hide a smile at her discovery. Another layer peeled back. Lynford was a
secret romantic. She didn't need a great imagination
to see how this story went: Rosenwyn and Cade Kitto
falling in love, but Kitto needing to leave Porth Karrek for the pursuit of his work, a lifestyle not suited to

the gently bred Rosenwyn. In order to help his friend, Lynford had supported her idea of a school. It was overwhelming, really. A whole school given in order to see his friend wed. 'I think that is the very grandest of gestures,' Eliza assured him.

'It was the least I could do for her. She'd been jilted in love before. I didn't want to see her hurt again.' It was a difficult admission for him to make. Eliza heard it in his tone. Another layer fell. Lynford was a humble man at his core. He didn't like attention being called to his good deeds.

They passed a worktable with tools and a book lay open beside a microscope. 'I apologise, I haven't picked up after myself,' Lynford excused the mess. 'I've been researching the healing properties of orchids. Ancient Chinese herbalists believed the orchid could heal disease. I've also been extracting vanilla from the orchids for cooking.'

'You're a gourmet, a botanist, a scientist.' Eliza studied him. She'd not been prepared to find so much underneath. 'The Marquess of Lynford is a Renaissance man.'

'Hardly. I am just me. Eaton. I do wish you'd use my name as I asked you to last night.' He steered them around a corner. 'Ah, here we are, the fountain and the aviary.' They'd reached the centre of the orangery, the source of the trickling water and the chirping birds. Birds hung in large, elaborate cages while others flew about unfettered, decorating the space with their bright colours. Eliza sat at the edge of the fountain, her skirts spread about her, watching in amazement as he held up a finger and a small green-and-yellow bird landed. Lynford—*Eaton*—dug in his evening-coat pocket and retrieved some seed. He let it eat, smoothing the bird's feathers with a gentle hand.

'This is a parakeet. Would you like to hold him? He's quite tame. Stick out your finger like a bar. He'll hop on,' Eaton instructed.

Thinking of him as Eaton was a dangerous step to take. It fostered a sense of intimacy as real as the intimacy they'd shared at the table, only this first-name intimacy was more portable. It would not be left behind with the dishes. It would go with them wherever they went.

The parakeet hopped onto her finger and Eliza gasped, delighted. 'I've never done anything like this,' she said. Eliza almost blurted out how much Sophie would love to see the birds, but her daughter was not a topic of casual conversation. Sophie belonged to her private world, the world she entrusted to few.

'You're a natural. He likes you,' Eaton assured her.

She looked about at the birds in cages. 'I wonder if they get jealous of the parakeets flying free?' As beautiful as the orangery was, she didn't like the idea of that beauty being at the expense of caged animals.

'Those birds can't fly.' Eaton followed her gaze. 'They all have various injuries. I brought them home from wherever I found them and nursed them as best I could.' He took the parakeet from her and set it to flying with its friends; Eliza felt her heart lurch in an unfamiliar way. Here was a man who was kind to animals, who built a school for a friend so she could marry the man she loved, who gave a stranger a home just because she asked for one, who mourned the loss of a dear friend. He was a rarity, like the orchids along the pathway.

'I fear too much of tonight has been about me. I didn't mean to monopolise the conversation.' Eaton reached overhead and plucked an orange. 'Dessert?'

She nodded. 'I was the one who asked the questions. You needn't feel guilty. You're an interesting man.' She could listen to him talk for hours.

'Well, you're an interesting woman and I'm wasting my opportunity to learn more about you by talking about myself.' He began to peel the fruit. 'I should have asked how the house is? If you have everything you need?' He passed her a section of the orange. 'I should also have had the decency to ask what has caused the change in your plans and whether I can do anything to assist? I hope it's nothing too serious?'

That depended on how seriously one took potential mutiny. Eliza took a bite of the succulent orange, buying time to gather her wits. Too often tonight she'd allowed herself to forget about business, to focus instead on being with him and the joy of simply being with someone who wasn't interested in her mines or her money. But his questions brought back reality and with it a reminder about how careful she needed to be.

'Just some unexpected mine business. We're timbering a new tunnel and I need to be on hand more than I'd anticipated.' She could see the answer disappointed him in its brevity, but she could not clarify further.

'Let me know if there's anything I can do.' He offered her another section of the orange with a smile, but she could see her lack of trust had insulted him.

'Thank you, but it's something I need to take care of alone.' A man like the Marquess, born to power, would never understand that she had to work twice as hard, had to be twice as strong as any man, that any weakness was enough to have her leadership called into question.

'Do you always handle everything alone?'

'Yes.' She met his gaze unabashedly. 'I've learned the hard way what happens to a woman when she doesn't.'

His eyes were on her, contemplating, his voice quiet and serious. 'Tell me, what happens to a woman who accepts help from a friend?'

'She becomes the target of society gossip. The worst of her character is assumed and the worst of her friend's character is assumed as well. Society does not tolerate men and women being friends.' It had started innocently enough with Miles Detford. She'd been establishing her control over the shareholders in that first year, unsure how to proceed on a matter. She'd gone to Detford for advice. She been naive in those early days. She'd not thought how others might look at those efforts with less friendly eyes. 'There were rumours that I was weak, unable to assume control of my husband's company. And that the gentleman in question was after my money, swindling me with kindness. I've never believed it. But I've made sure such a situation doesn't occur again.'

'Is this a cautionary tale for me?'

'No, it's for me. So that I remember what happens when I let down my guard.' Their eyes held for a moment before she rose. 'I ought to go. It's getting late and I've taken so much of your time today. Thank you for the evening.' If she left now, she might escape without offending him further, or without making herself vulnerable. She'd let down her guard too often tonight. There'd been only the one casualty for the indulgence—far better odds than she deserved.

'I'll see you out.' Eaton rose with her, but there was a stiffness in their politeness now—gone was the laughter in the carriage over spilled champagne, and the easy flow of conversation at dinner.

'My carriage will take you back to the dower house.' She understood the hidden message. He wasn't accompanying her, *unless* she asked. He was giving her every subtle assurance that he would not impose on her further in any way tonight. Eliza found the assurance disappointing and impressive. There wouldn't be any kisses tonight. He handed her into the carriage and stepped back. 'Goodnight, Eliza. Thank you for a lovely evening.' He motioned to the driver and the carriage set off, leaving him behind.

She ought to be glad of that. She also ought to be glad that he understood her need for formality and distance, that this was strictly a business arrangement, that she saw him as a business acquaintance only. Except she didn't. She saw him as a problem, a very attractive one. She'd only known him the sum of two days and three encounters. Already it was incredibly easy to let him shoulder her concerns and solve her problems. She could get used to that without even realising she was doing it. She preferred to keep her independence fully intact because she knew how this would end.

She had learned her lessons well and she would not repeat her mistakes with Eaton Falmage. She would not let these friendly encounters get out of hand or signal that she might be interested in something…more. She was worldlier now. She knew how her association with any man would look to others. She knew exactly what she risked in marriage to any man who might offer. And she knew how these stories ended in the real world.

Chapter Eight

The night had gone differently from what Eaton had anticipated. What had started as dinner and a chance to explore the connection between them had quite unexpectedly deepened into something more. Eaton made the long walk to the main house under the stars, hands in his pockets. It was chilly in the evening now, autumn had definitely arrived and he was without both his greatcoat and his carriage, having not brought one and having given the other to Eliza.

He'd not meant to talk of Richard Penlerick and yet once he'd started he hadn't been able to stop himself. Tonight had been about more than a physical connection between them. They'd both experienced great loss. Her words tonight had been a balm to him in a way the platitudes of others who'd not experienced such loss could not be. He was touched as well by what she'd shared, cognisant of the honour she'd done him by offering her own story in proof of her understanding. Yet there were other things she had not been willing to share, like the business that kept her in Porth Karrek. For all her openness about the loss of her husband, she'd withheld other things.

Eaton kicked at a pile of early fallen leaves. The restlessness that had tugged at him that afternoon was riding him hard now. It would be nice to enjoy autumn with Eliza Blaxland. They could pick apples, stroll the Trevaylor Woods, check on the boys at the school to see how the new curriculum was working. Perhaps they could work on her schools together. Perhaps he could persuade her that the first school should be right here at Wheal Karrek. Eliza would be a welcome distraction; an intelligent, discreet woman who could discuss the world and ideas with him. She would need persuading, though. Despite her abrupt dismissal tonight, she *did* respond to him. His attentions were not unwanted but he would need to take things slowly. She was not a merry widow but a very circumspect one, a woman who took her virtue seriously. He could respect that.

The sound of a dog howling in the distance brought a smile to his lips. Baldor, his hound, was out night hunting, restless like his master. Eaton whistled. The two of them could prowl the grounds together. He whistled again and Baldor bounded to his side, ready for an evening romp in the woods. A walk beneath the autumn moon would be just the thing to clear his thoughts, beginning with images of Eliza Blaxland as she'd been tonight—laughing in the carriage with him, her face inquisitive and glowing by the candle-light of their dinner, her exclamation of delight over the parakeet landing on her finger, her sincerity as they'd talked of Richard.

Tonight, he'd had a glimpse of the Eliza Blaxland who existed beneath her façade. But that glimpse had been fleeting. She'd remembered all too soon she had something to hide. That mystery would have to wait until tomorrow. He had business in Penzance that would keep him away most of the day, but he would look in on her later in the afternoon, perhaps invite her to another dinner where he could try once more to unravel her secrets.

The day had not gone as Eliza would have preferred. She'd wanted answers and she had none. She'd spent the day at the mine office going over books and peering out of the window at every noise, hoping to see Miles Detford ride in. But there'd been no news, not even a note. She hoped she hadn't erred in sending for him, that he wasn't raising the alarm among the shareholders. She was relying on his friendship to keep her circumspect message private between them. But Miles had not come.

There were plenty of grounds on which to excuse his negligence. It was entirely possible he was off to Scotland, shooting grouse. The message might not even have reached him. He might be delayed by other matters. Still, Miles's absence niggled at her against the backdrop of another who had far less reason to come to her aid and yet had arrived immediately.

Her mind whispered the comparison: *Eaton Falmage came and he owes you nothing, not even friend-*

ship. Eaton had responded to her note with his presence, with the offer of a home. She'd asked for nothing more than some answers from Miles.

Then again, perhaps Eaton Falmage had made the offer in hopes of getting something in return. He'd been disappointed in her last night. Would he still come if she summoned him today, or was he already regretting his generosity? She knew how these trades worked. She'd refused Detford's honourable overtures of marriage when society had confused their friendship for something more intimate. In retrospect, though, society wasn't the only one who'd imagined intimacy where she'd been blind. Detford had wanted more than friendship. There'd been a few kisses stolen in a moment of loneliness, of weakness, kisses that had meant more to him, signalled more to him, than she'd intended in her early grief. She wouldn't make that mistake again. It was why she'd left Lynford last night. To have stayed any longer in the orangery would have resulted in more kisses, more steps along a path she couldn't travel, no matter how handsome the companion.

Eliza looked at the wall clock and shut the ledgers with a resounding thump. Half past three. These were thoughts that made it impossible to work. She'd daydreamed the better part of the last half hour away and to no purpose. She was destined to be alone for Sophie's sake and for her own security. She'd decided this years ago. It was useless to persist in wasting time on such folly. It was time to go home. Sophie would be arriving and she wanted to be there. The day would be infinitely better once her daughter had arrived. Five days away from Sophie seemed like an eternity. She was never truly alone when they were together.

Eliza stopped at Chegwin's mercantile on Budoc Lane to purchase a kite and a doll for Sophie. She would leave the toys on Sophie's bed as a surprise. They could have a picnic tomorrow at the beach if the weather held. Her head was full of plans. This would be a holiday for the two of them. She would carve out time for fun even though she had business to look after. She was always so busy in Truro with the banks and the mines. A holiday would do them both good and the fresh air had much to recommend it.

Halfway down the drive to the dower house, she noticed the activity in the drive, an unfamiliar coach outside the house, servants bustling about hauling trunks inside. A tall, slim, young woman whom Eliza recognised as Miss Gilchrist—Sophie's governess—stood amid the chaos, looking about helplessly as progress was made without her. Eliza's mood lifted with realisation. Sophie was here! They must have arrived early. She spotted her daughter's dark curls bobbing in and out of the servants. 'Mama!' Sophie rushed towards her.

Eliza took her skirts in one hand and began to run. It was an awkward run, burdened as she was with a kite and a doll, but it served to close the distance and within moments Sophie was in her arms, her packages forgotten. 'Oh, sweet girl, you're here! How I've missed you!' Eliza held her tight. This was everything, her whole world right here in her arms.

'I've missed you, too, Mama, but we've had such grand adventures, Miss Gilchrist and I. The wheel on the coach broke just as we were almost here and Miss Gilchrist didn't know what to do. The driver said we should walk back to the last town,' Sophie rambled enthusiastically, 'but Miss Gilchrist said that was impossible because you were expecting us tonight and you'd worry if we didn't arrive. Then a man came by on a great big chestnut horse...'

Sophie paused for a breath, then continued in a rush to make up for lost time.

'We told him who we were and he brought us here. He said he was a friend of yours. He sent his coach back for our things and for Miss Gilchrist, who was too scared to get on the horse. But I wasn't too scared. I climbed right up and he held on to me tight so I didn't fall.'

A hundred thoughts hit her at once. Her precious child had willingly gone off with a stranger just because he said he knew her and Miss Gilchrist had *allowed* it. She ought to sack the woman for such a poor decision. Sophie was the Blaxland heiress. When she came of age, she'd be worth a fortune. In the right hands, or in this case the wrong ones, Sophie would be a powerful weapon to wield against her. Yet beneath Eliza's fears there was gratefulness, too. What a kindness the man had done them. 'Is your rescuer still here?' She searched Sophie's sweet face to assure herself Sophie had come to no harm. They would have to discuss the demerits of going off with strangers later.

'He's inside, giving orders. He's very good at that.

Almost as good as you, Mama,' Sophie averred, obviously impressed. 'But he smiles when he tells people what to do.'

A man was inside her house? Giving orders? That seemed a bit much. She needed to offer her gratitude and send him on his way. Eliza rose, remembering her dropped packages. 'I brought you presents. Why don't you go inside and unwrap them while I make my thanks?'

'There he is, Mama!' Sophie pointed at the archway of the arcade where a tall, dark-haired man emerged from the house, recognisable for his confidence as much as his greatcoat. *Eaton Falmage.* Eliza's heart skipped as he waved and strode towards them. He knew, then. Her secret. One of them, at least, was out. Would he be angry she hadn't told him?

'I see you've called for reinforcements. Have you tired of my company already?' He was all easy laughter and grins. 'I met this fine young lady on the road on my way home from Penzance. She was stranded.' He gave Sophie a wink and then fixed Eliza with his merry stare. 'You can imagine my surprise when she told me she was yours. For a moment I didn't believe her. How could that be possible? I thought. In none of our conversations had the mention of children ever come up.' He was teasing her and scolding her all at once. His gaze turned serious. 'But then I decided it must be true. After all, there are other things you haven't told me as well.' Such as her mine business. Or the fact that she was the *second* Mrs Blaxland.

'You must forgive me, I'm a very private person.'

She rested a hand on Sophie's shoulder. 'I do thank you for your timely intervention and your efforts. Once again, I am in your debt.'

Eaton shook his head. 'I am not keeping score, Mrs Blaxland.'

'Aren't you?' she replied coolly, a little frisson of awareness passing between them.

'A man of honour doesn't leave a young girl and her governess stranded on the road, score or not,' Eaton scolded and she demurred. She'd not meant to slander his honour. What was wrong with her? Had her life really become nothing more than tally marks in ledgers? A keeping of score between her friends and her enemies?

Miss Gilchrist bustled up, having recovered her senses, ready to take charge of Sophie. 'Shall we go to our rooms and see to the unpacking, Miss Sophie?' She ushered Sophie away, the girl chattering excitedly about seeing the house.

'Does she never stop talking?' Eaton asked with a laugh. It wasn't meanly said. 'I find it a marvel she has so much to say.' He slanted her a sideways glance. 'Unlike her mother, apparently. Why didn't you tell me, Eliza?'

'Would it have mattered? Would you not have offered the house?' Eliza answered swiftly.

'Of course it would have mattered. I would have offered *more*. There are toys in the nursery at Falmage Hill just gathering dust. I'll have someone clean them up and send them down. There are picture books, a boat, toy soldiers, my sisters' tea sets and dolls.'

'Your sisters?' Eliza interrupted, intrigued.

'Four of them, all younger than me, and a younger brother, too.' Eaton shook his head. 'They were the bane of my existence growing up, but now that my sisters are all married and live away with my darling nieces and nephews, I love them far more than I ever did when we were all together.' He chuckled. 'They don't come here any more. Falmage Hill is too far away and there are too many of them. It's quite the mobilisation. It's much easier for me to travel to them.'

'You miss them.' Eliza heard the wistfulness in his voice. He was always so confident, always in charge, always knew what to do. It was hard to imagine there were any voids in his life, any gaps he struggled to fill.

'I suppose I do, in my own way.' He grinned, but Eliza wasn't fooled. He'd grinned to hide the hurt. 'I'll tell Cook to send extra cake. Sophie told me her favourite dessert is chocolate cake, but that any cake will do in a pinch. Very practical, your daughter is, very sensible when it comes to desserts.'

'Perhaps Cook should send food for three.' The spontaneity of the offer surprised even her. The words were out before she could take them back. She was toying with temptation now, creating more time in his intoxicating presence, and she was being bold. Perhaps too bold. He might read an invitation in it. Eliza hastily backtracked, offering him a way out. 'That is, if you're not previously engaged or if Sophie hasn't already talked your ears off.'

Eaton continued grinning. 'Supper for three it is. I can't think of anywhere I'd rather be. I shall see you at seven o'clock.'

Chapter Nine

As dinners went, it certainly couldn't compete with the crystal and candlelight of the orangery. The food was plain, more appropriate for younger tastes than the sophisticated palate Eaton had presented her with the previous evening. Yet the meal had a dangerous charm of its own that Eliza was quick to recognise: the pseudo-image of a family gathered for an evening meal, simple foods and fresh cider in place of chilled champagne, a chatty young girl whose exuberant conversation carried an energy of its own. She was delighted in everything: the new house, her room, the gifts, her rescue—which had resulted in a ride on the 'most splendid horse in the world'. She was especially delighted in the chocolate cake, which, despite its promise, saw Sophie asleep at the table before it was even served.

'I suppose that's all the more reason to eat dessert first.' Eaton laughed softly in the candlelight of the dining room. 'We'll wrap up a piece for her to have tomorrow.'

We. How easy it was for this man to insinuate himself into their lives. She needed to put a stop to it before it went any further. Her debt to him was growing, as was her appreciation. 'I'm sorry,' Eliza apologised, 'I need to put her to bed.' She always put Sophie to bed, even though Miss Gilchrist was on hand. Eliza liked the ritual of bedtime, of closing the day together. 'There's brandy in the parlour, if you care to wait?' It felt awkward to act the hostess, as if Eaton was a guest in the house when he owned it and could do as he pleased. He *knew* there was brandy in the parlour. He'd instructed it to be put there.

'Let me help.' Eaton rose and lifted Sophie, who didn't stir at being hoisted away from her longed-for chocolate cake. 'She's done admirably for such an eventful day. Apparently, she's inherited her mother's tenacity.'

Eliza picked up a lamp and led the way upstairs, trying not to let her heart run away with her mind at the sight of Eaton Falmage's broad shoulder hosting Sophie's dark head. She told herself it was merely the paternal image of a man with a child that tugged at her, not the sight of that *particular* man. She might feel that way about any man offering a glimpse of his softer side. 'If you just lay her on the bed, I can tuck her in,' Eliza offered. Once the Marquess had left, she prepared her for bed, smoothed back Sophie's dark hair and kissed her forehead, arranging the blankets around her. 'Goodnight, my dear. Sleep well, we have more adventures planned for tomorrow.'

Downstairs, dishes had already been cleared by the efficient staff and a low fire in the parlour beckoned invitingly. One might find the scene cosy if one wasn't on edge. She hadn't been alone with a man in such an intimate, domestic setting for years. 'Will you sit with me while I have some brandy?' Eaton asked. How could she refuse after all he'd done today? It was a simple enough request, the only danger in it came from herself and the constructs she put on it.

Eliza took a seat while Eaton poured. 'Would you like a drink as well?'

'No, I don't drink spirits, but thank you,' she declined, hands folded tightly in her lap. Prolonging the evening like this was a poor idea. Such a setting begged for intimacies, for sharing things that should be kept private. She was merely passing through.

'You only drink champagne? You have exalted tastes, Eliza. I'd best remember that,' Eaton teased congenially, settling in the wing-backed chair across from her. How did he do that? How did he make it so easy to be with him? To laugh? To banter? One would have thought they were old friends instead of new acquaintances.

He sipped his brandy. 'Did you have a productive day at the mines?' he asked as if they were a married couple discussing their day. They'd be a very different sort of married couple. Wives didn't run mines. Cits didn't marry future dukes and *she* wouldn't marry anyone. Ever.

On those grounds, the fantasy wasn't only different, it was dangerous. Eaton didn't even have to try to seduce her, if that was his intention. She was seducing herself, seeing all sorts of domestic fantasies on her own: a family assembled at the dinner table, a conversation that veered and swerved with Sophie's enthusiasm, jumping from topic to topic, tucking Sophie in when the enthusiasm was spent. But it was a fantasy only, nice in theory, impractical in reality. She wasn't looking for a man to fill that role and she would not trade all she'd fought for simply to have a marriage. It wouldn't be fair to her daughter or to herself to have fought so hard for everything to simply give it over to a husband. 'The new tunnel is proceeding.' Her answer was succinct and she quickly turned the conversation to him. 'And your day? What were you doing in Penzance?'

'I was looking in on one of the school's donors, Mrs Penhaligon, the other widow. She's been very much alone since her husband died and she moved away from Porth Karrek, even though it's only a few miles.' Not just the other widow. The other *woman*. Eliza recognised the name now from that first conversation at the school when she'd made her surprise visit.

'You make a habit of collecting widows, it seems,' Eliza replied more sharply than she intended. Surely she wasn't jealous? She didn't even know this woman. Was she young? Old? Pretty? Did Eaton take her for carriage rides and pour champagne for her as well? They were unworthy thoughts when she'd just reminded herself there could be no pursuit here.

'I needed the name of a piano tuner.' Eaton eyed her suspiciously as if he sensed the envy beneath her sharpness. Too late she remembered Mrs Penhaligon was the donor of the prized Sébastien Érard. Eaton gave her a reprieve, turning the topic. 'Now, what adventures do you have in mind for tomorrow? The weather will be fine. Might I suggest a picnic at the beach? I can bring the carriage at noon. There's a cove at Karrek Sands with arguably the best beach in Cornwall. Sophie will love it. She can fly her new kite.'

He was going to come with them.

It was the last thing she needed. But also the first. Eliza didn't know how to make the arrangements for a picnic other than to burden the servants with the task, which she was loath to do since they weren't hers. His presence would be a great help. 'I've taken enough of your time,' she began to refuse. She really couldn't impose further, couldn't lead him on. She knew the rules of engagement. Most of all, she shouldn't lead herself on, pretending something was possible. How ironic that after all this time worrying about protecting herself from the external threat of men, the real threat to her own freedom seemed to come from her and her own longings.

Eliza rose. She needed to be clear with him now before this relationship of sorts spiralled out of control.

'It's no imposition on me.' Eaton rose with her, understanding her signal to depart.

'Perhaps it is to me,' Eliza said firmly, meeting his gaze. 'It occurs to me that you must really want something to go to these lengths for me. I will not kiss you for your efforts.'

Eaton's dark gaze became inscrutable, an indecipherable smile playing on his lips, part wry humour, part offended honour. 'I should hope not, Eliza, since such a trade would imply I am a man who has to buy a woman's affections and that you are a woman who would sell them. I think neither implication paints either one of us in a particularly good light.' He inclined his head, short and curt. 'Goodnight.' She had meant to put him off and it seemed she'd succeeded. If she didn't care for the terseness in his tone, she only had herself to blame.

Eliza wasn't alone. Eaton absently stroked Baldor's head as the two of them lounged by the fire in the library, Baldor standing at majestic attention beside his chair. 'She has a child,' Eaton said out loud to the dog. He'd not known about Sophie any more than he'd known about Blaxland's second marriage. Perhaps Eliza had got her love of privacy from Blaxland.

Eaton stretched his legs, resting his boots on the fireplace fender. Was Sophie all she was protecting with her privacy or was there something more? There'd been mixed emotions on her face when she'd seen him this afternoon. She reminded him of paintings of the Madonna, on her knees, clutching her child, her eyes closed in a moment of private joy at the reunion, yet when she'd opened them and seen him, there'd been a fleeting look of fear before she'd recognised him. She'd been expecting a stranger and the notion of a stranger had given her a degree of fright. Perhaps that was just maternal instinct. His own sisters were like that, panicking when a child disappeared into the woods for too long.

Eaton closed his eyes, reliving the pleasantness of the evening. He'd not had such a night for ages; no stiff evening wear, no need to be conscious of every word, only honest conversation and laughter. There'd been plenty of that. Sophie told funny stories—at least they were funny when told through a child's eyes. There'd been no terror for Sophie in being stranded on the road, only adventure and excitement. Eaton envied her that precious innocence. Eliza would guard it well if that look on her face today was any indication. She was a fierce mother. Fierce in love, fierce in protection.

His thoughts lingered on the word: *mother*. Eliza was a mother. He understood now why she felt compelled to resist the pull between them. A mother must always think of her children. Her reputation was their reputation. But she was also a woman, a young woman, with a young woman's desires and fantasies. He'd felt those fantasies stir in her when they'd kissed. She was a woman full of passions, not only for her child, but for living and for loving. Yet she was choosing to stifle the latter in order to protect the former. What a very difficult decision to make—to give up adventure and passion in its various forms for the sake of others. Unless, of course, she didn't know what she was missing.

Eaton's eyes opened slowly at the thought. He could help her there. If there was anyone who knew the value of adventure, it was him. But to what end? To coax her into a short-lived affair? He would be discreet, of course. No one outside the two of them needed to know. He could preserve her reputation and in exchange he could have a lover. He could even pretend to have a family. That was dangerous ground, to co-opt Eliza's child as his own even for a short time. In his opinion, it was the epitome of selfishness. No one should suffer from his affliction but himself. He'd not missed the instant admiration in Sophie's eyes this afternoon when he'd taken her up on his horse. Children often attached easily and quickly. Eliza might not be hurt when the affair ended, but Sophie would be. She wouldn't understand this thing they played at wasn't meant to last.

He was not an unkind man, nor a terribly selfish one. Did he dare pursue Eliza Blaxland now that a child was involved? 'And yet how can I not?' Eaton said to Baldor, who only perked up an ear. 'How can I let her go when I sense that she needs me?' Eliza Blaxland had secrets to keep and dragons to slay. She was in desperate need of a knight in shining armour even if an affair was out of the question, even if she didn't realise it. The strong ones never did. It was that very strength he admired most about her. He wanted her to keep that strength. It was the core of her. Eliza would have his sword, whether she wanted it or not. The trick would be in convincing her to accept it. A picnic tomorrow would be an ideal place to start. Perhaps once she accepted his help, more could follow.

It was not a good morning, despite the beautiful autumn weather outdoors. Miles Detford stared pensively at the papers spread out before him on the table before eyeing the other men with him. 'What we dare borders on treachery. To be caught would be tantamount to fraud,' he warned, but his words lacked conviction. There were benefits to the proposal as well, benefits that were worth the risk. He'd waited a long time for success.

'Do you think she'll accept our offer?' asked silver-templed Gismond Brenley, his gaze sharp. 'You know her best, after all, Detford.' There was a derisive undertone to Brenley's comment, a reminder that they'd tried and failed five years ago to take Eliza Blaxland out of the equation of mine ownership through a sentimental offer of marriage. Brenley held that failure over his head like the Sword of Damocles.

Miles shrugged to indicate indecision. 'She certainly should. The terms are generous. We are offering to buy out her shares in the mines at considerable profit to her. She can live in comfort without worry. But she's been offered such benefits before. She can take the money and invest it in some other venture if that's of interest to her.'

'Perhaps money will appeal to her more than a husband,' Brenley needled.

Isley Thorp, slender and sallow-faced, sitting on Detford's right, looked over the tops of his spectacles. 'Considerable profit under *today's* terms,' he reminded the group. 'If she sold today, the money would look generous. But against the future profits once that tunnel is complete, our offer looks paltry.' This was where they trod the grey area of defrauding. One could easily argue they knew it was a poor offer against the expected returns on the new tunnel.

Brenley pursed his mouth. 'Mining is a risk. The manager at the mine, Cardy, says there's a goodly amount of copper in that tunnel waiting to be plucked out. But there's a chance he's wrong. It's our bank accounts that take that gamble. We can't promise what we'll find there. She can't hold us accountable for future success if she sells out before then.' That would be their defence in court if it ever came to that. 'Any woman would be pleased with such an offer. She has a young child. Surely she can spend her time better raising her instead of running between her mines and meeting with shareholders.'

Miles raised smooth blond brows. 'When has Eliza Blaxland ever behaved like any other woman? It's unnatural how she acts, managing business, money and ourselves as if we're children unable to make decisions without her. If she doesn't take this offer, we'll be tied to her apron strings for life. How do the other shareholders feel?'

The third man, Isley Thorp, who'd been silent up until now, shook his head. 'Some are with us. But others are ambivalent. They say she's made us money, she's done a fine job of modernising. Why should she be ousted?'

'Not ousted, *persuaded*,' Brenley corrected impatiently. 'We're not forcing anyone out. We're simply putting an option to her out of consideration for her and her daughter.'

Thorp nodded. 'It sounds legitimate when you put

it that way. Perhaps you should be the one who presents the idea to her?'

Yes, Miles thought. Perhaps it was time Brenley stuck his neck out for this venture instead of making plans for others to carry out. But Miles shook his head. He wanted his revenge, his pride restored. No one had made him look as foolish as Eliza Blaxland had. 'No, that's my job. But not just yet. We'll let her stew for a bit in her own worries. We'll let her wonder why I've delayed answering her summons. The more unaware we can catch her, the more desperate she'll be. The shareholders' meeting is in just a few weeks at Porth Karrek.'

The meeting was being held there to celebrate the new tunnel. Miles exchanged a meaningful glance with Brenley. In this, they agreed. The meeting would be the ideal ground on which to launch their campaign against Eliza Blaxland, the woman who had refused him, who had made him look like a laughingstock when he'd gone to her with a decent offer of marriage. He would not let her play him again. He would go to her in the guise of a friend and she would not realise it was otherwise until it was too late.

Thorp spoke up. 'What if you fail to convince her as you've failed in the past? Are we willing to take more severe measures?'

Miles reached for the papers and rolled them up. Thorp was an icy businessman. He knew what Thorp meant by other measures: violence, kidnapping, mur-

der. 'We certainly won't rule anything out, but let's
hope for once that Eliza Blaxland will see sense, for
all our sakes.'

Chapter Ten

The cove at Karrek Sands was everything Eaton had promised and more; the picnic was a lavish but simple outing. Servants had gone ahead to set up a canopy and chairs and to unpack hampers of food so that all was ready when they arrived. Yet the preparations did not hinder the authenticity of the picnic. This was not a formal occasion. Sophie had brought her kite and immediately set about getting it aloft. Eliza watched her barefoot daughter from the shade of the canopy, envious of her licence to play in the sand and to tempt the waves sans socks and shoes.

Beside her, Eaton began to tug at his boots. 'Well? Aren't you going to take your shoes off, too?' He cast her a boyish glance as he divested himself of his footwear, revealing a long, narrow foot with a freckle in its centre. 'What? Have you never seen a man's foot before?' he teased before she could look away. 'This might be the last of the good weather; it's certainly the last of the *warm* weather. It would be a shame to waste it.'

Eaton winked and rolled up his trouser legs, showing off well-muscled calves. 'Come on, Eliza, no one will see. We've the entire beach to ourselves, all the privacy you could want.' He shucked off his coat and waistcoat, looking much as he had the first time she saw him, *en déshabillé*, moving furniture at the school. He rose and waved to Sophie, who was calling to him to come fly the kite. He gave her a smile that bordered on wicked. 'Come and play, I dare you,' he said, and then he was off, trotting to the water's edge to fly the kite.

Eliza smiled to herself as she removed shoes and socks and even her jacket. It would indeed be a shame to waste the opportunity to frolic on the beach, especially after all the effort Eaton had taken to ensure the beach was entirely theirs. Marquesses could do such things. Karrek Sands was theirs for the afternoon. Nothing could touch them here—not the mines, not her worries over the ledgers, not even propriety's whisperings that she should not bare her ankles in public or be interacting privately with a man. The beach was both public and private. It was also paradise and it was hers for the day—a precious day to enjoy her daughter. Sophie was nine and nearing that bridge between girlhood and womanhood. How much longer would she be allowed to wander shorelines barefoot before society deemed it unladylike? Her dear girl was growing up too fast.

Eliza tied up her skirts and went to join them. There

was a good breeze blowing and the kite was flying high. 'Look, Mama, we've used almost all of the string! I've never got a kite up so high before,' Sophie exclaimed.

'You're a natural flier,' Eaton complimented. 'Why don't we try some tricks?' His hair was mussed and his calves were speckled with sticky sand, proof he'd been running in the water, no doubt saving the kite from a soaking before Sophie had become a natural. Eaton stood behind Sophie, an easy hand on her shoulder, ready to intervene if needed. A gust of wind took the kite and it dived, dipping dangerously towards the waves. 'Oh, no!' Sophie exclaimed in panicked worry.

'Steady, Sophie.' Eaton's voice was calm. Instead of taking the spool and fixing the situation for her, he coached her in even tones. 'Reel in the string, just a little, don't tug, that will only make the kite jerk more and then it can't stabilise. There, see, you've done it. The kite has settled and you can let out the string. Well done, Sophie. Now, are we ready for some tricks?'

They were enjoying each other. How exciting it must be for Sophie to have the attention of an adult other than herself. Eliza busied herself gathering seashells, wanting to be close, but not wanting to intrude overmuch on the interlude. She surreptitiously watched Eaton show Sophie how to make the kite soar like a bird, swooping and diving in the sky before turning the kite back over to her. Sophie was clapping her hands and saying something to Eaton that Eliza couldn't hear. It must have pleased him. He smiled at Sophie and bent down to say something in return.

This was yet another sight to warm her. How different he was from Huntingdon. Huntingdon had been an old parent, too set in his ways to visit the nursery and play with a toddler. He'd adored his daughter, but he'd been unable to be the sort of father a child dreams of—a father who runs along the beach with them, a father who takes them for horseback rides and carries them to bed as if they were featherweights.

Eaton would be a spectacular father.

It was an unsettling and inappropriate thought. Eliza looked away from the kite flying. She could not give flight to that sort of fantasy. It was best to quell it before it got out of hand and the best way to do that was to think about reality. Argument one: a day with a child did not prove a man was good father material. It merely showed that he had a capacity for kindness. Argument two: Eaton Falmage had no intention of taking on another man's child. It wasn't what heirs to a dukedom did. Dukes' heirs made their own families. Argument three: she wasn't looking for a father for Sophie or a husband for herself. She'd made that decision years ago. She'd best get her emotions under control and rein in these fantastical constructions. She'd made her situation clear to Eaton last night. Today, he was merely being kind. He knew there was no hope in pursuing her. She was complicated.

Eliza allowed herself to glance at the duo again. Eaton smiled, this time for her. He strode towards her, collapsing beside her in the sand. 'She's having a good time.' He propped himself up on an elbow. 'Your daughter is wonderful. You've raised her well.'

'Thank you.' Eliza found herself blushing. 'I worry for her, being an only child. I was an only child and it's a lonely way to grow up. I would have preferred she had a brother or sister, at least one.' She drew an abstract figure in the sand, uncomfortable with the confession. It brought the conversation too close to other truths. She had not meant to say so much. She hazarded a glance at Eaton and offered a tremulous smile.

Eaton's dark gaze clouded, his brows knit as a shadow scuttled across his features. Perhaps talk of children unsettled him. It unsettled many bachelors. 'You could marry again. You're still young. You have much to offer.' A quiet intimacy settled between them at the suggestion. A new awareness of him unfurled in her belly, warm and inviting. She must resist.

'No.' Her answer was firm but barely audible over the waves. 'I've become too set in my ways these last five years. A husband would not find me biddable.' She shook her head with finality. 'I refused the last man who proposed.'

'Why?' Eaton did not allow her to dismiss the topic.

'I had nothing to give up when I married Huntingdon. But I have much to lose in a marriage now and I've seen what a woman gives up when she marries. It cost my mother everything. She turned her life over to her husband, who was only moderately good with money, and then to her husband's brother when her husband died. My well-meaning uncle was even worse with money than my father. By the time I was fourteen I knew with surety I'd do whatever it took to avoid my mother's fate. I started learning about the family business.'

'And then you married a man twice your age and more.'

'I was *not* after his money,' Eliza snapped.

'I did not mean to suggest that you were. I was merely curious as to what impelled you to marry as you did,' Eaton answered in sharp offence.

They were teetering on the brink of a quarrel. She would not be judged by anyone, certainly not by a marquess who'd had his perfect life handed to him, no matter how humble he seemed. 'Huntingdon Blaxland came to my uncle and proposed the match. And I took the offer. He was a good man and my choices were limited.' Not that it was any of Eaton's business. If she was upset over these disclosures, it was her own fault for having shared them.

Eliza blew out a breath, gathering her composure. She should not be discussing these things with a man she barely knew. She groped for a better topic of conversation, something lighter. 'Sophie will be spoiled after today. She'll expect to come to the beach every day.'

'Perhaps she should.' Eaton's smile returned, the shadow had passed. 'I think fresh air and exercise cannot be overestimated for children. You know what they say about all work and no play.' Eaton gave her a thoughtful look. 'It seems her home in Truro is a quiet place.'

Eliza looked down at her hands, wondering what Sophie had told him. 'We don't go out much. I have the mines to look after and before that we were in mourning and she was very young.' Sometimes she felt they'd never truly come out of mourning. It had been a convenient shield to hide behind, a legitimate reason to take herself out of the public eye. She went to business meetings and charity meetings, but she seldom went out at night to Truro's social gatherings. The few times she had gone out, Miles had been beside her and that had proved disastrous. Afterwards, it had seemed easier and safer to use mourning as an excuse not to engage.

'You're not in mourning any longer,' Eaton pointed out. 'Pardon my saying so, but it's been five years.' His gaze held hers and she knew he was doing the sums. Sophie would have been four, she wouldn't recall her father at all. He was thinking she didn't need to hold on to mourning for Sophie's sake. 'It must be lonely, living a secluded life with just Sophie for company.' His gaze studied her, unnerving her with the intensity of his dark eyes. 'Oftentimes people who choose seclusion see it as a form of protection.'

'And sometimes they simply value their privacy,' Eliza answered swiftly before she could take advantage of the opening and spill her troubles. How tempting it was, with nothing around them but sea and sand, to lay her problems on his shoulders.

'Should that cease to be the case, Eliza, I hope you would tell me.' Eaton pushed up from the sand with a burst of energy. 'Shall we eat? I have it on good authority Sophie is starving. I had the chocolate cake from last night packed and there might even be a few late-season strawberries.' He grinned at her and gave her his hand, banishing the seriousness of the prior moment; perhaps he also realised that a line had been crossed and a retreat into friendly acquaintanceship was necessary.

Lunch was an animated affair with Sophie talking of kites and seashells between bites of sandwiches and swallows of cider. As they relaxed on pillows beneath the canopy, Eaton fished through the bucket of shells. He held one up and shook it. 'Put that to your ear, Sophie, and tell me what you hear.'

Sophie did and her face lit up. 'I can hear the ocean!' She shook it again. 'Is the ocean in there?'

'No.' Eaton shook his head and took the shell, holding it on the flat of his palm. 'Do you see how the shell is curved? Air gets trapped in there and it makes a roaring, rushing sound when it bounces around inside the shell.' He looked over their heads and caught her gaze. 'Ambient noise is what it's called.'

'Let's try another!' Sophie was already digging through the pail, eager to test the hypothesis. This was an example of his curriculum, Eliza realised, the one he'd designed for Cador Kitto's conservatory. Learning by doing, by touching. How splendid it was to watch Sophie's face light up as she tried out the new word.

'Am…bi…ent…'

Eaton sorted through the bucket and pulled out one of the larger shells. 'Do you think you can spare these, Sophie?' He rose and went to his long-abandoned coat and fished in the pockets, discarding all sorts of bits until he drew out a length of twine and a penknife.

Eliza laughed. 'You have the pockets of a schoolboy. Are you sure there are no toads in there?'

Eaton gave her a wink. 'No toads, but plenty of useful items. Just watch.' He sat down beside Sophie and took the shell in hand, stringing it on a length of twine before tying it about Sophie's neck. 'There, a sea talisman for you. Now you can keep the ocean with you wherever you go, even when you're in Truro and miles away.' For a moment, the reminder lingered that this would all end. Then, Eaton leapt to his feet. 'Now, who wants to go exploring? There's an old smuggler's cave down the beach. Let's find it and see if there's any treasure left. You go on ahead, Sophie, and clear the way, while your mama and I follow.'

'You are as indefatigable she is. Do you never slow down?' Eliza laughed as they strolled at the edge of the beach, waves teasing their toes.

'Never. There's too much to do, too much to enjoy.' Eaton grinned and steered her out of the way of a large wave that threatened their feet.

It was her turn to probe as he'd done earlier on the beach. 'If we don't slow down, we often lose our chance to think, or perhaps that's the very reason we don't slow down. We don't want to think.' A whirlwind could be as effective a place to hide as the solitude he accused her of keeping. 'What's your reason?'

Eaton chuckled. 'What would I hide from, Eliza? I have everything I could want. Money, status, the power to do good in this world.' He bent down to pick up a pebble and skipped it out over the waves, perhaps to give himself something to do. He couldn't be still even in the moment. It made her wonder if she'd hit upon something after all. What could he possibly have to hide? What didn't he want to tell her?

'What will you do now that the school is underway? Are there other projects looming on your agenda?' She'd not meant to discuss the business of the mining schools today, but the opening was ideal.

Eaton shrugged and skipped another pebble. 'I'll plan my trip to Italy. I was supposed to go last spring, but then the school came along.' He smiled. 'I'll visit my sisters for the winter holidays, maybe spend a little time in London to make up for not being there this Season. I have experiments to conduct in the orangery. Perhaps Sophie can be my assistant. She has an agile mind.'

'You needn't feel you have to entertain her, or me,' Eliza quickly absolved him. 'I have work at the mine and a shareholders' meeting coming up and she has Miss Gilchrist to see to her.' Although Miss Gilchrist's lessons would hardly compare to the excitement of learning about ambient sound on the beach with Eaton or the physics of flying a kite. He might say he wasn't keeping score, but she was, and the ledger between them was becoming woefully unbalanced.

Eaton leaned close, whispering at her ear, 'Have you ever considered that maybe you're the one doing me the favour? That it's not the other way around, after all?'

'I fear we are a distraction, not a favour,' Eliza chided softly. She was not wrong. Eaton Falmage was a busy man for whom children were a passing fancy, not a priority. He had other things to consider: trips to Italy, London Seasons. His life was a collection of whirlwinds of which she and Sophie were merely one. Within a month they'd be forgotten.

They reached the cave. Sophie was already inside and Eaton had to duck to get through the entrance. 'I used to explore in here with my friends,' he told her. 'We once spent all summer looking for hidden treasure. We even had a map.'

Sophie's eyes went wide. 'Did you find anything?' she asked and Eliza found herself holding her breath along with Sophie, waiting for his answer.

'No, we never did.' He knelt down to Sophie's level and said seriously, 'But you know what that means.'

'That there isn't any treasure?' Sophie replied, disappointed.

'It means the treasure is still there. Waiting. Maybe for *you* to find it. Off you go, don't leave any rock unturned, no crevice unexplored.'

Sophie ran off and Eaton turned to Eliza, catching her frown. 'You disapprove? Or is it that you don't believe in treasure?'

'You're getting her hopes up. She'll be disappointed when she doesn't find it,' Eliza scolded softly.

'Disappointment isn't all bad,' Eaton replied, unconcerned. 'It's adds a certain flavour to life, as you well know. Certainly you're the better for your challenges, wouldn't you agree?'

It was hard to disagree with him at the moment. In the confines of the cavern, Eliza was acutely aware they were very much alone. In the cave, Eaton came fully into his height and breadth. His physique was not made for confined spaces. 'Do you speak from experience? You hardly seem the sort to have had disappointments,' she queried, slightly breathless. In such a space, it would be easy to be intimidated by him, or to think him invincible. She was not. She was enormously attracted to him. He filled the space entirely and her senses with it, reminding her, as he had in the garden, as he did *every time* she saw him, that she was more than a mine owner and a mother.

'Maybe I have found treasure, despite my earlier disappointments, after all, Eliza,' he whispered her name. 'These last two days have been extraordinary.' He leaned an arm against the rocky wall, bracketing her with his body. 'Maybe treasure doesn't come in an iron chest.'

'No, maybe it doesn't,' she answered, her breath catching, her imagination running wild. Maybe it came in the form of kisses stolen in a golden moment on a sun-kissed day. Her lips parted just a fraction in invitation and he took it without hesitation, his mouth commanding hers with a kiss, his body strong against her, and she gave over to it, surrendering herself to his mouth. How wondrous to lose herself just for a moment, to be swept away by another's touch, not to be an island unto herself.

There was a scream of glee somewhere beyond them, recalling them to reality. Eaton stepped back, but his eyes were hot even as his mouth curled in a smile. 'Sophie's found something,' he said softly with a laugh, but he took her hand, apparently as unwilling as she to break contact entirely. 'Shall we go and see? Then we'll have to head back. The tide will be in soon.'

Sophie didn't find any treasure, but she had found a starfish Eaton helped her throw back into the sea.

They headed back to the picnic area, their linked hands surreptitiously hidden in the folds of her skirts. It was a simple intimacy, one she should discourage, but it was less dangerous than a kiss. Perhaps that was why she allowed it. Perhaps there were other reasons, too. Perhaps she was lonely, starved for adult-human contact, although it did her no credit to admit it. It made her seem desperate, something she didn't like appearing even to herself. That was a craving she'd have to bottle. It had no place in her life now. She slipped her hand free.

'Where shall we go tomorrow?' Eaton asked as they gathered discarded socks and shoes.

'I have to work.' Eliza made her excuses before her willpower waned. Another day with Eaton was an intoxicating prospect.

'Not *all* day, certainly?' Eaton pressed irresistibly.

'No, not all day, but it's not just that.' She drew him aside with a meaningful glance and lowered her voice. 'One day is understandable, perhaps, if anyone saw us today. But a second day? I am a private woman by choice, Eaton, and by necessity. A woman in a man's company does not pass unnoticed, especially when that man is a marquess.' She arched a brow. 'Do you think because I am a widow that I am above censure?' It was precisely what he thought, she could tell from the rebuttal that died on his lips. The widows he knew were the former wives of aristocrats, who could afford, perhaps even welcomed, a little scandal to spice up their lives. 'What do you suppose happens to me as the head of the mining company if scandal is attached to my name?' She put the question to him point-blank. He did not run in her circles. She did not expect him to understand the knife edge she walked, but she could expect him to respect it. 'One false step and all I've worked for is forfeit.'

For a moment, she thought she'd convinced him, but his next words surprised her utterly. 'Then we'll go to the Trevaylor Woods. No one will see us and I can ensure complete privacy.' He was caressing her with his voice, low and seductive beneath the rhythm of the waves. 'Never say never, Eliza.'

Intuition told her this was the pivotal moment that would put her on a path down which she should not journey. She needed to proceed with business as usual. That meant no attachments. She needed to say no, but she didn't.

Chapter Eleven

Eliza hadn't said no. Eaton preferred to view that as a victory, despite having had to cajole an acceptance out of her.

He swung up on Titan. The day had been a heady one. It would be too easy to get caught up in the euphoria of it. A good canter over to the school to check in with Cade would help clear his head. Eaton kicked Titan into motion. He could appreciate a virtuous woman, but he couldn't resist her, although he probably should. There had been small victories today. Eliza had spoken of her marriage and he'd had a glimpse into her world. Into her.

One false step, one whiff of scandal.

Such a statement was not hyperbole to her. She knew it first-hand and, if he wanted to pursue a deeper relationship with her, the trick would be in convincing her to try again, that he could be trusted with discretion.

I'm a private person by necessity.

Detford had lacked that discretion and she was paying for it, forced to use the concept of privacy as a synonym for remaining apart, he thought. She was *alone* by necessity. Not unlike himself. He knew how hard it was to live that way. It gave them something terrible in common and it prompted the question: Could two people, destined to be alone, be together? Could two adverse situations result in a more optimistic outcome like multiplying negative integers to get a positive? It was a dangerous equation to consider.

Eaton gave Caesar his head on the long flat stretch before the school, letting the wind in his face obliterate any further thought. To travel down that particular road carried certain perils he did not wish to revisit.

At the school, he tossed his reins to a groom and went inside, listening unobtrusively at the open doors to the last lessons of the day in progress. He stopped at one door and smiled as bits of music filtered into the hall. Richard Penlerick would have been pleased.

He strode to the headmaster's office, poured a drink and settled in to wait for Cade. The dream was coming to life around him. Other dreams were coming to life as well, far less innocuous dreams—dreams of Eliza Blaxland and her darling Sophie, a family in need of completion. A Tantalus dream. That was what it was. Everything about today had whispered the old temptation. A widow with a child. A woman in need of a husband, a child in need of a father. On the surface, it could be the perfect arrangement. But beneath the surface, it wasn't. It was fraught with limitations and compromises.

Eaton took a long swallow of the brandy, letting it go down slow with his thoughts. Eliza Blaxland was not a widow looking for a husband. She'd made that extremely clear on the beach. She did not believe she could afford to remarry. She was unwilling to surrender her independence. It was for the best. He wasn't looking to marry her even if she were hunting a husband or a surrogate father. Marriage to him would be a death sentence for her dreams.

He took another long swallow, finishing the drink. He certainly couldn't marry her after her confession today that she wanted more children, that she regretted Sophie was an only child. Marrying him would mean trading her independence and getting nothing in return. The old pain rose again. Today had presented him with a mixture of emotions, from the excitement of pursuing an attractive woman, to the bittersweet glimpses of what could never be. Sophie was an energetic child with a keen mind. He'd loved creating adventures for her, watching her eyes light up, and yet that very response was a painful reminder of all he could never have.

Cade Kitto opened the door and entered, glancing at the clock. 'You're early. I apologise for the wait.'

'I needed a moment with my thoughts.' And now it was time to put those thoughts away. There were things he could not affect. He would never father a child. Medicine and science couldn't change that. But he could make life better for other children. He could love his nieces and nephews. He could create opportunities for students at his school and perhaps even help Eliza cre-

ate opportunities for miners' children. He needed to
focus his energies on what he *could* achieve. He knew
from experience it was the best antidote to his own loss.
And he'd spare some of that energy for planning an
excursion to the Trevaylor Woods. It occurred to him,
as Cade settled in to discuss the first week of school,
that a search for antidotes was something else he and
Eliza Blaxland had in common. They both dedicated
significant effort to helping others in order to ease the
emptiness in themselves—or perhaps to ignore that
emptiness altogether.

The Woods. The sea caves on the beaches. A visit to
the conservatory for a private recital from the upper-
level students. Eaton had filled her days with excursions. This was all new territory for her—someone
making plans for her, someone putting her first. Business as unusual had become business as usual, much
to Eliza's tenuous delight. Eaton had been as good as
his word; the outings were discreet. He'd ridden roughshod over her insistence that she and Sophie didn't need
to be entertained. 'I'm not interested in need,' Eaton
would say when she protested. 'Perhaps I *want* to entertain you and Sophie.'

Who was she to resist the smiles of her daughter
and the compelling grin of Eaton Falmage? And so
the days established their own pattern. In the mornings she worked at the mine office while Sophie did
her lessons. In the afternoons, Eaton planned adventures: autumn hikes in the Trevaylor Woods to collect
colourful leaves and mushrooms, with Baldor sniffing

at their heels; salmon fishing in the rivers; a carriage drive with the top down to old promontory forts. The list seemed inexhaustible, like the man himself. What drove him? Surely it wasn't simply the delight of her company. 'We'll save the adventures closer to home for when the weather turns,' he'd tell them whenever she protested at the distance and effort each outing took, fearing it took too much advantage of him.

Today, the adventure was the ruins of Bosrigan Fort, one of the many cliff 'castles' built along the coast. In truth, it was more of a wall or enclosure than a castle, but it provided adventure for Sophie. On the cliffs the wind was colder, the sky more grey, a reminder that autumn had arrived in full and time was passing. She'd been at the dower house for three weeks. The shareholders' meeting was in five days and she was dreading it. There'd been no word from Miles, which had inevitably led to her thinking he would arrive any day, only to have those hopes dashed each evening. She was entirely alone in her efforts.

'If the weather was better, we could walk from Bosrigan to the hotel at Gurnard's Head for tea.' Eaton helped Sophie and Eliza down from the carriage. 'I think today, though, we should take the carriage to the hotel when we're finished here. We'll walk another time.'

Eliza smiled distractedly. 'Be careful, Eaton, you are building dangerous assumptions with your excursions and future promises.' Eaton was always making plans for another time. Perhaps he did it unconsciously, a man used to leading, used to taking charge for others. But perhaps he did it for other reasons as well. In the weeks she'd known him, he seemed to be a man in constant need of activity. She understood the reason for it. He was grieving the loss of his friend, but he couldn't hide from it interminably. 'We will go home one day. Sophie will be disappointed,' Eliza cautioned. People without children seldom understood how carefully they had to guard their words, how they had to refrain from making promises that couldn't be kept.

'Sophie won't be the only one. *I* will be disappointed. What about you? Will you be happy to go home?' Eaton asked, in all seriousness. They came to a jagged section where rubble had accumulated. Eaton offered her his arm and she took it without thought. Touching him had become too easy these days, just like the outings, but no less devastating for its repetition. He'd fit into her life effortlessly.

'I will miss this, too,' she replied honestly. Truro would be drab compared to the brilliance of the last weeks. But the brilliance was due to the temporary nature of their association and it would soon be tarnished if they continued at length. It couldn't be sustained over the long term. 'I must thank you for your discretion and your regard for our privacy.'

'It's been a pleasure to spend time with you.' There was a caress in his words. 'Do you know when you might leave? I should not like to drive down to the dower house and simply discover you've gone,' he joked.

'The shareholders' meeting is in a few days. I suppose we'll leave shortly after that business is settled.'

'There is no rush.' Eaton smiled. 'Stay as long as you like.'

There was every rush, Eliza thought as he went to help Sophie scramble up to a lookout point. The longer she stayed, the harder it would be to resist the very natural temptation of giving in to him. He had not pressed the issue of kisses since the beach, but it was there in his eyes when he looked at her, it was in every attention he showed her. He was interested in her, in sharing more than conversations and outings. So was she, truth be told. She had a healthy curiosity about what it might be like to be with a young man, a man who held her in great regard, who wanted her for *herself.* The heir to a dukedom would not find her money alluring, nor would he find her child, her background, or her age an asset.

Of course, he needn't care on either account. An affair would be easy for him. He could love her and leave her when he chose. It would not be so easy for her or for Sophie. They would live with the memory of him for the rest of their lives. And yet, the longer she was with him, the more Eliza began to think it might have been worth it if there was only herself to think of, only herself to protect from the inevitable loss of him.

Already, it might be too late. Sophie adored him. Not just for the outings he planned, but for himself. Evening had become Eliza's favourite time of day. Eaton played cards with them after dinner, or Sophie would play the spinet in the parlour—sometimes he would read with them. Lately, he'd taken to reading excerpts of *The Odyssey* out loud by the fire. He was being reckless with them, leading them on, although perhaps unintentionally. She ought to be angry with him, but she was too addicted to the individual moments to relish ruining the larger picture.

Eliza looked out over the water. She didn't want to hurt Eaton. The longer they were together, the more she sensed he *needed* them. It was a realisation that had come upon her early in their stay. She was not naive. Eaton was grieving his friend. He was a man who thrived on projects to fill voids. She and Sophie were his current project. No wonder he wasn't in a hurry to see them leave. What would he do next? Was he merely hoping they would fill the gap until Christmas when he could visit his sisters? Perhaps he was attuned to her loneliness because he was lonely, too. The man who claimed to have everything had nothing with which to fill his time, to fill his heart. *Perhaps you're the one doing me a favour*, he'd said. Perhaps she was, but at what cost?

'The view is breathtaking, is it not?' Eaton was behind her, the bulk of him blocking the wind, the heat of him triggering an intense awareness of his body's proximity to hers. 'I feel very small when I'm up here. It's a great reminder of my place in the grand scheme of things to see the sky above me, the crashing sea below and to know that I can do little to affect either. It's quite humbling, yet sometimes it spurs me on to do more, to be more.'

How was it possible for this man to be more than he already was? She turned and looked up at him, studying his face, a new awareness taking hold—not a physical awareness but an emotional one. She was learning to read him, learning to know him and his life, the events that had shaped him. 'You're thinking about Richard Penlerick,' she said softly.

'Yes,' he confessed with a small smile as if he was pleased she understood this facet of his life, of his mind. 'I was thinking, too, how very finite life is, how every moment, every choice, counts.' His voice was low and intimate. It made her pulse race and her body warm. His words touched her, but here on the cliffs she wanted more than his words.

'I want to wrap you in my arms, Eliza. What would you think of that? Is it too familiar?' Ah, so he felt it, too, this need to connect physically, to have something tangible from this meeting of their minds.

'Hold me, then, just for a moment,' she whispered. Surely she could afford this one lapse? He did not hesitate. His arms were about her, gathering her in, her head against the strength of his chest, the breadth of his shoulders sheltering her. It felt good to be held, to be surrounded by someone else's power as the wind blew.

Out of necessity to be heard, his head bent to hers as he spoke, the wind wreaking havoc with his dark curls. 'It's only that I'm feeling my humanity, my smallness. Up here those things have a different meaning. The cliffs, the waves, the clouds, the wind, are all far more powerful than me. I cannot change them for all the money and land I own.' It was honesty that prompted his words, not vulnerability, not weakness, and she responded in kind.

'I've fought for every place I've occupied, knowing

full well I could lose it. When I married Huntingdon
I knew I would have him for a short time only and afterwards the mines were a fight. No one wanted me
to have them. Everyone encouraged me to give them
up. Even now, I must constantly prove myself.' It was
a lonely, wearying task she could never put down. But
perhaps just for this moment she could indulge.

She breathed him in, her head pressed to the lapels
of his coat, the scent of him, all man and wind, in her
nostrils. She closed her eyes, wanting to hold on to this
moment: the sound of the waves below, the feel of his
arms about her, as if he could keep out the world and
all of its threats. If only that were true. But to even test
that hypothesis, first she'd have to tell him her secrets,
she'd have to give up a piece of her control, she'd have
to risk letting him in, letting him see her vulnerability. She drew a breath, her decision made. She only
had five days left before the meeting and she had no
answers. She needed to reach out. 'Eaton,' she said,
letting her eyes open, letting them rest on his face, 'I
want to ask your advice on something.'

'Yes, of course. We can talk now or perhaps later at
the tea room at Gurnard's Head.' He was all immediate
concern, but there was something else in his dark eyes,
perhaps joy that she had decided to trust him at last.

'After dinner will be fine.' She didn't want to talk
about it in public where she might be overheard.

He nodded with a private smile. 'After dinner it shall
be.' When he held her hand on the way back to the
carriage, she didn't resist the gesture. A line had been
crossed and this time there would be no going back.

But it seemed there would be a detour. They never made it to the Gurnard's Head Hotel tea room. In fact, they didn't even make it back to the carriage before Eaton's tiger ran up to them with some news. 'My lord, it appears we have a visitor.'

Eliza looked beyond the boy's shoulder, hesitating involuntarily. There, standing beside the carriage, not a golden hair out of place even in the breeze, was Miles Detford, here at last, and most inconveniently so. There was none of the relief she'd originally anticipated his arrival would bring. Eliza dropped Eaton's hand, but it was an effort she feared came too late. From the look in Miles's eye, the damage was already done. How long had he been standing there and just what had he seen? Had he seen her one moment of weakness, when she'd given in to the strength of Eaton's arms? Was he going to hold that moment against her despite her years of strength and self-denial?

The visitor was unwanted. Eaton sensed it in Eliza's hesitation. She didn't want the man here any more than Eaton did. Damn the man for interrupting the outing now, when Eliza had been in his arms, when she'd finally let down her guard long enough to confide in him, not only the request to talk but that precious bit of information she'd imparted.

'I've fought for every place I've ever occupied, knowing full well I could lose it...'

It was the second insight he'd had this afternoon of what lay behind the impenetrable façade of Eliza Blaxland's smooth features. For just a moment on the cliffs she'd been vulnerable and that was as intoxicating as her strength. *To be needed by her*, the woman who needed no one.

Eaton strode forward, putting himself between Eliza and the intruder. 'Lord Lynford at your service, how can I be of assistance?' He would make it clear that this man would answer to him should Eliza so desire.

'I have business with Mrs Blaxland.' The man gave him a hard stare, the strength of his gaze was perhaps the most impressive thing about him besides his tailoring. All else was quite ordinary, from his middling height to his middling build. Here was a man who wanted to appear more than he was.

'I hope it is not an emergency? Although I fear it cannot be otherwise since you've chosen to seek us out instead of awaiting our return.' Eaton's polite tone was cold.

The man's gaze shifted over his shoulder, heralding Eliza's approach. Miles Detford would be awful at cards; his face gave away everything. 'Ah, my dear, there you are! I have answered your summons just as you requested.'

Summons? Eliza had sent for this man and then hesitated upon his arrival? Eaton had barely posed the question to himself when Eliza snapped, 'You are three weeks late.'

'Not without reason, my dear. I bring news from the shareholders that I am eager to discuss at once.' Something flickered in Eliza's eyes. Concern? Interest? Interested concern? Eaton intervened before curiosity could get the better of Eliza. He recognised a flanking movement when he saw one even if she did not. This man, this medium-sized, interloping, upstart thought to separate Eliza from the herd.

'We shall meet you at the dower house, then, sir.' Eaton held out his hand to help Eliza into the carriage and then he reached for Sophie, making it clear the carriage was full. *He* was driving home with Eliza, not this man who invoked hesitation and called her 'my dear' every chance he got.

'Who is he?' Eaton asked the moment the carriage was underway. A suspicion had blossomed at the familiarity between them. This was the friend she'd mentioned that night in the orangery. The man she'd mentioned on the beach, who had proposed and been refused.

'Miles Detford is a shareholder and the primary administrator of the Porth Karrek mine,' Eliza answered, but Eaton had already lost her. The open woman at the fort was gone, her thoughts racing ahead to the conversation to come with this Miles Detford, this man she'd sent for, her brain already wondering what news he might have brought.

'Do all the shareholders call you "my dear"?' Eaton was terse. He was not keen on men who made a habit of so fluidly mixing business with pleasure, perhaps with the deliberate intent of confusing the line between both.

Eliza's eyes flashed. Good. She understood exactly what he was asking. 'He's a shareholder and a friend. He's been a support since Huntingdon died.' It was telling that Eliza would defend him. How much of a friend was he? Eaton refrained from asking. To insinuate there'd been more than friendship was to do her a disservice, but that did not quiet the little green monster in him, or the doubt that began to mewl alongside. Was this why she resisted the spark between them? Because she had a lover back in Truro and it was this Miles Detford? He could not believe it of her, not after her protestations of privacy and the need to remain alone. Or was it that he didn't *want* to believe it of her?

When they arrived at the dower house, he helped her down and took his leave with a final question in his eyes. *Did* she want him to leave her with this man? He would not abandon her. 'I think I must see him, Eaton.' It was a softly whispered reminder that she had a life beyond the dower house, a life he still knew precious little about. The intruder was very physical evidence that she had a life elsewhere and some day soon she'd rejoin it.

He let her go. He had no choice. 'Come to me later. I'll be in the orangery if you still want to talk things through, or even if you don't want to talk.' He whispered the invitation as she moved away. *Even if you want me just to hold you like I did on the cliffs.* That had been a moment of heaven, the two of them against the wind. He would reclaim that moment if he could. Not just for himself, but for her. Miles Detford might call her his dear, but she did not welcome his attentions in that fashion, Eaton would bet his last guinea on it. He waited until Eliza and Sophie were inside, the door closed behind them, before he gave the signal to drive away. He would go to the orangery where he could be alone with his dog and his thoughts. And he would wait.

Chapter Twelve

'What were you thinking, Eliza?' Detford sputtered incredulously as he paced the front parlour in overt agitation.

Now that they were alone, he let loose his emotions, his polished veneer slipping. Sophie was upstairs with Miss Gilchrist having a bath and Eaton had decorously taken his leave at the front door, but not before slanting her a querying look that asked questions: Who was Miles Detford? Was he more than a business partner? But mostly, there'd been concern in Eaton's gaze, his dark eyes asking silently, *Should I leave you alone with this man, this intruder who has pre-empted our talk*?

But she could not afford to think of Eaton's dark eyes now, or the way his arms had felt about her. Miles was in the middle of a tirade and she needed her wits about her to keep him in check. 'For heaven's sake, Eliza, you were out there alone with him.'

'Sophie was with us. What is the crime, Miles?' Eliza snapped impatiently. If there was any crime committed, it was his. He'd kept her waiting for three weeks. She'd summoned him to help resolve a problem and he'd taken his time to make his way here. Now he had the audacity to act as if he had some claim on her.

Miles Detford stopped pacing and speared her with a stare. 'You know very well what the crime is. He's heir to a dukedom and you are a widow who can choose to be available to him without the benefit of marriage.' He folded his arms across his chest and she was struck by the dissimilarity between him and Eaton. Miles was a mediocre man in all ways: neither tall nor short, neither thin or large. His features were refined and finished, bland in their smoothness. He was nowhere near as rugged or as interesting as Eaton. Eaton looked like Cornwall. Miles looked like London. He thought like London, too, with his quick, wicked insinuations. He raised a blond brow and asked point-blank, '*Are* you available to him, Eliza?'

'Hush! Do you want the servants to hear you!' Eliza scolded. How dare he suggest such slander. She ought to tell him the truth, that absolutely no, she was not 'available' to Eaton, but that would only affirm for Miles that he had the right to lecture her on behaviour, that she answered to him, which *she* most assuredly did not. He answered to her. She controlled the mines. He was her employee, nothing more. 'Envy is unbecoming on you, Miles. Is that it? May no one have me because you cannot?'

Anger flared in Miles Detford's pale blue eyes, so very light where Eaton's were dark. Once, she might have found those eyes attractive, once she might have compared them to sea glass, but whatever nascent attraction had existed was long ago extinguished. Miles Detford might be a friend, but he could never be more. He sat beside her on the sofa, his anger banked now, his tone softer. 'It is your reputation I'm concerned about, Eliza, and the mines. This is not a good time for a dalliance. Too much hangs in the balance.'

'I don't think it's as dire as all that. I merely requested you to come and look over a few things for me as the shareholder primarily responsible for this mine. I have some questions about the tunnel,' Eliza chided him. He was for ever making mountains out of molehills and, while she appreciated his ability to think critically about situations, it was wearisome to have everything presented as a crisis. He glanced away briefly, and there was the slightest hesitation; but it was enough to put her on alert.

'There is something else?' she prompted coolly. 'Perhaps a reason why you delayed in coming?'

'You know I would have come immediately if there hadn't been a good reason to wait. I have news, something I hope you'll be happy to hear.'

'Good news, then?' Eliza probed. He seemed too tentative for it to truly be good news.

'I think it can be, my dear, but I need you to listen with an open mind.' He reached for her hand and she frowned at the familiarity, but did not withdraw. One could never have too many friends and she'd made her position with Miles clear. Surely there was no harm in allowing this simple touch and it would perhaps reassure him that nothing existed between her and Eaton, especially when there was something more important to consider. 'The shareholders want to put a proposal to you at the upcoming meeting,' Miles said. 'They want to make a generous offer to buy out your shares. Isn't that wonderful? You will be as wealthy as you are now without all the effort. You needn't be Atlas any more and carry the world on your shoulders. You can get on with your life.'

Get on with her life? This *was* her life. Every choice she'd made since the day Huntingdon died had been for this. But there was another implication, too, and that was the one that took her like a blow to the stomach. Miles thought the idea sounded splendid. He *wanted* her to take the offer. At the moment, she couldn't decide which news was more earth-shattering: that the board had concocted a secret deal to buy her out or that Miles Detford, someone she'd counted as a friend, thought the action ought to be allowed, accepted even, as a boon. She was betrayed on all fronts.

Eliza did draw her hand away, then, spearing Miles with the daggers of her gaze. 'The mines are my life. Why would anyone think I'd *want* to be bought out? Or that I would give up control of Sophie's inheritance?' She rose from the sofa, agitated. 'This is *not* generosity, this is a hard shove off a very high cliff. *They* are pushing me aside.' Her stomach was roiling. This was evil wrapped in a very pretty package. What was the cause of this? Had she not made the mines successful? Had she not lined the shareholders' pockets with profit every quarter?

Eliza racked her mind, searching for a reason, and

settled on one. 'This is about the tunnel. I thought we'd resolved that. We decided not to dig out under the ocean.' She'd thought a lot of things had been settled, though. Apparently not. The shareholders had been plotting against her behind false pretences of acceptance. For how long? How long had they faced her with smiles at the board meetings and nodded their heads while they whispered behind her back?

She faced Miles. 'Surely not everyone agrees with the decision to dig under the ocean? It's not safe for the workers and it's not safe for the investors. Who knows what we'll find out there? Maybe nothing that justifies the risk. One accident will be all it takes for poor men to lose their lives and rich men to lose their money. Are we all not rich enough as it is? Why do we need to grasp for more wealth and for such stakes?'

'Is anyone ever rich enough?' Miles countered with a patronising chuckle, sidestepping the real issue. Did he think she wouldn't notice? Did he think that she was so easily distracted? 'Perhaps this is exactly the reason you should take the offer and step away. I laud your concerns, Eliza, but money isn't made by playing it safe. I understand, though, that risk is not in your nature. You aren't made for it. No woman is.'

That had her bristling. 'You think a woman won't take a risk? You think it is my gender that makes me cautious as opposed to my good sense?' She whirled on him, making him the target of her anger, her disgust at the board's betrayal. Better to be angry than to be shocked. Shock made one weak, anger could make one strong, at least temporarily, and she needed to be strong now.

'It's not *my* opinion that matters, Eliza, but the board's. I am your friend. It's my job to help you see things as others see them. You have to understand what the board sees. They see steady profits, not rising profits—'

'At a time when smaller mines are shutting down!' she interrupted fiercely.

'At a time, my dear, when you are asking them to put funds into new safety equipment and schools for miners' children. There is no profit in those things. The board thinks it is too much coddling while we're not making enough of the mines' natural resources.'

'*People* are our natural resource,' she argued. 'They are not disposable.'

'That's where you're wrong, my dear. They *are* disposable. I know you don't like to hear it, but there it is. There are plenty of miners looking for work and willing to claim a pitch beneath the ocean. I wouldn't worry my pretty little head about it, if I were you.'

If he called her 'my dear' one more time, she'd scream or worse.

'I suppose I am disposable, too?' She saw what this was. A power grab, a chance for greedy men to seize more wealth at the expense of others. 'It would be a mistake to think so. I will fight this.'

'Then take my advice. Stay away from the Marquess. The last thing you need is for the board to hear you're having an affair.'

'Is that a threat?' She faced Miles squarely. 'Who

would tell them such a thing? Would you? Otherwise where else would they learn of it?'

Miles looked wounded. 'Eliza, be fair. I wouldn't need to say a thing. You know how it will look to the shareholders. You're living on his property, you were out gallivanting with him *en famille*. Dear heavens, it's like Prinny and Mrs Fitzherbert all over again.'

Her eyes narrowed; she did not miss the insult in his exasperation. 'I should slap you for that. You've no cause to assume anything of the sort.' But she knew what Miles did not, that her association with Lynford had progressed far beyond a trip to Bosrigan Fort. There'd been numerous outings, all discreet, all designed so that no one might see them together. She knew that Eaton dined in her home almost nightly, that he carried her child up to bed, that he'd kissed her *twice* now, he'd wooed her in his orangery with parakeets and champagne. Miles didn't know the half of it. Perhaps she needed to stop denying that other half existed, the half where her pulse raced when Eaton touched her, where she coveted each hot glance he sent her way and craved each kiss as if it were the treasure Eaton alluded to.

'If you want my counsel, Eliza, it is this: take the money, step away from the mines and you can tup whomever you like. No one will care. This offer is freedom, the one thing you crave above all else. I wish you could see it that way, my dear.'

My dear. It was the last straw. 'Get out.' She would not stand here and be condescended to, lectured, berated for sins she had not committed, not after all she'd endured. Miles's elegant brows knit in perplexity. 'Did you not understand me, Miles? Or is it that you can't believe I'd actually throw you out?'

Miles straightened and picked up his hat from the table with unhurried gestures that patronised her further. 'What I understand is that you're upset. We will talk again later when you've had time to think. We need to discuss the tunnel further.' Not any more, not after today's revelations, not when she was so suddenly aware that even Miles's loyalty might be questionable. If he was truly loyal to her, he would understand this was not an offer she could accept.

'It's nothing. I can sort it out myself,' Eliza lied. She wanted him gone before she broke down, before she showed how much his news had shaken her.

She saw him to the door and shut it firmly behind him. Miles might claim to be her friend, but he was a man easily swayed by the mind of the crowd. After all, he'd proposed to her out of social pressure to scotch mere rumours of their association. How long would he stand beside her now if he thought her decision a poor one? Especially if others were willing to line his pockets? She'd like to think better of him, but she could not. To award him attributes he didn't possess would be naive and it would make her vulnerable if she was wrong.

Eliza leaned against the door, exhausted. When would it end? When would she be left in peace to run her mines and live her life? She'd held up the world for so long. She was tired, but she could not relent. She climbed the stairs and checked on Sophie. She was asleep with a smile on her face. Perhaps her sweet girl was dreaming of their magical day. Eliza was envious. Her dreams would not be as sweet. But they were a far-off consideration. Her mind was still churning from Miles's visit. Eliza returned downstairs, occupying herself with a tour of the house, checking doors and windows, although the servants had already done it. There was little for her to do and she was restless. She needed exercise, something to ease her mind over the news and something to provide objectivity. Perhaps a walk?

Eliza took her shawl from a peg by the door and wrapped it about her shoulders. A moonlit walk would do her good. An emotional response to this latest gambit from her shareholders would not solve anything. She needed to be rational and she needed to be grateful to Miles, who'd told her the news. Friends risked much when they had to impart difficult news. The shareholders had meant to take her unawares by presenting the offer at the meeting and forcing her to a spontaneous response. But Miles, for all his differing views, had bought her time to think, time to marshal her troops even when she disagreed with him. Wasn't that the hallmark of a true friend? She had not treated him well for it.

The moon was bright and she walked without fear or thought of distance. After all, she was on Eaton's land and as long as she kept the main house visible to her right, she wouldn't get lost. She thought over the offer as she walked. Perhaps she *should* sell her shares? She could purchase an estate like this one, where Sophie could run and play all day and she'd never have to worry about leaving for a meeting. No, Eliza knew she'd be bored within a month. What would she do with herself all day without the mines to run? There wasn't just the activity to think of, there was the legacy as well. The shareholders would run Blaxland Mining into the ground if she stepped away. They'd pursue profit at any price.

The orangery loomed before her, the moonlight reflecting off the glass. Her feet had led her here even if her thoughts had not, at least not her conscious thoughts. Perhaps her subconscious? Perhaps she'd wanted to see Eaton all along, wanted to borrow his strength for a moment as she had on the cliffs that afternoon. Was it really so wrong to want to lay down the burden for a moment? Especially when one had been invited to do that very thing?

Come to me later...if you still want to talk, or even if you don't...

Eaton was not pressing her, he was giving her space and choices, two things Miles Detford was not keen to offer. Right now, those things looked like heaven. Or hell. Her hand stalled on the orangery door as her conscience whispered its final admonition.

Step in there and you will be tempted. The hour is late, you are tired, and he is persuasive. Who is the real devil, Eliza? Detford with his truth or Eaton Falmage with his fantasies?

Eliza turned the knob of the orangery door. To hell with it, then. Tonight she needed Eaton in his garden.

Chapter Thirteen

Baldor's ears pricked up and the big dog rose to his feet from beside the worktable. Eaton set down his tools, a satisfied smile taking his mouth. Eliza was coming. He could hear her on the path winding through the orangery, swishing skirts, staccato steps. She had not entered the orangery timidly despite the darkness, nor was she picking her way through. She was coming at full speed, straight and direct...*to him*. He wondered which Eliza had come to him tonight: the determined woman who'd ambushed him in his own school, or the woman he'd held in his arms on the cliffs today, the woman who was both strong *and* vulnerable. He was ready for either woman. He'd come to care for both. Goodness knew he'd waited longer for Eliza Blaxland than he'd waited for any woman. Not that three weeks was any great length to wait in general, but for a man who was used to having his every wish carried out instantaneously, used to having his pick of lovers, being in hard pursuit with no surety of success was something of a novelty—a very trying novelty. And yet these three weeks with Eliza and Sophie had been the best three weeks he could recall in his adult life.

'Eaton, thank goodness you're here.' Eliza emerged breathless and relieved, her mask of indomitability slightly askew.

'I told you I would be.' He motioned for Baldor to lie down. He studied her, following her restless perambulation about the atrium with his eyes. She was agitated, her colour high—perhaps from the evening walk or perhaps from some inner excitement? 'Have you come to talk, Eliza?'

She turned from the fountain, the distress on her face unmistakable. Eaton's gut clenched in primal protectiveness. Whatever Detford had said or done to cause that distress, the man would pay for it. 'The shareholders want to push me out.' The next moment, she broke, her voice trembling, her strength leaving her. 'I know I said I needed to do this on my own, but I need help.' She took a shaky breath. 'Eaton, they want to take the mines. They want to take everything. I'm not enough for them.'

Everything. His mind focused on that word. He knew what it meant to lose something so monumental that it felt like everything. He saw in an instant what 'everything' was to her: pride, hard work and long hours of toil to maintain her independence. All those things could be swept away in one act: his ability to have a family, to perpetuate the line of Bude, his purpose in the world. How long had he berated himself? What if he'd not sneaked off to Kilkhampton for the horse show? A single poor choice in a life full of good decisions had cost him. Oh, yes, he knew exactly how Eliza felt.

Eaton was beside her, guiding her to the bench at the fountain's edge, firm hands over hers where they lay clenched in her lap. He lent her the strength of his touch as he listened. The shareholders wanted to buy her out. Did Detford not understand this woman at all? Did Detford not see all it would cost her to take such an offer? That money could only cover so much. There was no price that could be put on her pride. 'How long until you have to decide?' Eaton asked calmly when she finished.

'It's five days until the shareholders' meeting.' Eliza shook her head, 'But I don't think I will have a choice. They will expect me to take the offer. I do not think they will take no for an answer.' She drew a shaky breath, emotion catching her again. 'How could they do this to me, after five years, after letting me think everything was all right, that they respected me?'

'I wasn't enough for them,' she'd said and now Eaton saw that the disappointment that overwhelmed her stemmed from more than the offer itself. This was about how it had been planned behind her back. This was a betrayal. Women saw the world so much differently to men. For them the world was built on a series of relationships. The relationships she'd counted on had been false. No wonder she felt alone.

'Eliza, I am sorry.' He stroked the back of her hand with his thumb, a soothing motion, as he thought. 'But surely you don't mean to take this lying down? What if you buy *them* out? Make a counter-offer and then find new shareholders who support your vision and admire your leadership.'

'If I were a man, such a thing might work. But if I were a man, this would never have been an issue to begin with. Besides, where would I find such investors, even if I could afford to buy everyone's shares? I could not sustain the business on my own for long.' Already, he could see her agile mind running the sums it would take and measuring them against the capital she had to hand. That meant there was a spark of hope and Eaton would take that spark over the desolation he'd seen in her eyes.

'What if I could find investors?' He was already thinking of Cassian and Inigo, and Inigo would have financial connections to others with capital. 'I will write in the morning.' Inigo and Cassian were in Truro for the autumn, just a half day's ride away. Arrangements could be made quickly. If the shareholders were counting on the isolation of Cornwall to work against her, the bastards would be unpleasantly surprised. They thought to hold her hostage to their offer, thinking they were all she had.

'Would you even need to buy out everyone?' Eaton began to hypothesise. 'Maybe these malcontents don't speak for everyone?'

'It's hard to say, perhaps not for a few.' She withdrew her hands from his and Eaton tensed. There was more. She was withholding something else. 'They may not wish to sell their shares to me, or they may drive the price up to a point where I cannot afford to purchase their shares. Those who are most interested in buying me out feel there is lucrative expansion for the Porth Karrek mine under the sea.'

She explained the recent quarrel over the tunnel with an apologetic nod. 'So you see, Eaton, I don't know that you can just throw money at the problem and make it go away. This can't be one of your projects.'

Those were fighting words, or they would be if Eaton didn't see what she was doing. She was pushing him away, pushing aside help because she thought it made her vulnerable, made her beholden to others.

'Eliza, my men won't fail you. These are good men with deep pockets.'

'And *you'd* be there to ensure their compliance. Not me. Why should I trade one board of shareholders—men I've known through my husband for years and by rights should have been able to trust—for a board of shareholders who are strangers to me? Men who owe their loyalty first to you, a marquess. How could I ever compete with that?' She sighed. 'Your offer is generous, Eaton, but it would cost me everything I'm trying to protect. It wouldn't be mine any more. It would be yours. Your men, your money, your plans.'

'The mines would be yours, you would still sit at the head of the board,' Eaton argued. 'I don't want to take anything from you, Eliza. I want to help you keep what is yours.'

'You want to slay my dragons.' She was quick to go on the defensive, or perhaps Detford had already put her there as the 'friend' bearing bad news. Did she not see Detford for the snake he was? Eaton had seen the man for all of a few minutes and had his measure completely. He was not to be trusted.

'What's wrong with that? Surely it has not escaped your attention that I care for you.' It was the first time either of them had given voice to their feelings and it ignited a powder keg.

'Everything is wrong with that! My mother lost all she had when she allowed a man to act on her behalf,' Eliza cried.

'I am not that man and you are certainly not your mother. You cannot compare the two situations,' Eaton argued, attempting to do battle with her ghosts and her dragons.

'But you *are a* man. People will not see your interference as chivalrous. How long do you think it would be before everyone concluded I was your mistress? A kept woman, propped up by your money and your friends? My reputation would be in tatters.'

Eaton gave a wry chuckle. Detford was a serpent indeed. Something else had happened in that awful conversation. 'It seems your "friend" has been poisoning the well. Is that what he said? Did he warn you away from me for the sake of your reputation? Convenient for him, don't you think? To isolate you, to cut you off from help, very powerful help, I might add. I doubt he and his friends have a marquess in their pockets. Perhaps he aspires to be more than your friend, Eliza?'

'Perhaps once, but not any longer. I disabused him of such thoughts years ago.' Eliza dismissed the notion, but Eaton did not. Did she really think she was so easily forgotten? His suspicions had been right. Detford was the man in Truro who had been the focus of the rumours. A man who had been after her money, if the gossips could be believed. Perhaps they should be believed. Eaton had suspicions anew.

'What did he do to earn such a rejection, Eliza?'

'Nothing more than offer an honourable proposal of marriage after Truro society made inappropriate observations about us. I've learned to be more discreet since then.' Did she really not see the man for the worm he was? Detford should have been more discreet years ago. Eaton would have liked to have wrung the man's neck for such behaviour. Detford should have known what it would look like to others even if Eliza hadn't. In the aftermath, she had not learned to be more discreet, she'd learned to be more alone, convinced that her freedom must always come at the price of intimacy. Detford was a cunning devil, ruining her for other men.

'You should not discount Detford so easily. I saw the way he looked at you today at Bosrigan.' Eaton brought a hand to her cheek. He knew the way *he* looked at her, how she brightened a room simply by being in it, how she captivated him. He was not willing to give her up. He imagined Detford wasn't either, although he suspected Detford's protective-friend act was fuelled by more than romantic notions. He stroked her cheek, his eyes holding hers. 'You are the sort of woman who drives a man insane, Eliza, the sort of woman a man sees at a dinner table and he wants to undo her—not just her clothes, but her secrets, too.'

'And you, Eaton? Is that what you want?' Her eyes searched his, wary and cautious, yet desire was there, too. She had come here tonight for more than talk of mines. She was on the precipice of surrender and so was he. He wanted her with an intensity that surpassed longing, but he could not take her lightly and he could not fail her in his answer to her question.

'I want to do neither, Eliza. I have no desire to undo you, to claim you, to remake you in my image. I want you just the way you are, the determined, stubborn, private, whole of you.' He took her mouth then, his hands cradling her neck, framing her face as his mouth testified to his want, his need. Once begun, he would give her no quarter, no permission to hide from her desire. He merely needed a sign from her that she had accepted his earlier invitation in full. He did not want her in his bed because she was mad at Detford or because she was desperate and upset. Those things might have been reason enough in the beginning when pursuing her had been a distraction. But she had not been a game to him for a very long time now. Before this went any further, he had to know. 'Eliza,' he whispered her name against her lips, 'what changed your mind?'

Her hands were in his hair, her gaze locked on his. 'I don't want to be alone any more. I used to think being alone was the price for my freedom, but I saw today that my sacrifice didn't matter.'

'Is that what this is about, Eliza?' His voice was hoarse, a sign of how tight the leash was he kept himself on for her sake. She would hate herself in the morning if that was what this was, but by the saints it was hard to do the right thing just now. 'Do you want me, Eliza?' Eaton breathed, his voice a low, seductive

husk at her neck, his mouth at her throat as she arched
against him.

'You know I do.' Her own voice was smoky with
desire.

'But do *you* know it? I want to hear you say it. Say
you want me. I won't tolerate regrets in the morning.'
She understood. He was gifting this to her, wanting
her to grant herself permission for claiming pleasure
after years of denial.

Her hands were moving through the tangles of his
hair, her mouth pressing kisses to his face. 'I want
you. Only you.'

'Then come with me.'

This was what she'd come here for. Deep at the
core of her, she'd known the moment she entered the
orangery this was how the evening would end. She'd
come here wanting more than to talk with him. She'd
wanted to be in Eaton's arms, wanted his mouth on
her mouth, his hands in her hair when he kissed her.
She fairly trembled with anticipation as Eaton led her
to a small antechamber hidden behind the foliage of
the aviary. It was a sparse room furnished neatly with
the necessities—a bed, a battered trunk at its foot, a
table—but she spared little time for the details. Her
attention was for the man who'd brought her. Tonight,
she would not be alone. It could not be more than that;
the world wasn't made for such things to last. This one
night would be temporary succour. She would take
tonight and hold it against all the nights to come. She

would not make excuses for this. In the morning, she would not claim seduction or false promises.

She wrapped her arms about his neck. She let her mouth answer his, let her body answer his, let her hips press against his. She would give no man dominion over her, but she would partner one, be the equal of one. He was dancing with her now, a slow sensual waltz of bodies against one another, his lips lingering on hers as they reached the bed.

His eyes were hot on hers as he whispered the solemn admonition, 'Watch me, Eliza.' He stepped back to pull off his boots and to tug his shirt over his head, revealing his body to her in the lamplight, as glorious in its nakedness as it had been dressed.

Yes, she would watch him. Eliza sat down hard on the bed's edge, every fibre of her being alive with hungry anticipation. He was riveting, all ridges and planes, with the chest of an outdoorsman who strode through woods and sands, with arms that hefted sleeping children upstairs with ease. Stark virility was etched in every hard line of him, particularly the two muscled lines that flanked his flat abdomen and disappeared into the waistband of his trousers with tempting invitation for her hands to follow. She bit her lip. Oh, to touch him, to trace those lines to their wicked destination.

'Do I please you, Eliza?' His dark eyes glittered, all too aware, no doubt, of the effect he had on her.

'I am drowning in how pleasing you are.' She swallowed, her mouth dry. She'd known from the first how out of her depth she was with this man and tonight only confirmed it. None of her experience with intimacy had prepared her for this moment. Lack of preparation did not make her shy, though; it only made her hungrier.

'Would you like to join me?' he drawled in low tones. 'I can play lady's maid, if you wish.'

'If you wish.' He wanted to undress her? The very notion made her heart pound with anticipation. She went to him, giving him her back. How long had she dreamed of such intimate play with a man, fantasised about it alone in her bed?

'I wish, very much.' His voice was a raw, heated whisper at her ear sending a trill of hot desire down her spine. 'You smell divine, like a summer's day, Eliza. It was one of the first things I noticed about you when you walked into the school.' She blushed in the lamplight at the compliment, overcome that he'd noticed such a minute detail about her from the start. While she'd been intent on calling him to account, he'd been intent on her perfume. Of course he had. He was a physical man in all ways.

His hands made short work of her lacing and he pushed her gown from her shoulders, letting it slide to her feet. Her stays followed as his mouth pressed kisses to the bare skin of her shoulders, her neck, her back. He reached for the hem of her chemise and her hand captured his in rote reflex, despite the fantasy. 'Wait.'

'Have you never been naked before a man, Eliza?' Eaton whispered at her ear. 'We shall be naked together, nothing between us, skin to skin.' His words nearly undid her. It was all the coaxing she needed. This was how she imagined lovers talked. Husbands and wives most assuredly did not speak to one another this way. Huntingdon had not. Eaton's hands cupped her breasts, drawing her against him, back to chest, the heat of his body warming her, calming her even as the hardness of him aroused her and the issue of the chemise was put on short hiatus.

'Shall I go first, Eliza? Shall you help me with my trousers?' he murmured, turning her in his arms. 'Slide them off, Eliza, free me.'

It was wondrous to undress him, to drink him in with her eyes, to touch him with her hands, to know he wanted her hands on him. Pushing the fabric away, his manhood rose strong and thick from a nest of dark hair, proud like its master. She circled him with her hand, delighting in the adamantine hardness of him. He had strength, even here at his core there was no weakness to him. He would need no efforts from her to ready himself. The thought shamed her. Tonight was not for comparisons or for remembrances. It was for fantasies.

Eaton's hand tipped her chin upwards, forcing her to meet his gaze. 'Does something displease you?'

'No, how could it? You are beautiful. Too beautiful. I hardly dare believe you're real.' Would he hear the unspoken comparison? That she had known a good man, but not a beautiful man. Her husband had been decades beyond the virility of a man in his prime. There'd been little hardness to his body.

'You are beautiful, too.' His hands were at the hem of her chemise once more. 'Allow me to show you.' He kissed her then, a deep, slow, abiding claim as he lifted the chemise from her and tossed it away. 'Come to bed with me. Let me chase away your ghosts.'

Eliza wound her arms about his neck. 'And let me chase away yours, too,' she whispered. How had she not seen it until now? It wasn't all her needing him. They needed each other.

Chapter Fourteen

⤫⤫⤫

Only his reverence for her kept Eaton's want in check. She stole his breath and very nearly his control, but this was too important to rush in the first flush of lusty pleasure, no matter how hungry they might be for one another. And she was ravenous, eager, and, despite the moment's hesitation with the chemise, she was determined to be the master of her own pleasure at last. Her late husband might have loved her, he might have given her a comfortable marriage and even comfortable companionship, but he'd not given her passion, had not made her pulse race and her breath catch. He'd not lain with her naked, had not worshipped her in the lamplight of an orangery.

Eaton levered himself over her, his arms taking his weight, his eyes meeting hers, offering promises of pleasure, offering encouragement. *Follow me down pleasure's path*, his body whispered to hers. He moved against her, her own hips rising to meet him. He gathered her close, making love with his mouth at her mouth, at the base of her neck where her pulse beat fast, at her breasts where his mouth suckled and his tongue caressed, at her navel where he tickled her skin with a feathering breath until her body arched in to him, a little moan escaping her pretty mouth.

From the intimate seat of her navel, Eaton hazarded a glance up the seductive line of her body with a wicked smile, thrilling in her response. She was bold in bed just as she was bold in life, a woman who knew what she wanted. 'Ah, just wait, my love. There is more, there is better than this.' His own voice was husky with anticipation. His hands bracketed the slim curve of her hips, his mouth moved down to the feminine juncture of her thighs, his body heady with the feel of her, the scent of her, his own arousal growing in response to hers, need driving him as hard as it drove her.

He teased her with his tongue at her seam, at her tiny, hidden nub, licking her, tasting her, until she cried out above him. Her hands wound tight in the depth of his hair as she rose to him, against him, her thighs tightening as if she would hold him there for eternity, reluctant to let him go, even as she trembled with the first shudders of burgeoning pleasure. His own breath was coming fast now from the excitement of his efforts. Had the giving of such delight ever been so fulfilling, so overwhelming? He lifted his head, panting hard, to watch climax sweep her, to let himself be undone. She was eroticism personified in her release, her hair flowing across the pillow, her long neck arched, her face thrown to the ceiling, eyes closed in rapture as the moment took her. Had anything, anyone, ever looked as beautiful as she did right now? Or as vulnerable?

In this moment, she was entirely without artifice and without armour. Something primal surged in him, the urge to claim this woman, to possess her, to protect her in all her guises. No other man should see her thus.

Pleasure ebbed, her eyes opened, meeting his, reflecting wonder and astonishment. Gone was the emerald-sharp hardness that so often resided in her gaze. 'Your eyes remind me of green Cornish sea glass,' he whispered, kissing her navel. He would get her a ring of that colour, perhaps a necklace, so that she might never forget such pleasure or the man who'd given it to her.

She stroked his head, her fingers combing through his curls, her tone coy. 'You have been selfless. You have not had your pleasure yet, my lord.'

He laughed against her belly, his grin wide as he smiled up at her. 'Oh, but I have. There is great pleasure for a man in seeing a woman enjoy his gifts so thoroughly.' Would she understand this was pleasure for them both? That he exalted in the giving of pleasure as much as she exalted in receiving it? He crawled up the length of her until they lay skin to skin. He pressed a kiss to the indentation of her shoulder, another to her neck, to the lobe of her ear; he could worship her all night. 'Besides, who says we're done yet?'

She met his whisper with a private, knowing gaze, as she reached for him, her hand wrapping possessively around him. 'Not me.'

'Have mercy,' Eaton breathed as she dragged her thumbnail over the tender head of his shaft.

'No,' she whispered, 'I think not.'

Eaton let her have her way—he was human after all and he adored an assertive lover. He loved the slide of her silken hair, the press of her mouth as she took her turn, sliding down the length of his body, exploring the ridges and crevices of him until her mouth took over for her hand at the hot throbbing core of him. She glanced at him once, her eyes burning, melted, lava-hot sea glass, as she tossed the long skein of her hair over one shoulder and went down to meet him, to take him.

Her teeth grazed his tender tip and he let out a wolf-ish groan at the contact, an intoxicating mix, part plea-sure, part pain. 'Vixen!' He ground out the word in a hoarse rasp as she licked the length of him and his blood surged, his release looming. Heady as her efforts were, he did not want to spill like this. He wanted to take her, wanted to be inside her, joined together in mutual pleasure.

Eaton shifted, disengaging her. She threw him an enquiring look and that nearly undid him. He reached for her, drawing her up his length, holding her against him until he could roll her beneath him. 'I cannot wait for you any longer,' he rasped, desire once again his master. She'd roused him to untold heights. He took her then, in a swift thrust that had her arching and moan-ing beneath him; a good choice for them both, then. She'd been ready, too. Her legs were locked about him, holding him tight, close, her hips rising to meet his as they joined in the pulsing rhythm of mating.

This was life, this was pleasure and it was coursing through her unabated. Eliza strained towards Eaton, her body pressing hard against him as if it could melt into his, as if they could be closer, joined more intimately than they already were. All she had to do was look into Eaton's face, his eyes obsidian dark; feel the tension of his arms as they bracketed her head, taking his weight, to know pleasure's wave was cresting. They'd be in it together this time when it came. It was the most exquisite sensation she'd ever felt, novel and yet innate, bone deep in its thrill, and it was coming again, more intense than it had been before.

'Keep your eyes open, Eliza, look at me when you come,' Eaton groaned, thrusting once more, eyes locking with hers, holding her accountable, before the wildness was upon them, covering them, claiming them, hearts racing, blood pounding with life, as if in that completion she knew the answers of the universe. Later there would be practical measures to take to ensure there were no consequences, but for now, she would revel in the ephemeral bliss of the moment.

It was another level of decadence to lie quietly in Eaton's arms, her head against his shoulder, her hand on his chest, as the night with its single lamp cushioned them. She would have liked to have stayed in that limbo for ever, ignoring everything except the pleasure, but her mind was not made that way. As pleasure ebbed, reality began to reassert itself.

'You are thinking.' Eaton's voice was a seductive murmur in the darkness, part question, part accusation.

She looked up at him. It was time to set the pleasure aside and define terms. She'd had her moment of respite. Now she had to think about the consequences.

'This was extraordinary but it cannot happen again.'
They could not be discovered.

'Why not?' Eaton nuzzled her ear.

'If the shareholders think I have indulged in an affair...'

Eaton reached for her hair, letting it spill through his fingers. 'Life is too short, and your passion is too splendid to be hidden away because some unimaginative men say it should be. If what you've told me is true, they want to break you in every way possible, Eliza. Don't let them.'

She fell back on the pillow, his words slamming into her with the weight of a newly revealed truth. The shareholders wanted to take her husband's legacy, wanted to take the mines from her—more than that, they wanted to take her soul. In fact, they'd been in the process of stealing that since day one. Only she'd not understood it that way. They'd tried to make a man of her by forcing her to adhere to the codes of a man's world and, when that had failed, when she'd still been very much a woman facing them at the boardroom table—a woman who would not be brought to marry one of them—they'd forced her into a half life where she could look like a woman, but she'd be pilloried for acting like one. And now they'd tired of even that.

She sighed. 'What shall I do, Eaton? Can I ever win?' She was so very weary of it all. She could not fight on enemy soil any longer, pretending she was gaining ground only to have it pulled out from under her. She'd never win. Perhaps she should walk away, after all? But the idea of giving up soured her stomach.

Eaton rolled to his side, facing her. '*You* do nothing. *We* fight back. You are right. As long as they are in power, you are in enemy territory. Replace them. Build your empire from a position of strength. Let me mount an army for you.'

'Have you forgotten what it will cost me?' Her eyes lingered on his beautiful face. 'And you,' she added. 'If you come to my aid, people will talk of us both.'

'Everyone talks about dukes.' Eaton was unfazed. She needed him to take this seriously, but all Eaton did was flash her a wicked smile and tackle her in a tangle of sheets and limbs until she was beneath him once more, her heart pounding as he looked down at her, all naked, powerful male, eyes full of wanting and play. 'Didn't anyone ever tell you not to discuss business in bed? There are punishments for that, you know.'

She laughed—how could she not? He was irresistible like this. 'What might those be? I think you'll have to show me.'

He nipped at her earlobe with a wolfish chuckle that had her forgetting about blackmail and ledgers. 'Damn right I will. Up with you, I have a horse that needs riding.'

Eliza let out an undignified squeal as she saddled up, taking him astride. 'You will exhaust me, sir,' she warned coyly, lifting herself up over his manhood, already hard and wanting her.

'No business in bed,' he answered firmly, his hands at her hips as she brushed the entrance of her core over the tip of his shaft. He moaned, the cords in his neck tightening. She took mercy on him then, sliding down his slick length and riding him to a short, explosive end that left her exhausted indeed. She didn't remember rolling off him, only slumping down on his chest, his satisfied length still tucked securely inside her.

He was gone from the bed when she woke, the grey morning peeping through the long window. She groaned, panic fuelling her into a full state of alertness. She'd not meant to sleep so long. She'd meant to be home before daybreak. She didn't want Sophie to wake without her.

'Good morning.' Eaton's familiar tones, still husky from the night, drawled from the other side of the room. She rolled over, following the sound of his voice, her effort rewarded by the sight of him, trousered but shirtless, sitting behind the little table as if it were a duke's desk, writing materials set before him. A dark curl fell across his face as he looked up. 'Sleep well?'

'You know I did, and too long,' she scolded him. 'You should have woken me.'

'It's still early,' he assured her as if he knew what prompted her thoughts. 'We'll have you back in time.' He nodded to the carafe at the corner of the table. 'There's coffee.'

'What are you doing?' Eliza sat up and began to make a plait of her hair, anxiety causing her fingers to fumble. He was working. She feared she knew on what. She had not given permission.

'I'm writing to a friend, Inigo Vellanoweth. He's in banking. He'll know men who are interested in investing.' Eaton smiled benignly as if he hadn't just upended her world. 'After you have Sophie up, I'll meet you at the mines. We can look over the books together and decide which shareholders to buy out.'

'Why are you doing this?' Eliza asked cautiously. 'I thought we'd decided last night…' Plans for outings had become plans for her businesses. This was what she'd feared. A man sticking his oar into her ventures, trying to sail her ship for her. It was not unlike Detford's efforts five years prior to save her from society's backlash. *But this man was different.* Was he? Perhaps because he was more powerful, more tenacious than Miles. That should frighten her, not reassure her.

Eaton fixed her with a dark stare, the imperious one, the one he'd used on Miles at Bosrigan to remind the interloper who was in charge. 'Last night, *we* decided we were going to fight back.'

She threw off the covers and gathered her clothes. 'The only person I want to fight at the moment is you.' She dressed in hasty motions, emotion overcoming her. 'I knew this would happen. The moment I gave in I knew you would try something like this, try to manage me and the mines. I can do this on my own. I *have* been doing this on my own.'

'And that's precisely *why* you came to me.' He left the desk and strode towards her in quick paces that matched the staccato curtness of his words. She stepped backwards instinctively but found nothing except the wall. 'You were doing it alone and you wisely realised you needn't. Only now, in the morning light, you're doubting that decision.' He rose and came to her, stopping her hands and taking over the laces. 'I am not one of your shareholders looking to usurp you. And I am not Miles Detford looking for marriage. It's high time you stop treating me as such.' He was scolding her and there was anger in his words. He did not like being classified with Detford and the mutinous shareholders. 'After all I've done, after all I've shown you, Eliza, do you truly still doubt my character? I can't believe you do.' His voice softened, the scold over. 'You *can* trust me, Eliza, you know it in your bones. You would not have come last night otherwise.'

Eliza swallowed. She *had* come to him because she had nowhere else to turn; because her own resources wouldn't be enough; because Miles Detford, the one friend she'd thought she had, would not help her in refusing the offer; because she was empty, her emotional and mental reserves sapped. She'd come to him because being alone was no longer alternative enough. Now it was time to own up to it. She lifted her chin and squared her shoulders. 'Of course. I'll meet you at Wheal Karrek after I check on Sophie.'

Chapter Fifteen

Eliza was late. Eaton gave the wall clock one more glance and decided to start without her while he had the element of surprise on his side. It had worked well so far. The manager at Wheal Karrek had been so flummoxed to have him on site he'd shown him to Eliza's office, unlocked the door and left him there unattended. Eliza should probably have a word with the man about such trusting behaviour, but for now, it suited Eaton's purposes.

He had the office to himself and her ledgers. He might as well start while he waited for Eliza to arrive. She'd wanted to stop by the house first to check on Sophie and change her clothes. There was no question of showing up at the office dressed in the same attire she'd worn the previous day. But even given that delay, she was running late. He was unbothered by it. His sisters were consistently late, trying to marshal their broods. Besides, it would give him time to appreciate Eliza in an entirely different context.

He toured the perimeter of the space, stopping at the window. This austere, grey office was her domain, when she was here. How often had she visited the mine and he'd been unaware she was near? It was hard to imagine she had been here all along and he hadn't known. It was like Plato's old argument on the subjective nature of reality: things did not become real until they were known to exist, regardless of whether they'd been there all along, just waiting to be discovered. The office was sparse, a testimony to many things other than the fact that she was not always here, that she had other holdings. Truro was the centre of her empire, close to banking interests and only a few hours away from any of her holdings. Perhaps her office in Truro was more forthcoming in its decor?

Or perhaps not, given what he knew of Eliza. Austerity was a type of privacy and she valued hers above all things. This office was giving away no secrets. There were no pictures of Sophie here to invite a visitor's comment as she made small talk with a guest. There were no crystal decanters from which to pour a celebratory drink, no carpet on the floor to brighten the space, no artwork on the walls, just a plain clock. Eaton thought of the headmaster's office at the conservatory with its Thomas Witty carpet, mahogany furnishings, the elegant sideboard with its assorted decanters and the art chosen for its adherence to the theme of music. The space had been designed to inspire conversation and confidence, to persuade donors to support the institution and parents to enrol their children in a fine school where they were surrounded by the trappings of wealth.

That was not the case here. This space was not designed to entertain or persuade. Visitors would not be inclined to stay long given that the room held the minimum of furniture: a desk, two chairs and bookshelves that contained only ledgers and legal paperwork. It was a boring room. There wasn't a braided rug set before the fireplace. He doubted even Baldor would find the space comfortable. Eaton tried to imagine her in the office, behind the desk, listening to reports, giving orders, her chestnut hair and green eyes the only sparks of colour in room. She would draw all eyes as she'd drawn his.

Eaton selected a shareholders' journal from the shelf and settled in the chair near the fire. Perhaps it was best she wasn't here. He was already having difficulty thinking about work instead of her. It would be deuced difficult to concentrate on the books with her providing a very physical reminder of what they'd shared last night. She dominated his thoughts. He knew with certainty that one night with Eliza wasn't going to be nearly enough for him.

She was a confident lover who made him feel like a partner, like something more than the embodiment of a title and a bank account, or a demigod to be assuaged in order to request something from him. Sometimes he felt like Scheherazade's genie in the lamp, granting wishes for others, but never for himself. That was the curse of the genie. Unlimited power to be used in the service of others. The school was for Cornwall, for

Cade and for Rosenwyn, the ducal estates supported the local economies of their regions, providing jobs and crops, homes and business for tenants and villagers. But Eliza was for him. What he had done for her was for him as well. He'd wanted to help. He'd not been obliged. Eliza was a woman he admired and whose admiration he wanted. And therein lay the danger.

He wanted more than her admiration. Eaton looked up from the journal and expelled a slow breath, letting the knowledge settle on him. He was falling for Eliza Blaxland and he was falling hard. This relationship was not a game and it hadn't been for a long time. Maybe never. She'd been clear from the start she did not play the merry widow. It heightened the importance and the honour she'd done him by coming last night.

She'd not taken last night lightly. What had it meant to her? What were her expectations? She was not looking to marry. She was not looking for an affair that might bring scandal either, which left Eaton adrift for an answer. Perhaps the better question was, what were his expectations? What did he want? But the answer to that would be very different than the answer to what could he have. The way he felt right now, he didn't want it to end. He liked who he was when he was with her and with Sophie. Perhaps because they had no inkling what it meant to be him—a man who could give no woman a future. They only knew he liked to fly kites and hunt for sea-cave treasures. He was at his best with them and he'd not been at his best for a long time.

Was that true? It was quite the epiphany and it set him back. How long was it since he'd been truly, deeply *happy*? Perhaps it wasn't that he was *unhappy*. He laughed with his friends, he had compassion for others. He knew he wasn't the sort to let disappointment shape him into a grumpy, reclusive hermit who groused at the world. But he hadn't realised his happiness hadn't gone bone deep, that his happiness hadn't been *joy*. Not until now. Not until Eliza.

There was joy and peace with Eliza. With Eliza he was content sitting before the fire at the dower house in the evening, strolling in the orangery and playing with the parakeets, or walking the surf line of the beach. He didn't *need* to be rushing from project to project or worrying about what came next when life slowed down and he had to face the void. Eliza was no longer another project, something to begin and end. *Eliza filled the void.* The realisation was followed by another just as stunning. He didn't want Eliza to go back to Truro.

He wanted her to stay. But he couldn't have that. To stay meant to offer marriage. She was not looking for marriage and she would not want the marriage he could give her. There was nothing inside that offer for her. He could not give her children, the one thing she felt she'd had to give up for the sake of her independence, and the only thing that might compel her to rethink her position on marriage. A certain inevitability settled on him. At some point, he would have to give Eliza up. But not today. Today, she was still his and there were still things he could give her. It would have to be enough.

Eaton returned his attention to the journal and set to work in earnest. He noted the different percentages owned by which shareholders. He began to work combinations that afforded Eliza the most leverage for the least amount of money. Before long, he had an arrangement that would suit her purposes. When she arrived, Eliza would be pleased. If they could convince these shareholders to sell, she would have a modicum of power against the mutineers. She should be pleased.

He hadn't waited for her! To say she was displeased was an absolute understatement. Eliza huffed up the stairs to the office, steaming with anger. This was precisely why she should not have got involved with him! What had Eaton been thinking? She threw open the office door—no need for a key apparently when Gillie Cardy was letting in everyone who waved a title around. She'd have words with him later, once she'd had words with Eaton—Eaton, who was lounging decadently in the room's one chair, long, booted legs propped on the fender of the fireplace, a ledger in his lap confirming his worst sin while he managed to look desirable in the world's most uninspiring room. It was not a space designed for desire and yet he'd succeeded wildly in transforming it with his presence. 'You! You started without me!'

'And finished, although I much prefer when we finish together.' He was all smug insouciance against her rage. Did he not understand what he'd done?

She marched over to him and grabbed the ledger off his lap. 'No! You do not get to be in a good mood after you've violated my privacy. What did you think you were doing? This is *my* office. You've flustered poor Gillie Cardy to no end. He had no idea to expect you.'

Eaton gave a hearty laugh. 'I was taking a leaf from your book, Eliza—the power of a surprise visit. Cardy was not ready for my unexpected arrival and I used it to my advantage. You're right, it does create a certain momentum. Instead of waiting for you and letting the day slip by, I found the answer.' He was unfazed by her scold, another reason she should not have indulged. She had no power with him. He ran roughshod over her usual strategies and then followed them up with an irresistible grin. 'It's a little different when the shoe's on the other foot, isn't it, Eliza?'

'You should have waited, as a courtesy,' Eliza snapped. This was not a game. Her future as the leader of the mining corporation was at stake.

Eaton glanced at the clock. 'So that it could have taken us four hours to discover what I did in two? Perhaps I was mistaken, but I thought time was of the essence with the shareholders' meeting looming in a few days? I thought the plan was to buy out the necessary shareholders by then.'

'It is,' Eliza acceded, untying the ribbons of her hat and hanging it on a peg. But she didn't have to like it. She was still uncomfortable with the idea that the plan was Eaton's, that the resources she'd be using to repopulate her board were Eaton's. Yet the decision to follow the plan had been hers. She should not take her frustration out on Eaton. 'What did you find?' After the morning she'd had, it was time to get down to business.

'In a moment.' Eaton went to the desk and lifted the room's second chair out from behind it. 'First, come sit and tell me why you were late.' He placed the chair by the fire, angling it to meet his satisfaction. 'I'm afraid a chair is the most comfort I can offer. This office is *most* incommodious. I do recommend stocking it with decanters at the very least and think about redecorating.'

There he went again, being charming, all the while he was stealing control away from her. 'No decanters. They'll just fall off the shelves and smash when we blast.' She'd known indulging with him would be hazardous, but she'd misjudged the depth of the danger and of her liking. She didn't want him to be charming, or considerate. Why couldn't he be an arrogant bully she could despise?

'I'll add it to the list of problems to solve.' Eaton grinned. 'Now, about your morning? Is Sophie well?'

'No, as a matter of fact, Sophie ate something disagreeable at supper.' A supper she'd not overseen because she'd been too busy arguing with Detford. Sophie had been asleep by the time Detford had left. 'She woke up sick this morning.' Which was something else she'd almost missed because she'd been in bed with her lover. She'd been home barely five minutes before Sophie had woken up retching and needing her. Eliza shook her head, trying to dispel her remorse. 'I should have been there.'

'You mean, you should not have been with me,' Eaton corrected.

'Yes, but I was with you and now things are just as bad as I knew they'd be.' She leaned forward, dropping her voice to a hiss. 'Detford is downstairs. Gillie Cardy told him you'd been here since nine. He knows you're up here *alone*, with carte blanche access to the office records.' She would look like the whore Detford had implied yesterday. Miles would think Eaton was her lover and *now* he'd be right. If Miles told anyone, she'd look immoral and weak. Would Miles expose her like that or was he still her friend? She fixed Eaton with a stare. 'This is exactly the kind of opening the shareholders needed and I've handed it to them on a silver platter.'

Eaton disagreed. 'Yes, I do know what this means. Those who plot against you will be very concerned about their duplicity when they realise a peer of the realm has taken an interest in their industry. Would you like to see the list? These are your best options for a buyout. If they sell, you can increase your majority in the company by fifteen per cent. Brenley's bunch can't muster more than forty per cent if anything comes to a vote. Even if Detford's five per cent sides with them, you'd still have a margin.'

The whirring of her mind halted at his words. 'Say that again?' Had she heard him correctly?

Eaton grinned. 'I said, Eliza, you can make yourself fireproof. But you'll have to act fast.' *You*. Eaton was empowering her, not taking anything away from her. It might have been his suggestion, but she had to enact it and the shares would be hers. Eliza smiled. It felt as if a weight had been lifted from her, her doubts evaporating in the wake of success. They had found a way through. She was on the offensive now.

Eliza Blaxland wasn't going to go down without a fight. Miles eyed the group assembled over ale, crumpling Eliza's note in his hand. 'She's refused our offer. Well, we expected as much. She's never been the most biddable of women.' Miles's dissatisfaction was palpable as he addressed the group. His interviews with Eliza had been disappointing. He'd hoped she would have found the offer more appealing. 'We never expected Bude's heir was in her pocket,' he said, trying to rationalise the refusal.

'More like he's in her bed,' Gismond Brenley supplied derisively. 'Looks like someone beat you to the finish line, Detford.'

'Hardly matters where he is, only that he's involved now and that makes him part of our problem,' Miles replied, redirecting their attentions back to the subject at hand. They could not blame Lynford's presence on him. 'We have three days until the shareholders' meeting. We have to make sure we have a case against her if she means to refuse our generous offer. If she won't step down for a nice offer, we have to force her out.' He liked the idea of force. He was done playing nice with Eliza Blaxland. It was time she learned her place.

'Lynford *is* the case against her,' Isley Thorp put in with a sly grin. 'If we put it about that she's his mistress, her reputation is in question. We can't have an immoral woman running the corporation.'

'It depends on how the rest of the board sees it.' Detford shook his head. Under regular circumstances, the current board would find such behaviour inexcusable. But if the board was under Lynford's thumb, it would hardly matter if Eliza walked down the street naked. Miles waited until he had everyone's attention. 'There's something else.' He pushed forward a letter. 'I got this from one of the minor shareholders last night. She's made an offer to buy his shares, at profit. I am assuming she sent similar letters to others.' If she were successful, this would ruin everything. It would give her majority control against their coalition.

Gismond Brenley seemed unconcerned. 'They won't sell. There's the money to be made from extending the tunnel once the widow is removed. Profits will go skyhigh, then. Surely these shareholders know that. Besides, she'd need to garner more than someone's three per cent. She'd need to buy all the three per centers. Odds are, not all of them will sell out.'

Miles wasn't as confident. He'd seen how resolute she'd been when he'd put the offer to her. 'Maybe. Or, perhaps those three per centers don't want the risk of an accident. Everyone knows nothing ever goes smoothly in mining. But that isn't the point. She's building a new group of shareholders, people who are willing to champion her, to leave her in power. Gentlemen, she's replacing us and it takes no imagination to know who is behind this.'

Miles met each man's gaze directly. There was a fortune in copper beneath the sea if they could just reach it. But they had to go through her.

Brenley thought for a moment. 'Then we have to get to her. She would never let a man control what she's worked for. We need to convince her that Lynford will take control away from her no matter what he's promised thus far.'

'And if that doesn't work?' Miles pressed. 'We may

need to remove her in a more permanent way.' A certain excitement roused in him at the prospect. Eliza Blaxland had crossed him too many times. Of course those methods were dangerous. There was too much money at stake for people to ignore her death. When those people included the Marquess of Lynford and the Duke of Bude, there would most definitely be an inquest. Yet, if it came to that, he would find a way to ensure the cards went his way. To be denied now, and by a woman who thought herself the equal of a man, would be an enormous loss of financial opportunity and pride. This was war. All was fair and the endgame was near. Eliza Blaxland would get a final chance to accept the offer at the board meeting and then she would get what was coming to her.

Chapter Sixteen

The game had started without her. Eliza drew a deep breath to steady her nerves and her anger before entering the upper room at the Ship Inn on Budoc Lane. She could hear voices within that confirmed what the innkeeper had reported: the shareholders were already assembled and had been for half an hour. How dare they begin the meeting before she arrived! She was the chairman, the head of the company. She would remind them nothing they did without her presence had meaning.

Eliza smoothed her skirts and squared her shoulders. She'd dressed to command today in a tailored ensemble of heather grey, the coat cut with military lines and trimmed in black velvet, a white stock peeking up at the collar. There would be no disputing that she was the one in charge. She ran through her mental list of resources, reminding herself what her goals were here today: to emerge with her leadership of the mines intact.

Eliza turned the knob and entered, gratified when the conversation faltered, when all eyes turned to her, some of those eyes looking guilty. Good. Six of those men had happily taken her money last night when she'd bought their shares in the company. Her chair at the head of the table was empty. Also good. They hadn't replaced her yet. To the right of her chair sat Miles Detford. Today, the sight of him didn't fill her with the usual comfort. But he was still her friend, still her ally, she told herself. He'd brought bad news, he'd counselled her to take an offer she didn't agree with— that didn't make him less of a friend. Perhaps it made him more of one.

'Now that I am here, we can begin.' Eliza strolled to her chair and consulted the watch pin she wore; ten minutes until the hour. 'That is, if no one disapproves of starting early? We did agree to meet at eleven.' She surveyed the room with a cool gaze before sitting. 'I do appreciate how very...*prompt* everyone is.' She took her seat. 'I officially call the quarterly meeting of the Blaxland Mining Corporation to order.' Miles Detford read the minutes and Eliza pasted on a cool smile as though nothing was out of the ordinary. They would see that their contretemps had not shaken her.

'A report from the treasurer is now in order. Mr Thorp?' Eliza called on the sallow-faced man, wondering if she'd imagined his Adam's apple bobbing nervously. She looked around the table when he finished. 'Are there questions for Mr Stinson on our expenses?' The question was met with silence. She stared at Isley Thorp, at Jerome Blackmore, at Sir Gismond Brenley.

Who was the betrayer? 'No questions?' She kept her voice frosty, her gaze returning to Thorp. 'I find that hard to believe when the lumber order for the Wheal Karrek tunnel was twice what it should have been. It is not our practice to deliberately over-order.'

'What are you suggesting, Mrs Blaxland?' Gismond Brenley patronised in a bored tone as if there was no need to be concerned.

She met him with a steely gaze, her own tone matching him in condescension. 'I am suggesting that someone countermanded our decision not to tunnel under the ocean. Why else would we purchase twice the required lumber? If that is not the case, I would think you'd be more concerned since it's your money that's been spent unnecessarily.' How horribly telling that he wasn't aghast. In fact, *none* of them was aghast, although a few of them exchanged looks. She did not give away her dismay. 'Very well, let the minutes show that no one was bothered by the expenditures.' She'd put them on notice, she'd gone on record in the minutes for having addressed the issue head-on. It would be harder to accuse her now of being inept, of having not been aware of what was happening in her own company. 'Now, on to old business, the Porth Karrek tunnel and the schools.'

'Ahem, Mrs Blaxland, I would like to table old business until we've discussed a proposal.' The interruption came from Gismond Brenley. 'I think it will affect how the discussion of the tunnel and the schools goes, which is why I'd like to have it introduced first.'

Eliza braced herself. So the ringleader was Brenley. She was not surprised. He was the most august of the shareholders. Under friendlier circumstances, he would have been her right hand just as he'd been her husband's. But he'd never been in support of her, having always fancied himself the heir apparent to the mining corporation. 'Mrs Blaxland, in honour of your fifth year as the head of the company, and in recognition of your extraordinary efforts, we have an offer to put to you to help relieve the strain you've endured. With the advent of the new tunnel, the corporation is entering a new era and it occurred to us that it is an opportune time for new leadership, a chance for you to step away and enjoy your life with your daughter.'

On her right, Miles murmured, 'These are good terms.'

Eliza suspected the murmur was for show. But whose show? For her benefit or for the board's? Would a polite refusal be enough? 'Thank you, gentlemen. I am sure the offer is made with my benefit in mind, however, I have no intention of stepping away from the mines at this time. It is an exciting period and, precisely for that reason, I will remain at the helm for the foreseeable future.' Eliza smiled her rejection. There was uncomfortable silence. No one spoke. For a moment, she thought she might have won, that all that had been required was a firm hand. Surely it couldn't be that easy. She waited for the count of five.

Brenley's eyes grew hard. 'It may not be up to you. The board believes it is time for you to step down. We want to go forward with the underwater tunnel. We feel financial resources are better spent on the pursuit of ore than establishing schools. We didn't want to do this as a vote, but we will if we must.'

'We definitely must. I want to see my betrayers, those who have plotted behind my back to bring about this moment,' Eliza snapped. 'The vote will be done by a show of hands and votes will be counted based on the allotted shares each member holds in the company.' There were no grounds for argument there; it was how votes had always been counted. 'Those in favour of new leadership?' Thorp, Blackmore, Brenley—the usual coalition—raised their hands along with Stinson. 'That's forty per cent, Brenley.' Eliza smiled coolly as she informed him, 'That is not a majority.'

'But Havens, Eldridge, Saxon, Halliday, Mycroft and Kincaid haven't voted,' Brenley replied.

'Nor will they. As of this morning, they are no longer shareholders in the corporation. They have sold their shares to me. That gives me a majority in the company.'

'Detford, you haven't voted.' Brenley skewered him with a prompting gaze.

'I only hold five per cent of the shares, so it wouldn't matter which way I decide,' Miles prevaricated. He smiled at her as if his abstention was some sort of victory for her. Was it? Was abstention a way of siding with her? She could hear Eaton's warning in her head. Detford was not to be trusted.

'So, we are to be a board of five, then?' Brenley challenged.

'Perhaps, or maybe I will sell my shares at some point. Not today, though, and not to you, although if you are jealous of your friends' profits made in selling to me, I am happy to purchase your shares at the same rate, as well as anyone else's here at the table.' That included Detford, who'd not declared his side, more was the pity, but that was not the main concern today.

'Replacing us will strain your resources.' Brenley glared. 'We are not so easily bought as these other piddling stakeholders.' No, they wouldn't be. Their shares would be expensive, but she did not flinch.

'I am offering to treat you equitably, as I have treated your colleagues, even though you secretly plotted a mutiny behind my back after I have spent years making you money.' Eliza rose from the table. 'As the single majority stockholder, I declare that the underwater tunnel will cease once it reaches the ocean and the schools will go forward as planned. This meeting is adjourned.'

She made it to the door of the Ship Inn before Miles reached her. He placed a hand on her arm as she stepped outside. 'Eliza, what do you think you're doing? Did Lynford put you up to this?'

'I put myself up to it, Miles. Since when does a man put me up to anything?' All she wanted right now was to be with Sophie, with Eaton.

'I've never known you to be reckless. Do you think you can simply buy them out and your problems will be solved?' Detford kept pace with her as she marched up Budoc Lane. 'Brenley's right, you can't buy out the rest of us without breaking your bank to do it. You'd have to sell those shares immediately.' It was as if a light came on in Detford's mind. 'Lynford has investors lined up, doesn't he? Don't be a fool, Eliza. He's setting up to take over the corporation. How long do you think you'd remain in charge?'

'As long as I like,' Eliza all but snapped. She was done discussing business.

'As his whore? Or will he seduce it out of you?' Miles snarled. 'You know that's what everyone will say. They'll say Lynford is propping you up because it humours him to let his mistress run mines. What do you think they're saying upstairs right now? It's already started, Eliza. They will come after you and this time they won't play by the rules. You should have pacified Brenley's coalition when you had the chance.'

She reached her carriage. 'Thank you for the advice, Miles.' She got in and pointedly shut the door behind her, leaving Miles alone on the street. She had much to think about. She'd poked a sleeping dragon and now it was awake and roaring. The meeting had gone as expected. She had what she wanted. But the fight had just begun. By tomorrow, the rumours would start. She had one last day of peace and she would spend it with Sophie and Eaton.

Eliza leaned back against the leather seat and shut her eyes. Eaton. She should not want him. He would be the undoing of her, perhaps not in the way Miles predicted, but there were other ways to steal her control and undermine the life she'd built. There was no future with him. They both knew it and yet they both continued to pretend it didn't matter. But it did. When it ended, she would be disappointed. Eliza sighed. Already she knew that word was too mild to encompass what she would feel. Intentionally or not, Eaton had given her a glimpse of heaven, a glimpse of herself, how she might have been if only things had been different.

'Mama! Mama! Come see the parakeets!' They were the sweetest words in the world to Eliza as Sophie tugged on her hand the moment she stepped inside the orangery.

Eaton emerged behind Sophie, jacket off, sleeves rolled up, a wide, open smile on his face. He'd been enjoying himself. 'You're just in time.' His gaze was intent, lingering on her, looking for signs there'd been trouble. 'We're going to feed the birds.' She smiled, offering reassurance that all had gone as well as could be expected. There'd be time to talk later. Eliza allowed Sophie to drag her off to the aviary, the tension of the meeting rolling off her with each step. Moments like this were what mattered. This was what she was fighting for, to protect Sophie's inheritance.

'Did the gambit work?' Eaton asked once Sophie was busy with the parakeets.

'Yes, the coalition was exposed and they were reminded I retain control of the board for now. But Brenley made threats.' She paused. 'Nothing we did not anticipate, but I'd hoped it would not come to that. He will say awful things about me, Eaton.' She watched Sophie hold up a finger for a parakeet to perch on and giggle when it did. She was so sweet, so innocent. 'I would not want her to hear those things said about her mother.'

'It will not come to that.' Eaton's voice was fervent and low. 'Once we have a new board in place, people will see the truth, I will see to it. Your reputation will remain intact.'

'It's not your responsibility, Eaton. It's mine.' Eliza felt the prickles of Miles's warning creep up her spine. No, she would not believe that of him. Doubt would only serve Brenley. What would Eaton do with a mining corporation? He didn't need it. There was no reason for him to take it over. *Any more than there was ever a reason to help her*, her conscience whispered. Why had he bothered at all? What did he gain?

'Your responsibility alone, Eliza?' Eaton queried. 'It doesn't have to be.'

'Yes, it does,' she insisted. What could he want? What could ever come of this association? Everything was so much simpler when she'd just been a patron of his school, a faceless widow who wrote cheques, who didn't know how handsome the Marquess was or how persuasive. This conversation was fast becoming about more than managing the board. This was about managing them—this relationship. Did one night in his bed constitute a relationship, or had that relationship existed long before they'd made love?

'I thought we'd settled the bit about being alone.' Eaton offered her a devastating smile. 'Can we argue about this later? I promised Sophie we'd pick oranges for tea. But I'd like to continue this discussion tonight?' She heard the invitation in that. She ought to decline. Accepting would make it harder to leave.

Just one more night, she promised herself. Then it

would have to be over and she would be alone again. The lines of demarcation were clearer that way. She'd had just the smallest taste of how easily it could all slip away if she indulged herself with him. To blur those lines was to blur her priorities. Eaton could not be one of them, no matter how much she wanted him to be.

Chapter Seventeen

One more night. One more night of torturing himself with a glimpse of what might have been, showing himself what could never be. Eaton would take it, whatever its guise. Sophie finished playing the spinet in the parlour and went up to bed, Eliza with her, while he waited downstairs with a glass of brandy. It was a fatherly, husbandly thing to do. Not for the first time he thought how different things might have been if he had not gone into Kilkhampton that day fourteen years ago. He might never have contracted the measles, might never have been stripped of his ability to reproduce. He wouldn't be faced with losing a woman he loved.

Up until now, the consequences of his infertility had been a theoretical concept. Certainly, he had agonised over what it would mean for his life as he grew older, how it shaped the choices he would make. That theoretical concept had become more real with Richard Penlerick's death and the overt pressure put on Vennor to marry. Now, with Eliza, that reality was complete. There were no more hypothetical dimensions to it. He'd met a woman he loved. A woman he wanted to marry. A woman who wanted children. A woman he couldn't have.

'Are you thinking about Richard Penlerick? You seem sorrowful.' Eliza entered the parlour.

'In part,' he offered. 'I was thinking of you and Sophie and how much like a little family we've become.' He gestured for her to join him on the settee.

'You've been good to her. She likes you.'

Eaton played with the stem of his brandy glass. 'And her mother? Does her mother like me?' Eliza was beautiful in firelight, the flames catching her chestnut hair.

'Her mother is very thankful for your support in this difficult time. You didn't need to give it and I fear your kindness has been repaid by dragging you into the quagmire.' Eliza's hands were tight in her lap. She was nervous. 'I think it might be time to leave. I don't want to be the guest who overstays her welcome.'

'Leave? Now? You can't leave now, not when you've just got control of the board. What about your school?' This was the worst possible time for her to leave— unless this wasn't about business but about *them*. Knowing he had to let her go was one thing. Actually letting her go was another.

'I control the board whether I am here or in Truro. The shareholders don't need me to be here for them to take their places. I won't see them in person until the next quarterly meeting, assuming I survive Brenley's character assassination.' It was coolly said, but for the first time, Eaton saw how worried Eliza was.

'You will survive it,' Eaton assured her. 'Why wouldn't you? Brenley and the others will sell out before long and walk away because they won't be happy once your new board members are in place. You simply have to wait them out, let them save face. You can afford to be a gracious victor.'

'I don't control the community. Even if I win this battle of wills, I wonder if it will be enough? I've wondered all day if I should have taken Brenley's deal. I wonder even now, at the eleventh hour, if I should write to him and accept the offer, as much as it would gall me to do it. Still, it might be better than what is to come.' Better than having her name dragged through the mud if Detford's information was right. Better than having Eaton's name dragged there, too. He deserved more for his assistance than a scandal. She'd been a poor investment to repay him thusly.

She gave him a sad smile. 'Victory at what price, Eaton? At the price of my good name? At the price of a scandal my daughter will hear of?'

'Is that why you're so anxious to be off to Truro? You want to avoid Brenley's next barrage?' Eaton drew her to him, wrapping her in his arms and tucking her head beneath his chin in the hope of giving her comfort. 'There's the principle of the matter, too, Eliza. If you accept Brenley's offer, you would be letting dishonest men win.' Eaton paused, allowing her to digest that piece.

'I can have peace. That is no small thing.' She sighed against his chest. God, he loved having her in his arms.

'But what of the miners? What peace will they have

when Brenley pushes the tunnel out into the ocean at their risk?' He had her there. He could feel her tense in his arms, another reminder of how multifaceted the fight was and how she was the shield maiden for so many. Perhaps it was for that reason her answer surprised him.

'I may reach a point very soon where they will have to fight for themselves. I can't hold up the world for ever.' There was a new weariness in her tone. 'Please don't talk to me about ethics and principles, Eaton. I *know* I should fight for them.' She looked up at him, her green eyes filled with regret. 'But Sophie needs my protection, too. At some point, a parent doesn't have the luxury of fighting for ethics. If I have to choose who to protect, I'll choose Sophie.'

But who protected her? Eliza Blaxland manned the wall of her defences alone. She needed a protector, an ally. He stroked her hair, his thoughts wandering down tangled paths. How could he make this right for her? How could he protect her and Sophie so that Eliza could fight?

'Does my choice disappoint you?' she asked, her eyes searching his face.

'No, it makes you honest.' And smart and brave, all the things he'd come to admire about her, *love* about her. It was not the first time he'd associated that word with Eliza. He loved her strength, her independence, her fierceness, her willingness to sacrifice everything for those she loved, and perhaps that meant he loved not only the characteristics that made her who she was, but he loved *her*, too.

Temptation whispered, *You can protect her. You can marry her, give her the protection of your name and your station. Save her mines, ensure her reputation, be a father to Sophie. Marriage to her gives you everything you've ever wanted.*

But it gave Eliza nothing. She would resist. She'd made her position on marrying clear. He would have to put it to her carefully and at the right moment. This was not that moment. She was too conflicted, too uncertain. His offer would look like charity coming now on the heels of her fear. And he'd have to tell her his secret, something he didn't discuss even with his close friends and family. They knew, of course, but he hadn't been the one to tell them. He had to tell Eliza. She had a right to know what marriage to him would cost her. It would cost her dream. Telling her might very well cost him his. He could lose her over this and that came with fears all its own. But loving Eliza demanded he take the risk. He'd not told a woman about his condition, ever. There'd never been a need to. How did one go about divulging dark truths and shattering dreams and hope to emerge intact? But those were discussions and considerations for another, better, time.

'Don't give in, Eliza,' he whispered. 'It will be all right in the end, I promise.' He would move heaven and earth to make it so. He'd created a school for Cade and Rosenwyn. Surely he could do at least as much for the woman he loved.

She smiled softly, something moving in her eyes. 'I shouldn't let you make impossible promises, but I don't want to think about it any more tonight.'

'What *do* you want?'

'I want to forget everything for just a little while. Do you have a remedy for that?'

Eaton grinned. 'I might. If you'd come with me, there's a place I know.'

She should not use him for escape, but it was hard to remember the reasons why as she reclined on the pillows in the orangery's antechamber, watching him disrobe. This little room had become their refuge, the place where the world could not touch them, where she was entitled to give her fantasy free rein. Eaton strode towards the bed, gloriously nude, all broad shoulders and muscled thighs, like a wild pagan god of old, desire heating his eyes with a fierceness that made her tremble. How phenomenal, how thrilling, that this man wanted her and how wicked that she should want him, too, with the same fierceness. Tonight she needed the pulsing, thrusting pleasure that drove one towards oblivion.

He came to her and she drew him down, bringing his length against her until they were skin to silk, her nightgown already sliding up her thighs, already revealing her eagerness, her desire. She welcomed him. His eyes reflected her own hunger. She was hungry to forget the day, hungry to recapture the passion that had flared to life in this room, hungry to be touched, to be cherished if even for a few moments.

'Tonight you are Breasal, the Celtic High King, come to earth.' She nipped at his earlobe, whispering the fantasy from Cornish folklore. 'You've come to claim a mortal maid for your pleasure.'

He gave a husky laugh, his hand running up her thigh, bending her knee. 'I will hope for better since his kingdom is only visible one night in seven years.' He kissed the inside of her leg, working up her thigh with his lips. 'Perhaps I am the mere mortal and you are the fairy Aeval, come to command my sexual favours.' He kissed the crease of her thigh where it met with the entrance to her private core.

'Hmm. I like that.' She stretched, cat-like, letting the warm thrill of him spread through her. 'I always thought the story of Aeval's midnight court was rather decadent, but secretly inspiring, that a woman might, nay, *should* command her own pleasure. Indeed, even hold a man accountable for it.'

'And did you? Command your own?' Eaton asked, his eyes dangerously feral as he kissed her navel, working his way up her body, heat following in his wake.

'Absolutely, or I would have had none.' She locked gazes with him, answering his look with one of her own just as wild, letting the implication settled on him. Married to Blaxland, she'd been responsible for her own pleasure alone in the dark after he'd claimed his rights. She'd never begrudged him that, but she begrudged knowing that there should be more, that perhaps she was entitled to more.

'And the holding-a-man-accountable part?' He sucked at her breast, drawing out a nipple with his teeth until she gasped.

'Only you.' She smiled wickedly.

He answered with a grin of his own. 'What does my Fairy Queen command of me this night?'

She shifted her hips, widening the span between her legs. 'Your Queen commands that you take her, swift and fast, that you drive her into pleasure's oblivion until the sun rises.' She kissed him hard on the mouth, reckless with desire and need, and he answered with a savage hunger that mirrored her own. She felt him move once and then he thrust deep, a bright spear that splintered her core. Yes, this was exactly what she needed. She gave herself over to it, knowing that oblivion awaited.

But so did the morning. Even Eaton's exquisite lovemaking could not hold back the sun, nor could the pleasure of waking in his arms, her body tucked against his, override the troubles of the day. She was no nearer to any resolution than she had been the prior evening. She and Brenley were still at odds and viciously so. His threats still loomed like ghosts on dawn's horizon waiting to take shape. But larger still was the issue of leaving Eaton. This had to end and she would have to end it. The longer she stayed, the more unfair it was to both of them. There was no expectation of a future, but there were feelings. How did one navigate the end of an affair neither party wanted to end? Last night had solved one need, but created others. If she wasn't careful, she would fall in love with Eaton. Maybe she already had. Maybe that was why she was still here.

Eaton's body stirred behind her, his voice warm at

her ear. 'Have I acquitted myself appropriately, my Queen?'

'Extraordinarily so,' she murmured, wishing to hold on to the night just a moment longer. They'd loved and slept, and loved and slept until they could conquer exhaustion no more as dawn crept up on them and the game had ended, taking oblivion with it. She was the Queen no longer, but a beleaguered businesswoman beset on all sides by those who wished to see her fail. Eaton moved against her and she amended the thought. Perhaps she wasn't beleaguered on all sides. Perhaps she had one ally, one person who wished for her success.

'Perhaps I might acquit myself one more time,' he whispered, his arm tight about her waist, hugging her securely against him. She would be his Aeval one last time.

Eliza moaned, her bottom wiggling against him. Morning pleasure was a habit one could easily get used to, addicted to. To wake like this beside such a man was heavenly indeed. No, not *such a man*. That suggested there were other men who could command such a response from her, that such a response was available on a whim.

No, only Eaton would do. Not Blaxland, not Detford. None of the men who'd tried to woo her had ever succeeded in wringing a response from her even close to this. Nor would any man ever, her conscience counselled. Eaton was one in a million and she knew why. He wanted nothing from her that she did not want for herself. She was safe with him. He did not want to take the mines by manipulation or by matrimony. He slid into her, faster this time, his slow, drowsy seduction increasing its urgency as she gasped, her hands gripping his arm where he held her close as she came apart.

She was reluctant to put the pieces back together. It would require getting out of bed, getting dressed, dealing with Brenley. It would also require putting distance between her and Eaton. That distance had to start today. That was what she'd promised herself and that was what the situation required if she was going to survive the scandal intact. Eliza sighed. She still had to be the one to do this. He could not fight this battle for her, although she knew he would insist otherwise.

'That sigh sounds ominous.' Eaton kissed her shoulder.

'I need to get up. I can't stay in bed all day.' For so many reasons.

'Why not?' Eaton propped his dark head on a hand, looking entirely too seductive by dawn's light.

'Because it solves nothing.' She shifted to the side of the bed and swung her feet over the edge, shivering now that she was away from the heat of his body.

'What can we solve today? We can do nothing more until we hear from Inigo.' She could feel his eyes on her as she moved about the room, gathering up her clothes.

She stopped her gathering and faced him. 'We can't solve the issue with the mining board, but we can solve what lies between us. This has to end. Even without pressure from the board, there's nothing here for us.'

Eaton sat up, hands behind his head, his torso with its dark hair on blatant display, a reminder of what she was giving up—all that masculine virility. He smiled and her heart thudded. 'Nothing here for us? Do you really believe that? I don't. If you do believe there is nothing here, then it seems you and I have very different understandings of what has occurred between us in the past month.'

Eliza set her clothes down, hands on hips. 'All right, you tell me what you think happens next.'

'I think we wait. We wait out Brenley. We wait for news from Inigo. I have no intention of deserting you in the heart of the storm, which is precisely where we are now. I am in no hurry to divest myself of you, Eliza. Yet you seem in quite the hurry to be rid of me. I am wounded.'

'You'll recover,' Eliza said sharply.

'I'm not so sure I will.' The lack of humour in his voice caused her to pause. There was no laughter in his tone; he was in earnest. Eaton crawled out of bed and wrapped a sheet about his waist. 'Let me help you dress. We can take Sophie to the woods today and hunt for another round of truffles. Baldor needs a good run. I'll have a picnic packed.'

'I have business in town, errands,' Eliza protested, but Eaton was adamant on this point.

'Do not go into town today, Eliza. Let Brenley do his worst. Your absence will simply show everyone how little you care for his accusations and how little you are worried.'

She wanted to argue, but his advice made sense. It would be best not to invite comment by going into town. Still, she did not want him making decisions for her. He'd already made so many. She'd known it would happen like this; first the house, then dinner, then the little entertainments with Sophie, all harmless in the beginning. But now, here she was in his bed, allowing him to repopulate the shareholders with his friends, allowing him to decide where she went. 'You have done too much.' It was a warning that he'd exceeded the allotment of favours she'd take from him.

His hands rested at her shoulders and she very much feared there was every chance they'd be back in bed before she got her dress on. 'Eliza, let me in.'

'You cannot fight for me. I've explained.'

'No, I cannot. But we can fight together. I can fight *with* you. You just have to trust me, Eliza.'

Eliza said nothing.

Chapter Eighteen

❧❧❧❧❧❧

The end of October was out in full, glorious colour. The golden leaves of the Trevaylor Woods crunched under their boots as they strolled beneath the autumn foliage, the sound serving as a reminder of the silence that had sprung up between them in the orangery. Up ahead, Sophie threw handfuls of leaves into the air, laughing and dodging among the trees, while Baldor wagged his tail and did his best to get in the way. Eliza envied the duo their romp, oblivious to the tension that had risen between her and Eaton. She had said very little to him since they'd left the orangery, focusing an over-bright smile on Sophie and getting ready for the picnic. In short, she was ignoring him. Did he not understand he was asking for the moon? The sooner she and Sophie left the better. This dalliance had gotten out of hand. She'd consented to the experiment, but now it had to end. She would retreat to Truro and clutch her fifty-five per cent majority to her for all it was worth. No matter what Brenley did, she would rise from the ashes.

Eaton stooped to pick up a particularly vibrant red leaf and twirled the stem in his hand, breaking the silence. 'Autumn has always been my favourite season. My father started bringing me truffle hunting when I was Sophie's age. We brought Baldor's grandsire with us. My father's hounds are bred for truffling. They have incredible noses,' he explained, casting her a smile, his dark eyes full of nostalgia. 'I loved those days when it was just the two of us, tramping through the woods. We'd stop by the stream and build a bonfire. That's where he taught me how to roast mushrooms. Sometimes we'd bring eggs and sausages.'

'It sounds delicious. Is that where your love for food comes from? You and your father must be very close.' She returned his smile warily, not wanting to be drawn into the story, this precious glimpse into his childhood.

'We are. In many ways, he is my best friend. He taught me how to be a man, how a man takes care of his family, of friends, of those less fortunate around him. He taught me how to be a duke, when the time comes, although I am in no hurry to lose him. In fact, I can't even imagine it. It will be so much worse than losing Richard Penlerick.' A shadow crossed his face and he looked away from her, clearing his throat against emotion.

'You're very lucky to have a father who cares for you,' Eliza offered, the wistfulness evident in her own voice. 'Sophie was four when Huntingdon died. She barely remembers him at all. I worry for her, growing up with a mother who must also be a father to her.' Eliza stooped to gather up leaves into a bouquet, aware she might have said too much, given the wrong impression. She didn't want Eaton to think she was angling for a proposal despite her previous arguments to the contrary. She didn't want to quarrel with him any more today. She'd rather enjoy this afternoon for what it was—a moment out of time where she could set aside her worries over the board and what came next.

'Do you honestly think being mother and father to Sophie is your only choice? That you absolutely must remain alone for the rest of your life? That there could never be a man worthy of your trust and respectful of your independence? Who could love you just the way you are?' Eaton was studying her. She was aware of his gaze, hot and contemplative. 'Humans are meant to marry, I think. You included.' Eaton handed her a golden fistful of leaves to add to the bouquet.

'And yet you haven't,' Eliza was quick to argue. 'You, who perhaps has more reason than most to marry.'

'I keep finding better things to do.'

'Like taking care of mining heiresses?' she joked, but it was as she'd suspected. She was a project, something to fill the void for this energetic man. She could be nothing more. He was meant for a different type of woman: a younger woman, a more innocent woman, a better-born woman. He was not for her, not in that way.

'I happen to like mining heiresses.' They stopped by a tree and Eaton distractedly chipped off a piece of bark. 'I used to think I wouldn't ever marry.'

She slanted him a questioning look. 'Why not? Surely it is expected of you?'

'No, not of me.' He slouched against the tree trunk, arms crossed, dark eyes serious. 'Can I tell you something, Eliza? Something I wouldn't want anyone else to know.'

He was asking her to keep a secret. A real secret. She'd learned to read him well enough to know this was not flirtation. She straightened, her leaf bouquet forgotten. She reached for his hands and held on. Intuition hinted whatever he wanted to tell her was difficult to speak of. 'You may tell me anything, Eaton.'

He would rather tell her anything but this. But honour demanded it. If he did not tell her, there was no possibility of moving forward. 'When I was fourteen there was a measles epidemic in Kilkhampton, which is not far from our family seat in Bude. I wasn't supposed to be there, but I was young, stupid and overly optimistic about my own immortality as many adolescent boys are. I sneaked away to take in a horse fair on the outskirts of the town. At fourteen I had no notion how illness was spread. I reasoned the fair was far enough from the village and I'd never been sick a day in my life, not the slightest fever ever.

'My luck ran out that day. I caught the measles. I took ill and almost died. We were fortunate. No one else in the family caught it and I lived. Many families around Bude lost loved ones that year.' Eliza nodded. Measles, mumps, any disease of that nature was a mother's nightmare. But her thoughts weren't for mothers in that moment. Her thoughts were for Eaton and where this story was headed and why she might need to know.

'It took most of that summer for me to recover. I've never been so weak. I hope I am never that weak again.' She squeezed his hands, giving him her strength once more the way she had that first night in the orangery when he'd told her about Richard Penlerick. 'I didn't realise it until a few years later, but it left me…unable to father children.'

Her brow knit. She was trying to be delicate and yet it was obvious her disbelief and curiosity were so much stronger. 'But, you don't seem to have any trouble…in the bedroom.'

'Sterility is not impotence. I can sleep with a woman as much as I like, but it will never result in a child.' Eaton gave a dry laugh. 'I know some men who wouldn't mind that sort of problem. I am not one of them.'

'No, you wouldn't be.' He could see the thoughts chasing across her face: how good he was with Sophie, how dedicated he was to the boys at the school. *Please,* he prayed, *don't offer me pity.* He simply wanted her to understand. He didn't need consolation. Eliza did not disappoint. 'How do you know for sure? Is there a test?'

'Just my own and some observations I made. There are other boys in Kilkhampton who caught the measles and have not sired children in their adulthood. I think it's unlikely there are that many barren females in Kilkhampton.' He shook his head. He knew what she was thinking. He'd once thought it, too. 'Eliza, do not give yourself false hope, that perhaps I am wrong, that there's a chance somehow.' This was the hard part, telling her about his experiment. 'I did a test, Eliza. My seed is dead. I put it under my microscope in the orangery and it didn't move. I know microscopic lenses are imperfect and I am no doctor but, taken with the other observations, there is no margin for hope. My father and I consulted a doctor in London and he was of the same opinion. He had made several studies of men who'd contracted measles in their childhood or adolescence. Not everyone was unable to father children, but there were enough to suggest it was a significant possibility.'

He waited for the pity, the platitudes. He waited for her to politely move away from him as if she could catch it. She would leave him now that she knew loving him, being with him, came at such a price. But Eliza did none of those things. Her words were full of gratitude for his honesty. 'Thank you for telling me. You didn't have to.' No, he could have kept the awful secret, could have let her believe their childless union was somehow her fault. It wouldn't have been a hard argument to make. She'd had one child in ten years with Huntingdon. Perhaps it hadn't been his age after all. Society would easily participate in that lie. But Eaton could not do that to her, this woman who wanted a family, who thought he might be able to give her one.

'The school isn't just for Cade and Rosenwyn, is it?' Eliza said softly. 'It's for you, too, to fill a void. All this time, I thought your life was perfect. The boys at the school, they're your children in their own way, aren't they?'

'Much like the miners' children are for you. It seems we must make families where we can find them.' He raised her hands to his lips and kissed each of them. 'You and Sophie have been a family to me in these weeks. I will always be grateful to you for that. Huntingdon Blaxland was a lucky man.'

Eliza laughed. 'He thought so, too, but I always thought I was the lucky one. He gave me Sophie and a second chance.' Baldor bayed in the distance, a reminder that the hound and Sophie had run far ahead of them. Eaton pushed off the tree trunk and they began to walk again.

'He did more than give me financial security. He gave me the ability to make that security for myself. Hunt enjoyed the fact that I took an interest in his mining empire. It entertained him to show me how to calculate tonnage and profit, to take me along when he explored the new shafts and to explain the new technologies that harvested ore faster. For our first anniversary I asked for stock in the company and for each anniversary after that, then as a birthing gift when Sophie was born. I don't know if he ever took me seriously, but it didn't matter. *I* took *me* seriously. In his will, he left me twenty per cent of the stock, but I'd amassed another twenty per cent in gifts during our marriage. I knew I'd outlive Huntingdon. I wanted to be prepared. I wanted to make every moment count.'

The very words of his toast from Richard Penlerick's funeral. Eliza knew the import of that. 'I thought you were extraordinary from the start and I was right. What a surprise it must have been for the likes of Brenley.'

'Oh, yes, you should have seen his face when the will was read. He'd been expecting to be named head of the corporation. He's hated me ever since. Now, he's having his revenge.'

Eliza Blaxland was remarkable for her strength, her tenacity, her foresight. If he'd been uncertain of his love earlier, he was certain of it now. The woman he wanted to spend his life with was walking beside him, but the wanting did not make her any more attainable. 'Eliza, I will keep you safe from Brenley. I will marry you if it comes to that.'

She gave him a kind smile and squeezed his hand. 'Let's hope it doesn't.'

Yes, that was probably the best to hope for. He wouldn't steal her dreams. She'd already had to choose between financial security and a family once. He didn't want her to have to choose again.

Eliza was hungry for proof of Brenley's treachery. Eaton could not keep her away from Porth Karrek another day, so he did the next best thing: he accompanied her when she went to the mine. He stood at her shoulder as she asked Gillie Cardy about progress on the tunnel, making sure that digging hadn't extended beyond *her* specifications. He went below ground with her as she inspected the new timbering in the shaft. He did nothing that would usurp her authority or give the impression that she took direction from him. But very soon he would have to intervene. There was a new tension when she passed the miners—gazes that slid away, or unfriendly bold ones that he was quick to dispel with a glare of his own.

'Sir Brenley and Mr Detford were here yesterday.' Cardy was distant but polite. 'They said we were to push the tunnel further out, after all.'

Eaton watched Eliza for the slightest hint of anger and found it in the narrowing of her eyes. 'They have no authority here, Mr Cardy,' Eliza reminded him in steely tones. 'Detford merely oversees the mine for me and Brenley is not the majority shareholder.'

'It wasn't clear whose orders we should follow, begging your pardon.' Gillie shifted nervously from one foot to the other and Eaton felt sorry for him. Dealing with an angry Eliza was not a comfortable experience. Gillie held out a crumpled handbill. 'Sir Brenley said you would be resigning soon.'

Eliza folded the handbill without a downward glance. 'Sir Brenley is wrong. There is to be no more work on lengthening the tunnel. Wheal Karrek is not extending under the ocean.'

Eliza waited until they were alone in the office before she gave vent to her fury. She pulled off her gloves, one fierce finger at a time, trying to hide her irritation, her hurt, and Eaton ached for her. This was another whole betrayal she had to face—loyal workers backing away from her, unsure who to take orders from—and it was worse than anything Brenley could have printed in his handbill. 'Give me the paper, Eliza.' Eaton took it, his own temper rising as he read. The man deserved to be called out for his vicious lies.

'Is it awful?' Eliza's cool sangfroid did not fool
Eaton. He crumpled the paper and threw it into the
fire. It was bad enough that Brenley had called her a
trollop for her 'immoral' association with the Marquess
of Lynford. She didn't need to see what else had been
written. Cade Kitto would not be pleased, nor would
the parents at the conservatory if word of this reached
that far. Eaton doubted it would have teeth in the long
run. A man like himself was allowed his peccadilloes,
but in the short term the conservatory could founder
until this was resolved.

'It is what we expected.' Eaton shrugged. 'Shall I
send a man down to gather the pamphlets up and burn
them? We could have a bonfire on the beach.'

'Like the king in *Sleeping Beauty*, who burns all the
spinning wheels?' Eliza gave a tired sigh. 'The worst
has probably already been done. Everyone will have
read them by now.' Eaton hoped not. If anything happened to the conservatory, Eliza would blame herself
and Eaton didn't want to be in the position of being
forced to remove her from the patrons' list. To choose
between Cade and Eliza would be an impossible situation.

'Perhaps I'd like to burn them for my sake, then,
if not yours.' Eaton smiled his reassurance. 'Inigo arrives today. In the meantime, remember that Brenley's
words can't hurt you. You control the company. He can
do nothing but rant.'

'And people can do nothing but listen,' Eliza
warned. It was hard to be patient. Waiting carried with
it its own risks—the school's viability, a scandal that

would last longer than it needed to. He wanted to quash it now before it ran rampant, before Eliza could be hurt further. Perhaps he should have framed his offer differently in the Trevaylor Woods. He'd just thrown it out there haphazardly as a contingency. Would it have been better to have asked her seriously then, before she'd seen Brenley's vicious pamphlet calling her a whore? If anything, the situation was more desperate now than it had been yesterday. He didn't want her facing his proposal from a vulnerable position. Perhaps he should ask her tonight after the meeting with Inigo. She would be more desperate still tomorrow, his window of opportunity slipping away exponentially.

Each day that passed weakened his own position. She would not believe he asked out of love instead of duty. And each day his doubt grew. Was proposing to her the right thing or the expeditious thing, a selfish knee-jerk reaction to a problem? It could solve her immediate problems, fulfil his own wants, but it did not change what he could offer her. He wasn't yet convinced either of them could live with that no matter how much his heart wanted it.

Chapter Nineteen

Eliza waited nervously in the grand salon of the school for the arrival of Eaton's friends. Sophie was in her element, thrilled at the chance to play on the Sébastien Érard piano. Eaton sat beside her, reading through documents. They'd decided meeting at the school would draw less attention and provide neutral ground. Anyone might think the arrivals were here as potential new patrons instead of in town to unseat Gismond Brenley.

'They're here, my lord,' Johns announced in hushed tones just after the clock struck four. Classes were done for the day and the boys were outside taking exercise on the back lawn. They would have the place to themselves. 'All four of them. Shall I show them in?'

'Four?' Eliza shot a querying glance at Eaton. 'Did you invite others?' They'd only been expecting two. But Eaton seemed as surprised as she.

'The Duke of Bude and the Duchess are with your friends, my lord,' Johns supplied and Eliza's nerves tensed. Eaton's parents were here! But there was no time to panic. The duchess sailed into the room.

'There you are, my darling.' His mother entered, tall and graceful. Anyone could see that Eaton got his looks from her and his bearing from his father. She crossed the room straight to him, embracing him warmly. 'Inigo tells us there's quite the stir down here.'

His father followed, shaking his hand. Inigo and Cassian clapped him on the back in turn. Cassian shot him a look that said, *I couldn't stop them.*

'We do apologise for surprising you,' his mother offered.

'I'm always happy to see you, Mother. Let me introduce one of the school's leading patrons, Mrs Eliza Blaxland, and her daughter, Miss Sophie.' Eaton ushered Sophie forward, keeping a hand on her shoulder. Sophie wasn't normally a shy girl, but one never knew when faced with so many strangers.

Introductions made, Eaton gestured for Johns to take Sophie to the kitchens for gingerbread and milk and to close the salon doors on the way out.

Eliza found herself with Inigo Vellanoweth on her left, Eaton on her right, and the Duke and Duchess of Bude across from her on a sofa. She was surrounded by powerful men on all sides. A frisson of foreboding ran down her spine. It was as she'd feared when Eaton had originally put his scheme to her. Had she simply traded one board of shareholders for an even more powerful one? How would she ever wrest power from these men if she needed to? She simply wouldn't be able to buy them out as she had some of the previous board. What else could she have done, though? She needed Eaton's friends. The board was still corrupt, it still plotted against her. Without them, she could not unseat her enemies.

Inigo was eager to share his information, 'Brenley has stocks in other mining ventures. He's buying up everything he can get his hands on. My sources tell me he's looking to establish his own cartel. If he succeeds, it will be a virtual monopoly.'

'Then Thorp and Blackmore are in on it, too,' Eliza mused out loud.

'It would seem so,' Inigo affirmed. 'You, Mrs Blaxland, are all that stands in his way.' It was not an enviable position to be in. 'Given what we now know, it's not surprising he made such a generous offer to buy you out, or that he's so angry you've refused.'

Eliza held up the sheaf of documents. 'Then we have to confront him now. We tell him we'll have him brought up on charges of attempted fraud, that he's buying me out because he knows there's more money to be made. My shares will be worth five times this next year. We'll tell Thorp and Blackmore, too, and see if we can't divide and conquer.'

Eaton nodded his approval. 'It looks as though we all have some writing to do. Inigo, you can draft the letters today informing Brenley of what we know about his actions. Eliza, you should send a letter of your own as well, introducing the new shareholders. Inigo tells me he deposited their funds in the bank at Truro where they are awaiting your permission to proceed.'

The sooner the better, Eliza thought. If they could

arrest Brenley and expose his crime, there would be no more threat. If she could get the new shareholders in place quickly, Eaton needn't sacrifice himself for her. The group rose, preparing to go their separate ways, she to the kitchens to retrieve Sophie. Bude smiled at Eaton. 'My son, if I might have a word?' Ah, Eliza thought. Speaking of dividing and conquering.

'I can see you're taken with her and why that might be the case. She's attractive and intelligent. She's certainly in need of protection. Even if we're successful in repopulating her board, her reputation may never recover without the benefit of marriage,' Bude said once the room had emptied.

Eaton blew out a breath. 'I can't give her that.' And the realisation was tearing his heart out. 'I can't do that to her. She wants children.'

'She has one.'

'She wants more. She dreams of a big family, but she insists on not remarrying in order to preserve her autonomy. Even if she were considering marriage, I can't take her hope from her.'

'You've told her?'

'Yes. She knows.' Eaton began to pace. A simple marriage would be the final coup de grâce to cut off the burgeoning scandal before it was out of control.

'Even so, most women would leap at the chance to marry a man of your assets,' his father pressed. 'Perhaps you underestimate her? She comes with her own limitations as well. She's older than you are. She's had her best childbearing years. It may be she won't have any more children regardless.'

Eaton studied his father. 'What are you saying?'

'Ever since we've realised what your illness took from you, you've looked at it as a curse. I know it is a disappointment, not only for yourself, but to your mother and me. Not for the succession, but for yourself. If ever there was a man who should have a family, it's you. You have so much to give in that regard. So, what I say next in no way makes up for what you have lost, but there is a silver lining.

'If you can withstand the gossip, you are able to wed where you wish. You can marry a rich mine-owner's widow if you choose. You needn't consider an alliance, a bloodline or an heir. You need only consider your heart. Do you know how many men with titles can do that? Very few.' His father's encouragement was overwhelming. Always, his parents had supported him in whatever endeavour he undertook. It was a feature that made the Falmage family unique, one that society often misunderstood. But never had Eaton felt his father's love more fully as he felt it in this moment.

'There's the family to consider. It will reflect on all of us,' Eaton replied. He'd never fully explored marrying outside the *ton* for that reason.

'Your sisters are all married and settled. I doubt your decision will affect them much at this point or that their husbands would allow any rumor against them. If you love her, don't let your assumptions about what you can't offer her stand in your way. Put the question to her, let her decide.' His father put a firm hand on his shoulder. 'You looked very natural with her daughter today. It was all I could wish for you.'

'What if she says no?' Eaton toyed with the inkwell. That was his greatest fear. He had to face it now that there was no longer family honour to hide behind. If Eliza said no, he would lose her. There could be no middle ground here.

'Then it's her loss. Eaton, you are worth loving. It's time you started believing it. Whatever her reasons for resisting marriage, she is attracted to you, she cares for you. I watched her at the meeting today, the way she'd look at you, study you, listen to you. Go after her.'

'I want to be sure. I don't want this proposal to be about the current crisis. Perhaps I should wait so that she knows my affections for her are not driven solely by resolving the situation with Brenley. I want her to know my love is constant.' But even he knew the argument was a stalling technique, a reason to delay the question. If he asked, then he would know. All would be resolved one way or the other. Eaton wasn't sure he was keen on such finality. If she refused, for ever was a long time to live with a broken heart. He would do it at dinner tonight. He'd already planned a special supper in the school's garden to take Eliza's mind off the situation. Now, the supper took on an additional import. It might be the most important meal he'd ever eaten.

Chapter Twenty

Saying yes to dinner had been a sound idea in theory, a seemingly natural extension of their day. How many dinners had they shared over the past month? There had been that first dinner, dinners with Sophie at the dower house, picnic suppers in the orangery. Dinners had taken many different shapes over the weeks she'd been in Porth Karrek, but no dinner was like this one.

For starters, this supper was not held in any of their usual places—not the orangery, not the dower house—but at the school, in the gardens where they'd first kissed. Secondly, the garden looked beautiful, far too lovely for a regular meal. The place was lit with paper lanterns strung overhead and candles on the table set for two. Beside the table, two smudge pots burned, creating heat against the autumn night. Eliza stood in the doorway leading to the gardens, taking it all in and wondering what Eaton was up to. What had he and his father spoken of after the meeting?

Eaton approached from behind. He was in dark evening clothes again, his hair combed, his manners impeccable as he placed a gentle hand at her back and kissed the side of her neck. 'You look beautiful, Eliza.' She'd worn a silk gown of peacock blue and taken time with her hair, and she was glad she had. Regardless of what Eaton intended for this supper, she would be leaving soon. There weren't many dinners left between them. 'Come this way, our fairy garden awaits.'

He held her chair and poured champagne. 'What do you think of the garden?'

'It is stunning. This is a lot of effort for a simple supper.' That worried her. What was this dinner really about?

Servants brought dishes and lifted the covers, revealing stuffed game hens and fresh vegetables. 'It's a truffle stuffing,' Eaton explained, offering her a tiny pitcher. 'And this is my very own truffle oil.' He drizzled a small amount over the game hen. 'I thought about having dinner at Falmage Hill. It's time you see the house, but it's been empty too long. It doesn't feel like a home, not right now, not like it used to when I was young. And what I want to discuss, I want to do here where we first met.' He reached for the champagne bottle and refilled her glass.

'Do you mean to seduce me with champagne?' Eliza asked, feeling off balance.

Eaton merely smiled. 'Perhaps, in my own way.' His eyes held hers and Eliza felt a frisson of desire course down her spine. No one would ever look at her the way Eaton did. No one would ever see her the way he did. 'I want to fill Falmage Hill with a family of my own—

with you and Sophie. Brenley cannot defy a duchess. Put Brenley's threat to rest before it truly takes hold. What I am asking you is to let me be a husband to you, Eliza. Let me be a father to Sophie. I cannot give you other children, but I can love you with everything at my disposal: my money, my influence, my name and my heart.' He reached for her hands. 'Marry me, Eliza.'

This was the purpose of tonight; a true proposal, one not as easily brushed off as the one in the woods. He wanted to marry her. He wanted to bind himself to her. She could not allow it. He was doing it for the wrong reasons. She was reeling, her thoughts turning in fragments like Brewster's kaleidoscope. 'You can't marry me. Dukes marry debutantes with immaculate pedigrees.' She was groping for arguments, for ways to protect herself, to protect him. How would she find the strength to resist, to say what she must when he was touching her? Reminding her of how he made her feel—strong, invincible, as if the world and its narrow-mindedness could indeed be overcome, as if she didn't need to fight alone. But the world didn't work that way. *She* couldn't work that way. To accept would cost her too much and him, too, if he stopped to think about it. He wasn't thinking now. He was worried about Brenley and he was reacting in the only way he knew how.

'You aren't meant for me, Eaton.' She locked her gaze on him, forcing him to look at her, as if her gaze alone could make him understand. 'You can't marry me, I'm not duchess material.'

'You will be a splendid duchess.'

She gave him a hard, querying look. 'A mine-owner's widow? Who would accept me? Maybe it doesn't matter here in Cornwall so much, but it will matter in London. I will not be an asset to your ambitions there.'

'Then we won't spend time in London,' Eaton answered easily. Didn't he see it wasn't that simple?

'You can't just say that. You will eventually have obligations in the House of Lords.' Eliza sighed. How did she make Eaton see reason when she didn't even want to? 'You will come to hate me, Eaton. I will be a barrier to the life you have now and the life you were raised to have. I don't belong in your world.' She gave him a soft smile. 'I will miss you, though.' Her heart was breaking. Couldn't he see this wasn't easy? That she hadn't the will for these arguments?

'The life I was raised to was drastically altered when I was a boy. Yes, I will be a duke, I will sit in the House of Lords, God willing, years from now after my father has had a very long life. But I will not be the usual kind of duke, Eliza. I needn't concern myself with heirs. I can marry where I choose and I choose you.'

She was silent. 'You are sacrificing yourself for me. It's too much. I can't allow it.'

'This is about love. I love *you*, Eliza. I would want this even if Brenley didn't threaten.' Eaton gripped her hands. 'What more can I do to show you that I care for you? Why won't you fight, Eliza? Why won't you fight for us?'

'Because there is no us, Eaton. I am just someone you are helping. You are doing this because you don't want to lose to Brenley. You want to protect me. You don't really want to marry me.'

'The hell I don't,' he growled. He pushed a frustrated hand through his hair, his carefully combed waves tousling under his fingers. 'You are exactly what I want.' He paused, eyes narrowing in thought. 'Why don't *you* want to marry *me*? Do you know what I think? I think you're the one who's afraid to lose. You think by marrying me you lose control, you lose the mines, your independence. But that's not how it would be. Eliza, you would be freer, more powerful than you've ever been. The mines would be yours entirely, Sophie's legacy protected always. Your money would be your own. I have no desire for it. Everything you've wanted—safety, security—would be yours. Think of the mining schools we could build. I can't give you children, but we can have a life together based on love and respect.'

It was a potent fantasy. She could have all she wanted. All she had to do was trust him, turn herself over to him in the eyes of the law and the church and hope he would be as good as his word. Nothing would stop him if he wasn't. In many ways he was above the law. Would any of it ever truly be hers again if she consented? He might mean to turn the mines over to her, but it would be his name on the deeds once they married. Should he, at any time, think to revoke her nominative ownership, he could take them from her.

Eaton would never do that.

She knew it in her gut and yet Detford's doubting words haunted her still. Perhaps Eaton did want the mines for himself? What better way to acquire them than to woo them out of her, to make her promises and then not keep them?

He'd offered her the moon and the stars and the planets to boot and she was still going to refuse him. Not just refuse him, but leave him. The game hen lay like a leaden rock in his stomach. Had he misjudged his strategy? He'd thought Eliza would want a balance sheet for a proposal. She'd want to see the assets such an alliance brought her. She'd want to weigh it against the disadvantages, of which there was only one— albeit an enormous one. He'd known she would resist, but he'd never dreamed he would come out on the short end of her analysis. He'd thought he could overcome it.

Eliza moved from her seat, her peacock silk swishing as she crossed the garden. She'd been beautiful tonight at the table. He'd been so hopeful when the evening had begun, but he was less hopeful now. He'd never met a more stubborn, more independent woman than Eliza Blaxland. How awful that the two qualities he admired the most about her were the very ones keeping her from him. 'Marriage is for ever, Eaton. It will last far longer than defeating Brenley.'

'Need I remind you that marriage may be the only way to beat him?' Eaton corrected. She was slipping away. If she wouldn't do this for love, perhaps she'd see the sense in doing it for business, for her own safety. He needed to reason with her, not beg. Eliza responded to strength.

'Eaton, I thank you for the offer. I wish it could be

otherwise, but my definitive answer must be no.' She was quiet and cool, the finality in her tone absolute, and his impatience slipped.

'We are all that stands in his way, Eliza. Brenley will be dangerous if he thinks he's cornered. Why can't you see that?' It was a growl, a yell. He was furious with her for not seeing the obvious and furious with himself for not being able to persuade her, for losing her despite his best efforts.

'Why can't you see that I don't need another Miles Detford? You don't need to sacrifice yourself by rescuing me. If you'll excuse me, I think I'll take my leave.' Eliza's tone was cold, her face blank as she picked up her skirts and walked out of the garden, taking all his hopes with her.

Eaton let her go. She'd all but slapped him in the face with her last remark, equating him with that snake. What was the point in chasing her down now? What would he say when he caught her that he hadn't already said countless times over in so many different ways?

I love you.

He could not change what he could not give her nor could he change what she couldn't give herself. He could not magically give her children. Tonight, he'd pushed her too far and this was the result. He could not erase her need for independence, her perception that marriage was about dependency, not love.

He did not know how long he stared at the doors leading inside, the very last space she'd occupied before she'd disappeared from his sight. It might have been hours or minutes. Time lost all meaning. What he did know was that he would see her everywhere, in everything. Every time he drank champagne he would see her as she was that night in the carriage. Every time he passed a mine, every time he stepped inside his school, his orangery. Every time a parakeet landed on his finger. No place would be safe. This was what happened when you let someone into the private parts of your life, into the corners of your soul.

He knew. This was what it had felt like to lose Richard Penlerick. Only that time, he'd been able to escape to the places that were his and take refuge. He couldn't do that now. Eliza had been his refuge, someone he'd emotionally invested in in the absence of his mentor. He'd not meant to. In the beginning he'd not intended it to be that way. But Eliza wasn't just any woman. She'd demanded more from him than a standard dalliance. Even then, it hadn't been enough. She'd gone anyway and he was left with the torment of knowing she was still in the world. He might see her again by accident on the streets of Truro when he went there on business. He might meet her again at an event for the academy. There would be correspondence from her regarding her patronage. She would be with him in a hundred different ways, but she would always be apart. In this new, post-Eliza world, he could not touch her, could not draw her close for a kiss, could not spend an evening in her parlour, could not walk the beach with her. Tantalus in Hades reaching for his ever-elusive drink would have nothing on him. It was to be expected when one wagered one's soul and lost.

'Are you going to spend the whole night out here?'

Cassian stood in the doorway, blanket in hand. 'I thought you might need this. It's cold out.'

'I hadn't noticed.' He noticed nothing but the pain that had taken up residence in his heart.

'Where's Mrs Blaxland?' Cassian took a seat on the stone bench—Eliza's bench, the place where he'd seen her watching the stars the night of the reception. Good lord, it was starting already.

'She's gone. I let her go.' She would be at the dower house, getting ready for bed. He knew her ritual by heart. She would have tucked Sophie in and read her a story. Sophie would have asked for one more. They would have giggled together and blown out the lamp beside Sophie's bed. He'd loved hearing that sound.

'Did you...ask her?' Cassian was trying to be subtle. It was not his strong suit.

'Yes, damn it.' Eaton's temper flared, sorrow turning to anger. 'I asked her to marry me. I gave her all the reasons, I made all the promises.' He had to stop to keep his voice from breaking. He took a breath. 'And it wasn't enough. I wasn't enough.' He'd never felt more inadequate than he felt now, not even when the doctors had told him he would never sire children, never be able to carry out what was arguably a duke's most important duty.

'That's not true,' Cassian said resolutely. 'You've always been enough for all of us, for your family, for me, for Ven, for Inigo, for the Trelevens, for Cade, for your tenants and for countless other people whose lives you've touched of which you're not even aware.'

'But not her, not the one woman I love, the woman I want to marry. I am not enough for her.'

'That's not true either. She just doesn't see it.' Cassian held his gaze. 'Are you going to let her go? Or are you going to fight for her?'

'I have been fighting for her.'

Cassian clapped him on the knee. 'Then carry on. You've just made a minor miscalculation tonight, soldier. You thought this would be the end of the battle when it was really only the heart of the battle and the outcome could still go either way. You, my friend, need a flanking movement.'

'No,' Eaton countered. 'I need to figure out how to go on without her. She has made her position clear.' There had been life before Eliza, and there would be life after Eliza where nothing would be the same, not even him. He would be a shadow, a ghost of a man who'd once fallen in love.

Chapter Twenty-One

'She means to divide us.' Miles Detford scoffed at the letters lying open on the table. They'd each received one. 'She has no proof. She just wants to scare us.'

'Well, I'm scared,' Isley Thorp replied honestly from his chair in Brenley's study. 'I could go to jail for this. It's your fault, you know.' He glared at Miles. 'You've been paid well for your part in this, as I recall. You had three tasks in all of this: marry the widow, get the tunnel built and take the fall if needed. You could at least manage to succeed at one of them.'

Miles sneered. 'Why are we allowing her to get away with this? We keep talking about drastic measures, but we never take action.'

'We distributed that pamphlet about her immoral character,' Brenley reminded him. 'No one will want to do business with her.'

Thorp laughed derisively. 'A lot of good that did. Now we have the Duke of Bude in town.' It was arguably the worst thing that could have happened, Miles acknowledged. He'd hoped the pamphlet would have caused Lynford to rethink his position as her champion, that Lynford would have chosen to distance himself. He hadn't. He'd closed the distance instead. That was what worried Miles the most.

He, like Brenley, wasn't afraid of the law. Bribes could work wondrous magic. But if they could not get hold of those mines, she would ruin Brenley's monopoly and Miles could not afford that. He would lose a fortune. He'd made promises, taken out loans based on gambling on Brenley's success. If he couldn't pay, very soon his credit would be cut off. Invitations to certain circles would cease, opportunities to invest in lucrative ventures would become non-existent. Lynford would consign him to a slow death in a social hell. He'd worked too hard to get where he was to let that happen.

'Lynford can't support a woman who isn't there to be supported,' Detford growled. Enough with talk. It was time for action. 'She marries *me*, or she…disappears. Perhaps I'll take her down to assess progress on the new tunnel and put the proposal to her there. Anything can happen in a mine. Not everyone who goes in comes out again.'

Brenley nodded. Miles hadn't worried about him liking the idea. Brenley liked anything that meant someone else was willing to do his dirty work, one more person to stand between him and the law. But Brenley wasn't stupid. A dead Eliza had implications, too. 'If she says yes, you'll control the mines, Detford.' He voiced the concern out loud, making it clear he wasn't terribly interested in someone else having all that coveted stock. Miles had to go carefully here. Brenley might be an enemy in the making.

'That is to your advantage. I want what you want,' Miles assured him. It was true, for now. But this was a dog-eat-dog world. How long would that last? He'd cross that bridge later if Eliza Blaxland came out of the tunnel alive and ready to be a bride.

Brenley offered his approval. 'Just be sure you get the job done if she says no. There can be no room for sentiment and it must be done soon.' Yes, speed was of the essence. He and Brenley could agree on that. They needed to act before the new shareholders were in place.

Miles gave a grim, satisfied nod. 'I'll go tonight.' One way or another, everything would be settled at last. This time he would make Eliza Blaxland a proposal she couldn't refuse.

She'd refused Eaton. It was the only thought that had claimed her attention since the moment she'd left the garden. Eliza sat in the front parlour, half-heartedly listening to Sophie practise her piano as the afternoon faded into evening. A whole day gone and nothing accomplished, no decisions made. She hadn't just refused Eaton. She'd hurt him. He'd told her he loved her. He'd been devastated last night despite his stoic show of strength to the contrary. When she'd not said the words in return, he'd not stopped fighting. Another man would have walked away and licked his wounds. But Eaton had come back for more. He'd opted to reason with her, to appeal to her pragmatic side. And she had wounded him twice. She'd equated him with Miles Detford.

She'd made a mess of something beautiful and well intentioned. His offer was nothing like Detford's. She'd not seen it at the time. She'd been too busy protecting her independence. It had not been her intention to set him up for failure or to demean his offer. Quite the opposite. She'd wanted him to see that she loved him, too, enough to give him up, enough not to trap him into a marriage that would ultimately disappoint him. She'd wanted him to see reason as well, that two people should not marry because one of them relied on the other. It created a toxic cycle of dependency. Her mother had never been more helpless than when she was married. For all her independence, Eliza feared marriage would strip her freedom away, wear it down over time until she, too, was entirely dependent on a husband. It was a solid reason. She had no real protection of her independence under the law. So, why did she feel as if she'd made a terrible mistake? Why did she feel as though she'd thrown happiness off the cliffs of Porth Karrek and it was drowning in the sea while she dithered?

'Shall I play another song, Mama? I have a new one from Eaton.' Sophie turned on the bench to face her.

Eliza nodded patiently. 'Please, play another.' Sophie started on the lullaby, encouraged by the praise, and Eliza smiled regretfully to no one in particular. How would she ever forget Eaton? Was that even possible? Eaton, whose presence was stamped all over the dower house and not because the house was his property to begin with, but because he'd tried so very hard to make them feel at home. Over the weeks, he'd brought dolls for Sophie from the nursery at Falmage Hill, sheet music looted from Cade Kitto's stores at the school, flowers sent down from the main house to decorate the tables and consoles.

It had worked. The place had taken on a comfortable, lived-in feeling. At some point they'd stopped becoming tenants and become residents.

More than residents, a dangerous wisp of thought curled in her mind. *You became a family here. Eaton gave you a family and you gave him one. You had a child with no father and he was a man thirsting to be one to your daughter and a husband to you. Together, you both were enough, you both had enough.* She'd taken that hope from him when she'd refused him.

Eliza made impotent fists of her hands. How could she not have seen it? His proposal wasn't only about Detford and Brenley and the mines. It was so much bigger than that. There'd been a chance to have more than a marriage of convenience. She'd thrown more away than just a business deal when she'd refused Eaton. She could have given him the family he wanted and he could have given her a family, too, although smaller than the one she'd imagined for herself. That would have been enough if she had Eaton beside her.

Eliza stilled, shame filling her. Eaton didn't know that. Did Eaton think he wasn't enough for her? That she'd refused him, using the business as a smokescreen for the issue of his infertility? Did he think she didn't want *him*? That he could never be *man* enough for her?

Just the opposite was true. She'd never known a man like Eaton, a man who was so thoroughly *enough* in every way. But there was no going back now. She'd made her position clear and he would not come for her again. She'd hurt, humiliated and walked away from the man she loved. It was enough to make her want to break down and sob, but if she started, Eliza feared she might never stop. She had lost Eaton. Now she was truly alone in a way she'd never been before and it was all her own stubborn fault.

Eliza swallowed hard. She would not give in to despair. She would move on from this and bury the hurt a little deeper every day until she could feel nothing at all. She'd done it before when Huntingdon died. She would do it again. She needed action, plans. She was not unlike Eaton in that regard. What did she do now? Her mind was occupied forming scenarios and options. Should she pack up Sophie and return to Truro and her comfortable town house, to the routine of her days? Life in Truro might not be exciting and it might be lonely, but at least she understood it and who she was in that life. She'd been gone too long. She was missing her bed, her office, her own things. But simply going back couldn't make things the way they'd been before. There would still be the business of the shareholders to deal with. But, to do so from the luxury of her own home, surrounded by her own things, might bring some balance. The sooner she got back to her routine, the sooner she could forget Eaton.

Sophie would miss the house when they left, but not as much as she'd miss Eaton. Her daughter adored him, not just his adventures, but *him*. Children had an innate sense of a person's inner character, they knew when they were sincere and when they were just attempting to flatter and win affection. Perhaps she should take her cue from Sophie? What could be so wrong with a man who was adored by his dog and her daughter? A man who had done nothing but empower her with the gift of his time, his home, his resources, even the resources of his friends? He'd not hesitated to introduce her to his parents. She could only imagine what the Duke had had to say about her.

It seemed unfair that Eaton had to defend her to his own father after having already had to defend her to so many others. Another reason why she should pack her trunks for Truro. Soon, Eaton would realise how much trouble she was for him. He'd realise, too, that she would always be trouble. His kind would never accept her. His beloved family would never accept her and she wouldn't allow him to give up his family for hers. Eaton deserved so much more than she'd bring him. Yet, there would be moments of wonder: picnics on the beach, rambles in the woods, suppers in the orangery, Sophie laughing as he cavorted with her, priceless moments. There'd be pleasurable moments, too, intimate moments just between them: lying abed in the mornings spooned against his hard body, endless nights of lovemaking, days of watching him flash that smile of his. Those moments would be worth the sacrifice. No. She could not be tempted and she would be if she stayed.

Sophie finished playing the lullaby and Eliza called

her over. 'I have something to tell you, my darling.' She pasted on a smile. 'We are going home to Truro. We will leave in the morning. Isn't that great news? Tomorrow night we'll sleep in our own beds and you'll have your own toys.' She hoped she sounded excited. If she was excited, perhaps Sophie would be excited, too.

Sophie looked crestfallen. 'But I don't want to leave. I want to stay with Eaton. We haven't found the treasure yet.'

'It will be winter soon and far too cold for treasure hunting. Besides, Lord Lynford can't always be on hand for adventures.'

'He was going to take me up to the conservatory for the holiday concert,' Sophie put in with slightly more diplomatic tact. Darn Eaton for making promises he knew he was unlikely to keep. Now she'd have to dry the tears left in his wake.

'Will we get to say goodbye?' Sophie asked.

'I don't know. You can leave a note for Lord Lynford, if you'd like.'

'He likes to be called Eaton. Not Lord Lynford,' Sophie corrected her with a slightly accusatory tone as if she was to blame for ruining their fun.

'Mrs Blaxland—' one of Eaton's loaned maids bobbed in the doorway '—you have a caller.'

'Who is it?' Eliza rose to her feet, clumsy with her skirts, her mind slow to shift gears between discussing leaving Eaton and trying to figure out who would call on her.

'Mr Detford.' The woman's tone was full of disapproval. The visitor was calling too late in the afternoon;

it was nearly five o'clock, well past visiting hours, especially when the visitor in question was a man who was not Lord Lynford.

What was Miles Detford doing here now? Instant worry overcame Eliza. Any number of issues might have brought him out. Was something wrong at Wheal Karrek? Was this about the mines? About Brenley? The shareholders? Surely things could have been handled during polite calling hours. He would not call at such an hour without reason, which meant something was wrong at the mine. 'Where is he? I will see him at once.'

'I've put him in your office, ma'am.'

'Thank you. Will you have Miss Gilchrist come down for Sophie? And instruct the maids to start packing. We need to leave for Truro in the morning.' She hoped Miles's business wouldn't take long. She wanted to have dinner with Sophie. With any luck, the visit would take ten minutes and she would send him on his way with an answer.

She reached the office door, straightened her shoulders and sailed into the room. 'Miles, what are you doing here?' He looked worried and that worried *her*.

'No good news, I am afraid.' He came to her, taking her hands in his. 'I want to talk you out of this madness of replacing the shareholders. This is Lynford's plan. He's using you. You've only known the man for a month. I've never known you to be reckless. I fear he must have some hold over you.'

Eliza pulled her hands away. 'Miles, I know what I am doing. Lynford has no sway over me.'

'Perhaps it's you who has a hold over him, then? I can't believe either of you have thought this through.' Miles drew a folded paper out of his pocket. 'Especially after the pamphlet. I assume you've seen it? Then you know how foul it was. I warned Brenley to hold back, but he would not. He's gone after Lynford, too, and that school of his.'

'What?' Eliza reached for the handbill, scanning it rapidly. Eaton had not told her the entirety of Brenley's treachery. There it was in black and white—Brenley was indicting the conservatory for taking funds and direction from the immoral Lynford and his mistress.

'I'm sorry, I thought you knew.' Miles took the handbill back while her mind reeled. She was not going to cost Eaton his conservatory. Not only Eaton, but Cade Kitto and his new wife. Perhaps it was indeed best that she was going home tomorrow. Just in time, it seemed. Perhaps being out of sight would put her out of mind, at least long enough to save the school. 'My dear, this is a deuced difficult situation and I dislike heaping more bad news on it all, but there is something else. The new tunnel at the mine. I think you should come with me, there is something you should see.'

'Now?' Eliza tried to steady her mind. All she could think of was Eaton and his precious school: his legacy, his boys, his memorial to Richard Penlerick. She was ruining everything she touched.

'Yes, I think now would be best. The fewer people around to notice the better,' he pleaded with her. She understood the need for exigence and even for secrecy.

Eliza put her hand on his arm. 'Yes, of course. I

don't forget how difficult it is for you to walk a fine line. Brenley and I, we've put you in an awkward position.' Over the years he'd had to balance his friendship and loyalty to her against his business association with Brenley as a shareholder. He was her friend now, wanting to warn her no doubt about Brenley's latest attempts to push through the tunnel against her express wishes. Dinner would have to wait and she would likely miss Eaton's evening visit—if he was even coming. But the mine needed to be dealt with. If Brenley had fuses down in the tunnel, or if Brenley had been giving orders again, she would put a stop to it. 'I'll just be a moment. Let me get my things and say goodnight to Sophie.'

Eaton was going to ambush her. He swung off his horse in the drive of the dower house, nerves drawn tight. He had the upper hand, but he also knew he was down to the last of his chances. He was risking everything on this final roll of the dice. Once the initial miasma of his disappointment—nay, his devastation— had lifted, he'd seen the flaw in his proposal. The formality of occasion, of his very invitation, had made her wary. She'd sensed something was afoot from the start and she'd been braced for it. She would not have that luxury tonight. He would catch her by surprise when she didn't have time to marshal her responses or be on alert. It was her own tactic, after all.

He'd given Eliza the day to sort through her feelings as he had sorted through his. Her rejection had cost her something. She'd not refused him lightly. He could see that now with the benefit of a day's distance. Refusing him had hurt her as much as it had hurt him. That recognition gave him hope enough to try one more time. There must be a way to get past her defences, her assumptions about what she needed. He'd searched all day for the words. He reached for the flowers in the saddle holster and for the small present he'd brought for Sophie. He dusted off his breeches and straightened his coat. He pushed a hand through his windblown curls for futile effect. No matter, he rather thought Eliza liked him wind-rumpled. The thought gave him courage. Eliza liked him. Eliza *loved* him.

He knocked at the door, taking a final deep breath as the door opened, an excited Sophie ducking past the footman and throwing herself at him. 'I knew you would come to say goodbye!' Eaton knelt down and she wrapped her arms around his neck in a hug. 'I don't want to go, Eaton. Won't you persuade Mama when she comes back?'

Eaton stood up and stepped inside, his mind fumbling over the words. Sophie had imparted so much information all at once. 'I'm afraid I don't understand. You're leaving?' His earlier confidence began to slip. Eliza meant to do it then, she meant to cut ties with him completely. If he'd waited another day, he would have missed her. The truth of it was in evidence everywhere. Trunks were open, maids were folding clothes and running up and downstairs precipitously to retrieve items. The pace at which the maids were working suggested there was an urgency to the task, that it was newly assigned. Eaton knew his staff. They were organised, they never gave the appearance of rushing anywhere because nothing was left to the last minute. They would not have deliberately delayed packing.

Eaton looked about, realising what else Sophie had said. 'Where's your mother? She is gone?' She was usually never far from Sophie, not with dinner so near.

'She's gone.' Sophie pouted. 'She said she'd be back for dinner but she's not. She never breaks a promise,' Sophie said solemnly. 'It's all Mr Detford's fault. I bet he breaks lots of promises,' she said sulkily.

'Detford was here?' Eaton squatted down again and drew Sophie close. 'Did your mama go somewhere with him?' Why would Detford come here? Why would she leave with him? And why was she not back yet?

'They were going to the mine,' Sophie supplied. 'Mama said it was urgent.' On Detford's word. But that might be enough for Eliza. Eaton's mind raced. She'd always viewed Detford as an ally and still did despite their recent quarrel. Eaton didn't like it. There were too many variables to consider. Detford would have received the letter regarding the new sharehold-ers joining the board. And Detford had yet to publicly declare a side in the little war between Brenley and Eliza. The bounder was likely playing both sides as it suited him. The man had already tried once to marry Eliza. Eaton didn't think the proposal had stemmed from affection for her as much as it had from an af-fection for the money and influence that would pass to him once they wed.

A few mad scenarios ran through Eaton's mind. Was Detford the lure? Did Brenley think to pressure her into some sort of deal through less than gentlemanly means? He didn't allow his thoughts to wander in that direction. There were all nature of dastardly pressures that could be brought to bear: kidnapping, threatening Sophie, dragging Eliza to the altar to marry Detford against her will and murder her if she did not. He could not stop his mind from raising questions: Who would inherit everything if Eliza were dead and Sophie so young? Probably Eliza's feckless uncle and her delicate mother. They would be easily overcome by the likes of Brenley and his cartel. The Blaxland fortune wouldn't last long in their hands.

Eaton's gut began to churn with his imaginings. If Eliza were to die before she were wed, Brenley would have a clear path to the holdings. Eliza's majority would be nullified and the new shareholders would be unable to stop him from taking control of the mines. But that was the least of Eaton's concerns. Eliza was out there somewhere with Detford. There was no guarantee they'd actually gone to the mine. That could be a ruse as well. At the moment, only two things mattered. Finding her and marrying her immediately to remove her—and Sophie—from such harm.

Unless he was wrong. Perhaps he was overreacting. Perhaps there was no evil lurking behind Detford's visit. Eliza valued her independence. She would not appreciate Eaton following her or interrupting the meeting. She would take such an interruption as proof that she'd lose her autonomy through marriage, that he would never truly let her run the business on her own. Did he wait here? She had been late before, like the day

Sophie had been ill. Did he go to the mine and hope she and Detford were there? Hope that he'd be in time to stop any nefarious undertakings? Hope that he'd have a plausible excuse if all was as it should be? And then he would take her to task for leaving him.

He rose and dusted his breeches. 'Shall I go after her?' he asked the darling face looking up at him. Sophie was worried. He'd caught her glancing at the clock, marking every minute her mother was late.

'Yes, please,' Sophie answered. 'One day Papa went to work and didn't come home. I want Mama to come home.'

Sophie would have been old enough to grasp the rudimentary details of that day. No wonder Eliza had sent for Sophie when her stay in Porth Karrek had been extended; no wonder she was never far from her daughter. Fears that were only somewhat irrational could play havoc with the young mind. That settled it. He would go to the mine and bring Eliza home, even if it meant bearing the brunt of Eliza's anger. He looked down at Sophie, thinking. He could not leave her here with only Miss Gilchrist for protection. Miss Gilchrist had been useless on the road when he'd discovered them. If there was trouble afoot, it might come here. Detford might be a decoy so that the way was clear to snatch Sophie.

Eaton called to one of the maids, 'Betty, get Miss Sophie's coat.'

'Am I going with you?' Sophie brightened at the prospect of an adventure.

'No, you are going somewhere far more exciting. The big house where I live. My parents are there and they love children. There are games and toys in the nursery and there's a beautiful banister to slide down.' Betty brought her coat and Eaton bundled Sophie into it. 'Betty will take you up to the house.' Over Sophie's head, he gave Betty strict instructions. 'Go straight to the house, have Sophie explain to His Grace what has happened. Stop for no one. Run if you have to.'

Betty would be loyal. Betty would follow directions. Eaton saw them off and swung up on his horse, going as fast as he dared in the dark, and hoped he wasn't too late—or better yet that he wasn't late at all.

Chapter Twenty-Two

It was getting later by the minute. Eliza had the distinct impression that Detford was stalling. Upon arrival, they'd gone to the office to discuss shares, a superfluous discussion that had had no urgency to it, in Eliza's opinion. Soon, the last of the crew would be gone, the mine empty. Perhaps that was what Miles was waiting for. Perhaps he didn't want to be seen by anyone. It spoke volumes about his fear of Brenley and even about the depth of his friendship for her, Eliza thought, that he would risk so much to alert her to whatever waited in the tunnel.

Sophie would be disappointed. Dinner time had come and gone. 'Can we go down now?' Eliza prompted. 'I need to get home. I did not realise this would take so long.'

Detford turned from the window with a mild smile. 'Yes, we can go now.' He took a lantern from the hook and she followed him downstairs, relieved at last to be making progress. But Detford seemed nervous, agitated or excited. Did she imagine a falter in his step? Once inside the shaft, he swung the lantern around, letting the light glance off the walls. All was in good order: strong timbers gave support to the rock; the floor was as free of debris as possible. She prided herself on safe working conditions, as safe as mining could be.

The shaft was deep and the deeper they went, the warmer it got. They reached the junction where the new tunnel had been started. Miles hung the lantern on a nail. 'This is what I want you to see, Eliza. Look at this rock.' He took up a pickaxe and a chisel from where they'd been propped by the wall and set to work, carving into the rock until the surface was chiselled away. 'Look at this. The copper is even more plentiful than suspected. It's right here on the surface, just waiting for us to pick it out. Every indication suggests the lode extends further than we have plans to dig.'

'You mean further than I have plans to dig.' Eliza met his gaze with a stern one of her own.

'Yes,' Miles conceded. 'We are leaving money on the table, Eliza. It's no longer just a hypothesis about what might be out here. This is the richest lode any mine has seen for some time.'

'And the riskiest,' Eliza argued.

'The technology exists. The Levant mine is using it—ventilation fans to help with heat, the pumps to disgorge the water. It can be done,' Miles pressed politely. These were old arguments. Ones she'd considered before.

'I don't know that submarine mining is right for us. The technology is still new, it is fallible.' Even now, she could hear the sea overhead, proof of how far out they were, how very close to disaster. Should a wall give way, no one would survive such an accident. There wouldn't be time to think, let alone to escape. She could not commit men to working under those conditions for hours and hours every day.

'If you pay them enough, they'll dig.' Miles read her thoughts.

'I will not bribe poor men to risk their lives just to feed their families.' Eliza knew the money would indeed entice men. She *could* pay them to take the risk. She *would* not. A man should not have to live in jeopardy simply to make a living.

'Don't be stubborn. You were right to get steam power in here to replace the horses. You know technology makes us more efficient.' Miles was cajoling now, flattering her. 'I thought if you could see the proof of the lode, you might reconsider.'

Eliza narrowed her eyes. 'Did Brenley put you up to this?'

'It's good business, Eliza.' He evaded the answer. 'As your friend, I felt duty-bound to show you the proof.'

'Now that you have, we may go.' Eliza turned to start the long walk back to above ground, but Miles's hand closed about her wrist.

'There is something else, Eliza.' The warning in his voice stopped her as effectively as the grip on her wrist. There was a hard edge to Miles Detford now. The cajoling friend was gone. 'Brenley will not appreciate your intractability on the tunnel. If you will not make the decision to extend the tunnelling, perhaps you would allow me to make it for you, as your husband.'

The thought was so outlandish Eliza almost didn't grasp it. 'What are you saying, Miles?' It was worded like a proposal, but it sounded like a threat.

'Marry me, Eliza, as you should have years ago. We could have avoided all of this. I have Brenley's word he will post a retraction about Lynford and his school and about you. Allow me to take the decisions regarding the mine from your conscience. I will consult you, of course.' She knew what that consultation would be like: patronising and useless. Detford would report to Brenley and Brenley would do what he wanted. Miles could not be her hero under those circumstances. Didn't Miles see that? As her friend, how could he think she'd even consider such an arrangement beneficial?

'Do not refuse me. It will go poorly for you,' Miles warned.

'I am not afraid of Brenley.' She wanted to get out of the shaft, back up above ground where she had space. She felt trapped, crowded by Miles and the rock walls.

'It's not Brenley you should be afraid of at the moment. It's me.' He pulled his coat back, revealing the weapon in his belt.

Dear heavens, Miles had a pistol. Didn't he know the dangers of firing a gun inside a mine shaft? Her heart hammered. 'Miles? What are you doing? What is this?' But she knew. Eaton's voice whispered again, *He is not your friend*. 'You can't fire that in here, you will kill us both.' A gunshot could bring down loose rocks, enough to block the way out.

'That's up to you. Don't make me use it.' He advanced on her until her back was pressed into the rock, his voice cold. 'I will ask one more time. Marry me. I have papers. You can sign them before we walk out of here and announce our happy news to the world. Or refuse and I will be the only one walking out of here.' Of course he had papers, something legally binding to ensure she couldn't lie to save to herself.

She was thinking fast now, realisations piling up in her mind. All these years, she'd thought he'd accepted her rejection when he'd really just been biding his time. She needed to get out of the tunnel. A new twist of fear turned in her stomach at the thought. Was Sophie safe? Should she have ever left her? Had this been an attempt to lure her away?

'Don't be stubborn, Eliza,' he admonished, the back of his hand skimming her face, his gaze dropping to her mouth. 'Marry me and all will be forgiven. You can walk out of here and into a new life. In time you will see that I am right, that it is for the best. This is not worth dying for.' His hips pressed into hers. She felt the hardness of his sex. Dear lord, this horror aroused him. 'Marry me and live.'

For a while. A cold chill came over her despite the heat of the depths. He would kill her first. A dead wife was so much more easily managed, her assets more easily acquired. The true danger came to her for the first time. Detford would not let her leave alive. 'We would be happy together, Eliza, if you would just allow it, if you would just allow me to show you.' He was fumbling with her skirts, his mouth slanted over hers, seeking a kiss.

She turned her face away, thrashing about. Detford pressed her to the wall, holding her captive between the rock and his body. His mouth came at her again and this time she couldn't avoid it. But she could fight him. She bit down hard on his lip. Detford cried out in surprised pain, losing his focus. Eliza shoved at him, hard, pushing past him, and began to run, scrabbling over rocky terrain in a dark landscape. She wasn't fast enough or far enough. She went down with a thud, something sharp in the darkness cutting her lip, scratching her cheek as Detford tackled her from behind. She screamed. Detford swore, the blow came and her world went even darker.

It was still dark when she found consciousness again. Her head throbbed, the waves throbbed. Then panic pulsed. The mine! She was in the mine! And she was alone in the dark, deep under the earth. Through the pain, she forced herself to think. How long had she been down here? Did it matter? Knowing the answer to that question seemed like a luxury. Light would be more useful than knowing the time. But neither luxuries were forthcoming. Did she dare call out? Would anyone hear? Or rather, would the right people hear? Someone who wasn't Detford or Brenley?

Eliza struggled to her feet, but only made it to her hands and knees. Whatever Detford had hit her with had left her dizzy and queasy. A sharp-edged rock, maybe? The butt of his pistol? She never should have come down here with him. She should never have trusted him. What a fool she had been! Her first clue should have been his insistence on secrecy, on waiting until everyone had left before they'd made an appearance in the shaft. She hadn't understood he simply hadn't wanted witnesses while he carried out his crime.

She crawled forward on all fours. She couldn't risk standing up, couldn't risk passing out again. Progress was slow and dangerous. She didn't know where she was going, or what she would find. Mines had all sorts of crevices and cracks one might fall into, or twisting turns one might accidentally take. People could be lost down here in this dark world and never recovered.

She would not think about that now. She would think positively. She would think about Sophie and how much her daughter needed her to get home. Sophie must be worried sick. Eliza calmed herself. She would not panic. She would think about Eaton and how grateful she was for everything he'd done. She'd never felt about any man the way she felt about him; here was a man to be relied on, to be trusted, who cared for the well-being of others, a man who loved her daughter, who loved her. A man she loved. A man she loved enough to give him up, yet she had not told him so. She had not said the words. She'd been too stubborn, too determined to be independent, to see that loving him didn't make her weak, didn't make her dependent. Why hadn't she seen it before?

To her left, gravel fell away beneath her hand. She reached out and felt only air. She stifled a scream. She was on a ledge. Horror rose. To her left there was nothing but darkness and emptiness. She'd taken a wrong turn. There'd been no ledge on the way down. Eliza picked up a pebble and tossed it, hoping to hear it clatter on other rock. Perhaps the ledge was really a slope, which was only somewhat reassuring. But she could not hear it land. How far did the ledge extend? Did it curve or go in a straight line? She didn't know. She couldn't see. Did she dare go on and hope the ledge didn't end? That it curved back towards the safety of two walls?

Eliza assessed her options. If she was wrong, she could pitch off the end into nothingness. If she stayed where she was, crews would return in the morning, she could call out and hope they would find her, hear her over the throb of the waves and noise of the tools.

The thought of spending a dark night in the mine carried a horror of its own. Eliza felt for the rock wall to her right and huddled against it, hugging her knees tight to her chest. It would be a long night either way. Morning was likely a long way off. She'd left home at five. It had been seven when they'd entered the mine. She would be missed by now. She was hours late. Would Sophie or Miss Gilchrist sound the alarm? Would anyone answer? Her one hope was Eaton, but she'd refused him in no uncertain terms. Would he come or had he washed his hands of her?

Eaton was alone in the yard of the mine. He wheeled his horse in a circle, letting the animal breathe as he took in the deserted property. He'd ridden as hard and as fast as he'd dared in the dark to reach Wheal Kar-

rek, only to find it deserted. What had he expected?
It was well after working hours. Then he saw it, a co-
vert flash of light in the office window, hidden away
quickly. Someone was up there and they didn't want to
be seen. Likely, they'd already heard him ride in. He
couldn't assume he'd escaped detection.

Eaton swung off and headed up the steps. With luck,
the person in the office was Eliza. But he didn't feel
that lucky. He reached for his pistol. Eliza would not
have dithered at the office, knowing Sophie was waiting. That left Detford. Eaton didn't like what that implied. If Detford was alone, that worried him a great
deal.

Eaton barged through the office door, deciding to
use brawn and surprise as his best weapons. 'Where is
she?' he demanded. He let the door bang off the wall
for effect. Detford looked up from the desk startled,
frightened. He had the ledgers out, but that was the
least of Eaton's concerns.

'I don't know what you mean.' Detford rose, putting
the desk between them.

'You left the house with Eliza hours ago,' Eaton
growled, advancing on Detford. Detford might have
the desk between them, but Eaton had the door behind
him. Detford would have to get through him first to
reach it. Detford wasn't leaving anytime soon.

'What have you done with her?'

'Does it matter? It's far too late.' Detford eyed him,
trying to concoct a plan and failing.

Eaton cocked the pistol and drew out his other one.

He fired the first at Detford's feet. Detford swore. 'You could have hit me!'

'The next one will. Consider that your warning,' Eaton ground out. 'I don't know how much Brenley is paying you to do his dirty work, but it cannot be enough to die for. It's probably not even enough to be wounded for.' With a pistol he didn't need to jump the desk, Detford was just now realising that. Eaton grinned as Detford paled. 'Now, let's try the question again. Where's Eliza?' He could see Detford weighing his options. But a man like Detford only ever arrived at one conclusion.

'She's in the mine. I didn't kill her,' Detford offered as a belated defence. 'I just left her there.'

Eaton's blood began to surge. He should shoot the bastard now. Detford had taken the coward's way out. He'd left Eliza in the dark, hoping she'd do the job for him. She just might. Eliza was too stubborn. She'd kick and claw her way right onto a ledge, or over a drop-off, and be lost for good. Eaton waved the pistol. 'You first, Detford. Lead the way and know that I'll shoot at the first sign of any trouble.' He nodded towards the lantern by the door. 'You carry the lantern.' He wanted one hand free in case Detford tried anything.

The mine was an eerie place to be after hours, the lantern throwing shadows against rock walls. Eaton fought back a bout of panic when he thought of Eliza without even the comfort of a lamp. They reached the tunnel and Eaton stopped. 'This is where you brought her? This is where you fought with her? Shine that lantern down there,' Eaton directed, his eye catching something dark on the ground. He bent down and tested it with his fingers, careful not to take his eye or pistol off Detford. The man was sweating and not just from the heat of the lower levels. He held his fingers up to the light and cursed. 'This is blood, Detford. What did you do?'

He steadied himself against the rage. Detford had harmed her. She was down here, hurt and lost. 'Let's retrace our steps, shall we?' Eaton ground out, shoving Detford before him. At each junction he paused and called out, 'Eliza!' But the only sound that came back was his voice. At the third junction he heard it, a faint answer. It was wide, a fork in the shaft, really. It would be easy in the dark to turn left instead of staying on the main path.

'Eliza!' Eaton called again, pushing Detford forward.

'We are not going down there,' Detford protested. 'It falls off into nothing.'

'I can shoot you here, then,' Eaton offered. If Eliza was down there, they were going even if it were the bowels of hell.

'You won't shoot. It might destabilise the roof.'

'Would you like to bet on that? You'll still be dead and the roof looks well timbered to me.' There was no way he was leaving Detford behind to wreak any kind of mischief while he located Eliza.

Eaton called instructions, hungry for the first sight of her, 'Eliza, wait for the light. Don't move until you can see.' He swung the lantern, his hunger for the sight of her turning to clammy horror when light hit the path-

Bronwyn Scott   271

way. It was as Detford had claimed, narrow and dangerous, falling away entirely on the left. It was a miracle
she was still out there. Then he saw her, pressed against
the rock wall, and his heart leapt. 'We're almost there,
Eliza,' he called out. 'Can you move towards us?' The
path looked unstable to his eye, as if too much weight
would send it collapsing. He didn't want to risk the
three of them out there.

Eliza began to move, crawling slowly, each inch taking an eternity. She was being careful, Eaton realised.
She knew the path wasn't reliable. Eaton kept talking,
kept her focused on moving forward. She was nearly
there, just a few feet to go when Detford turned on him,
swinging the lantern at his face. Eaton jumped back,
the lantern missing him, but Detford's motion caused
the lantern to go out, thrusting all three of them into
darkness. Eaton heard Eliza scream. Where was Detford? The darkness was the great equaliser. He didn't
dare shoot for fear of missing Detford or hitting Eliza
or starting a rockslide in the dark.

Eliza screamed again and gravel rolled. He could
hear the sounds of scuffling. Detford had her. If he
wasn't careful, they would both plunge to their deaths.
Eaton fumbled for a match, desperate to relight the lantern. The wick flared and he raised his pistol without
hesitation but there was no shot that didn't risk Eliza.
Detford held her against him like a shield with one
arm, his own pistol raised with the other. 'Put your
gun away, Lynford. You will get us all killed,' Detford
drawled. 'I'll throw her off the ledge.'

'You throw her off the ledge and you'll be dead before she hits the bottom. 'Where's the victory in that for you? All your hard work for nothing. Best to come up to the ground and take your chances at a trial,' Eaton reasoned. But Detford was beyond logic.

Detford's eyes narrowed. 'You say that because I am the only one with a decent shot.' And he took it without warning. The pistol report echoed throughout the cavern. Eaton felt the bullet take him in the left shoulder. He went to his knees. Eliza screamed as a rumble began in the depths of the mine. She was struggling, trying to reach him. The rumbling was getting louder. The ground began to shake. The path beneath Detford's and Eliza's feet was disintegrating, increments of shale sliding away. Detford couldn't hold her and maintain his balance at the same time. On his knees, Eaton levelled his own pistol, his left shoulder burning. If he could hold steady long enough, he'd have a clean shot and he could free Eliza. 'Eliza, stay down!' He called his warning and fired. Detford crumbled, clutching his arm, his pain consuming him entirely.

'Eliza, honey, come to me now!' Eaton held out his good hand, his eyes riveted on Eliza, lending her the strength of his gaze. The path was dissolving fast. Another shudder of the mine threw Eliza to her knees. She crawled towards him one lunge at a time and then he had her hand. He closed his grip around it as the ground beneath her gave out. She screamed, suspended in air with only the strength of his arm as an anchor. The rumbling was all around them, rocks falling everywhere. Detford was trapped on the other side, desperate and bleeding as his footing grew smaller, the path falling away beneath him. 'Help me, man!' Detford cried as the last piece of solid ground fell from beneath his feet, but Eaton could do nothing to help the other man as Detford's grip failed him and he fell into the abyss.

'Eliza, hold on! Look at me! Keep your eyes on me. Give me your other hand!' Dear lord, let him have the strength. Let his wounded shoulder hold. All he wanted was to get Eliza out of the mine, to see her safe. What happened to him didn't matter. Eliza would be free. That would be enough.

The tunnel was collapsing. One moment she was falling, the next Eaton's hand had gripped hers, the only piece of stability in the chaos around her. A body passed her and she was screaming as Detford fell, his hands clawing vainly for purchase. For a moment he had a fistful of fabric and part of her skirt tore away, but Eaton's arm held steady. How could it be enough? Already her fingers were slipping, sweaty and unsure. He was calling to her, his other arm bloody and slick as it reached down to her, his voice instructing her to look up, to give him her other hand. But to swing her body, to gain the momentum she needed, required courage. Any movement might cause her other hand to slip.

'Come on, Eliza! I won't let you fall!' There was urgency in his voice. She had to act now or she might doom them both. She was counting on Eaton as she'd never counted on anyone before. She would only get one chance. She drew a breath and swung her other arm. Eaton's strong grip closed about her wrist and he began to pull her up, hauling her against him, shield-

ing her from the falling rocks with his body, ushering
her to the sanctuary of the main shaft.

'Are you all right?' Eaton's arms were tight about
her. She was trembling, but there was no time. The
cave-in would trap them if they didn't move.

'We have to go!' But she stumbled, her efforts not
able to match her words. She was hurt, sick, her head
wound making it impossible to walk. She was going to
die here. She hadn't the strength left to get out. 'Eaton,
go. You can't stay here with me.' Already the corridor
was a thunder of falling rocks.

'Not without you.' Eaton was grim. 'You carry the
lantern and I'll carry you.'

'But your arm...'

'No arguing, Eliza. All I need is one good shoulder
to sling you over.' He swept her up and lumbered towards safety, strong enough for both of them.

Eaton staggered only at the last, collapsing as they
emerged into the fresh evening air of the mine yard,
surrounded by people and noise. *Help had come.* It
was the only thought Eliza could register. She was
dizzy and unsteady. Bude was there with Inigo and
Cassian. Someone draped a blanket over her shoulders, someone else pressed a glass into her hand. She
wanted none of it. 'Help Eaton, he's hurt. He's been
shot.' She wanted to stand up, wanted to go to him, but
she couldn't. 'Where's Eaton? Is he all right?' But no
one would answer.

'Shh...'

Someone—Inigo, perhaps?—soothed her.

'We've got him. We're taking him home. He's unconscious. A doctor will be waiting.'

'And Sophie? My daughter?' Eliza fought the urge to want to sleep. So many people needed her.

'She's fine. She's with my wife.' Bude knelt before her, taking her hands. 'We need to get you both home. I have my carriage.'

She was going to be all right. Eliza woke late in the afternoon the following day at Falmage Hill. Her head hurt, but she wasn't dizzy. That was an improvement. Sophie was beside her. She reached for her hand and smiled at her daughter, but Sophie didn't smile back. She went straight to the point. 'Mama...' her face began to crumple '...the doctor says Eaton might die.'

Eliza struggled to sit up, black spots swarming before her eyes from the effort. No, Eaton could not die. He would not die for her, or because of her. 'Sophie, find me a dressing robe and find someone to help me. Get Cassian.' She wouldn't be able to manage the walk alone. She needed someone to lean on. 'We must go to him. We're his family.'

The doctor had not lied. Eaton was pale and unmoving in his bed. She'd never seen him so still, this man who was filled with energy. Cassian helped her into a chair. 'He lost a lot of blood. An inch to the right and he would have died in the mine. The bullet was close to an artery,' Cassian reported. 'He developed a fever last night. He hasn't woken since we brought him home.' Cassian gave her a long look. 'It is my opinion that he'll wake for you, if you could find it in your heart to give him a reason.'

She heard the reproach in his tone. So he knew. Eaton must have told him she'd refused his offer. 'I was mistaken in that decision,' she whispered.

Cassian was tired and drawn from a long night spent at his friend's bedside. 'He is like a brother to me. I have known him since birth. Life has not always been fair to him, but he's never let it stop him. He would give his all for those he loves. He proved that last night. I know of no better man.'

Neither did she. Eliza's throat was too clogged for words. Eaton had protected Sophie last night with his quick thinking and he had not hesitated to come for her. 'I'll stay with him awhile. You should go and rest.'

Cassian took Sophie and closed the door behind him. Alone, Eliza reached for his hand where it lay atop the blankets. There were things she needed to say to him, things she'd realised in the mine—or perhaps she'd always known them and had been too afraid to admit it. 'Thank you, Eaton, for saving me, not just last night, but even before, by helping me see that I don't need to be alone.' She threaded her fingers through his, alarmed at how stiff they were, how unmoving. 'Thank you for looking after Sophie.' Her voice cracked and the words seemed inadequate. She would be dead now if not for him. Instead, it was he who was in danger. She laid her head on his chest, feeling the fevered warmth of him. 'Eaton,' she whispered, 'I love you. I need you to wake up so I can tell you I've changed my mind. I will marry you if you will still have me.'

* * *

Eliza was safe. Eliza was free. His mission was complete. He could go now, on to whatever was next. The next world, perhaps. There was nothing in this one for him now. Eliza didn't want him, didn't need him. Maybe this was why nothing had pricked his interest since the school opened. Maybe he *was* done here.

My boy, you're wrong. You're too young to be done.

'Richard!' He couldn't see anyone, but he could hear his mentor, his old friend's voice.

She loves you—aren't you listening?

'She doesn't want me. I can't give her a child.'

You can give her more than a child—you can give her hundreds of children. Open schools. Adopt. Make Falmage Hill a home again. I never thought you would give up so easily, Eaton. She's already lost one man. She can't stand to lose you, too. She needs you, her daughter needs you. Wake up, be a husband, be a father. Listen to me...

There was a new voice now. Eliza's voice, begging him, wanting him.

I want to tell you I've made a mistake, I want to marry you. I don't want to do it alone any more.

He pushed against heavy eyelids and coaxed his hand around warm fingers. He forced sound over his dry throat and was able to form a single word. 'Eliza.' And she was there, beside him, crying, kissing him, holding his face between her hands.

'Eaton, I was wrong. I made a mistake.' She was babbling through her tears.

'I know,' he managed to say hoarsely with a smile. 'I heard you. You want to marry me.'

'Yes. As soon as you're able.' She clumsily poured him a glass of water, slopping some of it on him as she tried to help him drink.

'You pour water the way I pour champagne in moving carriages,' Eaton rasped. 'What changed your mind, Eliza?'

'When I was lost in the mine, I realised I wanted to marry you not because I needed you or was dependent on you, but because I loved you. I. Loved. You. That's the only reason.'

'It's the best reason.' Eaton pushed back her hair with his good arm. 'It's the reason I came back. I wanted to have a life with you and with Sophie, and any children we might accumulate on the way, more than I wanted to die.'

Eliza smiled, the sweetest sight he'd ever beheld. 'You must be feeling better already. You're making plans.'

Eaton grinned. 'Can you plan a wedding in three weeks? The moment I am well enough to walk down the aisle, I want to marry you. Every minute counts, Eliza. I don't want to waste a single one.'

Epilogue

N̲ot a moment was wasted. Three weeks to the day,
Eliza stood at the doors of the school's grand salon,
dressed in a gown of pale blue velvet, a veil of cream
lace on her head. Blue for loyalty. Blue for truth. Blue
for eternity. Today, she was breaking one vow to take
another, far more important one. She'd sworn never to
marry again, but she'd not sworn never to love.

'Are you ready?' The Duke of Bude offered her his
arm. Eaton's father would give her away to the man
she loved in the place where they'd first met, the place
where Eaton had proposed, the place where Eaton had
given so much of himself to so many.

'You look beautiful, Mama.' Sophie twirled in her
new dress, blue as well, her hair done in long thick
curls. 'Is it my time to scatter the rose petals?' She
was excited for her part in the ceremony. Eaton had
insisted she be part of it. 'Today, I am getting a papa,'
she told the Duke proudly.

'Yes, you are.' The Duke bent down to tweak a curl.

'And I am getting a new granddaughter and a daughter-in-law. Who do you think is the luckiest? I think I am.'

Eliza disagreed. She was the luckiest of them all. She'd found love when she'd least expected it. She'd also found a partner, a man willing to be her equal, willing to fuse her dreams with his. Eaton had been true to his word, scrambling for a special licence as soon as he managed to get out of bed. He was marrying her three weeks after he'd awoken from his fever and she was ready. She didn't want to wait a day longer to start their life, not when she'd nearly lost the chance altogether.

From inside the grand salon, chords sounded on the Sébsastian Érard and the doors opened to a wedding march Cador Kitto had composed just for them, another three-week wonder. But love made so many things possible. Sophie went before her, happily spreading rose petals down the ribbon-festooned aisle, guests rising as she made her way towards the front. Eaton's friends were there; Inigo and Cassian smiled, the Duchess of Bude wiped tears from her eyes as she passed.

Reverend Maddern waited for her alongside Eaton but she had eyes only for her soon-to-be husband. Eaton stood dressed in a blue morning coat and fawn pantaloons, dark hair already unruly just as she liked it; his arm in a sling, a reminder of his bravery—a reminder, too, that whatever came their way, they would face it together.

She heard little of the service and would remember even less except the part where Eaton kissed his bride. The Reverend pronounced them husband, wife and family as Eaton gave Sophie his good hand and led them back down the aisle. Eliza did not think the world could feel any more complete. But Eaton had another surprise for her.

On the way to the wedding breakfast at Falmage Hill, the carriage turned towards Wheal Karrek, stopping a short distance from the mine yard. She tossed Eaton a questioning glance. She'd not visited since the night Detford had died. Inigo had kindly—and temporarily—taken over the reins of the business in addition to quietly investigating Brenley's attempt at creating a mining monopoly among other financial considerations. There was no proof Brenley had done anything illegal, yet, but it would take time. Already, she could see the effects of Inigo's efforts. He'd organised the recovery and stopped any further tunnelling. The damaged section of the mine from the rockslide was being pumped out below. Above ground, a section of land had been quartered off with stakes and string. She threw Eaton a glance. 'What are we doing here? What is this? No one said anything about a stop.'

'Consider this an ambush.' Eaton grinned and looked mysterious. 'Be patient. I have a wedding gift for you.' He jumped down and rang the bell, calling all the miners to assemble, all work forgotten for the moment as Eaton climbed back in the open carriage and stood up for all to see. 'Attention everyone! Today I celebrate my marriage to this woman, the new Lady Lynford and the future Duchess of Bude. In honour of that marriage, my gift to her is the Wheal Karrek school for miners' children, where everyone will be able to learn to read and write.' He turned to her. 'Eliza, would you do us the honour of breaking the ground?'

Eliza swiped at her tears. A school! He was giving her a school. Had there ever been a more wondrous gift? The gesture overwhelmed her as so many of his gestures often had from the start. She took the shovel from Gillie Cardy and dug out the first scoop of dirt to a rousing cheer from the miners. 'Thank you,' she whispered to Eaton.

He beamed. 'It was your idea.'

Her new husband certainly didn't waste any time. But she knew what he'd say to that. There wasn't any time to waste. There never was when you were in love.

* * * * *

THE PASSIONS OF
LORD TREVETHOW

For Ro, Catie and Brony.
I love living the fairy tale life with you.

Chapter One

The Elms, Cornwall, family seat of the Duke of Hayle—March 5th, 1824, St Piran's Day

'You can't have the land.' Those were fighting words. The surest way to guarantee Cassian Truscott's interest in a cause was to tell him something couldn't be done. That being the case, Inigo Vellanoweth, investment partner, best friend and utterer of said words, currently held *all* his attention.

Cassian looked up from the map spread before him on the long, polished surface of the estate's library table. '*What* did you say, Inigo?'

The dark-haired Inigo fixed him with a challenging blue stare from his desk near the wall of long windows overlooking The Elms's immaculate gardens. 'You heard me. You can't have the land. The Earl of Redruth won't sell.' He emphasised his point with a wave of the most recent letter in a series of failed attempts.

Cassian sighed. His solicitors and Redruth's had been meeting all winter to make arrangements for the sale, to no avail. Spring was around the corner and he was no closer to breaking ground on his Cornish pleasure garden than he had been last year. Without Redruth's acres, there was simply no ground to break.

'There's other land, Cass. Perhaps it's time we consider other options,' Inigo pointed out practically. 'There's the acreage over by Truro,' he said, reaching for the numbers on the property, but Cassian cut him off. They'd been over this too.

'No, not land like this,' Cassian insisted, planting his hands on either side of the map, his gaze lingering on the spot marking the coveted thirty-two acres. Damn. He needed that land. It was the ideal location for accomplishing the achievement of his own dreams and for rejuvenating the Cornish economy. The coastal views were spectacular and sweeping, the distance to Porth Karrek or Penzance close enough to engage workers from several of the villages and to access other needed supplies to run such an establishment. 'Doesn't it gall you that the earl won't sell?' Inigo was his partner in the Porth Karrek Land Development Company, yet Inigo seemed less bothered by the downturn of events.

'It's just business to me, Cass.' Inigo gave him a wry smile. 'What do I always say? Don't get attached to money, to things. It makes a person less flexible.'

Cassian looked up from the map and grimaced. 'You think I'm being stubborn. You think I should move on and take the land near Truro.' It might be just business for Inigo, but it was far more than business for Cassian. This project was redemption, a chance to restore a legacy, a chance to do penance to the community for his brother's mistake. It had to be here. Putting it in Truro couldn't accomplish those things. It was too far away from the people he wanted to help.

'Offer Redruth double.' Cassian sighed. He needed that land. He'd invested months in negotiation—he wasn't going to give up now.

'We've already offered double,' Inigo reminded him.

'I know. Double it again. I can't imagine why Redruth remains obstinate. It's not as if he's using the land. It's been dormant for over a decade.' But even as he gave the order, Cassian felt the futility of it deep in his bones. Money would not coerce a man like Redruth, a man much like himself, who had money aplenty to spend, to whom doubling or quadrupling a price was no great stretch. He shook his head, cancelling the suggestion. 'No. Don't offer the money. We'll look stinking desperate and then we'll never get that land.'

Lord, this was maddening. The earl was well-known for his philanthropy in London. He supported numerous orphanages, championed the veterans of the Napoleonic wars and other causes in Parliament and out. Couldn't Redruth see all the good that could be done here at home in his very own environs? It wasn't as if Cassian was asking for charity. He was willing to pay handsomely.

Cassian left the table and went to the windows. He studied the green lawn before him. The sun had broken through the grey skies of the morning marine layer to make for a tolerable afternoon in early March. 'If money won't impress him, what will? He's a hermit except for sitting his seat in London.' Even in London, the earl barely socialised. He left that work to his son, Phineas. Cassian knew the son by sight only since Phineas was a few years younger. As for the earl, Cassian knew nothing of the man except that he craved seclusion and preferred to wield his power from the behind the walls of Castle Byerd.

'It's hard to know how to appeal to such a private man, Inigo. I don't think he's gone out in years except to perform his duties and attend church.' And to host his annual charity ball, the only night of the year the doors of Byerd House in London were thrown open to society. Cassian had attended only once. Usually his father went.

'What does Redruth need?' Cassian mused out loud. 'More importantly, what does he need that he can't get on his own?' But nothing came to mind. Surely the man wasn't unassailable. Everyone had a weakness. 'Did your digging discover anything?' After the last refusal, Inigo had set about investigating Redruth's situation.

'Only what we already know. He is committed to the land staying in the family. I've said it before, but my professional advice is that you look elsewhere for your acres.' Inigo left the desk to study the map. He tapped a finger. Cassian didn't need to see the map to know the spot. 'There are benefits to being near a larger town, Cass.'

Cassian turned from the window. 'No. Absolutely not. That would be to admit defeat. It's too far away to provide jobs for the people here, the people I want to help.' There was nothing like telling a man who had everything that the one thing he truly wanted was beyond his reach. 'The people of Porth Karrek and the surrounding area need economic relief *now*.' His friend, Eaton Falmage and his new bride, Eliza, had begun establishing a string of mining schools to educate the children of miners so that the next generation might have a choice as to how and where they worked. Those benefits would be long-term. But in the meantime, something needed to be done about present conditions and he was determined to do it.

Having been raised on the Cornish coast, he was fond of the expression 'a high tide raises all boats'. An amusement garden could do that by supplying three hundred jobs directly and countless other employment opportunities indirectly for those more intrepid entrepreneurs willing to set up in business on their own. A project of this magnitude could revitalise the region.

More than that, an amusement garden was Cassian's dream, his grand vision to bring new experiences to people who never ventured further away from their homes than they could walk in a day. He'd had the luxury of travel. He'd ridden the ice slides of Russia, partaken in the grand amusements of the French. He'd seen and tasted the convergence of culture and food from all over the world in Venice.

Those experiences had enriched him greatly. He'd learned more from those encounters than he had from his time at Oxford. Why shouldn't others be enriched in the same way? Why not bring those experiences to people who couldn't go to the source? Why should such enrichment be limited to only the very wealthy? It was the philosophy that Richard Penlerick, the Duke of Newlyn, Cassian's mentor and friend, had imparted to him for years, encouraging him to have purpose in his travel. 'Travel for those who cannot. Bring it home for others,' he'd counselled. 'So that one man's experiences might enrich a community.' Richard Penlerick was dead now, the first anniversary of his death approaching in June, but his legacy was as alive as it had ever been in the schools Eaton and Eliza had founded. Cassian was determined to continue the legacy. Damn the Earl of Redruth for standing in his way on the basis of some reclusive shibboleths about keeping the land in the family.

'It's a noble goal, Cass. But are you sure that's the only reason you're holding on so tightly?' Inigo had a way of piercing through the truth to get to even deeper truths, darker truths. Heaven help the man who lied to Inigo. He wouldn't stand a chance. 'Don't tell me this is about honouring Richard Penlerick. You can honour his legacy just as effectively in Truro as you can here.'

Cassian bristled. He didn't like being called out. Inigo knew very well he was sailing in dark waters now, close to the things they never discussed. 'Why don't you tell me what my secret agenda is, then? What, pray tell, am I holding on to?'

'There is no need to be testy. Sarcasm doesn't become you.' Inigo gave him a hard stare, his voice like the fine, thin, steel of his favourite rapier. Inigo the fencer, with blades, with words. 'Tell me this isn't about Collin.'

Collin. His younger brother. Dead now for five years, yet the single word still had the ability to suck all the air, all the life out of him. Anyone close to him knew better than to pull out that particular skeleton from the family closet. It was the Truscott family's Achilles heel. Ducal families weren't supposed to have such disasters, such tragedies. Maybe his family wouldn't have had one either if Cassian had chosen differently when his brother had come to him. But he hadn't and now Collin was dead. It took Cassian a moment to still his emotions before he could respond. 'What does it matter if it's about Collin? We all have our obsessions, Inigo. Vennor's quest for justice regarding his father's death. I have Collin and you have Gismond Brenley. Don't pretend that you aren't driven to bring down Brenley.'

'The man has been a thorn in our collective sides for years. He deserves a reckoning, for the part he played in Collin's death, for what he tried to do to Eliza Blaxland, for what he's still trying to do to the industries of Cornwall,' Inigo argued.

Cassian gave a dry laugh. 'That's hardly sporting, Inigo. You can justify your obsession, but you won't validate mine? My revenge against Brenley is to build that park, to give workers a choice. They don't have to work for Brenley. They don't have to mine. They can work for me doing any number of things. Then, we'll see what Brenley has to say when he has no work force.' Revenge could be served in a variety of ways.

'Your revenge is only theoretical at the moment, thanks to Redruth,' Inigo reminded him. 'That land is meant to stay in the family. If you're not family, you don't stand a chance.'

'Then I need to become family.' That sparked an idea. Cassian strode to the shelves, searching for his father's copy of *Debrett's Peerage*. Cornish families were tight-knit and old, with lineages that went back to William the Conqueror. He set the book on the table alongside the map and opened it, running a finger along the list of names and stopping beside Prideaux. Perhaps there was some remote connection between the Truscotts and the Prideauxes, or perhaps, failing that, there was some remote cousin in need of marrying.

His finger stilled at the thought. Would he really be willing to marry for the land? It wasn't a preposterous strategy. His own lineage *was* something he could barter with. He was a duke's heir, a wealthy man with a title of his own as Viscount Trevethow. He could, maybe, entice Redruth with that. It was always worthwhile to have a future duke on the family tree. If he did that, though, what would be the difference between him and his last mistress? Cassian suppressed a shudder, unable to shake the idea that such a trade reduced him to a high-class whore and not even an honest one. It would be backhanded to marry without disclosing the truth: that he was the chief owner of the Porth Karrek Land Development Company, which Redruth had already discouraged in its pursuit of the very land available to him in the marriage settlement. Of course, it would come at the cost of Redruth despising his new son-in-law for the deception. Hardly ideal grounds on which to begin married life, to say nothing of what his bride would think of the situation.

Aside from that, however, a marriage between the Earldom of Redruth and the Dukedom of Hayle would be a grand alliance of two old Cornish families, Cassian thought wryly. Many men of his age and social standing married for less. At the end of the proverbial day, he'd have his land—perhaps the rest didn't matter as long as the dream could move forward. But the rest did matter. Achieving the dream by marrying for the land came with great cost, starting with his pride and ending with the loss of other dreams he held close, dreams that might seem fanciful to other peers. He'd like to fall in love with his wife. He'd like his marriage to be as grand in passion as it would be in politics. He'd like his marriage to be more than a contract, although that might be even more of a pipe dream than his pleasure garden.

In Cassian's experience, men of his station were regular targets for matchmaking mamas and pound-wise papas who saw the financial as well as social benefits of such a match. One had to be on constant guard in order not to fall prey to their schemes. His brother and that unholy mess with Brenley's daughter was indication enough that such caution was not misplaced paranoia.

Yet the notion persisted for Cassian that, despite the monumental evidence to the contrary, love inside of marriage *was* possible. His own parents were proof of it. The Trelevens were proof of it, Cador and Rosenwyn Kitto were proof of it as were Eaton and Eliza.

Why shouldn't he have the same? Why should he settle for a dynastic contract? Cassian scanned *Debrett's*
for the Prideauxes, his eyes landing on the list of the
earl's family members.

Countess of Redruth, Lady Katherine Prideaux,
née Dunstan. Born 1783. Died 1814.

She'd been young. He'd been little more than a boy
when she'd passed. There was Phineas Michael, the
son and heir. His finger stopped on the name below it.

Penrose, Margaret. Born 1803.

Inigo's gaze was steady on him. 'You think to marry
for it. I see it in your eyes and now you've found the
daughter. So many forget about her.' Inigo's eyes narrowed as they studied him. 'No one's seen her. She
doesn't go about in society.' Like father like daughter
it seemed on that note.

There was a wealth of implication in those words.
Cassian shut the book. Perhaps she was the reason for
the Earl's reclusive lifestyle. Perhaps there was a reason she hadn't been seen in public. Was she crippled?
Burned? Did she limp? Not that those things mattered
to Cassian. He was not as shallow as to determine
someone's worth based on their physical abilities. But
society was. Regardless of her potential afflictions,
it seemed Redruth's daughter wasn't bound to be a
beauty.

'Certainly, though, her father's title and her dowry

are enough to guarantee she has suitors regardless of her looks,' Inigo pointed out.

'But not me among them.' Not yet. Cassian wasn't willing to engage in such manoeuvring. To sacrifice one dream for the sake of the other seemed to demean both dreams. Perhaps it would come to that, making himself into a placeholder for an exchange of titles and lands. For today, he was out of ideas until he could figure out what might persuade Redruth. Tomorrow, he would write to the earl one more time, outlining all the benefits of such a sale.

Cassian put the book away and stretched. 'I'm going out. I'll ride into Redruth and take in the St Piran's Day festivities while the sun is shining. The town always puts on a good fair. The fresh air will clear my head. Perhaps I'll think of a new angle for getting that land while I'm there.' Maybe he wouldn't need to. Perhaps once the earl read all the benefits that could come from such a project, he wouldn't be so hard-hearted as to reject progress when it came with so many advantages and a substantial offer of cash.

Chapter Two

They were making no progress here. Lady Penrose
Prideaux stifled her temper behind the osculation of
her fan while Lord Wadesbridge conversed with her
father. She knew what was afoot. Her father was match-
making *again*. At first, it had only been a game to Pen,
one she could win. Since she'd turned eighteen, her
father had discreetly invited a select few men of good
standing to Castle Byerd and, over the past two years,
she'd repeatedly found something wrong with each of
them. In the beginning, her father had not pushed her to
reconsider. But with each rejected candidate the game
posed an ever larger obstacle to her freedom. Two years
in, it wasn't a game any more, but a threat.

Her father was in earnest over today's suitor, Lord
Wadesbridge, who had an estate not far from Byerd.
She could see why her father liked him. The latest can-
didate for her hand had more in common with the earl
than he had with her. It wasn't surprising considering
Wadesbridge was her father's contemporary, not hers.

He was at least twenty years her senior. She knew what her father saw in him: an estate outside Looe close enough to visit, security, stability, sensibility. There wasn't a more stolid man in Cornwall.

If she was an older widow with half of her life behind her, or a quiet, retiring wallflower with no eye towards adventure, she might find Wadesbridge more appealing. But she was none of those things. She was twenty years old and hadn't been allowed outside the walls of Castle Byerd alone for the last decade. Whatever escape from Byerd she'd had over the years, she'd engineered covertly. She was full of wanderlust and a passion for living. She wanted to see the world she'd read about in her father's library, wanted to make her own choices, live her own life. She wanted to do more than support unseen causes for the poor from behind the safety of Byerd's walls. She wanted to help them first-hand. She wanted to travel, to see the places on the maps she studied, to dip her toes in the warm ocean of the Caribbean, to smell the spices in the Turkish bazaar, to ride in a Venetian gondola, maybe indulge in ordering gowns from a French salon, at the very least, to have a Season like other girls of her rank, to dance with a handsome gentleman who wasn't her father's age, to flirt, to fall in love, to meet someone that made her heart pound and her pulse race, who understood her dreams. Some days, like today, she felt as if she'd burst from the wanting of it all. There was so much to do beyond the walls of Byerd and she was running out of time. She couldn't say no to every suitor for ever. Her father wouldn't permit it. If she didn't choose, she had no doubt he would choose for her. He was the most determined man she knew.

'My daughter is honoured by your attentions, Wadesbridge.' Her father shot her a sharp look, jerking her back to awareness. She'd missed her cue. 'She will consider your suit.'

Pen's eyes snapped to attention. What had just happened? She'd drifted for a moment and she was nearly betrothed. Wadesbridge smiled and rose, happy enough to conclude his visit on that note. He reached for her hand and bent over it. 'I look forward to showing you Trescowe Park, my lady. The gardens are at their best in the spring. Your father tells me you enjoy flowers.' She nodded non-committally, not wanting to agree to anything she might regret. She did like flowers, wild ones. She envied them their freedom to grow where they chose, to run rampant over hedges and moors, to climb stone walls and poke through cracks.

'I have a greenhouse that would interest you, my lady.' Wadesbridge was still talking. 'Over the winter, I perfected some grafts with my roses in the hopes of producing a yellow rose tinged orange on the edges. If you'd permit me, I could send a cutting over.'

Wadesbridge was being kind. She could not shun him for kindness, but she wouldn't marry him for it either. Pen responded carefully. If she showed too much interest she'd end up with a room full of cuttings tomorrow and both he and her father would take it as an endorsement of his suit. 'You are too generous, my lord.' Pen offered a polite smile. 'I will look forward to seeing your new rose when we visit and perhaps I can select a few cuttings then.' It was better to stall any potential outpouring of gifts. She smiled Wadesbridge out, but her smile faded the moment she and her father were alone in the drawing room.

'I don't want to marry him.' Pen spoke first, her voice full of sharp authority.

Her father sighed, looking suddenly weary, his voice tired. 'What's wrong now? Wadesbridge is rich, titled, stable, local.'

'He's old.'

'He's only forty-five.'

'He's closer to your age than he is mine,' Pen pressed. Only ten years separated her father and Wadesbridge, but two and half decades separated her from him.

Her father's dark eyes studied her in frustration. He had a temper too. They were alike in that regard. At the moment, they were both struggling to keep that particular character trait under control. 'The previous suitor gambled, another drank, another had debts. I should think Wadesbridge's lack of vices would appeal after that parade, or is it your intention to find fault with every suitor?' There was accusation in his tone. He was disappointed in her. She hated disappointing her father. She loved him and she knew he loved her. Too much sometimes.

'I want to do something with my life, Father.' She gentled her tone in hopes of making him see.

'Marry, raise a family. There is no worthier calling in life,' her father insisted. 'Family is everything, it is a man's life's work and a woman's too.' But it wasn't

the only work of a lifetime. There were other worthy
ways to spend a life.

'Maybe, in time I would like those things, but not
yet.' How did she convince him? 'I want to live a little
before I'm handed off to a husband. I don't want to go
from my childhood home to my husband's home without an adventure first. I haven't even been to London
for a debut.' Other girls her age, girls like their nearby
neighbour, Sir Jock Treleven's daughters, had all gone
to London for Seasons. Marianne was having her *second* Season this year and she was only nineteen, a year
younger than Pen.

Her father's eyebrows rose in censure at the mention
of London. 'The city is far too dangerous. Don't you
recall what happened last Season? The Duke of Newlyn and his wife were stabbed to death coming home
from the theatre. They were practically our neighbours
here all these years and now they're gone. I wouldn't
want to risk you. Besides, with your dowry and your
antecedents, what need do you have for a Season?' He
leaned forward and pinched her cheek affectionately.
'You have no need to hunt for a husband. *They* come
to you.'

'I want to choose for myself and to do that I need
time and a larger selection, Papa. How can I know what
I want in a husband if I haven't met anyone?'

'You should be guided by the wisdom of your elders.
I would not allow you to marry someone unworthy.'
No, he wouldn't. She would be assured of marrying
a decent man, but the thought of wedding a decent
man didn't exactly set her heart to racing. What about

romance? What about stolen kisses? What about *love*?
'I must insist you seriously consider Wadesbridge.'

'And *you* must seriously consider what I want. Does
it matter so little?' She felt as if an invisible noose was
strangling her. Her lovely home had slowly become a
prison over the years. If she stayed, she'd scream with
the futility of her life. She had to get out of here, if
even for a short time. She needed a walk, a chance to
clear her head.

'I don't want to quarrel with you, Penrose.' His tone
softened with love and she heard the old, familiar tinge
of sadness that had been present in his voice for over
a decade. 'You grow more beautiful every day, Penrose. You look so much like your mother. You have
her honey hair, her green eyes, like the Cornish sea at
summer. A stunning combination.' Her father was bi-
ased, of course. She might be striking in her features,
but she was not beautiful. There was a difference. Her
mother, however, had been beautiful and life had been
beautiful when she was alive, every day an adventure
from romping the hills to building hideaways in the
vast attics of Byerd on rainy afternoons.

Her looks were a blessing and a curse Pen had lived
with every day since the event that had claimed her
mother's life, a constant reminder to them all of the
woman they'd lost to a violent, senseless act and the
very reason her father was so protective. He feared losing her the way he'd lost his wife: instantly and arbi-
trarily. Pen felt her anger over the latest suitor slipping.
It was hard to argue with a man who was still grieving
after all these years, hard to hurt a father who loved

his children so deeply. She couldn't keep putting the discussion off, though. If she didn't stand up for herself soon, she'd end up married to Wadesbridge or if not Wadesbridge, the next suitor who walked through the doors of Castle Byerd. But not today. She would not fight with her father today. Today, she would do as she usually did and simply escape.

She moved towards the door, and her father looked up. 'Where are you going?'

'Upstairs, I think I'll lie down before dinner. I have a headache,' she improvised. There were festivities in the village, even fireworks this evening, and she didn't intend on missing them, especially if this might be her last time to see them. She wasn't getting any younger and her father's collection of suitors was only growing more insistent by the day. Desperate times called for desperate measures. She could either sit in her room and mope or she could go to a party.

Upstairs, Pen reached under her bed for an old dressmaker's box that had once contained a gown. Now, it was home to a plain brown cloak, a simple dark blue dress made of homespun wool and a battered pair of half-boots. Pen smiled as she pulled them out one by one as if they were made of the finest silk. The clothes were her treasures. Once she slipped these on, she was no longer Penrose Prideaux who couldn't leave the castle without an army for an escort. Now, she could be whoever she wished: a peasant girl, a farm girl, a girl who worked in one of the shops in the village, maybe even a stranger who'd walked here from another village. These clothes were freedom. She could be whoever she desired, do whatever she desired and no one would be the wiser.

Pen finished dressing and took down her carefully crafted hair, plaiting her long honey-hued skeins into a single, thick braid that hung over her shoulder. She critically studied her appearance in the pier glass, looking for anything that would give her away: a forgotten piece of jewellery or a silk ribbon in her hair. Satisfied that she'd erased any trace of Penrose Prideaux, she raised the hood of her cloak and set off to leave herself behind. Tonight, she would make some adventures of her own before it was too late.

Chapter Three

Cassian loved a good fair and the town of Redruth did not disappoint. It was a point of pride for the town as the nominal originator of the St Piran festivities. Many other towns in Cornwall had their own celebrations these days for the patron saint of tin miners, but Redruth had been the first.

Cassian stabled his horse at the livery, tossing an extra coin to the sulky young ostler left on duty while his comrades had gone off to join the festivities. 'You'll be rich when they come back with their pockets to let,' Cassian consoled him, but the boy continued to pout. Well, he knew a little something about that. He wasn't so far past boyhood himself that he'd forgotten how much he'd looked forward to an outing when he was younger. Fun was sparse in this part of the world. His pleasure garden could change that. It would have entertainments for all ages, unlike Vauxhall, which catered to an adults-only crowd. Children needed stimulation, too, especially when their imaginations were at their most fertile. Growing up, he'd loved adventure stories even though reading had been a labour for him. He'd loved any day that his father or Eaton's father or Richard Penlerick had taken the four of them out riding or exploring. But those days had been rare. Perhaps he'd bring the sulky ostler a pasty when he came back. Cassian's stomach rumbled at the thought of a hot pie, a reminder that he hadn't eaten since breakfast.

Outside in the street, happy townsfolk jostled past as he let his nose lead the way to a pasty vendor. He purchased a pasty and bit into the flaky crust, the savoury meat warm in his mouth. It took the edge off the weather's late afternoon crispness. March wasn't really spring in this part of the world. Cassian wandered the booths, stopping every so often to admire goods that caught his attention. It was at the leatherworker's booth, as he studied the workmanship on a bridle, that he noticed her out of the corner of his eye. He couldn't say what it was exactly that drew him: the swirl of her cloak, perhaps, or the way the woman beneath the cloak moved, all slender, straight-shouldered grace as opposed to the bustle of the fair-goers.

Cassian stepped back from the leatherworker's booth to study her. She moved as if she were savouring each sight, lingering over each of the items in the stalls, treating them as if they were luxuries. Maybe they were. Not everyone who came to a fair had coins in their pocket to spend. The hood of her brown cloak was drawn up over her face, her hair. Cassian found himself wishing it wasn't so. He wanted to see this woman who walked through a village fair with such reverence. More than that, he wanted to know her mind; what did the fair look like to her to inspire such awe? How might he capture that for his amusement park? It was precisely how he wanted guests to look when they visited. If he ever got it built.

She moved into the crowd and Cassian followed. Perhaps he would speak to her. She appeared to be alone, an odd condition for a woman at such an event. For all the excitement a fair could bring, there were dangers, too, if one wasn't careful, especially as the day wore on and the men were deeper into their drink. At the edge of the village green the booths gave way to the pens of livestock and the crowd thinned. Here, she halted, suddenly surrounded by a gaggle of children who'd swarmed her.

Cassian quickened his steps in concern. There were too many of them. These were not village children. These were street urchins, some of them older boys who likely followed the vendors from fair to fair. A smaller boy, likely the decoy, said something to her, tugging at her and claiming all her attention. Cassian could guess what he was asking for. The woman hesitated and then reached beneath her cloak and produced a coin for the lad. That would never do. The boys would either beg the rest of her purse from her or come back to steal it later now that they knew where she kept it. From the looks of her clothes, she hadn't the money to spare should she lose whatever her purse contained.

'Hoy there, lads! Be off with you!' Cassian strode into their midst, dispersing them with his sheer bulk. Smart lads didn't mess with men built with height and breadth to match. They scattered like swatted flies in the wake of his broad-shouldered, baritone-voiced barrage.

The woman straightened, becoming taller, more slender, more graceful than she'd been in the market-place. 'That was hardly necessary, sir. They were just hungry children begging a coin.' There was a slightly imperious tone to her voice. A proud woman, then, a woman who liked to be self-sufficient. He had two older sisters who had that same tone. He knew it well. A man had to tread carefully where such a woman's pride was concerned. It was a lesson he'd watched his sisters' husbands learn over the years.

'They'll have your whole purse off you if you aren't careful. Those were no ordinary children,' he scolded kindly.

'I know their sort very well. It doesn't make their plight any less pitiable. Out of concern for my fellow mankind, I'll take my chances, every time,' she answered staunchly.

Cassian nodded. 'A noble sentiment, although I doubt they'll extend you the same courtesy when they come back to take your purse. You exposed yourself, you know.' He wished she'd expose a little more of her-self, perhaps push that hood back from her face, show him the eyes, the mouth that went with her voice. In his experience, a confident woman was always attractive. He found confidence sexy in the bedroom and out. This woman's confidence stirred him, intrigued him. 'Perhaps I might escort you in case they return.' If he was beside her, he was certain they wouldn't.

'Where might *you* escort me? A dark alley?'

'Would you like me to?' He flirted with a smile. 'There are many things one can get up to in a dark alley, not all of them bad.'

'You might be more dangerous than the gang of boys,' she answered shrewdly. She was enjoying the exchange. 'How do I know you're not in on it with them?' She gave a throaty laugh when he raised an eyebrow in approval of her quick wit. 'See, I'm not as green as you think.' Sweet heavens, the minx gave as good as she got. The open boldness appealed.

Cassian chuckled. 'I never thought you were. I was merely concerned you were too kind-hearted for your own good. Might I interest you in a pasty or some other delicacy?'

'I don't even know your name, sir.' She was serious about that. He'd reached the limits of what she'd tolerate. However, he was enjoying her far too much to ruin it by announcing his real name. It would change everything if she recognised it. Even if she didn't recognise it now, she would be sure to recognise it later. A name was power, to be used for or against him. He would not put that kind of power in a stranger's hands.

'What would you like my name to be?' Cassian flirted. 'Choose one for me.' Beneath the hood of her cloak, green eyes lit in liking and understanding. The idea appealed to her as well. His intrigue ratcheted. His lady liked games.

'Matthew.' She chose easily and quickly. 'And what shall you call me?' It was an interesting woman who saw the benefit of an alias, who perhaps was just as eager as he to keep her identity hidden. Maybe because it made the little game between them more exciting, or maybe there was something more to it.

'Must I call you anything? I'd rather know your face than your name.' Cassian cajoled. 'Push your hood back a little farther so that I can see you better.' He was starting to like this game. This was a woman with secrets, a woman who liked her privacy. He respected that. He had secrets of his own.

With her free hand, she pushed her hood back just far enough to reveal hair the colour of caramel and honey and eyes like sea glass, a mouth that was full and inviting. Taken together, her features were starkly, intensely riveting. Memorable. In the right clothes, the right setting, she would be a beauty. Amidst the plain folk of Redruth, she was remarkable, a faerie queen among mere mortals. He understood why she stayed cloaked. Remarkable women drew attention and hardly ever the right sort.

'I saw an opal once the shade of your eyes, but I think Emerald makes a better name.' Cassian let her draw her hood back up. 'That way I can call you Em. It sounds friendlier.'

'Are we to be friends, then, for the night?' They'd begun walking back towards the stalls, the decision to share the evening already implicitly made.

'We shall be whatever you want, Em.' He let his voice linger on the last, the caress of his tone carrying the nuance for him; they could be strangers, lovers, friends. Em suited her, his cloaked minx with her throaty laugh and her bold mystery. He purchased two pasties stuffed with hot, sliced potatoes. He passed one to her and watched her bite into it.

'Oh, that is *good*.' Her eyes closed as she savoured the food, chewing slowly, and Cassian felt himself grow hard at the sight. If she looked this delicious eating a pasty, what might she look like in the throes of taking her pleasure? Her hair loose from its braid, her long neck arched?

A droplet of juice dribbled on her lips and Cassian felt the wicked urge to lick it from her mouth. She smiled coyly as if she guessed the direction of his thoughts, but before he could lean forward, the tip of her tongue darted out to claim the drop.

He wanted to kiss her, this handsome, dark-haired man. A little frisson of excitement raced through Pen at the realisation. She'd read enough novels to know. The drop of the eyes, the lingering gaze on one's mouth. Those were the signs. Only she'd beaten him to it with her tongue.

Perhaps she ought to have let him kiss her? But it was too soon. He'd think her easy. They'd only just met and she'd broken so many rules already: talking to a stranger, walking with him, accepting food from him, flirting outrageously, saying wickedly witty things she'd only ever practised in her mind and taking on a false name. *Em*, he'd called her, only when he said it, she imagined it as M. *M* for mystery, perhaps. Perhaps he might try for a kiss again when they'd known one another a little longer and she could oblige. It was naughtily delicious to think she might get kissed tonight; her very first kiss, and from a tall, dark, handsome stranger at the fair.

They finished their pasties and began to wander the booths, stopping when something caught their eyes: a belt here, a scarf there, a pretty bauble, a scented bar of soap and a never-ending stream of conversation. Matthew was easy to talk to and easy to listen to. He had stories about everything from how the French soap was milled to how many crimps of a crust it took to make a true pasty to how Brussels lace was made.

'You've seen them make the lace?' She fingered a delicate sample in renewed appreciation for the labour. At home in her wardrobe, she had several gowns with lace collars and yokes. She'd not stopped to think of the effort those yards had taken.

'Yes, it's a very elaborate, time-consuming process. It can take months to produce a design.'

She gave a sigh. 'I'm envious of you and your travels! How wonderful to see the world. I'd give anything to leave here, at least for a while. Where else have you been?' They stopped to sniff little vials of perfume. She held up a vial of sandalwood mixed with an exotic scent. She sniffed and handed it to him. 'Try this one. It's very masculine.'

He sniffed and put the stopper back in. 'It's nice. It reminds me of Russia.'

She smiled. 'So, you've been to Russia. Tell me. What is Russia like?'

He winked. 'I will, but first we need sustenance.' He was a bottomless pit, she discovered. The pasty they'd consumed earlier was followed by a sampling of every sweet available as they shopped and talked and he regaled her with stories of his travels. They ate, turning the night into a parade of scones with jam and clotted cream and saffron buns warm from the oven. When they stopped at a stall selling fairings, she gave a laughing groan as he bought a bag of the biscuits and offered her one. 'Oh, no, I couldn't eat another a bite!'

Matthew grinned mischievously and waved a ginger treat under her nose. 'Are you sure? I have it on good authority from my nieces and nephews that fairings are generally irresistible and these are fresh. Try one, for me, please.'

He smiled at her and it seemed to Pen that the crowd disappeared, that the whole world vanished when he looked at her like that with whisky eyes and long black lashes. She was lost. 'Well, perhaps I could find room for one,' she teased.

'Open wide, then, Em.' Her pulse raced as she divined his intentions. He meant to feed it to her from his own hand! She took the fairing from him with her teeth, aware of his fingers lingering on her lips, aware of the spark that leapt between them. Around them, the lanterns began to cast their glow as light faded, the day was changing and *they* were changing with it. There was a charge between them. Matthew's eyes were on her as she swallowed the fairing, searing into her as if his gaze could see into her mind, her very soul, into every fantasy she'd ever harboured of a night like this—a night with a stranger who wanted her, just her; a stranger who knew nothing of her family's tragedy, of her seclusion, her private fight for freedom; a stranger who didn't want her for her money, her land, her family's title, a man not curated for her by her father.

She was aware, too, that the fantasy had to end very soon. She'd already stayed longer than she'd intended. Matthew fed her another fairing and she took this one more slowly, revelling in the brush of his fingertips at her lips as she summoned the willpower for the words that must come. 'I have to go.' Her maid, Margery, would cover for her, of course, but she still had to walk back and that walk would now occur in darkness.

'Soon,' he said, taking her hand in his and beginning to stroll again. 'But not yet. We haven't seen the Venetian glass-blower.'

'One more booth and then I must go.' She could not resist the temptation of a few more minutes with him, a few more minutes of freedom.

The glass-blower did not disappoint. In the darkness, the flame of his forge was inviting and warm. They joined the semi-circle of onlookers gathered around the stall to watch him work his magic. Pen gasped as the man blew through a tube and a fragile shape took form at the other end. She'd never seen glass blown and the process mesmerised her almost as much as the man standing behind her. She was acutely aware of him, of his height, of his body so close to hers in the crowd, the breadth of his shoulders beneath his greatcoat, the heat of him rivalling the heat of the glassmaster's forge. She felt the gentle grip of his hand at her waist as they watched the demonstration. No man had ever dared touch her so intimately, so possessively, but he did it easily as if his hand belonged there, as if it had a *right* to belong there.

A hungry, curious, lonely part of her wished he had that right, but she knew better. She was an earl's daughter, a woman destined for a match that went far beyond the means of this whisky-eyed stranger. He was not a peasant. His bearing, his confidence was too grand for that with his greatcoat and boots. Perhaps he was a squire's son, a man of decent means, but no substantial wealth, a man who could never be a contender for the hand of an earl's daughter. She could only be his for the night. And who knew? Perhaps he had obligations elsewhere as well? Perhaps he could no more be hers beyond tonight than she could be his?

The glass-blower completed his demonstration to applause and the crowd dispersed. Pen lingered to look at the items on display in the case: a clever glass heart that could be hung as a pendant, a menagerie of little glass animals of all sorts, tiny thimbles and teardrops. 'Amazing,' she whispered under her breath. 'To think that Venice has come all the way to Redruth. What a world it must be.' It was worth it to be late getting back to have seen this and to have seen it with him, her Matthew. She slid a glance his way and smiled. 'I'm glad you insisted I see this.'

He did not look away, his gaze holding hers long after her words faded. 'Will you permit me to offer you a souvenir?' His voice was low and private, for her alone.

'I should not.' Her voice was equally as quiet.

'But you will. Your heart's not in the refusal,' he

said softly, gesturing for the glass-blower. 'The lady would like the pendant.'

Pen blushed furiously. It was too much, too intimate, far more intimate than Wadesbridge's rose cuttings. The necklace wasn't fine diamonds or even Austrian-cut crystal. She had a jewel box full of items that were more expensive, but she was cognisant this was a trinket of some expense for a common man. Yet Matthew handed over the coins easily. 'May I put it on you, Em?' He was searing her with his gaze, burning her alive here in public where everyone could see. Did *he* see what he did to her?

She gave him her back, pushing off the hood of her cloak and lifting the thick braid, giving him access to her neck. His fingers were cool against her skin where he tied the ribbon, where they lingered at her neck as he whispered, his mouth at her ear as if they were lovers, old familiar lovers who knew one another's bodies, 'You have the neck of a swan, Em.'

'Thank you.' Was that the right response? What did one say when one's neck was complimented? Somewhere in the distance, music began for dancing as he pushed up the hood of her cloak, covering her hair, his hands lingering at her shoulders.

'Do you insist on leaving? I would ask you to dance if I could entice you to stay?'

She fingered the glass heart at her neck. 'I must go now. Thank you for a wonderful evening.'

'Where are you headed? My horse is at the livery. I can take you.'

Pen hesitated. She was tempted. A horse would be

faster than a walk, yet her father's sense of caution and danger was deeply ingrained in her. Here at the fair, they were surrounded by people. Matthew couldn't do much to her here where she could cry out for help. But on a horse, on the dark road…her mother had died on a dark road.

'You're thinking of dark alleys again, aren't you, Em?' He chuckled softly. 'You don't owe me anything for the necklace. I'm not the sort of man who demands payment for trinkets. That wasn't why I bought it.'

'I know,' she whispered softly. She knew it was true in her bones. Fantasy or not, she was safe with him. *Em* was safe with him. Pen might not be, though. She didn't want him getting close to Byerd. He might try to find her there later. She couldn't risk him showing up, exposing her. 'Still, I must leave you here.' She had to insist although it saddened her to see the evening end. She would never see him after tonight. He would become a treasured memory.

But Matthew was determined. 'Can I see you again, Em?'

'I don't know.' She was faltering now, unsure. She hadn't thought further than tonight. How would she manage it again? Not just getting out of Byerd again without her father knowing, but keeping her identity secret? How would she explain if she were caught?

'There's an abandoned gamekeeper's cottage between Redruth and Hayle just off the coast road. Meet me there tomorrow at one,' he urged. 'I will wait all afternoon for you.'

She should absolutely say no now. No good could

come of meeting a man in an empty cottage. Instead, Pen found herself saying, 'I will try.'

'Do more than try, Em.' His eyes glittered dangerously in the lantern light, all hot whisky. 'I want to see you again. Tonight was magical, being with you, talking with you. I want more of that. If you don't come, I'll know you felt differently.' He raised her hand to his lips and kissed her knuckles. A bolt of white-hot awareness shot up her arm. 'Until tomorrow, Em.' Then he let her go, let her have her way to make the journey home alone with her thoughts. Her hand burned from the imprint of his touch, her heart wishing he'd dragged her into a dark alley after all and kissed her on the mouth instead of the hand. Her mind debated whether or not she was crazy enough to keep the rendezvous tomorrow with all its potential risks and whether or not he'd really wait all afternoon for the likes of her. He'd not struck her as the sort of man who had to wait on a woman.

Chapter Four

Em was keeping him waiting. Cassian snapped shut his pocket watch for the third time in fifteen minutes and retraced his steps back across the room to the hearth where his haphazard fire burned, built from the scraps of kindling he'd picked up on the cliffs. A half of an hour he'd been here, lighting a fire, setting out the parcels of his picnic on the scarred table and pacing the floor of the gamekeeper's cottage, first in anticipation, then in a little self-deprecating irony, reflecting on the intrigue this whole interlude raised in him. Certainly, he'd had more sophisticated affairs and yet this one had him vacillating between anticipation and anxiousness. Would she come? Perhaps she wasn't merely keeping him waiting—the very concept implied she *was* coming. Maybe that was a fallacy. Maybe she wasn't coming at all.

Perhaps she'd woken up this morning and realised the insanity of what he'd proposed—that two strangers meet in an isolated location for an afternoon of undisclosed activity. Such an adventure was always more dangerous for a woman. She would be taking all the risk. Perhaps last night had been risk aplenty for her and yet she'd enjoyed his company, that had been plain enough in her smile, her wit, the flash of her sea-glass eyes.

He'd definitely enjoyed her, the delicious directness with which she'd spoken. She'd been quick to challenge him when she thought he was too bold. She'd been open and unguarded when she'd told him of her dreams to travel. Her joy in the vendors had been natural, spontaneous. *Without artifice.* Those two words described her appeal completely. There had been no dissembling from her, no posturing. Everything between them— from eating messy, juicy pasties to wandering the booths—had been organic in a way no London ballroom or exquisitely coached debutante could replicate.

It felt good to put his finger at last on the source of his attraction. However, it felt less than good to realise *why* that had been possible. She didn't know who he was. If she did, all that naturalness might be sacrificed. She'd be intimidated into curtailing her open speech, into second-guessing what she shared, or maybe she'd realise the futility of meeting him. There was no future for a peasant girl and a duke's heir. Nothing could come of this except enjoyment of the moment, as it had last night.

Would the promise of continuing that enjoyment be enough to compel her out in the light of day to the cliff lands between Redruth and Hayle? He hoped it would be, but hope hadn't been his friend today when it had come to appointments. Today was taking on a potentially disappointing theme in that regard. The Earl of Redruth had written a vituperative letter in quick response to his latest missive. Redruth's letter had outlined his reasons for refusing to sell to the Porth Karrek Land Development Company. Such a project would attract 'outsiders', the earl's letter had cited with contempt. Redruth felt that such a plan would not only bring the desired tourists to the depressed region, but also strangers, people who would take jobs from the people the project intended to help here at home. Moreover, Redruth believed there would be other more nefarious types who didn't intend to work, but who came to prey on the unsuspecting, such as the families taking a holiday thinking they were safe, but instead finding themselves at the mercy of a cutpurse or worse, citing the tragedy of the Duke of Newlyn in London.

The last had boiled Cassian's blood. Redruth couldn't know how close to his heart that arrow struck. Redruth didn't know that the Duke of Hayle and his son, the Viscount Trevethow, along with Inigo Vellanoweth, Earl of Tintagel, and his father, the Duke of Boscastle; all close intimates of the late duke, were the driving force behind the Porth Karrek Land Development Company. Cassian had wanted to write back, to argue that the duke would have been the first to champion such an innovative project to restore the region's economy. But Redruth would not care and such a self-satisfying measure would risk exposing the land company's ownership. Other than being neighbours, Redruth knew little about the progressive thoughts of the Duke of Newlyn past or present. Redruth, in fact, knew very little of what happened outside the walled fortress of Castle Byerd. It was a pity. His own people would suffer for it.

Cassian threw another stick on the fire in the little hearth and watched it blaze. It was at times like these, where he could not effect change, could not break an impasse, that he felt most impotent. How could it be that with all his resources he could not breach the walls of the earl's disregard? He would try again. He'd find a way. He did not give up easily. He'd not given up when it had proven hard to read while others around him seemed to pick it up naturally. He'd not given up when the deans at Oxford had said he'd never complete his degree in history, a subject that required much reading. Instead, encouraged by his father, his close friends and Newlyn, he'd found a way to appreciate history through travel, to appreciate the world through other more experiential means than solely through texts. Newlyn was gone now, but he'd left Cassian with a legacy of perseverance and success. Hard work paid in rich reward. And, of course, he knew the opposite was true as well. Quitting, giving in, only bred more defeat. He had quit only once in his life. How might things have been different if he hadn't given up on Collin? Might Collin still be alive if he'd made different decisions where his brother had been concerned?

'Matthew?' Em's sweet voice broke into his darkening thoughts. Cassian looked away from the fire.

'Em!' Her presence chased away the guilt that was always present when he thought about Collin. His day was better already just at the sight of her. Her cheeks were rosy with exertion. Her hood had fallen back and her hair sparkled with droplets of mist. Her boots were muddy and her cloak damp. Cassian moved to help her out of her wet garment. He spread it before the fire, noting how thin it was. 'It will be dry by the time you leave,' he promised.

'You needn't fuss. It's only a light mist.' She held her hands out towards the flames, warming them, and Cassian felt a twinge of guilt. 'I hope the walk wasn't too far? I should have asked last night. I should not have presumed.' A slip on his part. He was privileged. He had sturdy boots to wear, a warm coat. He should not have assumed her shoes would be adequate for the task of tramping through the mud or that her cloak was warm enough for her to *choose* to be out of doors voluntarily.

'It wasn't too far. I like a good walk, rain or shine,' she assured him, but her smile was tremulous, her eyes glancing about the room, taking in the door and the two windows as if she might need to know their location for an escape. She wore the same blue dress he'd glimpsed beneath her cloak at the fair. The pretty glass heart was at her neck and it warmed him that she'd worn it. She was much the same Em in daylight as she'd been at the fair, but today she was nervous.

Cassian strove to put her at ease. 'I'm glad you're here. I thought you might not come.' He dragged over the two chairs from the table and set them near the fire.

'I'm sorry I'm late. I couldn't get away as soon as I'd wanted. I hope you weren't waiting for too long?'

She sounded flustered as she cast about for conversation. Perhaps she was realising how alone they were, how different today was from last night. There were no lights, no vendors, no fair magic to guide their conversation. It was just them.

'It's never too long to wait for you.' Cassian absolved her tardiness with the wave of a hand. The wait had been worth it to have her all to himself. Without her cloak to hide her, he could see the details of her face. Not just her eyes, but the minutiae of her: the tiny scar at her chin, the freckle at the corner of her mouth, the things that gave her features nuance and depth, that made them uniquely hers. When one struggled to read books, one learned to read people instead.

'Do you flatter all the strange girls you meet?' She blushed becomingly and dropped her gaze to her lap. 'Why did you think I wouldn't come?'

Cassian stretched his booted feet out before the fire and gave her a winsome smile. 'I thought you might have realised how insane it was to meet a stranger in a cottage.'

Oh, she had definitely realised that. She was still thinking it, in fact, now that she'd arrived and the very space they occupied seemed intent on reminding her of the remoteness of their location and the precariousness of her position. To be caught here would be devastating. Pen fidgeted with her hands in her lap. What did one say to that?

She jumped up from her chair and began to walk the length of the room, expending her nervous energy.

'It is crazy. But you're here, too, so I guess that makes two of us with questionable grips on sanity. Although, to my credit, I did turn around once.' It accounted for being late, that and the rather lengthy debate she'd held with herself on a rock overlooking the sea.

The admission seemed to intrigue him. She felt his whisky eyes linger on her, studying her as she moved about the room. 'Why *did* you come?'

'I had to know, for myself, if this was crazy. I'd never know if I could trust you if I didn't show up.' More than that, she didn't want her father to win. She didn't want fear to win, to steal her one chance at an adventure. But now that she'd come she hardly knew what to do with herself. What *did* one do on a rendezvous? Would there be kisses? More than kisses? She hardly knew the man she'd braved fear and rain to meet in an old cottage. For all she knew, he was a practised rake.

'Do you meet girls out here all the time?' It was possible she was just another in a long line of clandestine seductions. A hundred horrid thoughts had crossed her mind on the walk, thoughts not just about him, but about her. If he was a seducer, what did it say of her that she was still willing to meet him?

'No.' He sounded insulted by the idea. 'Why would you say that?'

'You've come provisioned, a man with a plan.' Pen opened the picnic basket at the table and sniffed appreciably. There were meat pies inside. Her stomach rumbled.

'We might get hungry. Bring it to the fire and stay

warm.' He left his chair and sat on the floor, taking the basket from her as she sat down beside him.

'You mean *you'll* get hungry. You're always ravenous. If I ate as much food as you did at the fair, I'd outgrow my clothes in a week.' Pen laughed, some of the ease of the prior evening returning to her. She'd not realised how much she'd relied on the fair last night to direct their conversation, to give them something to talk about.

'See, you already know me far better than you did yesterday.' He passed her a meat pie. 'You have an unfair advantage on me, I'm afraid. I don't know anything about you.' He slanted her a teasing look. 'I know what we'll do. I propose of game of questions so that by the end of it, we shall no longer be strangers.' He grinned mischievously at her, offering the jug of ale. 'First, the rules. Rule number one: we shall take turns asking each other questions. Rule number two: we must answer with the truth. Our honour requires it. Rule number three: our honour also requires the question cannot be refused. I'll go first.' He stretched out to his full length before the fire, his dark head propped in a large hand, looking indolent and perhaps a bit smug. He was too certain of himself for his own good and too certain of her. Perhaps he was used to women always following his lead. Her mother had always said a gentleman must never be too sure of himself when it came to a woman's attentions. A little dose of humility was a welcome quality in a man.

Pen decided to do something about that humility. '*You* will go first?' she teased. 'What happened to ladies first?' She lifted the jug to her lips and took a swallow before passing it back, wiping her mouth on the back of her hand. How many governesses would cringe if they could see her now? '*I* will start, thank you.' She cleared her throat in mock authority. 'Question one: Why did you notice me at the fair?'

Chapter Five

Matthew laughed at her audacity, a low rumbling sound that shot through her with a bolt of warmth, like his lips on her knuckles. 'You're just going to start with the hard stuff, aren't you, Em? No easing into it with the usual "what's your favourite colour?" or "what do you like to eat"?'

'No, absolutely not.' Pen shrugged, boldly unapologetic. Between the ale and the fire, she was losing her nervousness. Surely, if he'd wanted something from her, he would have taken it last night and forgone the trouble of a second meeting. 'Answer the question, Matthew. You're stalling.'

'All right.' His smile melted her and her boldness was in jeopardy. She'd poked the sleeping bear and now he was going to make her pay. His eyes lingered on her, amber pools, rich and deep, inviting her to drown in him, with him, for him. 'I liked how you moved. Even beneath that cloak there was grace and I liked how you looked at the goods. You had a reverent appreciation for them. I thought to myself, "There's a woman who knows how to enjoy herself, a woman who takes nothing for granted."' His words were as bold as his gaze, searing her with a heat that had nothing to do with the fire and everything to do with the man stretched out beside her. Good lord, she must be as red as one of Wadesbridge's roses.

He smiled, proof enough that she was flushed. 'You asked, Em. Now, it's my turn.' His grin widened and she held her breath. She'd been too daring with her question. He would make her pay. She'd have to be on her guard, careful not to give anything away that might alert him to who she was, or what she was. 'What was your favourite part of the evening?'

She let out her breath with a relieved sigh. There was nothing to fear there. She could answer simply and honestly. 'Watching the glass-blower. My turn. What is—?'

'No, wait. That's not fair,' Matthew broke in with laughing chagrin. 'You have to say more than that. I gave you details.'

'That was your choice. The rule was to tell the truth, not to offer details—that was entirely optional.' It was an option she could have exercised as well. She could have said she'd liked his hand at her waist as they'd watched the demonstration, that she'd liked feeling the heat and power of his body behind her, that it had made her feel safe despite not knowing him. But to say those things exposed her too thoroughly. Wasn't she exposed enough as it was? Perhaps he'd only said those things to trick her into reciprocating.

His amber eyes narrowed in speculation as he gave the issue feigned consideration of the most serious sort. 'Well, perhaps I must concede the point. *This time.*' The glint in his eyes said she wouldn't win that argument twice. He was on to her. She'd have to tread cautiously.

'In return, I'll take it easy on you, for now. I'll ask you something basic. What's your favourite colour?'

'Maybe I won't take it easy on *you*, Em, with my answer.' His reply was low, private, just for her. She loved the way it caressed her name. *Em.* But that wasn't really her name any more than Matthew was his. She couldn't lose sight of that. They might be telling each other bold things beside the fire, but they were still strangers. 'My favourite colour is sea green, the colour of the ocean on a sunny day, the colour of your eyes when they caught the glass-blower's flame, the colour of your eyes right now as you ponder whether or not my answer is flattery or truth.' He was definitely not taking it easy on her. Each answer he gave was a verbal seduction that went far beyond flirtatious banter. A lady shouldn't allow a man to talk like that. But she wasn't a lady, not here. Lady Penrose Prideaux was three miles away in the castle, lying down with a lavender cloth. Only Em was here and Em wasn't a lady. Em was just... Em. Em could allow the indiscretion, although she ought to protest just a bit to keep him honest.

'You shouldn't say such things.' She reached for the ale jug and took another swallow. She might start to believe them, that she was beautiful, enticing, that she could intrigue a man such as Matthew, a man who could have any woman he wanted on charm alone. The words would be easy to believe. She had nothing to compare them with.

'Why shouldn't I if they're true? You're a beautiful woman.' His hand reached out to stroke her cheek and she felt the game spiral out of her control, the conversation becoming one intimacy upon another: the fire, the floor picnic, the long stretch of his body alongside the hearth, the truth game. Even the rain outside had contributed to the cosy familiarity of their grey-skied afternoon.

'My question. If you could only travel to one other place in the world, where would you go, Em?'

She finished her pasty, thinking hard. When she had her answer she licked her fingers. No doubt somewhere in England another governess fainted. 'Venice.'

'Why?'

'That's two questions, sir,' she scolded, but there was no heat in it. 'I am willing to allow you this one transgression.' In truth, she might allow him more than one. Somehow during their questions, they'd moved closer together, their voices choosing to be low and private although nothing required it of them, their questions and answers becoming serious. 'I choose Venice because that is where the world still meets, where east comes together with west. I can find the silks of the Orient there, the spices of the Middle East, and the magic of Venice itself, a whole city built on a lagoon, with canals instead of roads. The best of the world is there.'

'Venice is past her zenith, an ageing queen,' Cassian probed. 'Perhaps you would be disappointed? It stinks in the summer.'

She shook her hair forward over one shoulder and began to comb through it with her fingers. 'No, Venice is like me. I, too, am an ageing queen. Girls younger than me are married, have children, while I am tucked away at home, waiting and waiting and nothing comes.'

'Waiting for what? What do you think will come?' His question was a whisper barely audible above the crack of the fire.

'For adventure, for life to start again or perhaps for the first time. My father is a man full of fear. He fears for me, he wants to keep me safe, but it has turned my home into a prison.' How freeing it was to talk to him, to tell him things she'd shared with no one, not even Phin, out of fear of making her father look bad to others. Perhaps sometimes it was easier to trust a stranger with one's secrets. Matthew didn't know Lady Penrose Prideaux, didn't know the father of whom she spoke, or the legacy of fear she referred to.

Matthew gave her a lazy smile. 'You didn't tell me the whole truth earlier, Em.'

'I told you I came here today to conquer fear, so that I would not be ruled by it,' she protested.

'Like your father? Yes. But you didn't tell me about the adventure part.' His eyes were on her mouth again. 'Am I your adventure? Remember, you must answer truthfully.'

She licked her lips, unsure how to answer. To say yes might be to objectify him. He might feel used. To say no would be a lie. 'I've never met anyone like you who has seen the world I want to see. You are my adventure in the very best of ways.'

'And you are mine.' He reached for her, drawing her down alongside of him, their bodies stretched out before the fire. 'In the very best of ways,' he echoed.

Her breath caught at the nearness of him, the sheer size of him. Matthew was a big man, built like a hero; broad through the shoulders, strong in the chest. Achilles or Odysseus, she thought, straight from the stanzas of the *Iliad*. This was not proper, to lie with a man before the fire, to see his every thought flicker in his eyes, to let him rest his hand at her hip, his thumb massaging low on her abdomen. It was not proper to resent the layers of clothing that kept them separated. But this had never been about being proper. If it had been, she'd never have come at all.

'Have you ever been kissed, Em?' His eyes were on her, intent on her answer. 'Remember, only the truth.' At his words, the game and its remaining questions were forgotten entirely. There was a new game to play.

Her answer was a mere whisper. 'No.' Who would dare to kiss Lady Penrose Prideaux, cloistered daughter of the Earl of Redruth? But here in this cottage, Em was a woman who belonged to no one but herself, who ate meat pasties with handsome men at fairs, who admired Venetian glass-blowers and met with strange men in abandoned cottages to play games of revelation.

'Would you like to be?' came the question, the dare. It would be easy to close the remaining distance, to part her lips, to issue the invitation he was asking for without a word. But he'd want the words. He would want to hear her consent. 'Would you, Em?'

She brought her hand up to stroke the stubble of his cheek, her own voice pitched low and throaty. 'You are terrible with rules. It's *my* turn to ask the question.'

His eyes darkened, guessing her game. 'Then, ask, Em.'

'Will you kiss me?'

A smile shimmered across his face. 'Absolutely. It would be my privilege.' A tilt of her head, a parting of her lips, and his mouth was there on hers, inviting her to join him in tasting one another. She gave him her mouth, all of it, savouring the remnants of sweet ale on his lips, the tease of his tongue as he explored her depths, the press of his hand cradling her jaw, the deepening of the kiss a reminder of their afternoon, an afternoon filled with simple pleasures, meat pies and conversations, and she didn't want it to end. A purr of desire purled up from her throat as she arched into him, her body wanting more of his touch, of him. She'd never been so warm, so hungry for another's touch. He would burn her and she would flame for him gladly.

She did flame for him, for a while, one kiss leading to another kiss and another as their mouths and hands explored one another. She could have lain there all afternoon, revelling in those kisses, those touches. She would have burned for him if he'd asked, but he did not. Instead, he separated from her, breaking the kisses, the touches, his own eyes dark.

A wave of desperation welled in her. She did not want the kiss to end. If she did not take her chance now, when? His hand brushed her cheek, pushing a loose strand of hair behind her ear. 'It grows late. We don't need to rush. We have tomorrow and the day after that and the day after that. We have as long as we need,' Matthew whispered his promise and helped her up from the floor, but his gaze said he was as reluctant as she to end the afternoon.

He gathered up her dry cloak and draped it over her shoulders, his hands lingering in his familiar gesture. 'Will you allow me to give you a ride home? I have my horse out back.'

She turned beneath his touch, called to action with sudden urgency at the risk of exposure. As tempting as it was, it was the one thing she could not allow. 'No. Please, Matthew, I must insist on this discretion. You cannot follow me home, not even the briefest of distances.' If anyone recognised her with him, word would reach her father before she even made it home and there would never be another afternoon like this. 'Please, kiss me goodbye here.' And maybe by the time she was home she'd have her wits back.

Chapter Six

He was going to need a new strategy to outwit Redruth and get the earl's attention. The bliss of the afternoon had given him a break from the situation with Redruth, but now it was time to get back to business. All the standard methods of persuasion had failed with the earl. Cassian drained his tankard and called for more as a tavern wench sashayed by with a swing of lush hips and a saucy smile. 'Another for my friend as well.' Cassian winked at Inigo seated across from him at the table. 'We have much to discuss, we've got to keep our throats wet.'

'You're in a good mood despite the setback today.' Inigo eyed him with his usual scepticism. 'You weren't this pleasant when you rode out this afternoon. Your mood was downright foul, if I recall. To what do we owe this change of disposition?'

'Fresh air.' Cassian shrugged non-committally, wanting to keep Em and his secret rendezvous to himself a little while longer. The afternoon had carried

a quiet eroticism in its simplicity—two people talking, two strangers moving from the unknown to the
known through conversation before a fire. That conversation had led to a kiss and that kiss to more kisses.
Cassian didn't kid himself that the setting alone had
been the chief contributor to the direction the afternoon
had taken. Not just any woman, not just any rainy day
would have kept him floating on air hours later. He was
too experienced for that. It was *she*, the mysterious Em,
who was responsible for his mood. He'd wrapped himself in the memory of her when he'd left the cottage: her
mouth, her touch, her voice when she'd whispered her
dreams: *'I want to go to Venice. I want adventure.'* He
would see her again tomorrow. He could hardly wait.
It had been a long time since he could hardly wait to
see a woman.

'All right, keep your secrets.' Inigo laughed. 'I can
see you're not going to tell me about it.' The serving girl came back with the ales and another round of
smiles that turned to a pout when Cassian didn't recip-
rocate. Cassian slid her extra coins for her disappointment and sent her away. Ales settled, they could return
to their discussion without interruption.

'I've tried letters of enquiry, I've tried raising my
offer, I've tried outlining all the benefits. None of it
has worked. He insists the land remain in the family even though it is unentailed. It was bought by his
grandfather and hasn't been used for anything since
his grandfather passed.' Cassian threw up his hands.
'I can't decide what upsets me more: that the earl is

intractable or that the land is just sitting there rotting for no reason.'

'Well, not really "no reason",' Inigo, always the voice of logic, put in slowly as if he knew the words would be upsetting. 'It's part of his daughter's dowry. Perhaps he cannot simply give it away without damaging her prospects.' Inigo knew money intimately. He made money, invested money, for himself and for others. Better than anyone, Inigo understood people's often intense, irrational attachment to things. Hadn't Inigo called him out on those very grounds yesterday?

Cassian rolled his eyes. 'Her prospects would be improved twofold if the money received for the sale was put back into the dowry. The company has offered twice what the land's worth.'

'Money can be frittered away, it can disappear before you know it, even a substantial sum like that. Perhaps her father feels that land will last where money will not. He's not wrong,' Inigo put in, playing the devil's advocate.

Cassian nodded, willing to concede the point. 'Perhaps. But that doesn't solve my problem. How do I convince him to sell me the land? He did not care for my plans at all. In fact, I think being open about what I wanted to do with the land hurt my case more than helped it.' Cassian took a swallow of ale and recounted the unpleasant letter, enumerating Redruth's complaints. 'He sees my plans as wholesale corruption, not progress,' Cassian concluded. The thought of not acquiring the land ate at him daily. What would he do if he couldn't break through to the earl?

'He doesn't want to lose control of the land,' Inigo ventured. 'That's what's at the heart of this. Have you thought of leasing the land from him? Perhaps a ninety-nine-year lease like they do with property in London? The land would still be his technically, but you would own any development that occurs on it. The land would be yours for three generations. Your grandsons could tussle it out with his great-grandsons after you're long gone.' Inigo laughed.

'And if he refuses?' Cassian queried, not entirely hopeful.

Inigo arched eyebrow. 'Plan B. I thought we settled that yesterday. You can always marry for it. It would be less of a tussle in three generations if it was all in the family.'

Cassian shook his head. 'I've already thought of that and, no, I just couldn't.' Especially not after this afternoon. He did not want to sell himself, not when there was such honest pleasure to be had with a woman he chose of his own accord.

Inigo leaned across the table and lowered his voice. 'Will you listen before you dismiss the idea out of hand? Consider all the pieces aligning at just this moment before you discard the option.'

'Are you a fortune teller now?' Cassian retorted sharply.

'Do you want to hear the rest of my news or not?' Inigo was undaunted. They'd been friends too long for him to be put off easily. It was what made them such good business partners as well. 'In fact, marrying for the land could be the piece of serendipity you're looking for. I did some more digging today after you left. The earl might not be open to selling the land, but he is open to marrying off his daughter, which could be the reason he isn't keen at this moment to separate the land from the dowry.' Inigo threw a quick glance around the taproom to be sure no one was listening in. 'He's been bringing suitors to Castle Byerd. It's all very hushed up. But Lord Wadesbridge was invited to tea yesterday.'

'Wadesbridge is too old,' Cassian shot back, but he didn't miss the smug gleam in Inigo's eyes.

'Perhaps that's what the daughter thought too. Perhaps that's why there's a dinner party tonight at Castle Byerd with some of the area's finest *young* gentlemen in attendance.' He smiled, pleased with himself, much to Cassian's chagrin. Cassian hated when Inigo might have a point.

'And we weren't invited? Who is finer than ourselves, if we're being blunt? It makes no sense that we're cooling our heels at the Red Dragon while young men of lesser standing are dining at Byerd.' Cassian played the devil's advocate.

Inigo chuckled. 'Actually, it makes perfect sense. I've made no bones about the fact that I've no intentions to marry in the near future and, if Redruth wants Vennor Penlerick for his daughter, the earl will have to go to London to get him, which would require Redruth doing the very things he hates the most: socialising and entertaining. If he wants a duke for her, you're the only real candidate out of the three of us who remains unwed. But it's too soon to go after you. If you'd shown up tonight, you would have intimidated the field. If he wants you, he'll want to draw your attention, make you inquisitive enough to want to meet the girl everyone else is meeting. Men are often attracted to something they have to compete for. It's simple supply and demand.' Inigo looked pleased with his analysis, and Cassian had to admit his friend was probably right. It did not, however, make the prospect more appealing.

'Perhaps I should just let all those swains have her.' Which suited Cassian just fine. He didn't want to marry for an alliance.

Inigo shrugged. 'That's up to you. All I am saying is that the window of opportunity is open at present. Redruth is eager to marry her off *this* Season,' Inigo pressed. 'If you're going to build that amusement garden here, you need that land now. Time is of the essence for the both of you. Marriage might be the way to convince him. He might not like your plans once he knows you and the land company are one and the same, but he will like your title. *That* hasn't been on the table in your negotiations. It could change everything and it would keep his land in the family where he feels as though he can assert *some* control. I'd wager in a few years' time, when he sees that his perceived harms haven't come to fruition and that you're making money hand over fist *for him*, he'll forget he ever disliked the idea. He'll think his son-in-law is a genius.'

Cassian shook his head, thinking of a caramel-haired minx kissing him beside the gamekeeper's fire with her hungry mouth, and her love of adventure. 'You make it sound so easy. I should simply walk in and trade my title for his daughter's dowry and break ground after my honeymoon.' It would give him everything he wanted.

'It can be that easy,' Inigo replied evenly. 'Other men do it all the time.'

'*Other* men.' Cassian threw the words back at him. 'Since when have we ever aspired to be like other men?' That was the flaw in Inigo's analysis. 'We're the Cornish Dukes, four fathers and four sons sworn to living by a higher code in life and in love,' Cassian reminded him. 'Or have you so quickly forgotten the legacy of Richard Penlerick?'

He'd gone too far there. Inigo's blue eyes sparked and narrowed. 'We all loved Richard, me no less than any of us,' Inigo snapped. 'Of course I haven't forgotten. I have not forgotten how he encouraged Eaton's pursuit of a conservatory or how he supported your endeavour to raise up the economy. Perhaps he would consider an alliance with Redruth a worthy investment for the goal.'

'A marriage without love?' Cassian spat the words with disgust. He was too raw from his afternoon with Em. Discussing the idea of courting another for monetary gain so soon after coming from Em's arms seemed a betrayal of their game in the cottage.

'Perhaps it's all in how you view it. Maybe you've been looking at it wrong? Why should we view the event of a wedding as the apex of love? Is everything else downhill from there? Why not view the wedding as the beginning of the journey *to* love? You have the next fifty years to fall in love with your bride,' Inigo counselled.

'Says the man who doesn't intend to wed any time soon.' Cassian gave an exaggerated sniff. 'Methinks I smell a little hypocrisy in the air.' He gave his friend a half-smile. 'You would have a hard time selling that rationale to Cador and Rosenwyn, or to Eaton and Eliza, or to any of our parents.'

'That doesn't make it untrue.' Inigo grinned, enjoying their debate too much. 'Now, tell me your secret. Who is she?'

'What makes you think a woman is involved?' Cassian felt a sudden wave of protectiveness with regards to Em.

'What other reason would you have to be so irritated over marriage and the principles of love?' Inigo was enjoying this too much. His friend called for another round. 'This one's on me. Tell me everything. How did you meet? How long has this been going on?' At Inigo's grin the tension that had underlaid the heat of their discussion eased. They'd been friends since boyhood, friends for too long to let disagreement sour the evening. They'd disagreed before and they likely would again, but they would still and always be friends.

'I met her at the St Piran's Day fair. We walked, we talked, I met her again today and we spent the afternoon together. She's incredible; she's beautiful, and witty, and she has a voice like smoke, low and throaty. I am meeting her again tomorrow.'

'Does she know who you are?' Inigo's scepticism was in full evidence, and Cassian knew where that line of questioning led. Inigo feared she was a fortune hunter. It was a well-meant sort of protection after Collin's ill-fated romance. But tonight, such caution was unnecessary.

'That's the best part…' Cassian leaned in '…I've taken precautions. We made up names for each other. She doesn't know I'm a viscount, heir to a dukedom. She is simply Em to me and I am Matthew to her. We can be ourselves.' Surely Inigo would understand why the principle of love mattered so greatly. 'Now you see why I can't simply storm Castle Byerd and carry off Redruth's daughter.'

'No, I don't see. You're not simply being yourself. You're being someone you made up.'

'It's not like that. We are still ourselves. *I* am myself, perhaps as I can never be with a society miss. We can talk and laugh and tell stories and share our dreams. Only the names are false, everything else is true,' Cassian tried to explain, but even as the words came the argument rang hollow.

'That's all well and good as far as it goes. But how far *does* it go?' Inigo asked. 'You can't possibly think anything comes of it. There can't be marriage. Even if the pleasure garden wasn't an issue, there couldn't be marriage.'

'Do you think I don't know that? Do you think I'm some green boy who falls in love with the first woman he lays down with?' Cassian snapped with more heat than he intended, perhaps because he knew Inigo was right, perhaps because those were the very thoughts he'd had today and had pushed away. He wanted to think only about today and tomorrow. If he thought beyond the day, beyond the immediate, he'd have to think about losing Em. He wasn't ready to think about that. He'd have to eventually, though.

'No, I don't think that. But I do see my friend perhaps hesitating on the brink of success and I have to wonder why. I have to wonder if this peasant girl isn't a distraction, a convenient foil that excuses him from not moving forward.' Inigo's voice was a low hiss. 'If today showed you anything it was that you are down to two choices. Marry the earl's daughter or build the park in Truro instead.' He paused. 'Or don't build it at all.'

'The last is not an option,' Cassian shot back. 'I know what my choices are, I don't need you to spell them out. I know the cottage affair can't last. But it's not May yet. I have until the Season starts to make up my mind.'

Inigo nodded. 'Fair enough.' A truce had been reached. Cassian knew his duty not only to his family, but to himself and to his brother and he would do it when the time came. But May seemed ages away from the cold March weather. There was always the possibility that Redruth might relent before then.

Inigo pushed back from the table. 'I think I'll call it a night. I have to be at Wheal Karrek early tomorrow to meet with the mine's shareholders to discuss Eliza's latest plans.'

Cassian rose with him, taking the change in conversation as an olive branch. He didn't want to part with his friend on poor terms. 'Eliza is keeping you busy. I thought she'd be back to the mines full time by now.'

She'd asked for Inigo's help with the mines six months ago when she'd wed Eaton and become Lady Lynford. It was supposed to have been a temporary arrangement.

Inigo laughed and shook his head. 'Her new mine schools and her new marriage are taking up more time than she anticipated. I've never seen Eaton happier and she positively glows. Her daughter, Sophie, is at Kitto's conservatory now as a day student. I heard her play the other day. She's very talented. Cador Kitto positively drools over her.'

The conversation carried them out into the crisp night air. They talked of the upcoming spring recital in April and Cador's impending fatherhood at the end of the month. Cassian clapped Inigo on the shoulder. 'Thank you for coming out with me tonight. Whether or not I agree with you, I appreciate your advice. As always, it is insightful, old friend.'

Inigo nodded. 'And as always, I am happy to give it. I don't envy you your dilemma. Just remember to think with your head.'

Cassian watched Inigo disappear into the dark before getting his horse and setting out for The Elms. Overhead the stars were bright white points of light in a black sky. At a fork in the road, the left steered towards home, but the right steered towards Castle Byerd and the little dinner party to which he'd not been invited. For several moments he played with the idea of just turning up, but it would accomplish nothing other than to risk further alienating Redruth. Cassian turned his horse towards home. Storming the castle would have to wait for another day. His heart wasn't in it. If his heart was anywhere, it was on the cliffs at the gamekeeper's cottage with Em.

The moment Pen returned to Castle Byerd, she wanted to be back in the cottage. Byerd was abuzz with more activity than it had seen in years. 'For the dinner party, my lady,' one maid said, rushing by with an urn of flowers. The dinner party? This was the first she'd heard of it.

Pen followed the maid into the dining room, a large, formal affair of a chamber that was seldom used. Today, the walnut doors were thrown open, polished silver and china marched the length of the pristine white linen on the table, urns of flowers decorated the sideboards in early spring splendour. The room wasn't being prepared. It was *ready*. For whom, for what? She hadn't done any menus. She counted the chairs. Dinner for fourteen? Pen began to panic. Had she forgotten? Was Cook, even now, wondering what she was supposed to prepare for the guests? Pen furrowed her brow, trying to remember. Had she even seen a guest list?

'There you are!' Her maid, Margery, hurried in. 'Thank goodness you're here. Where have you been? Never mind. It doesn't matter now. A new dress arrived for you and I've already drawn your bath. With luck, it will still be hot. You needn't worry, there's still time to get you ready.' Ready, like the dining room clothed in its best.

'Ready for what?' Pen whispered in half-horror. They never entertained. Yesterday it had been tea with

Wadesbridge and now a dinner party. It was as if the castle gates had been flung wide and the world let in.

'For you, my lady.' Margery took her by the arm, leading her to the stairs, her voice low. 'Your father has guests for dinner. All of them with sons.'

Chapter Seven

*A*ll of them with sons. Her father was throwing a dinner party and she was the main course, a beautifully
dressed lamb led to the slaughter with her hair a high
pile of curls atop her head and the rest of her turned
out in a gown of shot Parma silk whose iridescence
created the impression of being simultaneously equal
parts violet and blue. Pen fingered the pearls at her
throat anxiously as Margery dabbed the smallest bit
of rose-pink salve on her lips. 'There! You look a treat,
miss. No one would ever guess you were out tramping
the countryside all afternoon.'

No, no one would guess that she'd spent the afternoon sitting beside a fire, eating meat pies with a man
whose name she didn't know, playing a flirtatious game
of questions. Unconsciously, Pen's fingers drifted from
her pearls to her lips. The elegant woman in the mirror
didn't look at all like Em, like the woman who'd kissed
Matthew in the cottage with her mouth, her tongue, her
teeth, her body pressed to his begging for more than a

kiss. She would give anything to be back in the cottage now, wrapped in Matthew's arms, a simple dinner on the scarred table. It was a far preferable scenario than facing the glittering formality awaiting her downstairs.

'Careful, miss, or you'll smudge the lip salve.' Margery slid her a sly look. 'We're lucky the fashion is for a more natural complexion these days. No one thinks twice about a lady with a little fresh wind on her cheeks.' Margery pursed her lips when Pen said nothing. 'Whoever he is, miss, your secret is safe with me whether you tell me or not. We've been through a lot since I've been your maid. It's a little late to start with secrets now when you come home with them written all over your face.'

'Was it that obvious?' Pen looked away from the mirror, seeking reassurance from Margery in a moment of panic.

Margery gave her a knowing smile. 'A smart woman knows the signs, miss. Puffed lips, a faraway look in the eyes. You were grinning from ear to ear. I'd never seen you look so happy, or so confused. It was as if you'd fallen from the sky and crashed into reality.' She had. It was exactly how she'd felt. One moment she'd been in paradise and the next in a hell.

There was a soft knock at the door followed by her brother's voice. 'Pen, are you ready? It's time to go down.' The door opened and Phin stepped inside dressed in evening clothes, his walnut hair brushed back from his handsome face with its blue eyes and kind smile. He let out a sound of approval. 'You look stunning. All of Father's preparations will go to waste.

I doubt anyone will notice the china and the silver and the food once they see you. The gentlemen won't be able to take their eyes off of you.'

'Perhaps I should change, then, put on something less attractive.' Pen's anxiety rose anew. She didn't want to be the centre of anyone's attentions except Matthew's. Especially when the attentions of those downstairs were driven by avarice. Given that she hadn't met any of the gentlemen here before tonight, it was safe to assume they were here for her dowry—she merely went along with it, a physical embodiment of her father's land and money.

Phin took her hand, misunderstanding the source of her anxiety. 'I know you haven't been out among society much, but you'll be fine. You know your manners and you have good conversation. You've hosted a few of Father's guests—this will be just like that, only there will be more of them. Everyone knows you've been in seclusion.'

He meant it kindly. Phin always met things kindly, but the words rankled and she bristled at the insinuation. 'I am not a wilting wallflower. Seclusion has been Father's choice, not mine. If it were up to me—'

'Yes,' Phin broke in with a laugh. 'I know. If it were up to you, you would have come with me on a Grand Tour of your own. Whatever those gentlemen downstairs think, I dare say they will be pleasantly surprised by you...' he chucked her gently under the chin '...and you, Pen, might be pleasantly surprised by one of them if you allowed it. Hmm?' he said encouragingly with a gentle scold. 'You and Father are the two

most stubborn people I know. Make sure you are resisting his efforts for the right reasons. You are young
and untried. You know nothing of men. Why not allow
yourself to be guided by those who do? You can't think
Father would marry you to someone who would be
cruel, who wouldn't appreciate you as you ought to
be appreciated?'

He ushered her out of the room and into the hallway.
'Most of the gentlemen are friends of mine.' Phin was
still offering reassurances, but Pen felt as if she were
walking to her execution. 'Father thought you needed
to meet young men closer to your own age. He said
you felt Wadesbridge was too old.'

That sealed it. She was condemned by her own
words. The argument for younger men had been *her*
argument and now her father had answered it by serving up a room full of them.

'You're not helping, Phin,' she chided him as they
made their way to the curving sweep of the main staircase. Already she could hear muted conversation in the
drawing room. 'I want to choose more than my mate
when the time comes. I want to choose my own destiny.
Father seems to think marriage is the only destiny for
me and I disagree. There are too many places on the
map to see.' Matthew had not baulked at such a sentiment at the fair. He'd done the opposite. He'd encouraged it with stories of his own travels. Her hand went
to her throat, forgetting that she wore pearls tonight,
that her blown-glass heart was tucked away upstairs.

At the entrance to the drawing room, Pen paused,
taking a deep breath and settling her nerves. She was

not afraid to meet these men, she was only afraid of what meeting them represented. Her father had taken her request for younger men to heart, which meant only one thing: after two years of rather sporadic match-making efforts, her father was in earnest to see her wed. At her ear, Phin whispered final words of encour-agement. 'Don't worry, Pen, I'll be right beside you.'

Phin was as good as his promise. He stayed next to her, escorting her from group to group, making intro-ductions and ensuring that she needn't stay with any one group too long. She was a blue-violet butterfly in a room of neutral colours, flitting from one cluster to another as she tried to keep the names straight. When dinner was announced, she was taken in by Nigel Har-rington, heir to the Baron Lynton who seemed to know everything there was to know about goats and cheese, and nearly everything there was to know about fishing.

'But if you want real fishing, nothing beats salmon from Bodmin Moor,' an arrogant blond put in from across the table. He'd been trying hard to catch her eye all night and now she was forced to give it. 'The River Camel is cold, it makes for more fat on the fish, better taste,' the blond counselled. The footmen came and took away the dishes, replacing them with the next course. The conversation continued as the men de-bated the best rivers, and then moved on to debate the best fish—salmon or trout—with an enthusiasm that stunned her. Surely, they didn't think such a display *impressed* her?

Pen set down her wine glass and took advantage of a brief break in the discussion. 'If only men devoted such passion to the fate of the poor as they devote to their fishing, we might right a many great injustices in this world.' She smiled broadly, hoping to engage the support of the women at the table. Some of the young men, those who lived nearby, had come with their parents.

'That's why they have us, my dear,' Nigel Harrington's mother spoke up. 'Charity begins at home and the home is the woman's domain.'

'Hear, hear!' the arrogant blond's father toasted and the conversation moved back to trout and salmon. She was relieved when the table turned so she could speak to the gentleman on her other side, a Mr Abel Cunforth, but her relief was short-lived on that front. All he wanted to talk about was himself. At least after the first question, she didn't need to worry about carrying the conversation. In that regard he was as easy to talk to as every other man here was. One simply had to initiate and then the gentlemen picked up the conversation and ran with it. Was this their idea of getting to know her? Or of her getting to know them, not their bank accounts?

Pen smiled and nodded. She made the right noises in the right places. Didn't a single man in this room understand that small talk was more than rolling out one's pedigree and accomplishments? That small talk was about establishing a sense of ease? How did one *feel* when they conversed with someone else? It was about rhythm, about the give and take of the conversation. There was none of that here, only Mr Cunforth giving and giving facts about himself and her on the receiving end trying to be interested. Not a man in this room knew better. But Matthew had. At the fair and again today, they'd had real conversations.

It wasn't just the kisses she was looking forward to tomorrow, but the continuation of their talks. What would they discuss tomorrow? What might he ask her? What would she tell him? And the reverse as well. What would she learn about him? Talking with Matthew was like peeling back the petals of a rosebud until it was in full bloom. Talking with Abel Cunforth, to the arrogant blond or Mr Nigel Harrington was nothing like that.

What would Matthew think if he saw her in this room, dressed in silk, surrounded by these buffoons? What would he think if he knew she was supposed to marry one of them? Pen took another swallow of wine. He would think she was above his touch. He would think he had no right to her. Would he feel betrayed? He thought Em was a woman who could choose whom she spent her time with, perhaps the daughter of an artisan or a farmer, a woman who could welcome the attentions of a small, landowning squire. He did not imagine himself the subordinate in their relationship in regards to rank or standing, certainly not in experience. He could not find out differently. She liked that they were equals in the cottage. Yet, sitting here as Penrose Prideaux surrounded by suitors left her with a niggling sense of guilt that somehow she was misleading him. But she couldn't tell him or she'd lose him.

'I think the poorhouses do a great service,' Abel Cunforth was saying. 'They offer the poor two meals a day and give them employment to keep them off the streets. If anything, we need stricter laws and less hand-holding of the poor.'

'Have you been to a poor house, Mr Cunforth? Have you eaten the gruel that passes for food?' Pen broke into his political ramblings.

'Why, no, of course not.' Mr Cunforth gave her an odd look so compelling she began to wonder if she really had grown two heads.

'I think if people were paid a wage they could live on in exchange for their labours we might all benefit,' Pen offered. 'I hear London is expensive. I can't imagine earning a pittance *and* being expected to afford rent and food on it let alone clothes or medicines in a big city.'

'Then they shouldn't live there,' was Cunforth's answer.

'It's where the jobs are, sir,' Pen replied. 'How can they support themselves in the countryside when mines can no longer produce and land is being enclosed? What work is there for them? It is my opinion that Parliament is driving the poor to the cities like a herd of sheep.' A footman reached for her wine glass and turned away to refill it.

'Your opinion, eh?' Cunforth was salty. She'd upset him with her thoughts. He wiped his mouth with his napkin. 'Well, perhaps that's precisely why we don't allow women to vote. You'd all be tucking the poor in with beef stew every night if you had your way.'

As the footman made to return her newly filled glass Pen made a deliberately careless gesture with her hand and a fine white French wine drenched the thigh of Cunforth's dark evening breeches. 'Oh, I am so clumsy!' Pen exclaimed, making no move to offer a napkin. She tossed Cunforth a coy smile. 'Perhaps it *is* a good thing I don't vote. We can't have women spilling all of your male privileges to the masses. Looks like you might be the one tucking in early tonight.'

Across the table, Phin shot her a look and mouthed the words 'play nice'. But Pen didn't care. Anyone who set themselves above another simply because they'd had the luck to be born into wealth wasn't worth her consideration.

As soon as the last plate was cleared, Pen wasted no time rising and taking the women to the drawing room so the men could buttonhole the port around the table and congratulate themselves on having impressed her, no doubt certain that she'd been mesmerised by their ability to debate salmon and trout and insult the poor.

This would be her life if she didn't put a stop to it. For two years now, she'd been ignoring the reality, hoping that somehow things would simply change. But if there was going to be any change, it would have to come from her. If she didn't stand up and fight for what she wanted, no one else would. Pen surreptitiously fingered her lips and thought of Matthew. Now there was a man who knew how to treat a woman. She was hungry to be back in the cottage with him. Tomorrow couldn't come soon enough.

Chapter Eight

Pen arrived at the cottage first this time, breathless from a hard walk fuelled by rising distress as much as it was the anticipation of seeing Matthew again. Breakfast that morning had been a disaster with her father asking which of the fine *young* men she preferred and ended with him suggesting another round of dinner parties when she said none of them seemed to suit, or did she want to revisit the merits of an older, more stable gentleman like Wadesbridge? A visit could be arranged to see Trescowe in April. He would send a note.

Pen had barely kept her temper on a leash. She didn't want any of them. That had been the crux of their disagreement this morning. She saw clearly now it wasn't that her father didn't understand her argument. It was that he didn't accept it. He felt she should be guided by *his* choice. Would she never be free except in these clandestine moments? It made the prospect of seeing Matthew, a man of *her* choosing, all the sweeter even as it reaffirmed for her what she'd realised last night:

she had to stand up for herself. She could no longer be a neutral party in her fate.

Pen unpacked the basket she'd brought and spread an old checked cloth on the scarred table. She reasoned it was her turn to provide the picnic since Matthew had provided it twice now; at the fair and yesterday. The cloth was faded and the edges were showing early signs of fraying, but it suited the rustic quality of the room. The cottage was no place for pristine white linen even if she could have brought such a thing without revealing herself. Em in her plain dress and cloak was not a woman who had spotless Irish linen. It was all part of the fantasy. Or *the deception*, her conscience prodded. Fantasy and deception were fast becoming different sides of the same coin. Pen preferred not to think about the discrepancy today. If this was a lie, then it was the most exciting, most pleasurable lie she'd ever known.

She laid out bread, cheese, half of a mince pie she'd found left over in the kitchens and a jug of cider purloined from the cellar. Pen smiled, stepping back to survey her handiwork. The table looked homey with its food and cloth. She rubbed her arms to stay warm and wished she knew how to start a fire, but that would have to wait until Matthew arrived. *If he arrived.* Perhaps he'd changed his mind or something more important had come up, or perhaps he'd realised how silly this was, how futile. Now she knew how Matthew had felt yesterday when she was late. The worry was another reminder that they owed each other nothing, not even loyalty.

His big stallion came into view and the knot in her

stomach untied itself. She waited for him in the doorway as he tethered his horse, tying it out of sight from the road. In her relief, it took all of her willpower not to run to him, not to throw herself and her troubles into his arms. He would not admire that. They didn't have that kind of relationship, or any kind of relationship. They were simply two strangers. It was all she could allow them to be.

'Em, how are you? You're early today.' He kissed her on the cheek, pleased to see her, and her anxiety melted. This close to him, she could smell the masculine scent of wind and the earthy odour of a wet Cornish spring on his hair. She breathed it in. There was strength in simply being with him, in having these moments no matter how fleeting, no matter how contrived.

They stepped inside, and he smiled when he saw the table set with her small meal. 'You've been busy.'

'It was my turn to bring the lunch.' His appreciation made butterflies flutter in her stomach, his compliment meaning so much more than the false flattery she'd heard last night at dinner.

'I'll light a fire. You look cold.' His first thoughts were of her, so unlike the gentlemen last night. He set to it with an envious dexterity, producing flint from the deep pocket of his greatcoat. She told herself she watched to remember so she could do it on her own next time, but in truth she would have watched anyway just see him move. He was all strength and grace, so much grace for a big man. The fire came to life beneath his hands, warming the room and adding to the domesticity of doing for one another. It was an intimacy she was unfamiliar with in a house full of servants.

'Are you hungry?' Pen sliced bread at the table, putting pieces alongside hunks of cheese on the tin plates she'd brought. This was all part of the fantasy today—playing house, playing at being a commoner, at living the simple life.

He took off his greatcoat and hung it from his chair. She let herself imagine he was her husband, home from work, perhaps, from the fields overseeing a harvest. 'Yes, I could eat.' He laughed. 'I assume you guessed that. As you've noted, I can always eat. This is quite a step up from yesterday. We're progressing. We have plates today, mugs, a tablecloth, a knife. This is fine living.' He glanced at the fire. 'It would be a shame to eat this excellent food cold. Shall I grill the bread and melt the cheese?' He took the plates to the fire and Pen watched as he arranged the bread with its cheese on top of the grate. Satisfied, he turned to her. 'Come sit, Em. I've had a deuced difficult day. Tell me something interesting to take my mind off it. What did you do last night after you left me?'

Pen took her seat by the fire, that little pinch of guilt she'd felt last evening pinching her a little harder. She could not tell him what she'd done. She hated that, but even more she hated the idea of lying to him, so she said instead, 'Perhaps it would be best if you talked about your difficulty? We might find a solution together.'

He pulled the bread from the fire and put it on a plate for her. 'Very well, my trouble goes like this.

There is something I want to purchase, but the gentleman who owns it is unwilling to sell it to me no matter what price I offer.'

Pen bit into her toasted bread and cheese with a murmur of delight. 'Mmm, this is ambrosia.' She swallowed and turned her attentions back to his problem. 'Do you know why this gentleman resists?'

'He doesn't agree with what I want the thing for.' Matthew poked at the fire. 'I've tried persuading him, showing him that my purpose is beneficial to so many, but he only sees the bad. Worst of all, I feel we've reached a point in the discussion where he simply won't listen any more.'

Pen nodded. She knew the feeling all too well. She'd felt that way this morning at breakfast. 'I know. Sometimes I think my father has stopped listening to me. It's as if he's already decided my fate and he's just going through the motions now to placate me.' The only thing that kept her from believing that in full was Phin, who quite often stood between her and her father when they were at loggerheads, as he'd done last night. When Phin had an opinion, her father listened.

'What do you do when that happens?' Matthew pulled his own bread out of the fire, crisp and golden.

She thought for a moment. 'I find an ally. Perhaps you need one, too, someone whom your stubborn gentleman *will* listen to. For me, it's my brother. Sometimes it's not the message that matters, but the messenger. Two people can say the same thing, but be heard differently. Is there someone this man could be persuaded by? Perhaps he has a son or a friend who also shares your wisdom, but to whom he might be more receptive?'

He seemed to mull the idea over as he ate. 'An ally is a good idea, I just don't think I have one.'

'Then we'll keep thinking of a solution. Surely, between the two of us, we can come up with something.' She stood, brushing her hands on her skirt. 'I'll bring over the pie and cider.'

'You needn't wait on me.' He half rose, setting aside his plate, but she stalled him with a hand to his chest and a smile.

'Sit. You're still eating. Let me. I want to.' She did want to. She liked serving him, talking to him, helping him. He treated her like a partner, someone he could confide in. She was no one's partner at home. At home, she was swaddled, protected, something precious to be hidden away. No one would think of burdening her with their troubles.

Cassian sat back down with a laugh. 'You're bossy.' But he liked that she was assertive and willing to stand up to him, willing to solve problems with him even if he couldn't make use of her suggestion. So many of the women he knew were sycophants more interested in his title and what came with him than in *him*.

She returned with a large slice of pie and something primal stirred within Cassian. A man could find happiness in a simple life: a one-room cottage, four pieces of furniture, one good woman to partner him in life. Who needed ballrooms and titles when one had that? It was a potent fantasy he was spinning and an impossible one. Hadn't his conversation with Inigo last night been about this very subject? The finite limitations of this *affaire*? Dukes and their heirs weren't entitled to simple lives. Their lives were complicated, their alliances complicated; it was all part of their duty, their sacrifice for the greater good.

Despite his vast resources, this woman, like his land, was beyond him; she was a virgin he couldn't marry, a virgin whom he could not take to bed out of personal honour. No matter how low her birth, he would not risk leaving her with a child. Even if he compromised her, he couldn't marry her. Yet he wanted her: her company, her time, her kisses.

'Tell me,' he said once she'd settled in her chair. 'What does your father not listen to you about?' There was something different about her today. Perhaps it was that she was starting to grow used to him, more confident about their companionship, or perhaps it was something else he couldn't put his finger on. Maybe it was that the conversation was different today. At the fair, the conversation had been a general trading of tales. Yesterday had been a flirty game of questions. But today, the discussion was far deeper. This was about real life, things they dealt with in the world beyond the cottage walls, things their real *selves* dealt with. The line between the reality and their fabricated identities was very slowly starting to blur.

She shook her head. 'I don't want to tell you,' she demurred, perhaps in proof of that blurring. To tell would be to bring the other world too close, but Cassian was persistent.

'Why not? I told you about my problem. You can trust me.'

'It's not that.' She rose and collected the empty plates, suddenly restless. 'If I tell you, you will think I am fishing for something, although I assure you I am not.' She paused and set the plates on the table. 'This time here with you is important to me. I don't have much time and I don't want to ruin this.'

'You think telling me will ruin us?' Cassian was doubly curious now and worried. People only used phrases like running out of time when circumstances were dire. A horrible thought came to him. 'Are you ill?' Did she need money for a doctor? For medicines? A bolt of panic shot through him. Was Em dying?

'No, I am not ill,' she quickly disabused him. 'Oh, dear, I've worried you. I think I have to tell you now,' she blurted out the words. 'My father wants me to marry.'

Cassian should have felt enormous relief. To an extent he did. The tension that had welled so quickly in him had evaporated when she said she was not ill, but it had also been quickly replaced at the mention of marriage. 'To someone particular? Does he have the man picked out?' he tried to ask casually. It shouldn't come as a surprise. She was of age to marry, more than old enough, and it was the natural course of events. Yet, he didn't like the thought of his Em, his first-kissed Em, pledged to another.

'No one, not yet. But he's pushing for it.'

Cassian understood why she'd held back. She didn't want him to think she was looking for a proposal. 'It's all right, Em. We don't owe each other anything, no commitments.' This explained her need for the false identity, for the need to return home alone for fear of discovery.

'That's just it,' she said, 'I didn't want you to think you did.'

'We are just Em and Matthew,' he assured her. 'Nothing more.' The thought was less satisfying than it had been earlier, though. Em and Matthew could be nothing to each other. That had always been the case, implicitly acknowledged, never spoken of. It allowed them to be free. But it was less pleasant to contemplate when explicitly addressed. Freedom had suddenly become finite. This would be the ideal time to tell her about London, how he needed to leave at the end of April, but that seemed far off when viewed from the seventh of March, especially when it might end sooner. There might be no need at all to bring it up. He would bring it up, though, he promised himself, if the day drew closer.

She returned to the fire, and he drew her to him, pulling her on to his lap. He smiled, trying to take the new, furtive edge off the afternoon. Only three days in and already the clock was ticking. 'What else is your father stubborn about?'

She wrapped her arms about his neck and settled into him with a warm smile. Perhaps she, too, was eager to chase away reality and return to the fantasy. 'Pets. When we were growing up I wanted a dog badly, but he absolutely refused. No dogs in the house, he'd say. But I was desperate for one. I thought a dog could be my friend. After my brother left for school, the house was lonely.' It was the second time she'd mentioned her brother with fondness; her ally, her playmate. Cassian's throat thickened at thought of Collin. They'd been allies and playmates once too.

'I had great images of how it would be—my dog would wander around beside me, romp outdoors with me, lay by my bed at night, a constant companion, just like in the stories.' There was such wistfulness in her tone, Cassian suddenly wanted to shower her with a litter of puppies. Eaton's dog, Baldor, a magnificent hound with a nose for truffles, had just sired a new batch born a few weeks ago. She would love them.

'Since you didn't have a pup, how did you entertain yourself?' He liked the feel of her on his lap, her body against his. It was easy to talk to her, to listen to her. She was interesting and she didn't even know it. She had no need to dissemble and no desire to do it.

'I played with maps. You go to faraway places, but I dream of them. Seeing them on a map helps make them real.' She wasn't as lowborn as he thought. Somewhere in his mind, a silent warning bell began to clang. A brother sent to school, access to maps, the ability to read, a father who wanted to arrange a marriage. These were not the acts of a peasant or an artisan. Yet she seemed to want for certain things. Her dress and cloak were the same each day and they were showing their wear. *And she's a virgin*, his conscience nudged. Might she be the daughter of gentry down on their luck?

If it wasn't out of respect for the game of Em and Matthew, and out of respect for her need for privacy, he could probably determine her identity if she were gentry. It was tempting to try. But that would end the game. She didn't want to be exposed any more than he did. It was for the best. Knowing the truth of their identities would complicate things, especially now. If her father was eager for her to marry, and if her family was truly down on their luck, he'd look like a plum from heaven if they knew who he was. These two false names of theirs was all that kept the fantasy in place, a fantasy they were both desperate for, some time out of time to hold back the world.

He whispered against her ear, breathing her in, all sweet honeysuckle and rose water, 'Let me tell you a secret. I had an awful night last night after I left you, full of disappointments, and all I could think of this morning was getting to you. If I could get to you, if I could get here, everything would be better.' He kissed her earlobe and heard her breath catch. 'I was right. Everything *is* better even if it's just for a short while.'

He moved to take her mouth and she gave it, fully, deeply, as she'd given it before, passionately for a woman who'd not been kissed until yesterday, until *him*. *She was all his.* What a heady thought that was. He was the only one who had kissed her, who had tasted her like this, who had held her like this. It was an idea darkened by the thought that to be the first meant he wouldn't be the last. In the end, he would lose her to a faceless suitor yet to be named, one who was already on the horizon.

Em's hand was soft on his face. 'Are all kisses like

this? Consuming? Burning?' she whispered against his mouth.

'No, definitely not.' London debutantes didn't kiss like this with their whole bodies and mistresses didn't kiss like this, with every honest feeling burning in their eyes.

'Perhaps we should start here next time.' They were talking between kisses and it was quite the loveliest conversation Cassian had ever had. Em's hip moved against him at his groin. There was no hiding his arousal, no protecting her from it. 'I do this to you?' Her eyes registered wonder and shock at the hardness she found there.

Of its own accord, her hand seemed to find its way to the space between them, seeking him. Cassian put a stop to it, delightful as the prospect might be. 'Careful, Em. I am no saint. It would be too easy to take what you're offering and worry about regrets later.'

'Maybe I don't want to be a saint either,' Em pressed.

'You should at least think about it first. Those are easy words in the heat of the moment,' Cassian cautioned. He shifted her from his lap in a pretence of stoking up the fire. He was going to need some relief and soon.

'Don't worry about the fire, I have to go. It's later than I thought.' Em was already at the table, packing up their lunch and sounding flustered. He'd hurt her feelings.

He went to her and wrapped his arms about her, pressing a kiss to her neck in reassurance. 'It's not that I don't want you. I do. I want you more than I've wanted any woman in a long while. But I know the cost and I would not make you pay it for something that can never be more than it is now, a fantasy, a moment of escape from our real lives and selves.' He kissed the length of her lovely neck. 'I can take you part way on my horse.' He was reluctant to let her go, to step outside the door and back into that reality.

'No, I can't allow that.' She turned in his arms, her face alight with the same worry as yesterday, asking for the same promise as yesterday. 'Promise me you won't follow.'

'I promise. I won't follow you.' He thought he understood her fear better today. 'But you have nothing to fear from me, Em.' He whispered his wish. 'What would you say if I said I wanted to know the real you, Em?'

'I would say you already do.' She wrapped her arms about his neck, her hips pressed against him once more. 'Everything I've told you is the truth.'

'Except your name.' The one thing he wanted to know most. But he could not give his return.

'I didn't tell you my name. You gave me one,' she corrected. 'We have truth between us, Matthew, let that be enough.' Enough to bind them together? Enough to bring her back for as long as they could both stand it before inevitability tore them a part?

He nuzzled her neck. 'Can you come in two days?' He had business that required him in Bodmin. There was some disappointment in knowing he couldn't come tomorrow. It would be an eternity until Thursday, until he could return to heaven. 'I want to take you on an adventure. We'll be careful. No one will recognise us.' He assured her, knowing how important that was to her.

Her face lit up at the prospect. 'Where? What shall we do?'

He kissed her once more in promise. 'You'll have to show up to find out.'

Chapter Nine

He took her to Mutton Cove to see the seals. They were lucky. The rain had stopped and an early spring sun had found its way out for the afternoon, although she would have loved going even if it had been wet. She would have gone anywhere just to spend time with him. Pen rode behind Matthew on his horse, her arms wrapped tightly around his waist, her cheek pressed to his broad back, her body warm from the heat of his own despite the breeze. She was hardly noticeable sitting behind him, which was exactly what they'd intended. No one would pay them any mind.

At the cove, a sailboat awaited them, borrowed from a friend, Matthew explained. It was small but seaworthy, something a fisherman might use, or— the naughty, rather adventurous thought crossed her mind—a smuggler. 'The best way to see the seals is on the water.' Matthew grinned and handed her on board before shoving the little craft off the beach and into the surf. He splashed in beside her, the little boat skimming the quiet waters with Matthew competently at the sails.

'Is there nothing you can't do?' Pen admired him from the bow, the hood of her cloak thrown back, her face turned to the fresh air. Matthew merely smiled at her and shrugged out of his coat. He settled beside her in the bow seat, content to let the sailboat bob at will in the cove.

'Do you like your surprise?' He stretched out his long legs as they looked back at the empty beach. There were no seals yet.

'I love it. The wind in my face, the fresh air, no one around for miles.' She let her smile say it all. 'You have no idea what it means to me to be free for just a few hours.' Yet, she wasn't entirely free. Her smile faded at the realisation.

'But?' he prompted. 'Something is amiss?' His arm was about her, and she snuggled against his side.

'I'm not really free, even in these moments. There is so much I wish I could tell you, but I can't, not without giving away too much.' She paused, gathering her courage. 'Sometimes I wish we hadn't made the rule about names.' What would he say to that? Did he feel stifled too? Were there things he wanted to tell her, but couldn't?

His hand stroked the length of her arm. 'It's a type of freedom, though, Em. Knowing our real names creates a different set of limitations.'

All except one limitation. Pen sighed. Real names meant this could last, that she could find him. 'I wish we could stay here for ever. The water is peaceful.'

There were no worries here. She didn't have to think about her father, or the suitors, or what she was going to do for the rest of her life. She looked up at Matthew. 'How long do we have? Not just today, but how long…?'

He pressed a finger to her lips and shook his head. 'Whatever it is, it won't be long enough. Do we have to think about it now?'

'Yes, I think we do. I want to know. I want to drink every drop of joy out of the time we have. I don't want to be surprised one day to find you gone. I want a chance to say goodbye.'

Matthew turned his body horizontally and settled her against him so they lay along the length of the bow seat, the sun and the breeze brushing across them in pleasant strokes from the sky. 'I promise you, I won't leave without saying goodbye.'

'And I promise you the same.' She smiled up at him. 'May I tell you something? I haven't been to the beach for years, not since my mother died. She used to take me and my brother in the summers. I haven't been anywhere since she passed away.' It was the most personal thing she'd told him or anyone. Now that she'd started, she couldn't seem to stop. All the thoughts, all the grief that she'd kept to herself over the years, trickled out in carefully chosen words. 'At home, we never talk about her, not really, not beyond the odd remark about how much I look like her. Her death is why my father is so afraid,' Pen said quietly. 'Nothing's been the same since she died. Sometimes I think we all died with her.'

Then I met you. How will I ever go back to how things used to be?

Matthew's lips brushed the top of her head. 'My brother and I used to come here and swim in the summer.'

'You have a brother?' She hugged the idea to her, adding it to the facts she had about who he was.

'I did. He died.'

Em sighed against him, drowsy from the rocking of the boat and the heat of his body. 'So you know exactly how it is.' It was a tender but bittersweet thing to have in common with the man she was falling in love with. 'Would you tell me about him?'

Tell me about him. Cassian's throat tightened at the invitation. He'd not meant to say even that much about Collin, but he wanted to tell her, here in the boat, with no one around. It seemed the perfect place to do it, to whisper his secrets. Why not tell her, this woman who knew what it meant to lose someone, what it meant to never be able to share that grief? Her hand was drawing light circles on his chest, her fingers tracing him through his shirt, relaxing him as surely as the bob of the boat and the light breeze off the water. His throat eased and words came. 'Collin was my younger brother. He was dashing and reckless, fearless.'

He chuckled, remembering his brother. 'He'd dive into the water and swim with the seals. He'd swim so far we'd have to sail out to retrieve him. We'd warn him to stay close, but he'd never listen. Even in real life, he preferred to swim in deep waters. It didn't work out for him as well as swimming with the seals.'

'What happened?' She looked up at him.

'He made some poor choices in business and in love. Both played him false. People were hurt because of his decisions.' That was the condensed version, but it was the only one he could bring himself to tell. 'One night he walked out into the waters off Karrek Sands, swam out to the Beasts and never came back. His body washed up a few days later.'

The family had put about that he'd been caught in the undertow—the water was tricky around the Beasts—but Cassian knew what had really happened. Collin had just given up. He was to blame. He should have stopped Collin from going out that afternoon. He should have cancelled his own appointments when Collin refused to stay home. He should have followed him. He should have stopped Collin long before that afternoon. He shouldn't have let Collin invest money with Brenley. Looking back, there were so many places in the timeline where he should have stopped Collin, should have made him listen, and he hadn't. Collin was stubborn and he'd let his brother learn from his mistakes.

'I'm sorry, that's terrible.' She leaned up over him, kissing him lightly on the mouth. 'Thank you for telling me.' She held his gaze. 'Life is precious, it should not be wasted, yet I feel as if I've wasted too much of it, until I met you. You are so alive, so vibrant, and I feel that way too when I'm with you. Thank you.'

His hand moved behind her neck, sweeping aside

her hair. 'You make me feel alive, too, Em. More than I've felt in a very long time.' He took her mouth, their bodies shifting, hers moving beneath him, his moving over her, covering her, life and desire surging between them, demanding to be celebrated. But he had to be careful. He could not fall in love with her. This couldn't last. It served no purpose beyond the moment, yet he wanted…

She moaned beneath him, her hips rising up to meet his, her legs parting for him as if he were always meant to be there at the cradle of her thighs. Her eyes captured his. 'I want you, Matthew.'

'I cannot take…' he began to refuse, to counsel caution while he had any sense left. She was untouched and he could not marry her.

'But I can give.' She moved against him and he was nearly lost, so thoroughly did she arouse him. 'No matter what happens, Matthew, I want this first time to be with you, a man I choose.'

He kissed her hard on the mouth, his lips skimmed the column of her neck as he made his way down her body, every ounce of him wishing she were naked and every ounce of him thankful that she was not. It would be impossible to resist her then, impossible to find the intermediate ground on which he could satisfy her desire without ruining her. 'I will give you pleasure, Em,' he vowed fiercely, his hands sweeping beneath her skirts, pushing back the fabric, parting her undergarments until she was bare to him, her curls glistening in the sunlight. 'Sweet heavens, you're beautiful.' His own voice was hoarse with desire.

Her core was all dampness and want, yearning for his touch. He took her then, with his mouth, his lips, his tongue, his teeth, at the most private part of her. She was gripping him hard, her hands tangled in his hair, her legs wide for him. Em made a little sound in the back of her throat, his own body clenched in answer, moved by her ardent, open response. His tongue flicked over the tight nub within her folds, and she cried out at the exquisite pleasure of it. Again he licked and again the pleasure surged and ebbed, pushing her towards release. Soon it would be inevitable.

'I want…' she articulated only half a sentence before she lost the capacity for speech, her body focused entirely on pleasure and only pleasure now. But he knew what she wanted. He was pushing her towards a cliff, a place where she might fly, where he might give her a little more of that freedom she craved. He felt the moment she gave herself over to it, the point at which she let him push her all the way, until she claimed her release in a cry that filled the sky.

He might have held her for hours, both of them drowsing in the aftermath of the afternoon's intimacy, if it hadn't been for the seals. A thump against the boat had him upright and alert, his first thought that they'd drifted too far and hit something. But there was no need to worry. The seals had come out to play at last and one of them had bumped against the little boat. 'Em, come look.' He shook her awake gently. 'Seals.'

Em loved the seals, she loved watching them cavort in the water, diving and gliding through the waves. He brought out the dried fish and she revelled in tossing

them into the water and watching the seals swim after
them. When she laughed, her entire face lit up, taking
simple joy from this simple pleasure. Cassian didn't
think London offered a finer entertainment than this.
Em tossed the last fish and wiped her hands on her
skirts. 'I suppose this means it's time to go?' They still
had to sail the boat in and make the ride on horseback.
Cassian nodded and turned the boat around.

Neither of them spoke as they made the return trip
to the beach, but Cassian could feel her eyes on him
as he worked the sails. This afternoon had been more
than he'd bargained for: more revealing, more passion-
ate. At the beach, he took her hand and didn't let go.
They were together now in a way they hadn't been at
the start of the day. They'd shared important pieces of
themselves with one another, exposed a part of their
souls. He'd not intended that to happen. He was usually
so guarded, so careful with how he shared himself and
what he shared of himself. But Em had broken through
those defences with a simple question.

He helped her up on Ajax and settled himself behind
her, selfishly wanting to keep her close for as long as he
could. He wrapped his arms about her, his thighs about
her, and chirped to his horse. It was getting harder to
leave her and yet more likely that he must. His trip to
Bodmin for an ally had not born fruit. But he still had
time. The Season was weeks away yet. Anything could
happen between now and then.

Cassian had no sooner thought that than 'anything'
did. A rider came towards them on the road. Em's hood
immediately went up and her body tensed between his

legs, even as her head went down, her face completely shrouded by the hood. He did not know the rider, but apparently she did. Cassian nodded politely as the rider passed, throwing them a sceptical look. But Cassian did not stop.

'Who was that?' he whispered as the danger passed.

'Someone my father knows,' she whispered, still shaken by the close encounter.

She did not remove her hood for the duration of the ride, nor did she relax until they reached the cottage and he helped her down.

'He didn't guess who you were.' Cassian rubbed her arms reassuringly. 'Everything's fine. You spotted him before he spotted you.'

'But if I hadn't?' she asked sharply. 'Do you know what would have happened if he'd recognised me?' She shook her head. 'Of course not. You can't possibly know.'

The rest went unspoken, but Cassian heard it loud enough: *Because you don't who I really am and I don't know who you really are. This is what happens when time out of time meets reality. The two cannot mix.*

Cassian kissed her solemnly. He did know what would happen. She would be shamed and he would be forced to move on because dukes' heirs didn't marry country girls, gentry or not. That was not how he wanted it to end, not after today. 'We would have sorted it out.' At least they would have tried. 'Don't let it ruin today, Em.'

She smiled at that, some of her usual confidence returning. 'Nothing could ruin today, not even that.'

Despite the brave words, the rider on the road did serve as a warning to them both about the dangerous nature of their game. They stuck close to the cottage after that, venturing out only to the nearby meadows for long walks along deserted stretches of land, sometimes walking to the cliffs, watching the sea and talking, always talking, except for the days when all they wanted to do was kiss, to push the boundaries where pleasure and propriety might intermingle.

The cottage became their sanctuary in the weeks that followed. They stamped the little interior with their presence. The faded cloth and tin plates were joined by a chipped vase of wildflowers on the table and a pan for boiling tea water. A pile of neatly stacked wood stood next to the fireplace, old mismatched cushions taken from the Prideaux attics made the chairs more comfortable and a clean, worn quilt covered the bed in the corner. This was a place where they could be themselves, where they could share their secrets—all secrets but one.

Or perhaps two...

Cassian felt a change in her as April progressed. The tension in her grew apace with their passion, their interludes growing more heated, more intense. 'You're hiding something, Em? What is it? It's no good denying it, it's written on every inch of your body.' They were lying on the bed, wrapped in each other's arms, stripped down to their underthings in the warmth of the afternoon. It was as close to naked as he could afford to let them get. He didn't dare more, knowing that the end was near. He'd not broken Redruth. He would have to go to London, but he'd put it off until the last minute. Did she guess? Was that the reason for her tension? He'd tasted desperation in her kiss.

The bed ropes creaked as she lifted up on an elbow to look at him, her green eyes shadowed. 'Do you remember when I said my father wanted me to marry?' It was one subject they had expressly not revisited since the first time she'd mentioned it. 'There's a man he wants me to consider.'

His only thought was that he wasn't ready, never mind that she'd warned him weeks earlier. Somehow, he'd convinced himself he would be the one who'd have to walk away. The London Season and his chance to pursue his amusement garden loomed closer than ever on the calendar, forcing his hand. But it was her hand that was being forced now.

'Will you consider him?' Cassian's words were hoarse even as he strove for neutrality. He was already jealous of this unknown man and yet this or something like it had always been unavoidable. He and Em weren't meant to last.

Her next words spilled out in an apologetic rush. 'I'll tell my father no, of course, that the man is too old.' She bit her lip. 'I just wanted to be honest. I thought you should know.'

'What does he do?' Cassian imagined a merchant perhaps of some means. Her father probably consid-

ered it a great opportunity to have his daughter wed
a man already established in business. Cassian could
offer her nothing, not simply because he was a viscount
and she was a girl from an ordinary background, but
also because he could only make her unhappy. There
would be no joy for her in being a viscountess. She
would be under scrutiny for ever, for every little thing
she didn't know, every rule she inadvertently broke or
overlooked, every faux pas she made. There would be
no pleasure for her in that. He would not ruin her that
way. He wanted the Em who adored feeding seals, who
lay with him beneath the sun in a rocking boat.

'He grows flowers.'

Ah, a gardener then, someone who might work at
an estate or who might have some small patch of land
of his own. 'Is it a good match?'

'Not for me.' She smiled at him, her fingers touching
his face as they lay close together. 'I want something
different. Something more than an older man who is
dedicated to his roses.'

'Can you refuse him?' he asked. She'd said she
would, but was that possible? Her father seemed a very
determined man.

'In truth, I don't know. My father is very stubborn
once he sets his mind to something.' She gave a soft
laugh that warmed him. 'He's like your reluctant gentleman. Perhaps they should meet.' She sighed. 'I don't
want to go, Matthew, but the afternoon has slipped
away again.'

'Come tomorrow? We'll go down to the beach.'

Time was suddenly of the essence. There were a finite amount of tomorrows left between them.

She shook her head. 'I can't. Tomorrow…'

'…you go to see *him*, the man with the flowers,' Cassian finished her sentence, something fierce and competitive taking up residence in his stomach. But what could he do? He was a man with a false name. He was powerless.

She nodded. 'I'll come the day after.' She drew a fingernail down his chest, her hand hitching at his belt, her lips hovering close to his. 'And we'll make love, promise me. I meant what I said that day on the boat. I want it to be you, no matter what.' The desperation was back. She thought this was the end or very nearly so.

Cassian swallowed. 'Em, I don't know if that's wise.'

She silenced him with a kiss. 'You can't say no. It will be my birthday. You have to oblige.'

'Shall I bring you a present?' he teased, a thought already coming to him, something she'd like beyond anything, aside from lovemaking.

'If you like.' She snuggled against him. 'Do you know what I really want? I want to lie fully naked with you. I want to feel your hands, your mouth, on my skin. I want to put *my* hands on *your* skin, I want to know *you*, your body, your name, your *real* name.'

Cassian pressed a kiss to the top of her head. 'You can have all but the last.' It was hard to refuse. How many times had he wanted the same? To throw caution to the wind and announce himself to her, to know who she was. But to do so would be akin to eating the apple in the Garden. Once they knew who each other was, they'd be cast out of their little Eden. It was further proof that she thought this was ending. She thought names at the last couldn't hurt them. She was wrong. Cassian rose from the bed and put on his breeches. 'I think we need to keep this one secret, Em.'

Chapter Ten

'I know a secret.' Phin was all smiles in the drawing room before dinner. It was just the two of them. Father hadn't come down yet and there were no guests tonight, much to Pen's relief. She didn't think she could handle another night of feigned politeness.

'What is it?' A jolt of worry took her. Perhaps that *was* the secret? She scanned the room quickly, looking over her shoulder at the entrance for fear she might see a phalanx of gentlemen lining up for her attentions.

Phin laughed as he read her thoughts. 'Not more guests. It's just the three of us tonight.' His smile widened. 'We're celebrating your birthday early.'

'Oh. That's lovely.' Pen knit her brows together. 'Why? It's just two days away.'

'That's the other surprise, the one I won't tell you. Father would kill me for letting that particular cat out of the bag.' Phin cocked his head, his gaze lingering, inspiring a different worry in Pen. Did he guess she was meeting someone? She smoothed her skirts and played with the fan in her lap. Surely, what she'd been up to with Matthew didn't show in any way? She'd been careful to school her thoughts since the first night when Margery had caught her. 'I thought you'd be more excited than that,' Phin probed. 'Two extra days of birthday presents are not to be sneered at, yet you seemed underwhelmed, Pen.'

Pen looked up and forced a smile. 'Not at all, at least not at all if such largesse wasn't coming from our father. I'm merely wondering what he wants, how does this suit *his* plans?'

Phin frowned at her, disappointed with the cynical direction of her thoughts. 'He wants your happiness. Are you not pleased with the efforts he's made these last weeks? You've had the elite of Cornwall served up to you so that you may make your choice.'

'And tomorrow we're off to visit Wadesbridge,' Pen put in with less enthusiasm. 'We're back to where we started.'

'We wouldn't be if you'd pick one of them, show an interest. Toss Father an olive branch, Pen. He's trying,' Phin encouraged.

'If I toss him an olive branch, he'll take the whole bush and have me wedded to the first man I blink at. Did he put you up to this?' Pen sighed, disappointed in her anger and in lashing out at the least guilty party among them. Her brother meant well. 'I'm sorry, Phin. It must be difficult for you playing the liaison all the time.' She was reminded of the advice she'd given Matthew about his stubborn gentleman. Had Matthew found an advocate? She would ask when she saw him.

Two days from now. Despite the promise of birthday celebrations, the two days stretched before her endlessly.

'Are you well, Pen? You've seemed distracted of late.' Phin wasn't done with his scrutiny. She'd have to try harder to not give herself away. Margery had noticed and now Phin thought he was on to something.

'I'm fine. It's been a difficult few weeks.' It wasn't entirely a lie. The last month had been difficult as well as fantastic. She just wished the fantastic part didn't need to be her own secret.

Their father joined them and all personal conversation was set aside in lieu of small talk about the estate until dinner was announced, but Pen did not miss the undercurrent of excitement that jumped between her father and Phin. Whatever her surprise was, they'd planned it for her and it clearly pleased them. It would please her, too, Pen decided, looking around the table at her little family. Tragedy had shaped so much of their lives. Wasn't it time for a little joy to do the same?

'Well, Daughter, you will be twenty-one soon.' Her father approached the subject as the meal ended, a pleased look in his eyes. 'You've done as I've asked this past month, considering various candidates for your hand. But perhaps the process is still too contrived for your purposes.' He smiled kindly and for a moment Pen saw the father she'd known in early childhood, a more carefree version of himself, a happier version. 'Penrose, you've mentioned how much you long to see something of the world and your desire to go to London. So...' he slid a glance at Phin and winked

'...we have decided to give you a London Season for your birthday. We leave tomorrow. Your maid is already packing.'

Pen stared. Her father was beaming, looking entirely pleased with himself, and Phin was grinning from ear to ear. They were expecting her to say something. They'd just served up one of her wishes, a wish any girl would be delighted to receive. 'B-but,' she stammered, trying to organise her thoughts, 'I can't possibly go now.' If she left, she wouldn't see Matthew. She cast about for a reason to stay. 'What about Trescowe? Aren't we promised for a visit?'

'We'll stop there and continue on.' Her father was in high humour as he solved the little problem.

'But I need time to prepare. There are purchases I need to make.' She didn't have enough gloves or stockings for London and probably not enough dresses despite the influx of new ones for the dinner parties.

Again her father beamed. 'Buy them in London. You'll have two weeks to shop to your heart's content before the Season truly begins. You see, I've thought of everything. There's no reason not to get in the coach tomorrow morning and enjoy yourself.' He was waiting for her to say something, probably 'thank you'. 'Well? Aren't you pleased, Pen? It's what you wanted. We'll find you a fine husband in London.'

'She's stunned.' Phin leapt into the breach, covering for her lapse even as he slid her a questioning look. 'I never thought to see you speechless, Pen.'

'I'm overwhelmed.' She managed a smile. 'Thank you, truly, both of you.' Phin, no doubt, had probably argued quite hard for this chance. It was unfair of her to not appreciate it now. They couldn't possibly know how their gift broke her heart.

The rest of the meal passed in a blur. Her favourite dessert, a chocolate ganache cake, was brought in. Cook must have worked hours on it. Her brother and father laughed and talked endlessly of London; which entertainments they would take in, the people they would meet. Talk of balls and parties, decorations and food, flowed over her, but left her untouched. She made the appropriate noises, smiling and nodding in the right places. She ate the chocolate cake. She must have since her plate was empty. But all the while her mind was elsewhere.

How could she send word to Matthew? How did she leave a message for a man whose name she didn't know? That no one knew? If she could get to the cottage, she could leave a message there. But how to do that? She'd have to go tonight, in the dark. It would be almost impossible to get out of the castle and impossible to get back in, to say nothing of the risks of injury. In the dark it was easy to lose one's way, to turn an ankle in a hole. She'd not make it back home then.

Perhaps she could send someone else in the morning? But who would that be? Only Margery could be trusted with the errand and Margery was expected to travel with her. There would be no opportunity for a trip to the cottage. By the time Pen excused herself from the table, claiming the need for a good night's sleep, her heart was breaking. Her mind had moved on from thoughts of how to get to the cottage, to accepting the reality that she would not be able to reach Matthew. What would happen in two days when Matthew showed up and she didn't? All this time, she'd worried he would disappear suddenly, but it was she who would break the pact they'd made at Mutton Cove.

He would be hurt. He cared for her. Would all that caring turn to hate? Would he feel betrayed? Would he think she'd decided to wed the man she was visiting? Or would he understand that none of this had been her choice? That events had transpired that were beyond her control? Would he forgive her?

Would she forgive him if he simply stopped coming? That was a difficult question to answer. They'd accepted what they had couldn't last for ever, but they'd intended to say goodbye. Perhaps he'd think the worst of her. He would never know how much these weeks had meant to her, how alive she felt when she was with him.

In her room, Margery was busy packing, full of energy, her excitement at odds with Pen's melancholy. 'Isn't it wonderful? London, at last!' Her smile faded. 'What is it? Aren't you happy, miss? It's what you've wanted.' Margery set aside the pile of gowns in her arms and came to her, taking her hands. 'It is your young man, is it not?'

Pen sank down on an empty patch of bed. 'I'll never see him again. There's no chance to tell him, to explain.' But to explain what? To see him again would require she disclose everything. 'He'll think I left him,' Pen said forlornly. There would be no more kisses, no more of this afternoon's decadence, there would be no hope of lying with him skin to skin on the faded quilt. 'I was supposed to meet him there for my birthday.' She bit her lip as tears threatened. 'He was bringing me a present.' It would have been something thoughtful, something that spoke to the quality of their relationship.

'Perhaps it's for the best. It had to end some time,' Margery consoled softly. 'I know it hurts now, but this way it's over quickly and there will be no messiness. You'll be gone. He can't follow you, can't find you, can't make trouble for you.'

'I know.' Pen had been over all the silver linings in her mind, but that didn't make it better. Those linings were tarnished. She *wanted* Matthew to find her, but he was lost to her. 'Margery, make sure you pack my glass necklace.' She would keep it with her always as a reminder of what it had felt like to be loved for herself and what it had felt like to have a heart so she wouldn't be tempted to risk it again.

Em's birthday present, fifteen pounds of wriggling puppy, squirmed under Cassian's arm as he approached the cottage. It had been a feat of no small magnitude to carry the puppy on his horse. But the look on Em's face would be worth it. It was a rash gift, one she couldn't keep. But he would keep the puppy for her. The gift was the experience, a puppy of her own for the afternoon. They could take it walking in the meadow and it could gambol at her side just as she'd imagined growing up.

Cassian stepped inside the cottage and smiled. He'd

arrived ahead of her. Good. He set the puppy down on the floor. He wanted time to set the fire and lay out the picnic. He'd packed something special for her birthday. He wanted this afternoon to be perfect, quiet and private, a celebration just between them. They'd been together nearly five weeks and he was aware time was running out. Soon, he'd have to make good on the promise he'd made to tell her. It looked like he'd have to go to London, after all. There'd been no breakthrough with the earl. Tomorrow. He would tell her tomorrow. He'd would let them have today. One more brilliant day in the sunshine of their fantasy.

Half an hour later, the food was ready, the fire had warmed the room, but there was no sign of Em. The puppy snuffled at his boots and Cassian reached down and scooped him up. 'Just a few more minutes, Oscar.' He took the pup outside to do his business and came back in. The minutes came and the minutes went, collecting into an hour.

He got up and carried the puppy to the door, looking down the path for any sign of her. Perhaps she'd been delayed. Perhaps he should walk out and meet her on the road somewhere. But how could he? What direction did she come from? What might be the nature of her delay? Had she been unable to get away? Had she fallen ill? He wished he knew more about her. Right now he felt as if he knew nothing of her, nothing useful that would help him. He knew how she felt in his arms, how she kissed him, how she liked doing for him. He knew that she liked puppies, that she had a small family, that her father was stubborn. He knew that she liked melted cheese on toast, that she wanted to travel the world. But none of that would help him. If she didn't come to the cottage, she would be lost to him.

Cassian went back inside.

He waited another half an hour before admitting she wasn't coming. 'That's all right, Oscar.' He put out the fire and tucked the puppy into his coat against the cold and damp. 'We'll try again tomorrow.' Perhaps her visit with the gardener suitor had been delayed, perhaps she hadn't been able to get away. It was her birthday, after all—perhaps her family was celebrating. Cassian carefully rewrapped the food. Most of it would keep until tomorrow.

He came again the next day and the day after that, puppy, food and all, until the bread dried and he ran out of excuses for her delay. He had to face facts. Em was not detained. She simply wasn't coming. Cassian sat at the table, head in his hands. Was this how it ended? Suddenly and without warning despite their pact? One afternoon they'd been lovemaking on the bed, promising to do decadent things to one another, wishing for tomorrow to come quickly, promising one another to be here, and the next she was gone. He thought he'd have more time. A couple of weeks at least, time for them to prepare for goodbye together as they'd promised each other at the cove. He wasn't set to leave for London until the end of the month.

Why hadn't she come? A hundred horrible scenarios played through his mind. Did it have something to do with the gardener? Had she chosen him or been compelled to marry him? Had her family decided to keep a closer watch on her now that she might be betrothed? *To another.* The thought nearly made him sick. He didn't want to think on it: his Em belonging to another, kissing another.

He'd known an end would come—he could no more keep her than she could keep the puppy. So why did it hurt so much? He'd been wrong to think anonymity would protect his heart. He'd thought he couldn't fall in love with her, at least not fall too far. But he'd been wrong there. He'd fallen far enough for her leaving to sting. Damn, but the Truscott brothers were ill-fated in love. He'd been prepared and armoured, he'd warned himself against such a thing, and it *still* hurt. His brother had not been half as prepared when he'd fallen for Audevere Brenley, Sir Gismond's daughter. It was no wonder Collin had been devastated when she broke with him just weeks before their wedding. The Brenleys had played his brother false on all fronts.

From his vantage point of the cottage table, Cassian had a new perspective on how that loss must have felt. It also gave him a renewed determination to make sure he didn't let sorrow drag him down. He had to let go. It was time to say goodbye. Cassian took a final look around. The fire where they'd sat, the bed where they'd lain, where they'd flirted with lovemaking. He saw memories and he saw irony. He'd spent his adult life guarding against unscrupulous fortune hunters who would seek to use him as Brenley has used his brother.

But in the end, it was love that had done him in. Well, best to learn that lesson now.

Cassian took the note he'd written out of his coat pocket and propped it on the table against the chipped vase with its dried lavender. If she ever came again, at least she'd know he'd been here, that it hadn't been his choice to leave her like this. Beside him on the floor, the puppy whined. Cassian reached down a hand and stroked the puppy's soft head. 'It looks like it's just you and me, Oscar.' As cute as the dog was, the idea lacked a certain appeal.

Cassian rose and gathered up the pup. It was time to do his duty. He'd had a lovely spring reprieve, his project had been given every chance to succeed and it hadn't. Blind, arbitrary hope had failed to produce the results he'd wanted. Now it was time for hard work and sacrifice. They would not fail him. He stepped outside and closed the door behind him with a firm thud. Em was officially in the past. All there was to do now was to move forward. He needed to focus on his amusement garden now and courting Redruth's daughter. He could be married by autumn and he could break ground on the pleasure garden before another year passed. He was back in the game. The thought ought to have buoyed his spirits. It did not.

Chapter Eleven

The Redruth ball was well underway in all its glittering, chandelier-lit glory when Cassian arrived. He paused at the entrance to the ballroom. At his age, stepping over the threshold of a debutante's ball meant one thing: he was declaring himself interested in marriage.

Beside him, Inigo clapped him on the back in well-meant support. 'This is a momentous evening. It's a big moment. You're the first of us to really throw their hat in the ring. Eaton skirted the issue altogether marrying in Porth Karrek on the sly. Vennor can use mourning as a shield a little while longer.'

But not Cassian. He had no shields. Nothing protected his dreams but himself. If he didn't go after that land with every weapon in his arsenal, the dream would be lost. To not at least try smacked of cowardice. Tonight would be the first engagement in his campaign. He would dance with the daughter and see where it led. Campaign, engagement, arsenal. These were war words, not love words. He ought to have a less violent view of tonight's foray.

Cassian tugged at his ivory waistcoat and straightened his shoulders. The past three weeks had led here. There had been flurry upon flurry of activity since the night he'd committed to coming to London. There'd been packing to see to, appointments with his tailors, arrangements for rooms at the Albany so he wasn't underfoot at his father's town house and, most importantly, there'd been acquiring the interview with Redruth. He'd met three days ago with the earl to discuss courting the daughter and to garner an invitation to the ball. The earl had been pleased his daughter's presence in London had attracted the attentions of a duke's heir.

Cassian disliked the arrangement. He disliked being valued for his assets and titles. Even more, he disliked having to use that card to get what he wanted. Furthermore, he disliked the necessity for duplicity. The Earl of Redruth had no inkling that Viscount Trevethow was the man behind the Porth Karrek Land Development Company, the very company that Redruth had refused to sell to. Yet, when those avenues had failed to acquire what Cassian wanted, what choice did he have? He felt the scales of good teeter, balancing his deceit against the greater good. The people hurt by his brother's poor business sense were counting on him. Surely that outweighed his motives for courtship.

'Well, once more into the breach.' Cassian slid Inigo a look as they stepped inside. They wound their way around the perimeter of the ballroom, stopping to chat with friends as they made their progress towards the Earl of Redruth. Cassian was in no hurry and he certainly didn't want to look desperate. He wasn't desperate and nor was he nervous as Inigo seemed to think with all his 'throwing his hat into the ring, momentous occasion' talk. He felt nothing. His attendance here tonight was a professional business decision, nothing more. He wanted the land and he needed a different kind of currency to get it.

His memories of Em carried a dulled edge these days. Those weeks in the cottage seemed like a dream now, something that had been vivid once, but had begun to fade. Even the image of her; all that caramel hair and those sea-glass eyes, blurred into something unreal by necessity. He couldn't move forward if he focused on the past. What kind of a husband would he be if he spent his life mourning a woman whose real name he didn't even know? There might not be a grand passion in this marriage of convenience he sought, but he hoped there might be something milder, respect, perhaps, that would grow over time. That would have to be enough. The greater good would be served.

'Which one do you think she is?' Inigo nudged his elbow as they watched the dancers. So many smiling, hopeful faces. None of them Em's. A dangerous flash of her flared to vivid life past the dulled edges of his memory.

If you were here, Em, we'd dance beneath the chandeliers as if they were the stars in the sky, we'd stroll the gardens, I'd steal a kiss.

Em would look stunning in a silk gown of seafoam to match her eyes, an opal pendant at her neck, her hair done up high to show off the length of that neck.

His Em would be a swan among these downy young ducklings.

These were dangerous imaginings. Duty had no time for them. 'I have no idea.' Cassian pushed the thought of Em away. He wished he shared Inigo's enthusiasm for the venture. 'Is this what it's like to invest other people's money for them?' he joked. 'I suppose it's easy to be excited when the risk isn't yours.'

Inigo frowned, missing the humour. 'Oh, no, investing other people's money is positively nerve-racking.'

'And contemplating marriage to a stranger is not?' Cassian laughed in spite of himself. 'Perhaps that's why I brought you along. It's all about perspective.' He'd come to grips with that perspective over the past few weeks. In order for his dream to thrive his other dream would have to die. He would give up a romantic's marriage for a practical marriage in order to honour one man's legacy, to avenge his brother and to right wrongs. It was what the greater good demanded. Dukes lived to serve that hungry beast. It was the code the Four Cornish Dukes lived by.

They nodded to a group of young girls as they strolled. Four sets of eyes followed them along with a trail of giggles at their attentions. 'Speaking of perspective, it seems your presence tonight has brought a certain level of excitement to the evening,' Inigo pointed out. 'I wonder how many people Redruth rushed out and told you'd be here? You've been in town for three weeks, but you haven't been out yet. Redruth can claim he was your first stop. Quite the coup for him.'

Cassian shrugged. 'This wasn't the first stop. The

Trelevens' musicale was and I'll be sure to tell anyone who asks.' They'd spent the early part of the night with their neighbours from home, Sir Jock Treleven, his wife and his five unmarried daughters, all of who were talented musicians. Vennor had been there as well. It had been a quiet, low-profile way to start the evening. 'I wonder who will be the talk of the town tomorrow? Sir Jock with his smaller but tasteful and more exclusive affair with three ducal heirs present, or Redruth's ball?'

'Redruth is usually a hermit. Everyone will be attracted to this anomaly of his. I doubt the Trelevens will even get a mention in the columns,' Inigo offered honestly. 'But you will be mentioned for certain. Everyone is already looking at you. Once you dance with Redruth's daughter, no one will want to look away. I wager you'll be in the betting books at White's by morning.'

Cassian grimaced. 'If you think you're raising my spirits, you're failing. Just so you know.'

Pen was miserable. Everyone was watching her. Talking about her. She was the centre of every conversation. She didn't even have to guess at what was being said. Pen knew. She'd walked in on one such discussion in the retiring room, some silly girls being indiscreet with their gossip.

'There's the girl who is making her debut at twenty-one.'

'There's the girl no one has seen for years.'

'I wonder what's wrong with her?'

Curiosity could be a cruel thing.

She'd exchanged the prison of Castle Byerd for the

glittering prison of London of her own accord. She stood with her father and her aunt amid the splendour of the Byerd House ballroom; the chandelier dusted, the floor polished to a walnut gleam, surrounded by silks and jewels and all she could think was 'This is all my fault.' She'd asked for London and she'd got it. Her father had spared no expense for her debut. Food had been delivered in endless waves today: cakes from London's finest pastry chefs, chocolates in the shape of Castle Byerd and crates of champagne that had been chilling since early this morning. There were flowers, too, white roses in cut-crystal vases tied with pale pink ribbons everywhere in the house, except for the one bouquet of roses tinged with yellow-rimmed petals which had already arrived from Wadesbridge. It was set in pride of place on the mantel in the drawing room, perhaps as a subtle reminder of what her fate would be should London not inspire a different choice.

Her father had very subtly drawn a line in the sand with his birthday gift. He'd given her London, as she'd asked. Now, he would expect something in return— that she choose a suitor, that she make a commitment to marriage. If not, a suitor would be chosen for her: Wadesbridge, solid, predictable, stable, close to home, far from her dreams. It would make her father happy. He would have succeeded in keeping her safe until he could hand her off to a husband.

There would be no travels, no grand adventures, no danger. No *passion*. She could not imagine Wades-bridge's kisses exciting the same response as Mat-thew's, could not imagine lying on a faded quilt with

Wadesbridge, yearning to be naked, yearning to put her mouth on him as he'd done her. Surely, Wadesbridge or whomever she selected would not expect her to do such a thing with them, or expect to do such a thing to her. She didn't want to think about it. She only wanted to think about Matthew: his hands, his kisses, his touch, the way he talked of seeing the world. Pen swallowed hard and fought back a sudden rush of tears.

In the weeks she'd been in London, she'd spent hours pondering how that visit had gone. How long had Matthew waited for her? Had he gone back to the cottage after that? What had he brought her for her birthday? What might they have done in the cottage that afternoon? More kisses, more mouths—would they have consummated their relationship as she had wanted? Once, she'd thought such a thing inevitable. Every time they'd met had led them closer to that conclusion. She'd wanted to. She'd made up her mind. She'd wanted a memory to hold against all the nights to come.

Pen fingered the glass heart tied about her wrist on a pink ribbon with her dance card. She was decked out in her mother's tiara and diamonds, but the glass heart was the most precious thing she wore tonight. She'd wanted it with her, a talisman, perhaps, to bring her luck, to keep Matthew close a little while longer. Her dance card was filled with the names of strangers, men only interested in her dowry.

Men, perhaps, like the Duke of Hayle's heir who was claiming the seventh dance. She could picture how delighted her father would be over that—a duke's heir dancing with his daughter and a man from their part of the world at that. It quite positively put Wadesbridge in the shade. She ought to be relieved. But she wasn't. What did it matter who she danced with or who she married if it wasn't Matthew?

At the thought of Matthew, her gaze unerringly picked out the tallest dark-haired man in the room and not for the first time that night. She'd noticed him immediately even though he'd arrived late. He hadn't been in the receiving line—she would have remembered. But her gaze, it seemed, had made a habit out of looking for him once her memory had decided he reminded her of Matthew with his height and his breadth. His shoulders were exquisite. She wished she could see his face, or maybe not. If she saw it, she would have to give up the fantasy. It wasn't Matthew. He was perhaps country gentry, not the sort at all to mingle among the glamour of the *ton*. That didn't stop her, however, from thinking about how different this ball would be if Matthew *were* here, how she'd look forward to every dance in his arms, how he would look at her if he could see her in this ballgown, her hair done up, his common girl transformed into a princess. He would tell her she was beautiful and she would believe him because Matthew didn't flatter.

Matthew didn't lie.

She would not be the only one transformed. How wonderful Matthew would look in evening clothes, a tail coat cut to his physique. No woman in the ballroom would be able to keep her eyes off him. Not even the presence of Hayle's heir could compete with Matthew.

Her father nudged her elbow. 'Trevethow is coming, my dear.' Her stomach sank. The dreaded seventh dance was here, the one with the much-anticipated heir to the Duke of Hayle. Of all the dances, she was looking forward to that one the least. Trevethow was bound to be a pompous cad. Tonight, when people weren't talking about her, they'd been talking about him. Apparently, he was handsome and rich and every woman in the room was dying of love for him, never mind he hadn't been to any grand balls yet this Season. It was enough to make the girls swoon to know he was in London, that they might run into him at any time, on Bond Street, at the Park.

'Trevethow is the big fish tonight. Penrose, please, be nice to him. He would be a good match, perhaps the best we could hope for.'

She only half-heard him. The tall man she'd spied throughout the evening was on the move. Her gaze had found him again and it was far more interesting to watch him than it was to listen to her father enumerate the benefits of an alliance with the house of Hayle. Pen stilled as the tall man drew near, her breath catching at the growing possibility that the tall man who'd captured her attention *was* Trevethow. Someone touched her arm to ask a question and Pen stepped aside for just a moment to answer.

'Allow me to introduce my daughter, Lady Penrose Prideaux.' Her father tapped her elbow, reclaiming her attention. Pen turned, her gaze and her mind struggling to register who stood before her. It was her tall stranger from tonight, but there was something of the familiar about him, sans greatcoat and dusty boots, but the same broad shoulders and square jaw, the same warm amber eyes. Pen's stomach plummeted and her mouth ran dry while her thoughts were assaulted with a hundred realisations, the foremost among them was that Matthew was *here*, the very fantasy of her thoughts brought to life in vivid physical reality. How? Why? What did it mean?

Pen's shock was overwhelming as he bent over her hand and kissed it, the little glass heart dancing on the ribbon about her wrist. His eyes were no longer the warmed whisky she remembered, but hard amber flints instead, full of their own shock. 'Lady Penrose, how charming to meet a neighbour so far from home.' His words were edged in an irony meant just for her. So he knew. He recognised her too. So much for the protections of secrecy.

Other realisations assailed her in a relentless barrage: not only was Matthew here of all places, he'd lied. The son of a country squire was in truth a duke's heir! He'd gone slumming, hoping to turn a simple country girl's head with all those pretty lines, all the professions of affection. Had he just said them to steal kisses? All this time while she'd been in London worrying over Matthew, worrying over the hurt she might have caused him, he wasn't hurting in the least! He was attending balls and asking permission to court earls' daughters. He'd not been languishing for her. While she'd felt guilty about dancing with other men tonight, he'd been coming to court a faceless girl he'd never met with deadly intent, simply because she was Redruth's daughter.

He'd already been to visit her father, he'd already asked to court her. He'd made his intentions known to her father. He quite obviously had one goal in mind, which begged the horrible question: How long had he known he was going to court Redruth's daughter? Had he been contemplating it during their time together? Had he known the whole time he would be going to London? Had he always known *exactly* when their affair would end? It seemed so. He'd known it would never last beyond April because he would be gone.

The other set of realisations were not flattering: *she'd* been played for a fool and that was all her fault. She'd been naive to believe in his protestations of affection, that she could trust him, that she *meant* something to him. Noblemen toyed with common girls all the time. Had it all been a game to him? What had he meant to do? Set her up as his mistress? Or perhaps not even that courtesy. Perhaps he thought to marry well and keep a little country mouse on the side.

Worse, what did he mean to do now with that information? Her mind ran wild with dark speculation. Would he use their secret affair to coerce her to the altar? To take away all choice? What if he told her father she'd been gallivanting around the countryside meeting strange men under aliases? There would be no place for her to hide if that happened. Her father would insist on marriage.

He managed a cold smile so unlike the smiles she was used to, his voice tinged with irony as he said her name. 'Lady Penrose, I believe this dance is mine.'

Chapter Twelve

He'd found Em. For just one brilliant, sparkling moment, when she'd turned around, the world had been perfect. If only he could have held on to that singular moment, frozen it in time, Cassian would have gladly lived in it for ever. But then he'd seen her eyes, seen her look of stunned surprise turn to something akin to loathing and fear and the moment passed, perfection shattered by the hammer of reality. Em didn't want him here. Em hadn't wanted to be found. Em had left him. Only it hadn't been Em leaving him, it had been Lady Penrose Prideaux, the woman who held his land. It could not be worse. How could he marry the woman he had loved for her land? How could they recapture what they'd once had when everything about them reeked of rank distrust?

Her hand lay on his sleeve, barely brushing it as he led her on to the dance floor, as if she could treat him as a ghost. 'You used to like touching me,' Cassian whispered low at her ear as he placed his hand at her waist and moved them into position for the waltz.

'Not you. Never you. Only Matthew.' The ice of her tone matched the ice in her eyes as the music began and they started to move. 'I should slap you for your deceit.' Her hand curled into the fabric of his coat where it lay on his shoulder. For a moment, he thought she might do it. It would be deuced unfair of her since *he* was the wronged party.

'As I recall, you were the one who left me.' Cassian took them through a turn at the top of the ballroom with a nod to a passing couple.

'You were always planning to leave and you said nothing! I told you from the start my father wanted me to marry,' she hissed through gritted teeth.

'Smile, Lady Penrose, people are watching. They've talked of nothing else all night but your debut and my presence at a ball for the first time this Season. You can imagine what they'll talk about now that their two favourite subjects are united as one.' This was not the way he'd envisioned finding Em, of dancing with her, of having her in his arms again.

But this wasn't Em. This was someone else entirely, someone he didn't know. This was a woman who'd no doubt found Matthew dispensable, a man of no consequence compared to the match she was expected to make. She'd discarded him without a thought. There'd even been a man in mind, not a gardener as Cassian had originally thought, but a man of rank. Yet she'd kissed him, touched him, seared him with hot looks and hotter promises, all the while using him to cuckold another.

Be fair, his conscience prompted. *You participated willingly. She told you her father wanted her to marry.*

But it stung. She'd used him and discarded him without saying goodbye. She'd broken their pact and now she wanted to call him to account. He should resent her, but he couldn't bring himself to it, not without reason. Not until he heard her story. This woman in his arms wasn't Em and yet Em was inside those sharp green eyes somewhere. He just had to get her out from behind this wall she'd built. He couldn't do that in the middle of a ballroom with the *ton*'s gaze on him unblinking, assigning nuance to every move.

'We can't talk here.' Cassian put his mouth close to her ear, breathing in the vanilla sweetness of her, a scent he thought he might never smell again. 'Meet me in the library. We need privacy.'

She pulled back, fixing him with a look of pure disdain. 'So that you can compromise me? You forget I know what happens in private with you.' Her words carried a bite. Is that what she thought of him? Em would never have thought twice about being alone with him. Em would have relished every moment. But Em had no reputation to protect, no consequences to think about should they be caught. He understood: Lady Penrose Prideaux had everything to risk.

'Please, give me five minutes. There are things we must say to one another, questions that need answering.' Five precious minutes to change their trajectory. 'If you don't give me those five minutes now, I will be back tomorrow and the day after that. You will not be rid of me until you hear what I have to say.'

Logic flickered in her eyes as she weighed her decision: to see him now for five minutes alone, or to allow him to come back where his time might be unlimited, where he might have a chance to speak with her father. 'All right,' she said, relenting. 'The library. But only for five minutes.'

Victory lit him up from the inside. Cassian returned her to her father and bowed over her hand. He made his way casually to the library, stopping to talk here and there with friends, making sure no one would align his disappearance from the ballroom with hers.

The library was thankfully dark, signalling its emptiness. Cassian turned up a lamp and stirred the fire. He poured himself a drink while the mantel clock ticked off the minutes and he waited. By the time she arrived he'd begun to doubt her intentions. She'd made this promise before and broken it. 'You're late,' he ground out from his chair by the fire.

'How can I be late? We didn't set a time.' Penrose shut the door behind her but kept her distance. Perhaps their dance had affected her more than she'd let on, perhaps she was the one who didn't trust herself with him. One touch, one kiss and she'd crumble. But there was too much to settle between them before he could contemplate such actions.

'Forgive me my doubt, but you have something of a track record in the absentee area.' Cassian rose and poured another drink. Redruth kept excellent brandy. The clock chimed half past eleven.

'Your five minutes are starting.'

'Then let's cut to the chase. Why did you leave

me?' Cassian fixed her with a stare over the rim of his tumbler.

'Why does it matter? What we had between us was never going to last. We were going to leave each other sooner or later.'

'But why *then*? We had plans.' He wanted to melt the glacier of her exterior with a reminder of the heat that had passed between them, of what he'd done to her, of how she'd felt when he'd done it. Surely, she didn't think the passion between them was usual? 'You'd wanted to—'

Pen's cheeks flamed in the darkness. She cut him off sharply. 'I know what I wanted. A gentleman wouldn't mention such a thing.' It was a wanton desire, one she'd not likely forget.

He moved nearer, closing the distance between them, his voice a sibilant seduction in the firelit darkness. 'You lied to me. You told me you would come and you didn't.' His voice lulled her toward confession, his words dragging her back into the fantasy where Em and Matthew could ignite each other with a touch. Beyond him the fire crackled and popped.

Pen shook her head. 'When I made you that promise, I meant to come.' She covered her mouth. No. She would not explain to him. Em might have explained. But Em and Matthew were no more and neither was what had existed between them—that had been as great a fiction as their names. She'd made a grievous mistake and now her little adventure had come back to haunt her. 'No, I won't apologise.' Pen straightened her shoulders and fixed him with a stare, hardening her resolve and summoning all the reasons he was dangerous, all the reasons she detested him. He was everything she wanted to avoid in a husband. 'You're acting like the wronged party here, but I never lied to you. Even as Em, I told you my father was pursuing a match for me. You knew.'

'I thought it was a merchant, a tradesman. When you mentioned the roses, I thought perhaps a land steward, a landscaper. You led me to believe—' he fired back but she was quick to interrupt.

'I never told you that, I never misled you. You did that all by yourself, drawing whatever conclusions you wanted.'

'What else was I supposed to think?' Anger was growing now. The viscount had a hot temper. 'You let me think you were a commoner. You knew that's what I thought and you allowed it to go on.'

Pen gave a snort of disbelief. '*Who* was in disguise? It was not only me. You presented yourself as a squire's son with your dirt-caked boots and your greatcoat and your windblown hair. You weren't half as put together as you are tonight. Where were your silk waistcoats and watch fobs then?'

'One does not wear such finery when tromping the cliffs of Cornwall. I was unaware there was a dress code for that.' His eyes narrowed, scrutinising her, and she felt a flush of heat go through her. 'Besides, those were our rules, Pen. *Anonymity was our rule.*' Her heart raced a bit at the use of her name, her real name. She could not afford the attraction. 'We wanted our secrets. Do you deny it?'

No. She couldn't deny it. The fantasy had been intoxicating, only now did she realise how far out of her depth she'd been. 'I never thought…' She couldn't finish the sentence without admitting her stupidity. Even in the dim light of the room, her cheeks betrayed her with remembrances of the things she'd done with him, of the things he'd done to her, thinking she would never see him again, that she'd never need to be accountable for them.

Cassian—that was his name, wasn't it? It was how he'd been introduced to her tonight. Cassian Truscott, Viscount Trevethow. It was strange to think of him that way—chuckled softly. 'Never thought what? That we'd both be masquerading as someone we were not? Never thought your little indiscretion would come back on you?' It was exactly what she'd thought. Never mind the false names. She'd thought there was truth in how he'd presented himself. Even if she didn't know his name, she'd been confident she knew what he was.

He reached for her, close enough now to touch her, his hand skimming her cheek. Her body thrummed at his caress, remembering other touches, other caresses. She had to keep herself in check. She could not repeat her mistakes. 'Can we get past this, Pen? I know you were surprised to see me again tonight just as I was surprised—*stunned*—to see you. I'd given up hope of finding you again.' His voice was low, intimate. 'I was devastated when you didn't come. I waited for hours that afternoon. I went back for three days hoping you would be there. I didn't want to believe you'd left me. But now, we've found each other and this should be a happy occasion. We don't have to pretend any more. We can be ourselves, we can continue to explore what we can be together. Pen, what I'm saying is that I forgive you. I want to try again.'

The cad! How dare he make this disaster out to be of her making? She'd almost been drawn into the fantasy, almost. Pen swatted at his hand, pushing it away. 'Do not touch me. Do not think you can waltz in here, ask me to shoulder the blame and then offer me forgiveness I've never asked you for as if this is all my fault.'

She was blazing now, but with the heat of an anger that had nothing to do with the warmth she'd felt earlier. 'There is a liar in this room and it's not me. I've been nothing but honest about having a match being made for me, about going away to visit the man my father chose for me. But you were never honest. You made all these protestations of love when we were together and tonight you profess to have been devastated when I didn't come, but here you are in a ballroom hunting a wife and contemplating marriage just weeks later. Those are not the actions of a devastated man in love.'

He stood there, unmoving. There was no reaction and that only made her all the angrier. 'Say something, Cassian. Argue with me, shout at me. Hate me.'

But Cassian did none of those things. He was perfect in those moments; perfectly controlled, perfectly contained. He looked every inch the duke he would one day be while she was acting nowhere near a lady. 'I don't want to argue with you. I don't want to shout. I don't want to hate. I want you to see the good in this.

Matthew and Em had something special and now Cassian and Pen can have that too. You can have Matthew, Pen. He's not gone.'

She shook her head. She would not be taken in again. What did he want from her that he was willing to set aside his anger and his earlier sense of betrayal? 'No, I can't. Matthew doesn't exist. He never did and that means the man I thought you were isn't the man you are.' She'd nearly given herself to a pretence. She'd had a lucky escape even if she hadn't realised it at the time. What would have happened if her father and Phin hadn't whisked her off to London?

'What is that supposed to mean? If Matthew doesn't exist, then how do you know anything about me? You can't have it both ways.'

'I know you're here and I know *why* you're here. You are no different than any other man in the ballroom tonight. Do you think any of them care about me? They care about the Redruth alliance and the dowry that comes with it. When they dance with me, they're already calculating how they can pay off their debts or they're wondering why I've been hidden away in Cornwall for years. I'm a thing to them, a curiosity.'

'Not to me, you *know* that,' Cassian insisted. 'What about Mutton Cove and the things we told one another?'

'What I *know* is that you played with me in the gamekeeper's cottage, knowing that you would leave at the end of April. You started the affair knowing full well the Season would take you away. Dukes' sons dally with common maids all the time, intending to discard them.'

'That's not how it was,' he broke in, but she stalled him with a shake of her head. She wanted to believe otherwise, but the facts wouldn't allow it. Her heart was breaking all over again.

'It's exactly how it was. I was nothing to you then but a plaything and I am nothing more than that to you now. Viscount Trevethow came to court me sight unseen. You had an audience with my father, the two of you arranging my life without any consideration for how I might feel about it, all so that my father might have husband with a title for his daughter and so that you might have an alliance you find in some way useful. That is all the proof I need that you are no different than any other man here tonight. The one thing I thought Matthew could be capable of was liking me for me. You've taken that away.' That was what hurt the most about this whole debacle. She drew a breath and smoothed her skirts, calming herself. 'You've had more than your five minutes. I need to return to the ball. I would like you to leave the premises when you've finished your drink.'

She walked to the door and slipped out into the hall without a backward glance, letting her anger sustain her. It was better than giving in to other emotions. She felt as if someone had died. Matthew, and who she thought he was, was gone. Cassian Truscott could never replace him. He must be resisted at all costs. He might look like Matthew, but he did not share the values she'd associated with Matthew. She would not take a husband that was settled on her by her father, but that wasn't Cassian Truscott's greatest sin. His greatest sin was that he was supposed to have been different from the others and he wasn't. He'd gone to her father without even knowing who she was. He'd been willing to buy her sight unseen. It reduced her to a sack of potatoes in the market place, something to be bartered and traded while he'd pretended to have a different code of honour with a different girl in the cottage.

She would not set herself up for failure and heartbreak. She didn't want to marry a man who would hurt her. She knew already Cassian Truscott had the power to do that. She'd loved that man in the cottage and that man had moved on to another woman, a woman he'd never seen, with no regret. She could not give her heart again to such a man, knowing what she risked. He would hurt her over and over again. He would say whatever it took to win her in the moment, but he could never be true. He'd proven it tonight.

Chapter Thirteen

He'd not proven himself worthy of her. She'd dismissed him for a cad, a man who was pursuing her only for her money, and she wasn't entirely wrong. He had come courting the Redruth girl for those very reasons. Cassian was still reeling from her set-down the next morning over coffee in his rooms at the Albany. He deserved everything Pen had said last night. He couldn't recall the last time or *any* time a woman had not responded favourably to him. The evening could not be termed as anything other than an utter failure.

'Another resounding success for you, old chap!' Inigo strode into the dining room and slapped the newspapers down on the table, pages already creased back. 'One night back in action and already you've made the columns. Allow me to read aloud.' He cleared his throat dramatically. '"Viscount T. set hearts to fluttering and tongues to wagging when he took to the floor at Earl R.'s long-overdue debut ball for Lady P.

with said lady in his arms." Then there's this charming little mention.' Inigo reached for another newspaper.

Cassian shook his head. 'Stop. It was a disaster, Inigo. She's all but refused to see me. She threw me out of the ball.'

Inigo pulled up a chair and poured a cup of coffee, becoming instantly serious. 'Well, at least no one knows.' He nodded towards the papers. 'Everyone thinks a St George's wedding is imminent. So, she's refused you. We can work with that. Once she knows you, I'm sure she'll find you charming and your height less overwhelming. You can cut an intimidating figure, Cass.'

'That's the problem. She does know me.' Cassian leaned close to whisper, 'Inigo, she's Em.' There was some satisfaction in watching Inigo's face process the information, moving from confused to dawning realisation to stunned.

'Oh, damn.' Inigo whistled low. 'I'm not sure if that's lucky or not.'

'It's *not*,' Cassian growled. 'I've found her, but she wants nothing to do with me. She thinks I was merely toying with her in the cottage, a nobleman taking advantage of a commoner. Worse, she feels now that I'm here pursuing a wife so soon after our encounter that nothing I said was true, that my feelings were a sham just to seduce her, that I'll say anything to get what I want.' Cassian pushed his plate away—what little appetite he'd had was gone. Guilt was eating at him hard: guilt over Pen, guilt over Collin. He couldn't satisfy one without being untrue to the other. 'It seems I've become the unscrupulous fortune hunter I've guarded myself against.' That thought had haunted him long after he'd left Byerd House.

'May I? If you're not going to eat this?' Inigo reached for the discarded plate still full of warm food. 'Your cook does the best eggs.'

'I'm glad someone can eat,' Cassian replied pointedly. 'The rub is that for a moment last night, when I saw her face, I thought everything would be perfect. We'd found each other and we could pick up where we left off. Then, everything fell apart. The only things I'm picking up now are pieces. I need to win her back. I need her trust.' He needed Em.

'You need her land.' Inigo waved his fork.

'I need her attention before I can contemplate that. How do I pursue a woman who doesn't want to be pursued?'

'You go back. If you don't go back, she'll know you were all fluff and no substance. But...' Inigo dropped his voice conspiratorially '...if you go back, she'll know you're willing to fight for her, that you're serious.'

Cassian chuckled. 'I told Eaton something similar when he was certain he'd lost Eliza. It's a lot easier to give advice than it is to take it.' He fixed Inigo with a sombre stare, his mind working. He had to show Pen the man who was concerned for his people, for his region, a man who was willing to create an industry, to create jobs and income, a man who was willing to come down out of his ivory tower and put his privilege to work for others. Most of all, he needed to show her the man she'd fallen in love with at the cottage. 'What time is it?'

Inigo flipped open his pocket watch. 'Half past eleven. Why?'

Cassian set aside his napkin and rose. 'That's just enough time.'

'Time for what?' Inigo looked up from polishing off the plate.

Cassian grinned, feeling more optimistic than he had in a long while. 'To win her back.' Lady Penrose and her aunt held at-home on Thursdays from three until five. He had four hours to make himself presentable and to acquire the appropriate 'accessories' for his visit. He'd have to time his entrance just right. If her attitude last night was a solid indicator about her husband hunt, she wasn't enamoured of it. She'd had a cynical view of why the young men had flocked to her. Cassian would bet she wasn't looking forward to an at-home the night after her debut. It would be crowded with sycophants. By quarter past four, he'd wager she'd be looking for a way out and he'd be there to provide one. Even the strongest damsel needed to be rescued sometimes. He called for his manservant. 'Send to the stables, have the horses and Oscar ready at four.'

Pen felt her pasted-on smile start to waver as yet another gentleman paid homage to her eyes, her hair, her gown, her laugh, with insipid words designed to appeal to her. Flattery did not impress her. Honesty impressed her and that had been in short supply. She'd almost welcome the man who'd burst into the drawing room and declare in loud terms, 'I'm here for your dowry, Lady Penrose, and you can come along too.' At least she'd know where she stood with that man. She had to be honest, too, though. That man, should he exist, might be welcomed for his truthfulness, but she wouldn't marry him for it any more than she'd marry Wadesbridge for his kindnesses. It didn't change the fact that she wanted to marry a man of her choice for love, his antecedents and her dowry be hanged.

She glanced surreptitiously at the clock. It was four. An hour to go. It might as well be an eternity. The minutes seemed to drag. Her jaw actually hurt from endless smiling. Her brain hurt from trying to remember all the names. She'd danced with most of these men last night. They'd sent bouquets this morning until the house was bursting with vases full of roses, carnations and lilies of the valley filling up every available mantel and tabletop in the townhouse. Her father had beamed with delight when the morning papers had joined her name with Cassian's. Her father would be disappointed when her aunt reported Cassian was the only one not among the crop in the drawing room today.

As to her own disappointment, Pen wasn't certain. Part of her had hoped he might come even though she'd been quite clear last night that she didn't want to see him again. Part of her was glad he'd taken the set-down to heart and stayed away. But no part of her believed that was the end of it. So, here she sat, waiting for the other shoe to drop, as if discovering that Cassian was Matthew wasn't shocking revelation enough.

Even this afternoon, with time to process that reality, it was still stunning. He was not lost to her after all. Oh, how she'd felt last night when she'd seen his face and knew it was him, not a mirage! For a moment, it had been a miraculous discovery. There'd been a split second of pure joy before reality had swept in, bringing with it all the consequences of what his presence meant: for him to be here meant he'd not been honest with her and he was dangerous to her. He could expose what they'd done in that cottage and she'd be ruined. Furthermore, he wanted something from her father enough to court her sight unseen. That in itself should be frightening. Logic proposed she ought to be glad he hadn't come to the at-home.

But it wasn't that simple. Her heart, her body, disagreed with what her mind recommended. Last night in his arms, she'd been hard put not to press herself against him as they waltzed, convention be hanged. It had been torture to be close to him, but not close enough to feel the hard muscles of his chest beneath his clothes, to not be able to lay her head against his shoulder, to feel his arm around her, folding her to him. She'd had to resist those temptations not only for propriety's sake, but for her own sake. He would take advantage of those feelings and the stakes were so much higher now. Marriage. For ever. Her father would be ecstatic. His daughter, a duchess! He would gloat that Father knew best after all. Yet, her eyes still drifted to the doorway and she had to remind herself of all the reasons Cassian wouldn't come through it.

The largest reasons of course was that Cassian wouldn't come today after that scathing set-down and that was as it should be, needed to be. Second, she didn't *want* to see him. At least that was what she told herself as she raised her fan to hide a yawn. Young Daniel Strathearn on her left was telling another story about his grandmother. He was very fond of his grandmother. This was the fourth story this afternoon. What she would give to be whisked away. She wondered if she could plead a headache and leave her aunt to manage the rest? But, no, a headache would land her in bed with one of Cook's odious possets.

There was a commotion at the drawing-room door, enough to excuse glancing away from Daniel Strathearn. Her fan stopped oscillating and her breath caught. Cassian had arrived. He'd come, after all. Her set-down had been nothing but a paper tiger and he'd charged right through it, which meant he didn't believe there wasn't anything left to say. That both consoled and concerned her. He wouldn't have come back if he didn't want something.

Her aunt caught her eye with a quiet look of approval, a little smile of delight on her lips. In fact, every woman in the room, every cousin, every sister, every mother who'd accompanied their male relatives here today to make the visit look more altruistic, was smiling as he wove through the room. How could they not? He put every man in the room to shame. He was taller, broader, better dressed, more at ease. More everything. There was an energy that rolled off him and permeated the room. He made no secret of his intentions. All that masculinity was headed straight for her. Pen held her nervous hands still in the depths of her skirts. What did one say to a man she'd sent out of the house the prior night?

He bowed before her, dressed for driving in immaculate in nankeen riding breeches, polished tall boots and coat of claret superfine with pristine linen beneath a cream waistcoat that sported a pattern of twining poppies. His jaw was new-shaven and his hair brushed back, exposing every sharp angle of his face: the strong jaw, the hawkish length of his nose. His whisky eyes were on her, a challenge on his lips. 'Lady Penrose, you look a tad wilted today. I hope last night didn't take a toll on you.'

Wilted? Did he just say she looked wilted in a room full of men who'd been praising her beauty? There was a moment's silence as if the rest of the room couldn't believe what they'd heard either. 'Perhaps we might rectify that with some fresh air.' His eyes sparked. 'May I interest you in a drive? You're nearly done here. I'm sure the gentlemen won't mind me stealing you since they've had you all afternoon. My phaeton is waiting outside.'

Escape! Even if it was with Cassian. She was desperate enough to take it and perhaps it was the chance she needed to determine what his intentions were. If there was to be a battle between them, it was best to know her enemy. Pen glanced at her aunt for permission. 'Air does sound wonderful,' she prompted, earning a nod from her aunt. She put her hand in Cassian's and let him lead her from the room while her guests looked on in varying degrees of disappointment.

Cassian's phaeton was a gorgeous bright blue lacquered affair with a black leather seat and pulled by two matched blacks jingling in their harness. They were groomed to perfection, coats gleaming and blue plumes dancing from their head gear. Hours of effort had gone into preparing the horses and the equipage. His tiger in blue livery rode on the rear bench beside a large wicker basket. 'We'll be noticed by everyone we pass,' Pen commented as he handed her up to the high seat. Perhaps that was what he intended, to be as conspicuous as possible. She wasn't sure she liked that.

'That's the point.' Cassian grinned as he vaulted into the driver's seat and picked up the reins. 'I want everyone to know I went driving today with Lady Penrose Prideaux.'

'The wilted flower of the *ton*? Are you sure you want to be seen with her?' Pen queried.

'I had to say something to get you out of there.' Cassian turned the horses into the traffic. 'We'll take a turn through the park.' That was what she feared; that he was a man who might say anything to get what he wanted. Had that been the case at the cottage? Were his words just pretty persuasion?

'Why did you come at all? I thought I'd made myself clear last night. Are you a glutton for punishment?'

'I'm a glutton for *you*.' Cassian slid her a look that melted her resolve. 'I came because I don't want to give up on us. Matthew and Em had something special. Maybe Cassian and Pen can have that, too, but we have to discover it, to discover each other all over again or perhaps for the first time. Now, we can do it without pretence. We can be ourselves, all our cards are on the table. We don't have to hide.' He was so impassioned in his plea, she wanted to believe him. But she couldn't, not yet.

'Why would you want that? You were clearly ready to settle for less.' She'd already accepted him at face value once before, to her detriment, she feared. She couldn't afford to do that again.

'Because I didn't have a choice, Pen. You were gone. I had to move forward.' They turned into the park, joining the line of carriages parading down the lanes, and Pen tried to summon the loathing, the sense of betrayal that had given her strength last night, but found her defences lacking.

'And you chose Redruth's daughter to move forward with. Why?' The best she could do was wariness and caution. She needed her answers. He made it sound easy, but it wasn't. There were things they couldn't change, like the fact that he was willing to marry a woman he'd never met after he'd professed love to another. She needed a loyal man. Could he be that?

'Redruth is close to home. It made sense for me to seek a Cornish alliance. I'm not out to hurt you, Pen.' Cassian steered the phaeton into the park, choosing to enter through the Kensington Gate at the north-west corner as opposed to the much busier Cumberland entrance.

'Where are we going?' Pen twisted in her seat, looking around and noting the relative absence of people, of horses and carriages. The public had suddenly become quite private.

'The north-west enclosure, some place where we

can talk. It will be less crowded and I have a surprise for you. Do you trust me?'

'I don't know.' She was suddenly at sea. Did she dare trust him again?

'That's not a no, so it's a beginning. I'll take that.' Cassian parked the phaeton and called for his tiger to hold the horses. 'We'll walk from here. Horses and carriages aren't allowed in the enclosure.' Cassian climbed down and came around. He reached up for her, his hands at her waist, and swung her down with an impressive ease that was not lost on her. She was nothing for his strength and she relished the feel of his hands on her, confident and warm. She'd missed his touch. 'First things first, there's someone who wants to meet you.' He tucked her arm firmly through his as led her to the back of the phaeton and the big wicker basket. It rocked as they approached and a sharp bark escaped.

'Oh! What is it?' Pen exclaimed, startled by the sound.

'Your birthday present.' Cassian reached inside and lifted out the pup. 'This is Oscar. I brought him with me when I went to the cottage. I'd wanted to give you a day with a puppy. Here, hold him.' Cassian deposited him into her arms as the puppy wiggled.

This was no good at all—how dare Cassian not play fair? One look at those dark puppy eyes and she was lost. How was she to resist Cassian and a puppy, too? 'I can't keep him,' she stammered.

'I know.' Cassian grinned boyishly. He fastened a leash around Oscar's collar. 'I'll keep him for you.'

'I'll be forced to visit you,' Pen pointed out, another unfair move.

'Yes, exactly.' Cassian took the puppy and set him on the ground. 'Now, Lady Pen, would you like to walk your dog?'

Oh, she did! This was a childhood dream come true. She shouldn't accept it, she *knew* he was bribing her. It scared and exhilarated her. He'd brought the puppy all the way to London. She furrowed her brow and stopped. 'Why did you bring the puppy to London if you didn't know I'd be here?'

Cassian stopped too. 'Because I missed Em that much and the puppy was a way to keep her close. Why do you wear that glass heart?' She reached up to finger it with her free hand.

'Because I miss Matthew,' she admitted. 'But that doesn't mean…'

'I know what it doesn't mean, Pen,' Cassian said softly. He ushered her and Oscar through the front gates of the enclosure, his hand light at her back. 'There are benches inside where we can sit.' He laughed, a low, familiar chuckle at her ear. 'I know a game we can play. Twenty questions. Maybe you've heard of it?'

'Like old times?' Pen asked, immediately wary, not only of him and the easy assumptions he made with his hands and his words, but also of herself and the ease with which she'd gladly glide back into the old behaviour if she wasn't vigilant.

Cassian shook his head, his gaze resting on her. 'No, like *new* times. I don't think we can go back, Pen. We can only go forward.' But the past *would* come for-

ward with them. It would always be between them, reminding them of the potential for passion, for loss, and
the consequences of risk, both the good and the bad.
'Give me a chance to know the real you. Give yourself a chance to know the real me before you decide to
throw happiness away with both hands.'

Chapter Fourteen

Pen could see why he'd chosen this spot. It was peaceful and green. There was a pasture with deer and cows to one side and a keeper's lodge to the other. The Serpentine served as one border and Kensington Gardens served as another. Within the enclosure, two springs contributed to the country coolness of the space. 'Would you like a glass?' Cassian offered as they strolled past an old woman sitting at a table beside the springs. Oscar gave her a friendly high-pitched puppy yap. 'One of the springs is a mineral spring.' Cassian stopped and fished out coins from his pocket for two glasses. 'You should try some. The water is always cold. Perfect for a warm day like today.' He gave her a glass and they went to the spring to drink.

Pen sipped the water, tentative about the taste. She smiled, pleasantly surprised as the cool water slid down her throat. 'It's so much more refreshing than hot tea. What's the other spring for? Is it mineral water, too?'

'People come to bathe their eyes from it. I don't

know if it works. Do you have weak eyes? Should we try?' Cassian laughed and the sound made her smile. This was the man she'd wandered the St Piran's Day fair with, to whom everything was an adventure.

'I'll pass on that today. My eyes are fine.' She could feel herself starting to relax, starting to remember how it was between them, how easily they talked, how comfortably they moved together. Surely those things weren't lies? Remembering made it easy to forget the wariness she'd armed herself with, the knowledge that this man, who wasn't dangerous to Em, was indeed dangerous to Pen. She needed to determine how dangerous and in what ways.

'I think the enclosure's gamekeeper has the best job in the world,' Cassian nodded towards the lodge with its picturesque gardens. 'To be able to live here, surrounded by the feel of the countryside, and still be in one of the world's most vibrant cities. Anything he wants or needs is within his grasp without sacrificing tranquillity.' He gave her a smile. 'How do you find your first time in London?'

'In a word, overwhelming. There are so many rules, so many people, so many things to do and to see, and everything seems to require a change of dress to do it. Phin is determined that I see it all. He's taken me everywhere: the Tower, Astley's, Gunter's, we've seen the cathedrals, the British Museum, the art at Somerset House. I've shopped on Bond Street incessantly and excessively. I've never had as many clothes or needed as many.' This was safe conversation. It was personal but not terribly probing. There was nothing dangerous in it, no disclosures, no secrets.

They stopped beneath a shady oak. Cassian brushed off the bench, freeing it of tree debris for her to sit. Em would not have cared, but Em hadn't worn expensive Bond Street gowns. 'Can't have you ruining your dresses,' he teased. 'London suits you. There's an adventure around every corner. Isn't that what you wanted?' Oh, there it was, the danger, in just a few words, there was the reminder that she'd shared her innermost thoughts with him. That he was the keeper of her secrets, the things she told no one else.

'It does suit, in a way.' She was contemplative as they rested, enjoying the view of the pasture as Oscar romped in the grass. 'But London takes some getting used to. It's thrown several things into sharp relief for me.'

'Like what?' Cassian whispered the prompt, coaxing the intimacy to life between them, overriding her misgivings.

'Do you truly want to know? They're rather dark things.' She cocked her head and fixed him with her green stare, challenging him. 'Along with the adventure, there's also noise and danger lurking around every corner, especially for a woman.'

'Is that your father speaking or is that you?' Cassian queried to her surprise.

'You remembered.' She softened, touched that he'd recalled the story she'd told him in the cottage. 'Perhaps it's both. However, I wonder if it's really true or if that's a construct men have made up to keep women dependent. Even in London, a supposedly civilised city, I can't go anywhere without an escort. Apparently, even a gentleman of my own class can't be trusted to not be a ravening beast, unable to control his urges in my feminine presence. My very femininity is enough to tempt him. To make his lack of control my fault is ridiculous.' She sighed.

'You're safe with me, Pen.' His hand was warm on hers, his thumb stroking her knuckles. This was her opening and she took it.

'Am I? It occurred to me, after the shock of seeing you again had settled, that I might be in the greatest danger *from* you. You would only have come back today if there was something you wanted and you have the power to get it.' She let her eyes linger on him, watching his face for any reaction, that she was right. 'The cottage, Cassian. You could blackmail me with it.'

A slow smile spread across his face. Apparently, he found some humour in her very serious suggestion. 'And you could blackmail me with the same. Have you thought of that?' He raised her hand to his lips and kissed her knuckles. 'Perhaps *I* am the one in danger? Perhaps, now that you know who I am, you will go to your father and say I compromised you. I know many girls who would do it to be a duchess.' He chuckled. 'Yet, I risked coming back today.'

'But *I* wouldn't do such a thing!' Pen protested, aghast at the thought. In her fear and in her haste, she'd not thought of that.

'Maybe that's why I risked it. Because I knew you wouldn't any more than I would do it to you,' he assured her with a laugh. 'What suspicious minds we have, Pen. No wonder we decided on false identities.'

But it was no laughing matter to Pen. She studied his face for a moment, a thought coming to her. 'Is it because of your brother? You mentioned he was thwarted in love.' It would have been a high-born alliance, she could see that now.

'In part.' Cassian shifted on the bench and crossed a leg over one knee. Ah, the topic made him uncomfortable. Well, good. It was his turn for a change. 'He fell in love with the daughter of a man he made investments with, only she was a decoy. He loved her, but her love for him was not real—it was an act to draw him in. It destroyed him. I would prefer to avoid such hardship if I could.'

'Is that possible, though? I don't think love works that way. Love is hard, it demands sacrifice. If it was easy, the poets would have nothing to write about,' Pen said softly. 'I am sorry for him and for you in the losing of him.'

'I'd most likely be cynical any way, just as you are.' Cassian offered her a wry smile. 'It's not much fun being hunted. It's why I could not give you my real name.' She'd not forgotten how the women in the drawing room today had looked at him, with naked hunger in their eyes. They would devour him if given the chance, all for his title, with little thought for the man who bore it, the man who could build fires and sail a little boat among the seals of Mutton Cove. What she would give to be back in Mutton Cove now, with him.

'No, it's not.' She gave him a meaningful stare.

'Do you think I'm hunting you?' he asked quietly.

'Like you, I have to assume everyone is hunting me,' she answered. 'We are just animals in the great cage of London. The longer I'm here the more I realise I've confused adventure with freedom and what I really want is the latter. I want to be free. Free to make my own choices, to go where I want to go, to marry how I want to marry. To be who I want to be.'

'Is that why you went to the fair?' They were talking softly now. Birds chirped in the background.

'Yes.' The old intimacy flared to life between them, stoked into being by his touch, his voice, his words, the very nearness of him a source of support and solace. She offered him a smile tinged with mischief. 'Do you want to know a secret? The fair wasn't the first time I sneaked out of the castle.'

Cassian laughed, a low, deep rumble just for her. 'You minx. Where do you go when you sneak out?'

'To the hills. I like to walk and pick flowers and look for the little animals.' She looked down at their hands. 'How do you do it? How do you convince me to tell you all of this? Whenever I'm with you everything just comes out: my secrets, my fears, my hopes. I don't talk to anyone the way I talk to you.' And maybe she shouldn't. She didn't want to give him any more power than that which he already had.

'I'll take that as a compliment.' His eyes were on her. She knew that look, the one that lingered on her eyes and caressed her lips, just before his body leaned in, his head tilted to capture her lips, his mouth on hers, reminding her. A little mewl welled up in her throat as his hand cupped her jaw, encouraging her to open to him entirely. 'I mean to prove myself to you, Pen. I want you back,' he murmured between kisses. In those moments, she wanted that too. She wanted to pretend that he had no other agenda, that there was no danger here on the bench, just pleasure, just them and that a man could love her just for herself. Later she would remember all the reasons to resist.

The first invitation arrived the next morning along with a bouquet of wildflowers. The flowers had looked out of place in their simplicity against the enormous bouquets sent by others, but they meant the most, just to her. Even in this bouquet they had their privacy, their secrets. The flowers were a reminder of their visit to the enclosure. They were also proof that he'd listened. He'd remembered that little detail from when she'd confessed to sneaking out of the castle. 'Put them in my room, please.' She handed them off to a footman while her father was still agog over the invitation.

'The theatre, my dear, tonight if we're free. We are, of course. I'll have your aunt cancel any plans. We'll go. It will be a show of force. All of London will see that we approve and encourage Trevethow's attentions.' Her father handed her the note so she could read it too. After all, it was addressed to her. '*Pizarro* at the Covent Garden Theatre, it's a tragedy.' For a moment her father looked dubious. 'Hopefully it's not too bloody for you? Daniel Egerton plays Rolla and is said to do a passable job.'

'I'm sure I will enjoy it,' Pen put in quickly before

her father could change his mind. They'd not been to the theatre yet and Pen was excited to go, no matter what the show, a treat that was marred only by her father's satisfaction. He was getting what he wanted—a suitor hand-picked by himself.

'London will enjoy seeing the two of you together again.' Her father returned to his breakfast. 'What do you make of him, Pen? I have great hopes for Viscount Trevethow, although it might too early to disregard a few others. Viscount Wilmington, for instance. He's been most insistent. Your aunt said he was overtly disappointed yesterday with your disappearance. He told her he felt you should not have left with Trevethow.' He'd also been quite overt about his intentions with the largest bouquet of them all usurping Wadesbridge's pride of place on the drawing room mantel.

'I think it's too early to discard anyone.' The last thing Pen wanted was the field narrowed. Narrowing fields meant funnelling *her* towards making a decision.

'Still, being seen at the theatre with Viscount Trevethow will certainly boost your cachet.' He smiled. 'A duchess, Penrose. Just think how proud your mother would be if we could pull it off.'

Pen only smiled. She didn't want to argue with her father although she disagreed. She did think of her mother. Was that all her mother would have wanted for her? To marry well? That wasn't the mother she remembered. Her mother would have wanted her to marry for love, for happiness. Her mother had been full of laughter, she'd had little use for rules and society. She'd insisted on raising her own children instead of turning them over to a bevy of nurses and governesses. She'd hated leaving them for time in London with her husband. She'd invented games and taken them on picnics in the hills and told them stories; Cornish fairy tales or tales she invented as they looked up at the sky. Her mother was fearless. She climbed rocks with Phin and swam in the ocean. She filled Castle Byerd with colour, with life. Then one day she was simply gone, taking all that colour and life and laughter with her. But her mother would never have meant for her to live imprisoned by fear. Her mother would have wanted her to live vibrantly, and Pen would, starting with the theatre.

The theatre was bustling with life as Cassian's carriage pulled to the kerb in front of the Bow Street entrance, taking its turn to disgorge its passengers. Cassian handed Pen down, watching her face light up as she surveyed the Doric-columned facade. Cassian felt as if a shaft of sunlight had warmed him from the inside out. She stood still for a moment, letting humanity swerve around her as she studied the building. 'They've modelled the theatre after Minerva's Temple, haven't they?' she exclaimed, recognising the likeness. 'I saw a picture once of the Acropolis in a book about Greece.'

'I knew you'd like it.' Cassian tucked her hand through his arm, feeling inordinately pleased. This was one adventure he could give her. There were other plays and other theatres, but he'd chosen this one on purpose for her appreciation of such details. He might not be able to take her to Greece, but he could show her a bit of Greece right here in London.

He loved her enthusiasm. Inside, she wasn't afraid to look around as she exclaimed, 'I know it's not polite to gawk, but I want to see everything!' And everyone wanted to see her. Cassian kept a strong hand at her back, ushering her up the grand staircase on the left, stopping every few steps to greet people. Her enthusiasm was contagious, everything fresh and new through her eyes. When was the last time he'd been interested in the Box Saloon or the coffered ceilings or even noticed them? But with Pen, it was all brand new. He fed her excitement with stories and bits of information whispered at her ear. 'The theatre was rebuilt after a fire in 1808—this one is larger than the original.' Or, 'There were riots here when the seat prices were raised to cover the building the expenses.'

She looked over her shoulder at him with a smile. 'Are you as well informed on every subject?'

'There are some subjects I'd like to be better informed about,' Cassian flirted, his eyes dropping to her lips. Too bad her family was near. He'd like to steal a kiss right here in the box for all of London to see, claiming her as his own. But for now, it was enough to be here with her, to give her this night, to prove to her that he was worthy and to hope that all else would follow.

He settled her in a seat at the front of the box and saw to her family's comfort before taking the seat beside her as the lights went down. Under the cover of darkness, he felt her hand grope for his. A moment later her head bent to his with a whisper. 'Thank you for this.'

His heart swelled at the simple praise even as his mind counselled caution. Would she thank him later? Would she believe all this truly had been for her if she found out about the land? This was the shard of guilt that had lodged itself in his conscience as he'd planned his campaign. His heart wanted her back, land or not. But his mind, his dream, his legacy, the guilt he needed to assuage over his brother, needed to win her. She was the key to his land. Without that land there was no plea- sure garden, no boost to the Cornish economy, no jobs for hundreds of unemployed workers, no atonement. Perhaps he should tell her about the land. But how could he? This new burgeoning trust between them was too fragile. He couldn't tell her. Not yet. There would be a better time, a time when she would under- stand, a time when she would know that he cared for her apart from the land. If she knew too soon, it would only prove to her what she already thought was true: that he was no better than any other suitor come to trade titles and money in a political alliance.

Those suitors came in droves at the intermission, crowding the box to such an extent that Cassian felt obliged to move the party out into the Box Saloon so that no one was crushed. Viscount Wilmington was one of the first to arrive, levelling daggers at Cassian for his interruption yesterday. 'You've stolen her from us twice now, Trevethow,' he joked loudly enough for the other gentlemen nearby to hear in hopes of garnering an ally with his feigned bonhomie. 'It was a bold move, taking her for a drive in the Park. Perhaps I might try it myself.' He arched an enquiring eyebrow Pen's direction. 'Might I steal you away for the last act, my lady? My box has a rather unique view of the stage.'

Cassian was prepared to intervene, but Pen was cool beside him. 'I think you've misunderstood yesterday's events, Lord Wilmington. No one steals me. I make my own decisions about where I spend my time and with whom.' She smiled to take away the sting.

Wilmington gave a curt nod. 'Another time, then. If you enjoy the theatre, I also have seats at Drury Lane.' He bowed and made his farewells.

Cassian watched him retreat with careful eyes. 'He is quite intense where you are concerned.' He might have made an enemy. He'd have to ask Inigo about Wilmington tomorrow. What was the source of Wilmington's interest in Pen? Was it just the competition of the Season or did it stem from something more? The lights dimmed in warning for the final act and Cassian returned Pen to her seat. She'd been a revelation in the Saloon. Despite her claims of being overwhelmed by London, she'd handled the attention well, just as she'd handled it splendidly the night of her ball.

Cassian leaned close. 'Have I told you how beautiful you look tonight?' She had opted for a gauzy gown of rose-gold with satin striping. The effect was stunning. She looked softly alluring, managing at once to present the image of the debutante while also projecting intelligence and sharp wit. It was no wonder every man in the theatre had been drawn to her. Her hair was twined with a rope of pearls and behind one ear was a small, pink wildflower. 'You're wearing one my flowers.'

'Yes. It was the most thoughtful bouquet I received. Wherever did you find them?'

'I rode out to Hampstead Heath.' He grinned. 'We should picnic there and you can pick flowers to your heart's content. Shall we? Tomorrow? I'll call for you at one.'

'Don't we get to discuss this?' she scolded.

But Cassian simply smiled as the stage lights went up and replied, 'No, the play is starting and we wouldn't want to be rude.'

Chapter Fifteen

This was progress; lying on a blanket in the sun, the smell of sweet grass in the air, watching Pen weave a flower chain while bees buzzed, Oscar napped on the blanket and the May day behaved perfectly. Beyond them were her maid and his tiger, but they had privacy enough should they want to behave less properly than the weather.

Pen held up a necklace of daisies. 'There, I've made a lei in honour of King Kamehameha's visit to London.' The newspapers had been full of the Hawaiian King since his arrival on the eighteenth. But he'd been confined to his suites at Osborn's Hotel until King George could receive him, or *chose to* receive him as some less favourable news reported. Some papers suggested the English King had no intention of meeting the Hawaiian King, or the Sandwich Island King, depending on which paper one read.

'Are you interested in meeting them?' Cassian propped himself up on one arm. 'Secretary Canning is giving a reception for them in a few days. The Foreign Office has taken over the visit since the King drags his feet on meeting them. Canning has invited several dukes, Wellington included, along with the Duke and Duchess of Hayle and their son.' He watched her eyes light up as she grasped his intentions.

'Really? I could meet them? People from halfway around the world? People from a place I've only read about?' She gave him an infectious smile. 'Perhaps I should make some more English leis.' Then she sobered and reached out a hand to touch his. 'I fear you are spoiling me. First the theatre and now this.'

He took her hand and threaded his fingers through it. 'Why do you fear it? I mean to win you back, Pen. I am serious about that. You told me the other night at the ball that I was not worthy of you, that I was no better than any other sycophant in the ballroom. I want to prove to you that I am better, that I am worthy of you and your dreams.'

'Please don't.' Pen tugged at her hand and he let it go, feeling as if a shadow had scuttled across the sun. 'It's not just that. I don't want to be traded in marriage. I don't want to be a pawn between my father and a man he's chosen for me, or my husband's pawn because my marriage settlement possesses something he wants. Marriage should be more. It should be trust, and honesty, and respect and love built between two people who *want* to share a life together, not just live in the same house.'

Yes! Yes! Cassian's soul wanted to cry out a chorus

of yeses. Wasn't this exactly what he sought in a mate? What he thought he'd lost when he'd come to London to claim Redruth's daughter? Someone who wanted those things, too? But her next words dampened that enthusiasm. 'I don't know that you and I can have that, that we can get there after everything that's happened, not just between us, but with my father. He chose you, the Viscount Trevethow. He picked you out for me. And you picked out Redruth's daughter sight unseen. You were going to choose her over Em, always. No matter what you say about love, you chose duty first.'

This was the argument he dreaded, the one for which he had no good answer. He had chosen duty over love when he'd come to London. Even if he hadn't lost Em, he would still have chosen duty. How would she feel if she knew about the land? Perhaps he wouldn't have to tell her, if they chose each other voluntarily, if she fell in love with him the way Em had with Matthew? It was the coward's way out, but it was also the only way in which he could have both Pen and the land.

He reached out and smoothed back a strand of caramel hair that had fallen in her face. He didn't want to quarrel with her today, not with the sun out and this rare peaceful moment of privacy between them. London made it deuced difficult for them to be alone. He didn't want to waste the opportunity. He picked up the lei in her lap and changed the subject. 'How did you learn to make these? They look difficult.'

'They're not that hard.' Pen plucked two daisies and handed them to him. 'Copy me. First, you need to break off some of the stems to shorten them. Then, you can take your fingernail and make a slit right here on the stem.'

'With a fingernail?' Cassian arched a brow at the request and she laughed.

'Or a knife if you have one. Ladies so seldom carry knives, you know. We must make do with what's on our bodies.' She passed him a second flower. 'Now, you slide the stem of this flower through the slit, and repeat until you have a chain long enough.'

Bodies, slit, sliding and repeating.

Cassian shifted on the blanket. Daisy chains had suddenly become a rather sensual activity. 'Who taught you how to make them?' He was more interested in watching her face as she worked than in making his own. The task absorbed her entirely.

She looked up with a soft smile. 'My mother taught me. We used to make them when we went walking at home.'

Ah. The hills. The place she went when she sneaked out of the castle. 'And now you walk the hills alone.' The afternoon became intimately quiet, the buzzing of the bees in the nearby lavender more pronounced in the stillness.

'I'm not alone. I feel closest to her there. It's where I have the most memories of her.'

'You miss her.' It was a statement. He could hear the longing in her voice—it was a tone he recognised too well. 'What happened?' Their fingers were flirting with one another again, slowly moving to the middle ground between them on the blanket. He reached for her hand. Sometimes touching helped people to open up, to feel safe with their disclosures.

She didn't pull away. 'My mother was travelling to Truro to meet her sister. It was a sudden visit. Word had come early that afternoon my aunt, who was expecting a baby, was doing poorly and the child was imminent. My father was busy with the estate and couldn't accompany her on short notice. He asked her to wait, but my mother felt she couldn't delay. It had been a difficult pregnancy and my aunt was older.' She looked up at him, the memory giving her gaze a far-off look as if she was seeing beyond him into the past. 'It was one of the few times I'd ever heard them fight. My father denied her nothing and in the end he didn't deny her this. He called for the coach and off she went. But the quarrel had delayed departure and part of the journey would be made in the dark. Her coach was set upon by highwaymen.' Her voice caught and Cassian waited as she gathered herself.

'You needn't say any more,' he assured her. He knew how hard it was to talk of the dead, how stirring the memories stirred other aches as well.

'There's little more to say. The coachman and the outriders were killed defending her. One of them lived long enough to report my mother had drawn a pistol on the leader and shot him through the shoulder. She'd gone down fighting.' Pen smiled a bit at that. 'I wouldn't have expected it any other way. My mother wasn't afraid of the world or of anything or anyone in it. She always said, "Live your life, Pen, and don't worry if anyone else likes it. It's not their life.'" She sighed. 'It's not easy to do that. I wish it was.'

Cassian heard the unspoken regret behind her words. Just the opposite had occurred. Pen's life had become the life her father chose for her. She wasn't free to explore the world. The world beyond Castle Byerd was limited to books and atlases. 'Did they ever catch the highwaymen?' Cassian asked quietly.

'No. It's been ten years. There's no likelihood of that now. Perhaps they've been caught by someone else and found justice that way. Criminals don't last long. That's what I have to believe, at least, if I want consolation or if I want to move forward and not be paralysed by fear.'

'Like your father?' Cassian prompted. He was starting to see now how large of a role fear had played in her life in the years. Fear had been her ruler whether or not it had been her choice. So much had been decided for her out of fear.

'Yes. My father regrets not stopping her. He regrets he wasn't able to catch them, that he didn't go with her.'

Cassian nodded. 'I felt that way when Collin died. I should have been there to stop it. I don't know if that kind of regret ever goes away.'

'That regret is eating him alive and the rest of us. He's taken that regret out on me, ensuring that nothing will happen to me. If he can keep me safe, then somehow he is making up for not keeping her safe. In the meanwhile, in his attempt to save my life, he's robbed me of it.' Her words were raw with resentment. At last, here was the source of the cynicism he'd heard as they'd walked in the enclosure at the Park, the bitterness he'd heard the night they'd quarrelled in the library.

'So you sneak out of the castle to remember, to escape, to live.' He saw more clearly what he was up against: her desire to choose her mate was more than selfish defiance. This was about reclaiming the freedom she'd been denied. She'd been locked in a castle for ten years like a princess in fairy story even if it had been done without malicious intent. Now, she was breaking free, only to risk being tied down again the moment she'd tasted that freedom. From that perspective it seemed almost cruel to have brought her to London, to let her taste freedom only to snatch it away.

Cassian leaned in, claiming her mouth in a sweet kiss. 'I can show you the world, Pen,' he promised.

'I know,' she breathed, her lips brushing his in return, the fire between them starting to ignite. The world was more than places…it was passion and pleasure. 'That's what scares me. How can I go back in the cage after I've seen it?' They were kissing in earnest now; mouths and tongues competing with words, air coming in ragged breaths.

'You wouldn't have to go back.' Cassian rolled her beneath him, his gaze intent on her face watching for any sign of capitulation.

'Don't make promises you can't keep, Cassian,' she warned softly. 'A duchess is the most gilded cage of all.' But there was no heat to the argument. The only heat was that which sprang between them on the blanket and warmed them overhead. Nature's heat, passion's heat, but not anger's.

'My duchess may do as she pleases.' Cassian nipped at her neck, feeling her pulse race beneath his mouth, his own desire rising hot and fast for this woman, for this moment. He would make her any promise.

'May she?' Pen's words were laced with sensual purpose. She pressed a hand to his chest. 'Shall we test that theory? Lie back.'

'Pen, what are you doing?' Cassian said warily, but it didn't stop him from complying. She gave him a wicked look full of meaning and he went hard. Dear sweet heavens. She meant to use her mouth. It took only the insight of a moment to understand her intention. She worked the fall of his riding breeches open, her eyes already wide at the prominent evidence of his arousal. There was smug pride in her gaze, too, a woman's pride that she could rouse him so effortlessly. Perhaps there was surprise too. 'I had no idea a man could be so big, so hard.'

'Does it please you that I am?' Cassian levered upwards on his elbows and stole a kiss. Gone were talks of dead beloveds and regrets. This afternoon was for the living.

She leaned up over him and kissed his mouth. 'What do you think? Now, hush. I have it on good authority it's rude to talk when the show is starting.'

'Show, is it?' He couldn't resist one last tease as she wiggled down the length of him, her mouth closing around the tip of his shaft, the heat of her lips reducing him to a moan. Dear lord, she was good at this. It just proved one didn't need experience when one had curiosity and ambition, and Pen was ambitious in the extreme. She explored him with her tongue, licking at his length, lapping at his tip, tasting and testing, as if he were a fine, well-aged vintage and she a connoisseur who knew that one did not gulp such a wine, but sipped it, savoured it. Which was all well and good up to a point.

She'd licked him to a frenzy. He dug his hands into the folds of the blanket, feeling the give of the grass beneath the fabric, his head arching to the sun, his eyes closed tight, the cords of his neck exposed and taut, every muscle in his body exerting themselves in a bid for restraint. He was not alone in the struggle. From his thighs, her own breaths came in ragged pants, her artful seduction degenerating into the primal. He gave a sharp groan as her teeth bit too hard in her excitement. Her head came up for a fleeting second. She was a wild thing, her hair falling forward, her eyes green fire before she took him again, working his length with her mouth until restraint could be held no longer. He let out a warning growl, giving her time to move away and take him in hand instead before he spent quite thoroughly against her palm, against his thigh, his stomach.

'Fireworks,' Pen murmured as she took a handkerchief from him. 'Or a great fountain.'

'Do you like fireworks?' Cassian adjusted his breeches, drew her up to him and settled her against his shoulder. Her efforts had left him pleasantly drained and drowsy. He wanted to hold her, wanted to feel her warm body against his.

'I like yours,' she teased gently.

'Tuesday is opening night at Vauxhall. I have a supper box. There will be dancing and fireworks and a hundred other entertainments. Will you come?'

She lifted her head. 'My father says Vauxhall is full of danger.'

'He can come with us. Perhaps if you're with me, he'll feel there is less to fear.'

'I think you are the danger.' But she didn't mean it. There was only joking in her words this time as she snuggled against him, her hand comfortable and familiar on his chest. For a moment they were Em and Matthew, lying together once more in the gamekeeper's cottage, content just to be. No, Cassian thought drowsily. Today they'd become more than Em and Matthew. Em and Matthew had nothing to lose, nothing to risk by being together. It was easy to share secrets with a stranger. But Cassian and Pen had much to risk and they had shared any way. It was a significant step forward towards winning her trust.

'I wonder what my mother would have thought of you?' Pen traced a circle on his shirt and Cassian regretted the invention of clothes. How wondrous it would have been to feel her finger on his skin, to lie beneath the sun naked with her, to feel the sun's heat on their bodies. Her finger stopped tracing and he could sense her gathering her thoughts. 'I talk to her a lot, not just when I'm out walking. Do you think that's crazy?'

'No.' His hand played idly through her hair, lifting it and dropping it. He liked lying her with her, listening to her think out loud. What a precious gift this was, a gift he thought he'd never have again.

'I think losing someone close changes your relationship to them. They're gone, but they're not gone. They're with you, in your mind, in your heart. Does that make any sense? Have you ever lost someone close to you besides your brother?'

'Yes. Last year, I lost a mentor, the Duke of Newlyn, Richard Penlerick.'

'I heard of it.' Pen rose up to look at him. 'You were close to him?'

'Our families were close. My father was lifelong friends with him and he was like an uncle to me, a mentor. He encouraged me to travel, to pursue my dreams. I hear him sometimes in my head, telling me to go on, to not give up although I've done a terrible job of pursuing those dreams, of honouring his legacy.'

'Tell me your dreams. What are they? I want to hear every last one of them.' She smiled at him, a sundappled Circe in her yellow muslin and the temptation was great to lay all of his dreams at her feet, to see what she'd make of them, but the practical dreamer in him warned he could not risk it, not yet. Today had been perfect, he didn't dare tax that perfection any further.

He reached for her hand and kissed it. 'Perhaps I will tell you at Vauxhall with fireworks overhead.'

'I will hold you to that.'

'And I will hold you.' His arm tightened about her and he breathed her in, all vanilla and sunlight and daisies. Somehow, against the odds, he'd find a way to make this dream and the others come true.

Chapter Sixteen

The reception did not disappoint. The Gloucester Lodge gardens were beautifully lit, the scene of ladies and gentlemen strolling beneath the late-night glow serene as soft strains of summer music played in the background. Later, there would be a performance from the Life Guards band, but for now, all was a fairy land and she was part of it. Pen smiled as she looked about. When she thought of all that had happened since she'd come to London, she had to pinch herself.

'I can't believe it's all real,' she murmured to Cassian as they joined the promenade about the gardens. Most of all, she couldn't believe he was real.

It's too good to be true, whispered the unbelief in her head. *He wants something from Redruth and you're the key.*

'Believe it.' Cassian laughed, her enjoyment of the reception pleasing him.

'I'm not sure I dare for fear it will disappear. I'll wake up and discover it's all a dream.' She laughed up at him, but her words weren't entirely in jest. The last time she'd believed in him, he'd been snatched away without warning.

'Lord Trevethow!' A tall man with long dark hair drawn back called to them from beside a fountain where he stood with an elegant woman who nearly matched him in height. 'I thought I might find you here tonight.' The man's English was perfect, although his voice was tinted with an accent.

Cassian nodded the man's direction and ushered her over to make introductions. 'Prince Baklanov, Princess Klara, allow me to present Lady Penrose Prideaux. Lady Penrose, this is the esteemed Prince Nikolay Baklanov and his wife, Klara Baklanova. The Prince is lately of Kuban, formerly a captain in the Kubanian cavalry. Now he runs a riding academy in Leicester Square. His wife is the daughter of the Russian ambassador to Britain.'

'I'm pleased to meet you, Your Royal Highnesses.' Pen managed a curtsy, feeling overwhelmed. Of course a prince and a princess were just sitting here out in the open. It simply added to the magic of the night.

'Do you know of Kuban?' Princess Klara asked. 'Most people don't.'

'Yes, it's in the south of Russia. It seems very wild and magnificent.' Pen could see it in her mind on her maps where east met west along the border of the Ottoman Empire. She could picture the port at Ekaterinador and the long strip of the Kuban River running inland towards the capital.

'Magnificent. That is exactly the word for Kuban,'

Prince Nikolay said approvingly. 'Most call it desolate but they don't know any better. I like her, Trevethow.'

Cassian placed his hand over hers, his gaze sliding towards her, warm and adoring. 'I like her too.' Then he lowered his voice. 'How is Prince Shevchenko? I heard it was a near-run thing. An abominable business in Shoreham, I'm afraid.'

Nikolay nodded, all seriousness. 'He and his new bride are well away. They've sailed off into the sunset, quite literally, but his neck is intact and the officer in charge of the farce will be court-martialled.'

Pen didn't pretend to understand, but Cassian nodded his approval. 'I'll miss Shevchenko. He always had good vodka. You will, too, no doubt. There's only you left of the Russian Princes to do the diplomatic duty when called upon.' Cassian chuckled. 'I think every foreign prince in the city has been called upon to turn out tonight and the diplomatic corps as well.'

'Yes, the Foreign Office was insistent there be a Russian presence here tonight so that nothing looks underhanded,' Nikolay affirmed. There'd been great speculation in the newspapers about whether or not the Hawaiian King meant to seek British protection against a Russian attempt to establish a settlement in the islands.

Two other men, Sir Liam O'Casek and Lord Preston Worth with their wives, May and Beatrice, strolled over to join the group and introductions were exchanged before Cassian politely disengaged from the group, whispering to her, 'There are others I want you to meet before the royals arrive. My close friends, Inigo Vellanoweth, the Earl of Tintagel, and his father, the new Duke of Newlyn, Vennor Penlerick, and my parents.'

That particular group was gathered by a rose arbour near the French doors that led indoors, well positioned to be one of the early groups to meet the King. Pen hesitated as they approached. This was different than a chance meeting on the path. Meeting foreign royalty was exciting. Meeting Cassian's parents was daunting. She smoothed the skirts of her pale blue silk gown. Cassian squeezed her hand. 'You look fine. They will adore you, as I do.'

There was another round of introductions. Inigo Vellanoweth was dark and cynically enigmatic with a sharp wit. Vennor Penlerick was golden and charming. He used that charm like a shield, Pen thought, a shield to keep others at bay along with his grief. Not unlike Cassian. It was rather intriguing to watch the two of them together. She'd not thought of Cassian as having a shield. He was always easy to be with—he drew people in with that ease, and made it easy for others to talk to him.

Perhaps that ease was Cassian's shield. He was all dazzle and grand gestures; the theatre box, tonight's reception, the upcoming tickets to Vauxhall. But behind the glamour of his invitations, he seldom talked about himself. He had done so with Em, certainly. There'd been no risk in that. Em was a stranger who had no idea who he was. He could tell her anything he liked. But the picnic the other day had been the first time he'd shared anything deeply personal with her. She treasured that disclosure all the more for its rarity even while wishing there were more moments like that where the shield was down.

She could see where he got the easy charm from. Both of his parents were charismatic, both of them dark-haired and tall. His father had Cassian's strong, chiselled jaw and his mother, the amber eyes. The Truscotts were a handsome family. The group exchanged pleasantries until a gong announced the arrival of the Hawaiian court. 'Are you ready to see some more of the world?' Cassian whispered beside her as the Hawaiian King, King Kamehameha II, and his Queen, Kamamalu, entered the garden.

Pen's eyes went wide. They were spectacular, dressed in European-styled clothing, which only served to emphasise their majesty. Both of them had thick dark hair and skin, and both stood over six feet tall. Pen had never seen such a big woman before. And the King! He managed to make Cassian's usually intimidating height and breadth look merely average. Some of the newspapers had styled the Hawaiian court as savages come to town, but Pen saw none of that as the King moved from group to group, respectfully greeting dukes and diplomats. He stopped for a long moment with Wellington, sombrely nodding as the hero of Waterloo was introduced to him. He'd done his homework, Pen thought. He understood the import of Waterloo in this part of the world. Impressive.

The royal court approached their group and Pen felt giddy with excitement. She made her curtsy, and, to her surprise, Cassian gestured for two footmen to come forward with two long boxes. 'Lady Penrose has been teaching me about leis and the custom in the islands.' Cassian opened each box to reveal two fresh leis made of roses. 'Lady Penrose tells me the flora on the islands are used for the leis, so I present you leis made of English flora, to welcome you. There is nothing as English as the English rose.'

The King nodded his thanks and the Queen looked touched by the gesture, but no one moved for an awkward moment. Yes, the greeting! She'd read about it once and hoped she'd remembered it right. Pen took a deep breath, eager to avoid creating an international incident with a misstep, especially with the visit off to a difficult start as it was. Pen lifted the first lei from its box and stepped forward. She reached up and put it about the Queen's neck and kissed her cheek. The Queen beamed with pleasure and Pen knew she'd done well. She repeated the process with the King, who graciously bent down to accommodate her.

'*Mahalo,*' the King said. 'That's how we say thank you on the islands.' A little round of applause went up from the onlookers that had gathered, but what pleased Pen the most was the look of approval on Cassian's face.

The Life Guard Band's performance began soon afterwards and everyone drifted inside to take their seats, but Pen was loath to leave the garden. 'Can we stay out a bit longer?' she asked as Cassian made to usher her inside. 'I want to linger in this fairy land a few minutes more.' In truth, she wanted to linger with him. For all the magic the night had provided, nothing compared to the magic of being with Cassian, of having his hand at her back, his words whispered at her ear, the delight he took in introducing her to his friends. They hung back from the crowd, finding their way once more to the fountain where they'd met the Russian Prince. Pen sat at the edge and trailed her hand in the water.

'Thank you for tonight, Cassian. You promised to show me the world and you did. We didn't even have to leave London. Tonight I met a Russian prince and a Hawaiian king.'

'You saved the day with the leis.' Cassian rested a foot on the fountain's edge. 'I had no idea what to do.'

'You brought the leis. That was inspired. Thank you for that.' They'd been specially designed. He'd gone to some effort to see it done. It was further proof that he listened when she talked, that he remembered what she shared, that he made what was important to her important to him.

'We make a good team, Pen.' Cassian gave one of his easy laughs.

There was more she wanted to say, more she wanted to thank him for: for introducing her to his friends, for the chance to meet the Hawaiian royals, for *listening* to her, but Cassian was looking at her in that intent way of his with smoky amber eyes. 'Am I proving myself to you, Pen? That I am more than any man in the room?' His voice was low and intimate as his hand raised her chin up to meet his gaze. 'I have always wanted you as Em or Pen. It doesn't matter. They're both you. Tell me I have a chance? That we're building something new and strong between us here in London. The magic is real, Pen. Believe in it. Believe in me.'

'I do want to tell you that. But it's hard.' Maybe she'd lived with the fear so long it had begun to be part of her without her realising it? Her father's fear had worn off on her. 'Magic spells are often broken, Cassian. Magic comes with costs in all the tales. Everyone gives up something in order to have it, if only for a little while. I'm afraid of what I might have to give up.' But even now she was thinking whatever the cost might be, it would be worth it when he looked at her like that, like he saw the world in her eyes.

'I won't push you, Pen. Tell me when you're ready and I'll speak to your father. It's not the world's most romantic proposal, but perhaps it's the one you need.' Lack of romance aside, the words took her breath away. This man who would lay the world at her feet, who wanted to marry her, wanted to give her every one of her dreams. And yet, he was still a man with secrets, who hadn't shared any of his dreams with her.

The fountain made little splashes in the silence that rose between them. 'So soon? It's only been a couple of weeks and yet you are willing to make an extravagant offer.' An offer as extravagant as the entertainments he'd lavished on her.

'It's been nearly three months since St Piran's Day,' Cassian corrected.

'Do you think you know me well enough to spend for ever with me?' She hated herself for speaking the words, hated the doubt that surged in her despite the feelings she carried for him. How was it possible to care and to doubt at the same time? Most of all, she hated that she couldn't simply accept the miracle that had been given to her.

'Yes.' Lord, how she envied him his confidence. There wasn't a bone of doubt in that whole, hard-muscled body of his. He took her hand and drew her away from the fountain, into the shadows beyond the lantern lights. 'Let me show you how sure.' They were out of the light, at the fence that ran the garden's perimeter. He was kissing her, the hard wood of the fence at her back, and she was burning hot and fast for him. His kisses obliterated all reason. His hand was in her hair, another at her breast, her own hand slipping low between them to cup him through his trousers, to feel the hard, wanting length of him.

Whatever she doubted, she could not doubt this, that there was truth in his wanting. He desired her, his own desire as hot and as rampant as her own. But the stakes were different this time: they could not be anonymous lovers any more. He had said he'd not push her for a decision, but to make love with him now would give him every permission to push her. It would be implicit consent to marry.

Cassian's hand pushed up her skirts, his voice a hoarse rasp at her ear. 'I will not take you against a fence, but I would give us some pleasure tonight.'

'Yes,' she breathed, her teeth sinking into the tender lobe of his ear in her hunger. Then his hand was at her juncture, his fingers seeking her in the tangled thicket of her damp curls. She gasped when he found her, hot, slick at her core, the little nub at her centre throbbing for his touch. He stroked it with his thumb and she cried out as a trill of pleasure took her. She pressed her mouth to his shoulder as another wave took her.

'Let it go, Pen,' he counselled, his voice rough with his own desire, his hips moving against her thigh even as his hand moved against her. 'Scream all you want, no one can hear you except the moon.'

And she did. She arched her neck, turning her face skywards, and cried out her pleasure to the moon as release swept her. She was going to have to decide soon. But perhaps that decision was already made for her. How could she live without this? How dreary her world would become once more without him in it. Did she dare seize the happiness Cassian offered? Did she dare believe in the fairy tale and her very own happy ever after?

Chapter Seventeen

'She's a lovely girl, Cassian. When do you mean to tell her the truth?' his father asked over drinks at White's the next afternoon. They'd made a habit ever since Cassian had come of age to meet once a week during the Season for drinks and talking, catching up on news of the family and their friends.

'The truth?' Cassian prevaricated. 'That I'm crazy about her? I would think she already knows.' White's was still quiet. The late-afternoon crowd hadn't strolled in yet and they had the place to themselves.

His father gave him a hard stare. 'The truth about the land, that you need her acres.' His father tapped his finger on the tabletop in a disapproving tattoo. 'You have to tell her. She will feel betrayed if she discovers it after the fact.'

'She'll feel betrayed if I tell her now. All she wants is to be loved for herself. If she thinks the land prompted my suit, I will lose her.' The outcome was unthinkable.

His father studied him with hazel eyes. 'I've never

thought of you as a sly man, Cassian. Marrying her without full disclosure is dishonest.'

'It is necessary,' Cassian replied, not caring to have his motives questioned in such unforgiving terms. 'For the greater good. I must have that land.' But the rationale sounded more hollow these days than it had in the beginning. At what point was his happiness, Pen's happiness and a successful marriage built on honesty and trust worth more than the greater good? How much longer did it need to be sacrificed?

The duke took a swallow of brandy. 'Would you marry her without the land?'

'If I could, but that's not relevant because I need the land. I must marry for the land.'

'And not for love? Why?' His father would have made a fine barrister with his soul-piercing questions.

'You know why. For the gardens, to help those who lost their jobs when Collin's venture went under, because I promised Richard Penlerick to restore the Cornish economy. Because the dream demands it,' Cassian ground out.

'What if the dream becomes a nightmare, son? This dream of yours was noble and good at the start, and it might be again under the right conditions, but not now. Now, it is consuming you. That's not what Richard wanted. He would not want you to sacrifice love and personal happiness for this. Nor would he want you to commit to dishonesty. Many men have started down a dark path, thinking to do good, only to discover that they've lost their integrity along the way.'

Cassian stared into his glass. There was nothing

quite like being a man of thirty and being called on the carpet by your father. Yet he couldn't shake the notion his father might be right. When had he become the very monster he'd sought to protect himself from—the unscrupulous fortune hunter? 'Are you suggesting I give it up?' He raised his gaze to his father's, looking for clarity.

'If it comes to that, I would certainly consider it.'

'What about Collin? What about all those people?' Collin's death had devastated his parents; Collin the baby, the youngest of four children, dead at his own hand before the age of twenty-five.

His father shook his head. 'You cannot carry the blame for that. It was not only up to you to stop Collin. Perhaps we all should have been more vigilant. Any one of us could have stopped him and none of us did. He acted rashly, foolishly when he invested in Brenley's scheme. Yes, people lost their jobs. But he would not have wanted us to let our lives be defined by his mistakes. He's paid dearly enough for them.'

Cassian nodded. How differently his father dealt with regret than Redruth or even himself. He'd seen so much of his own reflection the other day when Pen had talked of her father's regrets; of wishing he could turn back time, that he'd stopped Collin. But perhaps his father had the right of it. No one could dictate another's choices. Redruth was trying to dictate Pen's choices. The man wanted to control everyone as a means of protecting them. All the while never seeing how that was hurting the people he loved.

'I worry for you boys,' his father said gently. By

boys, he meant Inigo and Vennor and himself. 'You're all so driven. It is a fine line between ambitions and vendettas. Vennor insists on pursuing his father's murderers even though the trail is cold. Inigo insists on finding justice against Brenley. And you insist on atoning for your brother's sins at the expense of your own happiness. Richard would not want that for any of you any more than I do.' His father looked at his watch and rose apologetically. 'I promised to meet your mother. But before I go, I want your word that you will you tell Lady Pen everything.'

'I might lose her,' Cassian warned again. His father's wisdom was sound, but it formed a pit in his stomach. He'd already lost her once.

'You might. But you will lose her for certain if you don't. It will just be a matter of when. What kind of marriage can you have without the truth between you from the start?'

Cassian hated it when his father was right. He was making Pen promises he could keep: a life of adventure, a life of passion. All of it was honest and true. Except for what he'd left out. Would she think his promises nothing more than barter for her acres? Would she once again think his compliments false when nothing could be further from the truth? He would tell her, but when? Perhaps it would be best to say nothing of the land until their relationship was more stable, where they could weather a storm, or at least a light squall, where the smallest of dents wouldn't destroy their hard-won trust in one another. Everything was so new and fresh between them, fragile like a baby. Cassian let out a breath. He would wait to tell her about the land, but perhaps he could start tonight with smaller truths to pave the way. There were other things he could share with her, things that might win her to his side so that when the time came for the land to be discussed, she would understand. Tonight, he would tell her about the park. Vauxhall would be the perfect setting.

Vauxhall dazzled from the first impression of the lights from the Thames as their wherry pulled alongside the stairs, to the concert and supper with the infamous thin-sliced ham. Pen couldn't stop gazing at all the marvels and there *were* marvels around every corner: paintings, lamps in trees, acrobats and fortune tellers.

'This is even better than the St Piran's Day fair,' she whispered to Cassian, careful for the others not to hear. If there was any imperfection on the evening it was that they weren't alone. Her father was there with Phin and her aunt. Cassian's friend, Inigo, was there along with Vennor Penlerick, who was escorting Miss Marianne Treleven and her sister, Ayleth, friends from home. It made for a merry party in the private supper pavilion Cassian had arranged, but it afforded little intimacy.

'Would you care for a stroll, Lady Penrose?' Cassian offered his arm, his eyes suggesting he'd read her thoughts. 'You haven't seen the paths yet and there's just time before the Cascade and the fireworks.' He courteously nodded to her father. 'We won't go far or be gone long, sir.' The other message was also clear. Company was not invited.

Once outside, Pen breathed deeply. 'The stars are even out tonight. They so rarely are in London. I must thank you for another magical evening.'

'You haven't seen the best yet.' Cassian steered them down a path lit with colourful gas lamps. There were others strolling as well, but they were alone in the conversation. Out here, they might talk about anything. 'There are still great things to come.'

'I think the lights are my favourite part. I can't imagine this many lights and yet here they are.'

'Twenty thousand of them,' Cassian supplied.

'Impossible. How do they light them all?' Pen argued in disbelief. 'I would need all night to light them.'

'Not by hand, I assure you.' Cassian laughed. 'They're lit by linked fuses.'

'Like daisy chains?' She smiled. 'This place is a fairy tale. I had no idea such a place could exist.' Her smile faded. 'I wonder if I will love Cornwall half as much when I return? I think it might be hard for Redruth to compete. I fear it will seem desolate.' It was already June. A month in London had slipped away, a month of freedom and she was starting to dread what that meant. Every day that passed was a day closer to returning to Castle Byerd and every day closer to making a decision on a suitor, committing to be passed from father to husband. Cassian had already suggested he could make the decision an easy one, that he would offer for her.

She slid an unobserved look at Cassian's strong profile. Would it be so bad if that husband was Cassian? Could the fun of being with him be enough to overlook

that he'd come wife-hunting despite having declared
love for Em just weeks earlier? If she had to marry
one of *them*, one of the *ton*'s titled gentlemen—why
not choose him? Her father would be happy. She could
imagine his face now when she walked into his study
and announced she'd accepted Viscount Trevethow.
And she would be happy, as long as she protected her
heart, as long as she didn't give it entirely, but kept
one small part for herself. That way, she couldn't be
hurt if her faith in Cassian proved misplaced. It would
be a worthy compromise and it might be the best she
could manage.

They stopped outside a small building to listen to the
Turkish band inside. 'It sounds exotic,' Pen said wist-
fully. She could imagine hot nights and harems in the
sounds, something straight from Arabian Nights. She
danced a couple of steps, rolling her hips, and halted,
self-conscious. A decent English girl didn't dance like
that.

'Why did you stop?' Cassian looked disappointed.

'It's music for veils, not skirts, I think.' Pen blushed.
'But never mind that. I've been waiting to be alone
with you all night. We have to finish our conversation
from the picnic. You promised to tell me your dream.'
She'd not forgotten despite the allure of Vauxhall. She'd
spent most of the evening trying to guess, running
through theories in her head. What did Cassian Truscott, a man who'd seen the world, a man with a title, a
man who would be a duke some day, dream of? What
was left to want?

It was his turn to be self-conscious, something she

would not have associated with this confident man if she hadn't seen it. They started to walk again, her hand tucked through his arm as if it had always belonged there. Then the words came. 'I want to bring Vauxhall to Cornwall.'

'You mean a pleasure garden at home?' She cocked her head to look at him with curiosity. 'What would it be like?'

'It would be exotic like the Turkish pavilion. There would be music from all over Europe and food, too, so people could hear and taste other cultures. Each pavilion could house a country, a culture. The Turkish pavilion would have music, carpets and mosaics, and robes. People could eat kebabs and *kofte*. In the evening there could be a show with Turkish dancers and fierce Turkish warriors with their curved swords. In the Russian pavilion there would be Cossacks with their trick riding.'

'Wherever would you find people who could do that?' Pen couldn't get her head around the logistics of acquiring people and supplies. The magnitude of the concept was bewildering, but exciting.

'It wouldn't be that hard. London has managed to find Turks for Vauxhall. Nikolay could help with the Cossacks.'

'It sounds wonderful. It would certainly bring entertainment and education to an isolated part of the world.' Pen was starting to see the vision, the dream. 'People who never leave home could experience the world.' What a gift that would be for those who couldn't travel, people like herself.

'We'd have amusements too.' Cassian was in his element now. He made an expansive gesture with his hand, encouraging her to imagine with him. 'I want to have a "mountain" like the one in Russia, a coaster. The problem with it is that it doesn't stop reliably. But I studied a model in France, the Russes à Belleville— it's a little cart you can sit in and it has a groove that's inserted into the track that guides it. It can go up hills, down hills, around corners, and at fast speeds so that there's some thrill to it.'

'Just to ride around a track?' Pen wasn't sure she saw the appeal that excited Cassian so much.

'A set could be designed. We could recreate mountain peaks: the Alps, the Matterhorn, Mont Blanc or the Dolomites. People could pretend they were coasting through those locales. It would be a reality fantasy.'

The Alps, the Dolomites, the Matterhorn.

The words were as seductive as the man, as the night alight with Vauxhall lamps. In her mind, she could see each peak, each range, on her maps. But the magic she was caught up in was all him. 'Maybe there could be a river and we could sail down the Nile and see the pyramids, or camels on the shore, or the Egyptian desert by moonlight.' She sighed and leaned her head against his shoulder.

'We could. We could have rivers and boats and a thousand adventures at our fingertips any time we wanted them.' Cassian whispered at her ear.

'When I was young, I had great plans to sail to China.' She laughed softly in the darkness.

'We'll bring China to Cornwall until you can go yourself,' he assured her. 'It's more than entertainment, though, Pen.' His tone was sombre. 'It's about jobs. Amusement gardens don't run themselves. Think of all the musicians and waiters Vauxhall employs, to say nothing of the gardeners and caretakers who manicure the grounds, or the set designers who paint the scenes and the pavilions, who create the fantasies we see tonight, and the acrobats. Admittedly, some of those jobs are very specialised and will need to come from outside Cornwall, but many of the jobs aren't. Gardeners, caretakers, waiters—all of those jobs can be filled by Cornishmen. They can make a decent wage, take care of their families without leaving home. And that's just the direct employment. People with inns, people who can supply the park with food, they'll all benefit too. People with carts to carry the food.'

'And it wouldn't be charity.' Pen was nearly as dazzled by the thought of employment as she was by the park itself. 'There is so much need. People are happy to work, but there are no jobs to be had.' The charity baskets she made weekly barely had an effect on families and what stop-gap they did provide was short-lived. But a project of this magnitude could create long-lasting change. 'I think you must build your park, Cassian. Whatever it takes,' she whispered, looking about her for the first time since he'd begun his impassioned dissertation. 'There are fewer lights here. You, sir, have taken me off the well-travelled path,' she scolded lightly.

'Because I wanted to do this.' Cassian's hands were in her hair, tilting her face up, his mouth on hers, and she welcomed him whole-heartedly. 'No night at Vauxhall is complete without a little seduction on the paths.'

'Hmm.' She licked her lips. 'I think I was seduced well before the dark paths.' She put her arms arounds his neck and let him dance her back to the trunk of a wide discreet tree, claiming more kisses as they went. She ought to be more careful, but tonight she didn't care. Tonight, she could pretend she was Em again at the fair, a woman with nothing to lose.

There was the famed Cascade at ten o'clock, a mechanical cataract that simulated a waterfall most artfully with a verisimilitude that made Pen applaud enthusiastically along with the Treleven girls who were equally amazed and, following that, the sky lit with fireworks in blue, green, red and violet while the band played Handel. Under the cover of the crowd, she was aware of Cassian's hands at her waist where no one could see, aware of the heat of him as her back brushed his chest. She looked over her shoulder at him, watching his face wreathed in enjoyment and contemplation. He was thinking of his park, his dream as he watched the fireworks and the sight of the determination on his face moved her, inspired her. 'I can hardly wait to see your amusement park,' she whispered with a smile. If there was any man who could bring such a thing to Cornwall, it would be him. If there was any man she could marry, it was him, as long as she was very careful not to fall in love with him completely, again.

* * *

'I told her about the amusement garden,' Cassian said carefully to Inigo over coffee and toast the next morning. Inigo had made it a habit of joining him for breakfast. Cassian didn't mind. He welcomed the company. It kept him from being alone too long with his thoughts—thoughts that ran almost exclusively to Pen these days.

'How did that go over?' Inigo enquired, buttering his toast and reaching for the marmalade.

'Very well. She liked the idea.' She'd more than liked it. She'd been impressed by it on all of its levels. She'd seen its potential. Her eyes had lit and in turn the sight of her excitement had lit something warm in Cassian. She could share his dream, they could be partners in it. Except for one thing. Cassian tapped his fork on the table distracted, barely hearing Inigo recount the action at White's.

'The betting book is exploding with speculation after last night. Everyone knows you took her to Vauxhall. Your courting of Redruth's daughter has outpaced even the public's fascination with the Hawaiian King.' Inigo lifted his coffee cup in a saluting toast. 'She's falling for you. You should be pleased. You'll have a wife and an ally.'

An ally. At last. But an unwitting ally to be used against her father when the time came. By the time she understood the dynamics, they'd be married and there would be little she could do except reconcile herself to it. The thought sat poorly with Cassian, even more so after last night. When he'd originally thought of courting Redruth's daughter, he'd not planned on falling in love with her, never imagined she'd be Em. The girl, whoever she might be, had been a means to an end, a sacrifice he'd make for the sake of his dreams. But now, Redruth's daughter was Pen, a woman he loved. A woman who could hurt him with her rejection, with her hatred if she turned against him.

'I didn't tell her about the land.' Cassian blurted out the words. There it was, the one thing that had eaten at him after he'd taken her family home last night. 'She doesn't know I need her land to do it.' His father would not be proud of his decision to hold that back.

Inigo considered this thoughtfully. 'Perhaps she wouldn't mind? If she favours the idea, perhaps she'll want to contribute the land as a partner, not as someone who felt she was courted for the sole purpose. If she trusts you, it shouldn't be an issue.'

That was the crux of the matter, the one thing that held Cassian back. *Did* she trust him? Had she overcome her earlier misgivings about him and his reasons for having sought out the earl's daughter? Had he proven himself worthy of her? Or when she heard what he wanted, would she think not only that he was no better than the other men begging for her attentions, but that he was worse because he'd betrayed her a second time? 'I can't tell her, not yet. We're not strong enough.' But the question remained: When? When would they be strong enough to let his secret out?

'Don't wait too long. Rumour is, Wilmington is displeased. He is looking to discredit you. I would hate for him to stumble across any evidence that might be made to look incriminating.'

'Understood. But there's nothing to worry over. The identity of the owners of the Porth Karrek Land Development Company is ironclad. There's nothing he can discover. I won't rush my fences for the likes of Wilmington. It's too soon, the relationship is too fresh. I want to dazzle her a little while longer.' But in truth, it was himself he wanted to dazzle. He wanted to bask in the fantasy that Pen loved him before he tested it with reality.

Chapter Eighteen

⸎

The Season became a whirlwind of one fantasy after another for Pen with Cassian by her side. The Hawaiian Royals invited them for a day touring the Exeter Exchange and the Royal National Menagerie topped off with an evening in the King's box at Drury Lane for a performance of *Rob Roy MacGregor*. Cassian took her to the British Museum to see the Elgin Marbles where they debated Elgin's right to have plundered them. He took her to the National Gallery, for drives and walks in the Park, he drove her to Epsom to watch the big horse, Cedric, win the Derby. They revisited the Enclosure and rowed on the Serpentine, Oscar howling from the bow. They attended a Riding Night at Prince Baklanov's equestrian school in Leicester Square. Cassian escorted her to balls and musicales without end.

June passed in a flurry of excitement of new activities and new acquaintances. Cassian had promised to show her the world and he had most spectacularly. She was dazzled by the experiences, but she was more dazzled by the man. He'd not only shown her the world, he'd shown her a glimpse of what their life could be together, of what they could build together. They could be partners. His dream slowly became her dream.

Together, they could bring entertainment and economic recovery to Cornwall, give the people an industry to rely on besides mining. Diversification was what the region needed more than anything. A region could not leave itself vulnerable to the caprices of sea-based industry or the industry of mines. Fish migration routes changed over time and mines played out. She could really live, really give meaning to her life through those projects with Cassian. There would be tangible results for her efforts. Pen fairly trembled with the prospect of possibility, it was that exciting to contemplate. But contemplating it required marriage. She had to decide. Cassian was waiting for her to give the word. She'd wanted the right to choose and he'd given her that too. But always, came the whisper of doubt: *What did he want?*

'You seem happy today,' Margery commented, fixing a comb in her hair. 'You've seemed happy for several weeks now, ever since the handsome young viscount has been squiring you about.'

'Yes.' Pen smiled in the mirror. 'He certainly knows how to keep a girl on her feet.'

'Or sweep her off them?' Margery enquired with an impish grin. 'Do you think he'll propose? Everyone downstairs is talking about it, if you don't mind me saying so. It's the most exciting thing that's happened in the household for ages.' She could hardly begrudge Margery and the others their own joy. It was a reminder that she was not the only one whose life had been changed when her mother had died. Her father's choices had affected everyone.

Margery held up a necklace for her approval. 'It's like we're an enchanted castle coming back to life after the spell has worn off. We're entertaining again, Cook is preparing teas and cakes and meals for more than just the three of you and the odd guest. Maids have a reason to polish the silver. *You* have a reason to wear beautiful clothes It's just wonderful, that's what it is, miss.' She made a little frown. 'I don't know how we'll manage to go back home after this. Everything will seem so ordinary.'

Hadn't she thought the same? Yet, she could change that. Cassian had made no secret of it. He was waiting for her. She would have thought *knowing* the outcome would have made things less tense. Instead, knowing had brought a tension of its own. The choice was hers and she wasn't ready to make it, not yet, although the case Cassian built for marriage was a strong one. Would what they could build together be enough to make a successful marriage? He cared for her, but he had never said he loved her. Was passion enough to sustain them in the absence of mutual love? The passion seemed assured, the latter did not. Cassian wanted her, but love and want were two different things.

What happened to them once the passion and the wanting waned, trampled by the wear of real life? What would be left? Would a common cause between them be enough? In some ways the dazzling display Cassian had laid at her feet didn't help the case, but obscured it. What would life be like after the promise of the Season was gone? Would that life be different, *better*, than what she'd have with any of the others? Or was he just a superior salesman? He had plans where others had platitudes. The questions chased themselves around in her head endlessly these days and she was no closer to an answer. Perhaps she never would be. Perhaps she just needed to take the leap.

'What shall you do today?' Margery moved to the wardrobe, laying out a hat and a light shawl to match her dress, a fetching white muslin sprigged with pink flowers.

'Lord Trevethow is taking me for ices at Gunter's.' It was one of her favourite things to do, to sit on the high seat of his phaeton and eat ices. It gave them a chance to talk, a chance to be private even in public and she was so desperate to speak with him today. It was just the outing she needed to clear her head and her heart.

The outing had gone wrong from the start. Cassian had not driven the phaeton after all, but had borrowed Inigo's carriage to squire not only her but the Treleven girls. The girls were pleasant and she enjoyed their company, but she wasn't in the mood for it. Soon, the outing would be over and she wouldn't have had a chance to speak with Cassian alone. She would not see him tonight. Her father had a long session in Parliament, Phin was out with friends and her aunt had suggested it would be good to rest for an evening, so they were spending it in.

Cassian shot her an enquiring look as he finished his chocolate ice—he had, she was not surprised to note, quite the sweet tooth. 'I am in need of stretching my legs. Lady Pen, would you care to accompany me?' It was not the most subtle of gestures. From the knowing smiles on their faces, Marianne and Ayleth were not fooled. Pen took his hand and let him help her down. 'I fear Gunter's has disappointed you,' Cassian said without preamble. 'You're out of sorts today.'

'No, I'm sorry if I haven't been good company.' She turned and faced him, let him see the need in her eyes. 'Is there some place where we can be alone? I need to speak with you. I had hoped to do so today.'

Cassian nodded, his whisky eyes darkening to agate with concern. 'It can be arranged if you're willing to take a little risk. Pen, are you all right?'

'I will be.' She managed a small smile and let him lead her back to the carriage.

They took the Treleven girls home and Cassian gave instructions to his driver, 'The Albany, please.' Pen swallowed hard. They were going to his rooms.

'Unless you'd rather talk here?' Cassian asked in the wake of her silence.

'No. What I need to discuss should be done privately.' She worried her lip. 'We won't be caught, will we?' Everyone knew the Albany had strict rules about women on the premises. Her reputation would be ruined. She'd have no choice but to marry Cassian then.

'We won't be caught. I know all the secret passages,' Cassian offered with a laugh, but Pen wasn't assured.

'You've done this before? Sneaking a girl into your

rooms?' The old worry surged. Of course he had. He was an experienced man of the world. A man who'd loved multiple women, a man who gave his heart to no one. Hadn't he told her as much?

'I'm no virgin, Pen, and you know it,' he scolded her. 'That doesn't mean I'm not capable of fidelity and feeling.' He directed the driver around back at the Albany. 'This is the best time of day. No one is back yet to change for the evening and the servants are all at tea.' He led her up a warren of staircases to the third floor and expeditiously ushered her into a set of plush rooms done in pale blue and cream, firmly locking the door behind them. 'We're safe now.' Under other circumstances, he might have winked or made a joke, but his tone was serious.

'These are nice rooms.' Pen commented, suddenly nervous. She had him alone and now she hadn't any idea where to start. Why did she make a habit of wishing for things she didn't want?

'They do well enough. I'm hardly here.' Cassian strode to the console and poured a drink. 'Would you like one? I can't offer you any tea, but perhaps a little brandy might help you relax?' He poured her one anyway. 'You've got me worried, Pen. You're as tight as a bowstring. Come, sit and tell me what's happened.'

She took the glass from him. Perhaps having something in her hands would help. 'June has happened. The Season is slipping away and I still don't know what you want with me, with Redruth's daughter.' She turned the tumbler about in her hands. 'But it must be extraordinarily important when I consider the lengths you've gone to, all the balls and outings, boxes at the opera and plays, Vauxhall, meeting royalty. You've laid the world at my feet. No man does that without hoping for something grand in return.'

'I do hope for something grand, Pen. I hope for *you*. I hope that one day, you will tell me you are ready for my proposal. I promised you I wouldn't push and I haven't.' No, but he'd certainly persuaded. Dear lord, when he looked at her like that, like she could be the sum of his world, it was hard to remember caution.

Cassian took a long swallow of his drink. 'I am willing to dance to your tune, Pen. I know what marriage means to you and I know what I want.'

Her. He wanted her. He could make it no plainer. She'd never been courted so forwardly, so bluntly before. Not that she'd been courted a lot in any way, but she'd grown used to the suitors like Wadesbridge who went through her father, or the young men at the at-homes and on her dance cards who couched their affections in metaphors and clichés, who never spoke to her directly, fearing to upset her sensibilities.

Pen ventured a sip of the brandy, letting it burn clarity all the way to her stomach. 'You are the most single-minded man I've ever met. Why me, Cassian? Why do you want me? Why do you want Redruth's daughter?'

This was the moment of truth. But which truth? 'I've never met anyone like you, your spirit for adventure, your passion for living. Your tenacity to live by your convictions. Whether you've been Em or Lady Penrose, those things have remained constant.' That was the higher truth, the one that transcended all others. He would want *her* even without her thirty-two acres.

She blushed. 'You do know how to flatter a girl.'

'Does the girl believe me?' he whispered softly, his mouth at her ear, kissing the soft space between her ear and neck. 'I've done my best to be worthy of her. She's very stubborn.'

Pen tilted her head, giving him full access to the length of her neck and he took it, sweeping aside her hair with one hand. 'Is the girl beautiful?' She sighed as he kissed her neck, her throat where her pulse beat fast beneath his mouth. 'You didn't mention that in all your flattery.'

His own voice was husky with mounting desire. 'She is more than beautiful, more than the sum of her physical features.' His mouth moved to other side of her neck, laving it with equal attention. Their game of questions had evolved to something more dangerous, something that exposed them both at their cores. They were testing deep waters.

'Do you love her?' The question should not have surprised him. Hadn't everything been leading to this?

'I want her, body and soul,' Cassian whispered the words against her skin.

'It's not the same,' came the whispered reply.

'It is the same,' he replied hoarsely. 'Does the girl love *me*?' Pen's arms were about his neck, her body pressed close to him of her own accord, her own heart racing against his chest, her green eyes dark.

'The girl wants you, body and soul.' She kissed him hard on the mouth, fervent and hungry. 'I don't want to ask any more questions, I don't want any more answers. I just want you. Today. No matter how this ends.'

There was desperation in that hunger. Cassian ought to heed it—he was the one with experience here. He knew the pitfalls as well as the pleasures of giving in to the moment. 'There's only one way this ends, Pen. This is not the cottage.'

'It ends in your bed. I know.' She moved against his hips, against his hardness, making reason impossible for them both. How long had he wanted her like this?

'It doesn't just end in bed, Pen,' he cautioned. If he took her this would end in marriage. He was not in the habit of divesting virgins of their maidenhood and discarding them as a casual affair.

'It would have for Em. Bed would have been the end for Em.' She rose from the sofa. She undid the laces of her walking boots and tossed them away. She lifted a leg, resting her foot on the edge of the sofa. She wiggled her toes, her skirts falling back to reveal a length of silk stocking tied with a pink ribbon. 'Shall I untie them or shall you?'

'You.' Cassian's breath caught. Clothes were so much more erotic when they were about to come off. He set aside his glass, his eyes fixed on her as she undid the ribbons and rolled the stocking down. Did she have any idea what this was doing to him? This tantalising show of bare flesh and promise of more?

Stockings off, she lifted hands to her hair and pulled out the pins, one by one, until the rest of it fell. She looked innocent and wicked all at once, her hair falling forward and loose like a schoolgirl's, but her eyes blazed like a woman who knew what she wanted. 'You'll have to help me with the rest.' Her tongue licked her lips in invitation. 'I can't manage the gown alone.'

Temptation whispered between them: *come undress me, come touch me, come be with me as you wanted to be in the meadow on the heath, naked, skin to skin.*

Cassian went to her, working her laces loose, pushing her dress from her shoulders, her chemise, her stays, all discarded until his mouth could feast on bare skin, until he could hold her naked against him, soft buttocks to his hard groin, filling his hands with her breasts, each caress bringing pleasure to them both. His thumbs ran across her nipples and she gave a mewl of delight at the sensation.

He moved his hand lower to her curls, intent on bringing her pleasure as they stood. She covered his hand with her own and turned in his arms. 'Not until you're naked, too,' she whispered against his lips, her hands working his cravat loose and unwinding it. 'Whoever said women wore too many clothes never undressed a man. Cravat, coat, waistcoat, shirt, boots, breeches. There are so many layers between me and the man I want.'

'Be thankful I don't wear smalls.' Cassian laughed against her mouth.

'You think to shock me,' she whispered in feigned horror. 'You forget, I already knew that. I've already held you in my hand, in my mouth, straight from your trousers.' Dear heavens, he'd spend far too soon if she continued talking like that. He was rock hard with wanting as it was.

'Pen,' Cassian replied in a voice that cracked from desire. 'Do you think you could hurry?'

'Waiting is the best part,' she teased, pushing down his trousers.

'No,' Cassian ground out, pulling his shirt over his head and tossing it into a corner. '*This* is the best part.' He drew her close and danced her through the room to the chamber beyond, the one with the bed. It was time for him to take charge of this seduction.

Chapter Nineteen

Pen disagreed. She rather thought that the best part was seeing Cassian Truscott entirely naked, all broad shoulders and muscle narrowing to a lean waist and long, hard legs. His was a body that clearly espoused the benefits of outdoor living. No London gentleman of her acquaintance had physique that even hinted at a body like that beneath their tailored clothes.

A moment later, she rethought her position. Maybe *this* was the best part—the way he pressed her back to the pillows and came up over her, covering her with the power of his big body. His walnut-dark hair fell forward, framing his face, giving him the look of a savage. A trill of excitement raced through her as his hands bracketed her head on either side, carrying his weight. She liked the thought of being his captive.

'What are you thinking, minx? You've the look of mischief about you.'

Pen licked her lips. 'I never noticed how long your

hair was.' It wasn't a blatant lie…she had been thinking that too.

'Hmm…' Cassian teased. 'Somehow I doubt that's all that was going on in your head.'

Pen wiggled beneath him. 'I was thinking that I wouldn't mind being your captive.'

Cassian gave low growl of a chuckle and reached for her wrists, drawing them above her head and shackling them with his hand. 'No more talk, captive.' He moved against her in blatant prelude of what was to come, hips to hips, his hardness to her softness, and her thighs opened of their own accord as if his being there was the most natural thing in the world. 'Are you sure, Pen?' he whispered hoarsely. It was a last bid for caution, for surety.

'Yes,' she breathed. At her core this was what she wanted no matter what happened afterwards, this was right. This was what they'd intended at the cottage, what would have happened had her father not taken her away so abruptly. It was as if fate had ordained they would be together. This had not been avoided, only delayed.

Pen felt his hand move between them, low at her entrance, his fingers testing, caressing, intimately, searching for readiness. Oh, he would find her ready enough. She was warm and she was wet, proof that her wanting was in more than words. She wrapped her arms about his neck, and breathed at his ear, 'Cassian, I want you.'

It was all the permission he needed to press forward, to press into her. 'Hold on to me, Pen,' he urged at her gasp, the pain of the breaching catching her by surprise. She felt him still, felt her body stretch to accommodate him so he could press on. Her body learned him as he moved, his pace like a gentle wave on the shore, surge and ebb, surge and ebb until he was there at her core, filling her completely, her body shaping around him until he was part of her.

He moved within her, and she gave an exclamation of wonderment. There was no more pain, just… pleasure. If pleasure felt like something, this was it. She looked up into his face, his eyes dark, his strong jaw set with the tension of passion restrained as he moved, evidence that desire was riding him hard, each thrust driving him towards pleasure's brink as much as it drove her. Wherever they were going, they were going together. She held him to her, with her arms about his neck, her legs about his waist like a vice as if she could lock him in place, keep him within her for ever. Her hips picked up the rhythm, joining him as his thrusts came harder, no more the long, languorous surge and ebb, but shorter, faster strokes full of exigence. They gave themselves over to the relentless urgency of them until they were there at pleasure's cliff, falling into warm abyss.

Pen knew, before she opened her eyes, she was in uncharted territory. This was not a place on her maps. She'd never known anything like it and she'd never find her way back on her own. This was a journey for two and perhaps not for just any two, but a journey specifically for her and Cassian and no other.

Pen opened her eyes slowly, savouring the idea of lying in bed, naked, in the middle of the day, with him. This might be the best part, watching Cassian sleep, his strong face in rare, relaxed repose. She reached for a sheet to wrap about herself and slipped from the bed. She was content to let him sleep, but her own mind was too awake for drowsing. There was too much to think about, to reflect on.

Pen padded out to the parlour, careful not to wake him. She wandered the small room, running her fingers over the small collection of books on the shelf. A person could tell a lot about another by the things they surrounded themselves with. He read books about travel, accounts of far-off places, not unlike herself. She had her atlases; he had his travelogues. The similarity made her smile. The only difference was that these books were sort of a remembrance for him, a way to recall the things he'd seen and done in person whereas, for her, the atlases were all she had. In the corner, leaning against the wall, was a leather cylinder, the kind used for storing rolled-up documents like maps. She left it for now, moving her tour around the room to the little machines scattered on empty spaces.

On a small table by the window sat a vertical wheel that rotated when the handle was turned, not unlike a miller's water wheel, only this one carried little people in its buckets. On the windowsill sat a brightly painted canopy under which a circle of painted porcelain horses could rotate. She picked up the piece, searching for the winding mechanism. Once found, Pen set it back down on the sill and watched the horses turn. They moved not only around the base, but up and down as well to a tinkly little tune. She understood what this and the wheel were; they were hopes for his pleasure garden, attractions he wanted to create for his guests just as Vauxhall had created the Cascade. Her lover was an ambitious man.

Her lover. She liked the sound of that. When she'd awoken this morning she'd not had a lover. But now, she did. Outside, beyond the window, it was still daylight, of course, although it seemed odd. More time should have passed considering the significance of what had happened. She'd made love with Cassian Truscott, lain naked in his bed. What did it mean? Anything? Everything? What did she want it to mean? Her little tour of his parlour had revealed so much to her about this man. He was clever and creative. The park he dreamed of was a work of the heart for him.

Her gaze returned to bookcase and the cylinder in the corner. This time, she didn't resist curiosity's lure. She picked it up and opened the lid, squinting to see inside. There were papers, long thick papers like the type maps were drawn on! Surely Cassian wouldn't mind if she looked. Pen took the tube to the table and carefully removed the rolled papers. She spread them on the table, anchoring each end with a paperweight. Oh, it was a map!

Pen studied it, her finger tracing the neat lettering beneath each object as she whispered each word out loud. Turkish pavilion, the Pavilion of Kuban, and there, right at the edge, overlooking the sea, was the word 'coaster'. Her breath caught as she realised what she was looking at. This was Cassian's Pleasure Garden, plotted out in minute detail. Seeing it on paper made it all the more real. He truly meant for this to happen. This was not an intangible dream, a theory.

She felt his eyes on her before she even looked up. She smiled and turned. Cassian was watching her, dressed in a paisley silk robe that hung open loose, teasing her with his nakedness. She breathed her approval, 'It's beautiful.'

She'd found it. He wasn't sure how he felt about that. Cassian crossed the room. 'You've been snooping, minx.' It was part-jest, part-scold. She'd helped herself to his secrets without asking. Perhaps he wouldn't mind if this particular secret didn't mean so much to them. This was the one that could break them and he didn't want to be broken, not yet, not after this afternoon, not when, in his mind, there was no going back.

Her admiring smile wavered. 'Do you mind? I didn't think you would.' He'd made her hesitant, doubtful of *them*. She'd thought they were closer than that. He hated himself for it. He'd worked so hard to earn her trust, her respect, her admiration, her love, and in a single sentence he'd managed to put a dent in it. Perhaps it was a sign of how fragile their relationship still was, how new. He'd been right when he'd told Inigo it was too soon to tell her, that he needed to wait for the right time and the time wasn't yet.

But if not now, then when?

His conscience poked at him. There would come a time when it was too late to tell her. There was such a possibility of waiting too long and that would be just as damaging as telling her too soon.

He wrapped his arms about her and drew her against him, nuzzling her neck. 'No, I don't mind.' It was only a small lie. What did it matter if she saw the map? He'd already told her about it. He was overreacting. His only excuse was that he knew just how close to the edge they skated on the issue. 'I haven't shared my grand design with very many people, that's all. I suppose I'm protective of it.'

And you, he thought. *I am protective of you and us and what we could have together if given the chance.*

She leaned her head back against him, unaware of the internal turmoil this moment caused him. Her smile was back. 'Did Richard Penlerick see it?'

'Yes.' His voice cracked on the word without warning. That she'd known to ask touched him to the core. She'd listened to him, deeply, not just to the story he'd shared, but she'd listened to how much Richard had meant to him.

She turned in his arms and took his face between her hands. 'Then why isn't it built? This is clearly not some wild imagining. You've travelled the world, studied parks and entertainments. You've put considerable time and energy into this, thinking about it, designing it. But not implementing it?'

Another moment of truth. He couldn't seem to get away from them. 'No land, at least not the right piece of land,' he added when it seemed she was going to correct him. Of course, the Dukedom of Hayle had land, but not the land he needed. 'I need centrally located land so I can maximise access to and for a labour force and for supplies as well, yet I need space around it for new businesses to develop, for those entrepreneurs who want to try their hand at innkeeping. The setting must be picturesque, a view worth leaving London for, something that shows Cornwall at its best. And,' he added to his lengthy list of requirements, 'I don't want to displace anyone. It defeats the purpose if we take land away from people, which rules out most of the Hayle holdings. I don't mean to dispossess our farmers and tenants.'

'You're very specific. Have you thought of building near Truro?'

'Yes, and I've discarded that idea since it's too far to help the people at home. The people in the Hayle environs won't be helped by a pleasure garden three hours away in Truro.'

She thought for a moment. 'I see your dilemma.' She ran her nails down his chest and he shivered delightfully. She moved against him, her hips brushing his groin in suggestion. 'Sometimes when I have a problem, I think about something else and, while I'm busy thinking about that something else, a solution presents itself. Perhaps we should think of solving a different problem.' He could think of several problems he was about to have very shortly.

'Like how to get you out of that sheet you're wearing,' Cassian growled playfully. 'I could spin you out of it, or I could lay you down and roll you out of it, or...'

'Or, I could just slip out of it.' Pen gave a single tug to the sheet and it fell to her feet, leaving her gloriously, deliciously naked, like Venus from the sea. There'd not been time before to really study her, he'd been too intent on the bedding, but there was time now, time to take in her breasts, high and firm and yet full enough to fill his hands, the flare of her hips, the caramel hair between her thighs. Oh, she was a delight to look upon and an even greater delight to bed in her eagerness and her curiosity.

'Come back to bed with me—' Cassian swept her up in his arms '—I like solving problems this way.' He settled her on the bed and drew her on top of him. 'Would you like the reins this time?'

'Can I?' Her eyes widened in excitement.

'Most definitely. I think, for the man, the sensation is even greater this way.' Cassian lifted her hips and helped her into position. She eased down his length and swept her hair over one shoulder, looking like the world's greatest temptress. She wriggled, testing the fit.

'I didn't know it could be this way.' She was suddenly shy as Cassian settled his hands at her hips. 'I didn't know people talked about lovemaking like this, as though it's not a duty, but a privilege, a feast for the senses.'

Cassian levered up on his elbows, careful not to dislodge her. 'It can be like this and better. It can be any way we want. In bed, we make our own rules.'

'I like the sound of that.' She pushed at his chest, knocking him back against the pillows. 'Do you know what else I like the sound of? You taking your pleasure and knowing I was the one to give it to you.' She began to move and Cassian was happy to oblige, pleased to make all the sounds she required.

He let the lovemaking exhaust him, drain him of all strength, of all thought, of all worry. He lived only in the abyss of climax where his body was capable of surviving only moment to moment. He didn't want to think beyond the now, didn't want to contemplate what happened next. Next was complicated. Now was not. Next had consequences, Now did not.

'Cassian—' her drowsy voice broke through his pleasant fog '—I was thinking.'

'You have the strength to think?' Cassian jested. 'I do not.' He played with her hair, idly sifting it through his fingers, his mind not fully functioning, not wanting to. He wanted to lie in this pleasant state for a while longer.

'A little.' Her head was nestled in the hollow of his shoulder and she shifted to look up at him. 'I have land that would be perfect for your gardens. It's part of my dowry. Thirty-two acres on the coast not far from Redruth.'

Cassian's fingers stilled, his mind forced into full awareness of the moment. He did not want to think about the damn land now. 'Is this a proposal, honey?' He tried to play it off with humour, but Pen was in earnest.

'No, you've already proposed. You said you were just waiting until I was ready. I am telling you, Cassian, that I am ready. Propose to me. Go to my father and ask for my hand. I will say yes. We'll be married, we can lie abed all afternoon every day of the week and you'll have your land.'

'And what will you have in exchange, Pen?' Cassian rose up on one arm. Why was he arguing? Wasn't this what he wanted? His land was within reach and Pen was within reach. He wouldn't even have to tell her about the land, about why he'd been courting Redruth's daughter specifically. She was giving it voluntarily—she was his partner in all of this. He hadn't needed to seduce it out of her after all. There needn't be any trickery. It could not have worked out better. So why did he feel dirty? 'You don't think it's too fast any more?' he hedged.

'It's been over a month since my debut, we've been together almost every day since then and, in truth, we've known each other longer than that, just as you said,' Pen insisted.

'But what about your doubts regarding me?' Cassian pressed. He needed her to be sure.

'You said you came to London because there was nothing left to do but pursue your duty. I believe you.' Pen reached for his hand and laced her fingers through his. 'You proved yourself worthy. You've shown me the world and you've shown me what a life with you could be like. This is what I want, Cassian. You are what I want. Together, we are going to make a whole new world.' When she put it like that, they seemed unstoppable.

'Very well, then, Penrose Prideaux, will you do me the honour of becoming my wife?' It was too good to be true. Cassian didn't allow himself to think about the other end of that adage. When Pen whispered yes, tears shining in her eyes, and he rolled her beneath him in celebration, it was easier and much more pleasant to think that love had triumphed against the odds.

Chapter Twenty

Cassian was going to marry her! *Matthew* was going to marry her! What were the odds her true love was also an eligible suitor? 'It's perfect! It's like those stories where the girl kisses a frog and he turns into a prince. Only Matthew was never quite a frog.' Pen gushed to Margery the next morning. She felt giddy and silly. She could hardly contain herself. 'He's coming to talk to Father today. Father will be so pleased!' She grabbed Margery's hands and spun her around the bedroom. 'Just think, Father and I agreeing on a suitor! I would have thought that was impossible.'

Pen plopped down on the bed. 'Now, what shall I wear? The primrose? That gown reminds me of the sun and I feel all sunny inside.'

'I have yellow ribbon for your hair and your little heart charm too. Today would be the ideal time to wear it, a token of his affections.' Margery picked up a brush just as the sound of a carriage harness jangled outside.

'Is he here already?' Pen rushed to the window over-

looking the street. It was only eleven, too early for
a call, but perhaps he couldn't wait either. She was
sure she'd slept last night only out of sheer exhaustion.
Lovemaking, it turned out, was fine exercise.

Pen pulled back the curtain just enough to spy on the
street. It was not Cassian's bright blue phaeton parked
at the kerb. She shifted her gaze to the door, recognising the straight-backed posture and sombre clothing of
the man on the front step. Wilmington. He was an odd
visitor at an odd time—perhaps her father had Parliament business with him.

'Perhaps he wishes to propose too, miss,' Margery
suggested.

Pen dropped the curtain with a breezy confidence.
'He can propose all he likes. I will accept only Cassian.'

Half an hour later, there was a scratch at her door.
Margery opened it, exchanging hushed words with a
footman. Pen did not care for the look on her face when
her maid turned around. 'Miss, your father wishes to
speak to you in his office immediately. Your brother
is with him.'

Something was dreadfully wrong. Pen shifted her
gaze between her brother and her father and back again,
looking for a clue as to what, but all she received in return was the briefest shakes of a head from Phin. Her
father's face was stoic and blank. He was ashen with
restrained emotion. It took only a moment to realise he
was angry. Angry beyond words. She'd only seen him

this mad once before, when the news had come of her mother. 'Father, what's happened?' Pen took the one empty chair in the room.

'Viscount Trevethow has asked for an appointment this afternoon. I believe he wishes to discuss marriage. What do you say to that, daughter?'

Pen smiled—perhaps she'd misread the emotion. This should be pleasing news for him. 'I hope he does. I would welcome his proposal.'

Her father's hard gaze softened for the briefest instant, but with sorrow, not happiness. 'Then it is as I feared. We have been played falsely, you most of all, Penrose.'

'How so?' She furrowed her brow and glanced at Phin for clarity. He offered none. 'The Viscount and I are very much in love,' she tried to explain to them, to herself. How could falling in love mean being played falsely?

Her father shook his head. 'Trevethow does not love you. He would have courted you if you'd been an old crone. I have it on authority from Wilmington this morning that Trevethow is only after your dowry.'

'Nonsense, he has wealth of his own. He'll be a duke some day,' Pen argued. It was as if they were talking about a different man. 'You can't take Wilmington's word. He despises the viscount. Wilmington would say anything.'

'It's the land, Pen.' Phin spoke quietly from his corner. 'He wants the land to build a pleasure garden.'

'You misunderstand, I'm the one that told him about the land,' Pen countered hopefully. This was all a misunderstanding. She would put it straight, although she had to do it carefully.

'When?' her father asked.

'Yesterday, on the way home from Gunter's.' It wasn't technically a lie. They'd just made a stop by the Albany first.

'Yesterday? You're sure?' her father pressed her.

'Yes, absolutely.' Pen smiled, feeling confident this solved her father's riddle. But her father was more stoic than ever.

'Then it seems Wilmington is right.' Her father held out a pair of letters. 'Trevethow was after that land long before yesterday.'

Pen took the papers and read them. It was hard to focus with her pulse racing and her emotions high. She could barely comprehend the import of the words. 'This is a land development firm, the Porth Karrek Land Development Company. What does this have to do with me?'

'Read what they want to do with the land,' her father coached. 'And note the date.'

Her eyes scanned the top of the letter. 'This was written last autumn.' She read the letter, past the salutations and expressions of politeness. There it was, in the fourth paragraph after the request to buy the land— the desire to build a pleasure garden. She moved to the second page, her stomach tightening as her eyes moved over the arguments for the park: to boost the economy, to create jobs, to educate people—all the reasons Cassian had given her.

'It's the first letter.' Her father passed her a packet

of papers. 'If you like, you can read the subsequent correspondence. It will show that the Redruth estate rejected the first offer and the second. It will show that the development company doubled their offer and was refused. The last refusal was first of March.' Her father held her gaze with angry, weary eyes. 'I know you think your heart's engaged, Pen, that's why I'm showing you this. You don't have to believe me. Believe the proof.'

She set the letters in her lap. 'What is this proof of? That two people had an idea for an amusement garden? What does this have to do with Viscount Trevethow?' But she knew, as she said the words, that the coincidence was too great for it not to be connected. She just didn't know how.

'Pen, Viscount Trevethow and his father own the development company,' Phin explained.

The room spun. As pieces came together, her world slowly unravelled. She stared at the date on the last letter. Absolute refusal had been in March. Word fragments spun through her mind: *'There's a gentleman I wish to purchase something from... He is stubborn... he doesn't see all the good it could do...' 'It sounds like your gentleman and my father have much in common.'* They were one and the same. Her mind was reeling now. When Cassian had spoke of his problem, it was the problem of acquiring land for his pleasure garden. Why hadn't she seen it sooner?

Cassian's first outing of the Season had been her debut ball in May. The society columns had remarked upon it. Dear Lord, he'd come straight after her, whoever she might have been, knowing that marriage was the only way he was going to get that land. Pen swallowed hard. Now she knew what it was he'd wanted so badly. He'd been after her land all along.

Oh, he'd been relentless and crafty. He'd not even mentioned the pleasure gardens until she was well and duly impressed with him, besotted with a man who laid the world at her feet and overcome her resistance in the most spectacular of ways, all the time knowing what he wanted in exchange for his efforts: thirty-two acres on the coast.

She'd made it easy. He hadn't even had to trick her out of the acres. She had offered them to him yesterday, in his bed, thinking she'd come up with the perfect solution, that it was all her idea. Her throat tightened. This was her nightmare come true. Her worries from the start had come to life: that Cassian or Matthew—the distinction hardly mattered—was nothing but a flirt, who would say whatever was required to get what he wanted. In this case, he'd not wanted her, but the land. She just happened to come with it. No, that couldn't be right, that couldn't be all there was to it. She couldn't accept that it had all been a lie. 'He loves me. He wants to marry me.' Pen made the feeble argument.

'He wants to marry you, that's true. But not for love.' Her father was stern. 'At least we know before it's too late. Imagine how much worse this would have been if you'd actually wed him.'

Pen shook her head. 'There is room for love and land, Father. He loves me. I know it. The land is just an extra benefit.' But the sun was going out of the day, her happiness turning to grey doubt. He had come straight from Em to court a girl he'd never seen with the intent to marry her. She'd accused him of it that night at the ball. He'd denied it, but it was exactly what he'd done. Had he truly only courted her for the land, had he not loved her at all? Had he not fallen for her? She thought of yesterday. She'd given him everything. Had it meant nothing? Just a means to an end? Had he meant to compromise her in case he failed to persuade her to marry him legitimately? Pen pressed her hands to her stomach. She wanted to be sick at the thought of such treachery. No, she couldn't give in to such belief. She knew better. She had to fight.

'I don't believe it and I don't think you should either. You should talk to the viscount and hear it from him.' Pen pushed on, frantic to make sense of this turn of events. 'What's so wrong with marrying for love *and* land?' She was desperate now. 'You picked Trevethow yourself, Father. In May you were over the moon about the prospect of me becoming a duchess. I invested in him, emotionally, and now that I've decided on a man I wanted to marry, you are pulling him away.' Pen lowered her voice, determined to not become hysterical. She played her ace. 'You said I could come to London to find a suitor. Well, I have. I choose Trevethow.'

'And I refuse to sanction the union.' Her father's answer was sharp, cold and fast. He hadn't even taken a moment to think. The speed of his answer rendered Pen temporarily speechless. That had been her ace and he'd trumped her without hesitation.

'Father, I choose him,' she repeated dumbly.

'My daughter will not marry a man who seeks to so blatantly mislead her about his intentions. It is one thing to arrange an alliance through marriage, as long as both parties understand that's what it is. It is another thing entirely to feign affection and deceive a young girl with no experience in the world, who was susceptible enough to fall for the first man who showered her with attentions.'

Pen's temper flared and she rose. 'That is not what happened. I am not a young girl. I am twenty-one years old and I am not naive. I might have lived behind castle walls, but I am not ignorant of how the world works.' Tears stung and this time she could not stop them. 'How dare you think I am too stupid to not know the difference between love and cheap flattery. Mother raised me better than that.'

'You leave your mother out of this.' Her father rose, too, bracing his hands on the desk. 'I have had the task of keeping you safe for the last ten years and I will not falter in that duty now. Your marriage to a bounder like Trevethow would disgrace her memory. That's the end of it. We are going home tomorrow. I've already instructed Margery to pack your things.'

'No!' This was Em and Matthew all over again—she was being pulled from Cassian. Would he think she'd changed her mind? Would he think she didn't love him? 'I won't go.' Not until she heard from his lips he didn't love her, that he'd used her. Only then would she believe it had been a lie.

'You will go. We are going home where it's safe. There's measles at the Royal Military Asylum. The

Hawaiian court has come down with them, including the King, and there's been talk of a strange vigilante walking the streets at night, meting out justice as he sees fit. These are not conditions I want you exposed to. Besides, Wadesbridge has written once more, expressing his continued interest in marriage. I will accept the offer on your behalf. You'll be settled with a decent man close to home who won't break your heart.' He smiled, trying to soften the blow. 'I know it seems disappointing now, but in a few months you'll see this was the right decision. We'll have a grand wedding at Trescowe among the autumn leaves and you can wear your mother's wedding dress. It will be the biggest party Cornwall will have ever seen.' He was trying to placate her. This time it wouldn't work.

'Pen,' Phin said, trying to make peace. 'Trevethow isn't honourable.'

She shook her head. 'Please, Phin. Don't. You can't make this better. Not this time.' She gathered her skirts and her dignity and left the room. She would not let them see her cry. She would save those tears for when she reached the safety of her room and hope that at some point she would be able to stop. She doubted it. Her heart was breaking, shattering into a thousand pieces. She'd been betrayed not by one man today, but three and all of them claimed to love her. If that was love, she wanted nothing to do with it.

The hall clock at White's chimed three. Redruth was late, but that did not dim Cassian's spirits, nor had the request that they move their meeting to the club

as opposed to Redruth's town house. He was going
to marry Pen. He'd meet Redruth at the tailor's if that
was what it took.

'You're cheery today.' Inigo sauntered over and took
a chair. 'What's the reason?'

'I'm asking for Pen's hand. Redruth is meeting me.'
Cassian kept his voice low, well aware of how the news
would affect the betting book.

'He's meeting you here?' Inigo was surprised.
'That's rather public for him.'

'It's how he wanted it, but he's late.' Pen had been
'late' once, too, and she'd never come. He was starting
to wonder if it was a family trait.

'Well, then, congratulations are in order.' Inigo
waved for a waiter. 'We'll have an anticipatory drink
while we wait and I'll tell you all my news. All anyone
wants to talk about aside from your courtship is the
Hawaiian King with the measles and the vigilante—
apparently this week hasn't been the first time he's
struck, merely the first time someone has put all the
pieces together. Interesting, don't you think? A man
who goes about dealing out justice on his own?' Inigo
took his drink from the tray. 'Cheers, my friend.'

'Is it any different than what we do? Eaton with his
school, me with the pleasure garden, you with your
loans and investments, all of which are guided by the
principle of making Cornwall better? This man apparently wants to make London better, one night at a time.'
Cassian mused, one eye on the door. Any moment, Redruth would walk in. A group entered and Cassian's
nerves eased only to tighten again. It wasn't Redruth,

merely Wilmington and his cronies. Wilmington gave him a sardonic nod as he passed.

'We don't wear masks.' Inigo chuckled at the analogy. He jerked his head towards Wilmington's group by the window. 'What was that all about?'

'I don't know. He's been angry over Pen for weeks.' Cassian smiled and looked beyond his friend's shoulder. 'You'll have to excuse me, Inigo, Redruth is here.' At last. Only a half hour late.

Inigo clapped him on the shoulder. 'Good luck, then. I'll be over there reading my newspapers if you need me.'

Cassian motioned the earl over and summoned refreshments, playing the consummate host in his little part of the club. 'French brandy is your drink, I believe.' Cassian shook the earl's hand. 'It's good to see you. Thank you for coming.' Although by rights, the earl ought to be the one thanking him for making this accommodation.

The earl was taciturn as he took his seat, ignoring the offer of brandy. 'This won't take long.'

Chapter Twenty-One

An odd little chill crept through Cassian. The earl wasn't known for his social graces: he ought not be unnerved. Still, 'things' were starting to add up: wanting to meet outside his home, a desire to make the meeting brief, no apology for being late, the refusal to drink with him.

Cassian opted to plunge in. Clearly, the earl was no lover of small talk, and probably not a lover of sentiment. 'As you are aware, your daughter and I have become quite close during the time we've spent together. I have developed an affection for her and I believe she's developed one for me.' That was an understatement based on yesterday afternoon. 'One that has led me to want to ask for her hand in marriage and make her my duchess.'

Sharp green eyes with dagger tips met his gaze. This was not the look of a man who welcomed a proposal for his daughter. He'd seen that welcoming look just weeks ago. Something had changed. 'I am well aware where your affections lie, Trevethow. They are not with my daughter as much as they are with her land and your damnable amusement garden. I will no more consider your suit for her hand than I did your land company's offer for the land.' He ground out the last words.

'I'm sure I don't understand,' Cassian replied coldly. He was frozen inside, paralysed by the revelation as his mind grappled to make sense of it. Redruth knew. How could he have known? But, more importantly, Redruth did not believe his feelings for Pen were genuine. 'Your daughter discussed the land with me yesterday. She voluntarily suggested it as a site.'

'After you turned her head with opera boxes, nights at the theatre and weeks of dancing dazzling attendance on her. She is not worldly, Trevethow. You took advantage of her. You did not tell her you deliberately targeted her for her dowry.'

'She is more worldly than you think. I mean that as a compliment, sir. She is a fine woman, intelligent, thoughtful and kind. You underestimate her.' Cassian kept his voice low. People were starting to look, to wonder. It had been bad enough to know eyes had been on them covertly since Redruth had walked in. This was the meeting the *ton* had been waiting for since the Redruth ball. To have it take place in public was a gossip's dream come true. Cassian had no doubts stories of this would regale dinner tables around London tonight. He'd been jilted just like his brother.

'She is not for you. I do not want that land in your hands, bringing all nature of strangers to Cornwall. You will corrupt our part of the world. You will bring

strangers and strange ideas, and violence and crime.
Tell me, is Vauxhall a safe venue? You cannot do it.
Women are assaulted there…cutpurses roam the paths.
It will be the same for you. The venture will fail to produce the results you want. I will not give my daughter
to that. Let me be clear. Your association with her is at
an end. We will not welcome you at Byerd House or at
the Castle. Good day.'

Redruth rose and Cassian rose with him, letting his
height remind the slighter man that he was a peer, too,
that he could not be dismissed so callously. 'Who told
you about the land company?' Cassian asked, barely
keeping his emotions leashed.

Redruth gave a brief nod in Wilmington's direction.
'A better man than you.'

Cassian wondered when White's had last seen a
brawl. He was going to kill Wilmington. At the moment, Cassian did not mean that metaphorically. A duel
suited him. The jealous prig had deliberately set out to
ruin him and in the attempt the man had managed to
ruin Pen too. Certainly Cassian was seething for what
amounted to Wilmington ratting him out on the land
company like a snotty-nosed schoolboy playing teach-
er's pet, but he was positively livid over what Wilmington had done to Pen and the man didn't even realise it
although the bastard professed to care for her, to have
her best interests at heart.

He could imagine too well the despair Pen must
have felt when her father told her. Redruth would not
have spared her feelings, would not have sugar-coated
what he thought was the truth, that his daughter had

been misled by an experienced man of the world all for the sake of her property. It would have triggered all of Pen's old doubts about him, all of her fears about marriage. Pen, with her broken heart, thinking he didn't love her, that he had never loved her, that he'd taken her to bed to force her hand if it came to that.

That beautiful afternoon seemed dishonourable in the aftermath. Now Pen was ruined, her heart broken, her trust in him shattered, her maidenhead gone, given to a man her father forbade her to marry. Cassian only hoped that was all, that their afternoon hadn't left her with a child. He was regretting not taking precautions now. He'd been so sure of himself, of *them*, or he wouldn't have done it. All that surety was gone now. Across the room, Wilmington looked his direction with a triumphant smirk. He knew exactly what had transpired. That did it. Cassian was out of his chair and striding across the room. Wilmington was going to pay for what he'd done to him, but most of all for what he'd done to Pen.

Inigo met him halfway across the room, blocking his way with a hand on his chest and low-voiced counsel. 'Don't do it, Cass.'

'Do what?' Cassian growled.

'Stir up more trouble. You cannot brawl in here. Remember yourself. You are a duke's son. You outrank that *pissant* in every way.'

'This is about Pen, about what he's done to her.' He tried to push past Inigo, but Inigo stood his ground.

'Cass, you cannot brawl in here and you can't duel out there. Duelling is illegal.'

'No one will convict me, assuming I'm caught,' Cassian growled.

'Assuming you aren't *killed*. Cassian, think!'

'By Wilmington? I will not be killed by that rat.'

'Listen to me, you're angry. You're not thinking straight. Let's go somewhere else for a drink and talk it through. You can't duel a man for telling the truth. He didn't tell Redruth lies. Wilmington is a symptom of the problem, he's not the problem. What do you solve by duelling him?'

Cassian heaved a sigh, reason asserting its slow tentacles.

'Let's go back to my rooms,' Inigo suggested, 'it's quiet there.'

It was too quiet at Inigo's rooms off Jermyn Street. Cassian could hear himself think and he had only one thought. He'd lost Pen. The more he thought it, the more devastating the concept became. He hadn't just lost the land. In fact, he barely thought of the land. He'd lost *her*: her trust, her affection, her laughter, her stories, her passion for living. 'I had a second chance with her and I failed. She will hate me for ever.' Cassian slumped in his chair, his drink untouched. Not even Inigo's excellent brandy could tempt him. 'My father was right. I should have told her about the land.' He'd misjudged everything. He'd tried to take the easy way out.

'Give her the night to calm down. Go over tomorrow and ask to see her,' Inigo counselled. 'If you love her, you can't let Redruth be the one who decides this.

Perhaps a show of strength on your part will persuade the earl you love his daughter.'

'He'll refuse me. He told me as much this afternoon. I am not welcome.'

'Then get a note to Pen. She'll be worried sick over you just as you are worried over her. Do not let Redruth keep you apart.'

His friend was trying hard to alleviate his suffering with solutions. But no solution would matter if Pen had given up on him, if Pen believed what he felt for her was all a lie, a strategy to get at the land. Cassian managed a small grin of appreciation. 'Thanks, Inigo.'

'For what?'

'For not letting me punch Wilmington in the face, or call him out or make a scene. There was scene enough as it was.'

'That's what friends are for. Now, why don't you come with me to the Treleven monthly musicale? Vennor will be there and it will take your mind off things. I don't want you sitting in a dark room brooding. You *will* see her tomorrow.'

That's exactly what he wanted to do: sit in his rooms and sulk, to give over to the pain of loss rocketing through him. He couldn't lose her, not now when he'd just won her back. Cassian barely suppressed a groan. 'Going out is the last thing I want to do, Inigo.'

'That's why it's the first thing you *should* do. Tonight, the best you can do is go out and show the gossips you aren't beaten. I'll send my man over to the Albany for your things. Remember, while they are all thinking this is the end, you know differently.'

He knew he was going to fight for Pen, for *them*, even if meant giving up the land. His father's wisdom came back to him. He could not let the dream consume him, blind him to what was truly important. This wasn't over.

It was truly over this time. Pen watched out the coach window as London gave way to dirt roads and countryside. Cassian had gone out last night. The early-morning papers had reported it just as they were leaving. Her aunt thought the papers would make good reading on the journey. Pen wished she hadn't seen them.

> *Viscount T. was spotted at Sir J. T.'s monthly musicale just hours after having a tense encounter with the Earl of R. at White's.*
> *Reports say Viscount T. and Lady P. are officially off.*
> *One might speculate that the Viscount is already hunting a replacement from among Sir J. T.'s many unmarried daughters.*

Good heavens, why didn't they just come out and say it? The column wasn't even trying to be discreet.

How could she have misjudged Cassian so badly? Twice? There was no one to talk to about it, not even Margery. She was riding with the other servants in the second carriage. Phin was out riding with her father and she certainly didn't want to talk to *him*. This was a mess of her father's making, of Wilmington's making.

Men. Wrecking her life again with their suppositions about what she wanted, what she needed and there was still Wadesbridge to contend with. Her father seemed more determined than ever to see that match happen now. She didn't want to marry Wadesbridge. She didn't want to marry anyone.

Not true, her heart reminded her. *You still want Cassian.* That was the beginning of a very dangerous game she played all the way until lunch. Would she still marry him, knowing all she knew now, if he pulled up beside this carriage and asked her to come with him? Would life with him be worth it? Would it resemble at least in part some of the glamour he'd displayed for her or was her father right? Once he had the land he would forget about her, see no reason to dazzle her and she would be forgotten, discarded.

Would it be worth it to defy her father in order to find out? It was an enormous risk, and a hypothetical one, given that they'd reached their lunch stop and there was no sign of Cassian, although there were plenty of reminders of him. The heath they stopped to lunch on was like the place the two of them had picnicked and where Oscar had played himself into exhaustion. She missed Oscar. Would she ever see her puppy again? The tears started. Better to cry out here on the heath alone where her family couldn't see than to hear once more how Cassian wasn't worth her tears.

She couldn't possibly explain to them the tears were for the fantasy, for what she'd *thought* they'd had. In the moment, that fantasy had been very real and, in it, she'd been real. She'd been alive. She'd given her heart, her body, her soul to it. When she was with Cassian she was alive for the first time. He made her laugh, made her think, made her feel. The world was brighter, she had purpose. Hadn't he felt the same? He'd claimed to. He'd told her about his brother, about his guilt over his brother's death. Those were not things idly shared. Which was why it was so difficult to believe Cassian didn't love her. Had he really shared those things just to get her land?

Pen sat down in the meadow and plucked a handful of daisies, playing a new game, a more dangerous game than the one she'd played in the carriage: if he'd been real, he wouldn't give up. If he loved her, he would come for her. Perhaps even now, he was at Byerd House, discovering that she'd left. He would know she'd gone home. In this way, things were better than when she'd left Cornwall. He hadn't known where to find her then. He did now. He could come. It was a rather awful test, though, a blunt one that would not allow her to hide from the truth. If it was true that if he loved her he would come, it had to also be true that if he didn't come, her father was right. He hadn't loved her, only the land, and he'd been willing to do and to say anything to acquire it.

She pulled a petal off the daisy. *If he loves me, he will come.* She pulled another petal. *If he loves me not...* Then he wouldn't. It was as simple as that.

Day one of the journey had passed with no sign of Cassian. Of course, Pen reasoned, he needed time to catch up with them. Day two had passed and she reasoned he couldn't possibly leave the city immediately. He'd have business to wrap up, farewells to make, plans to cancel. She had reasoned the same on day three and day four, and on into the full first week she was home. July was careening to a close, pleasantly warm for Cornwall, the sea impossibly blue from the cliffs of her thirty-two barren acres. Every time she stood there, she thought of Cassian's gardens, of his coaster speeding by and looking out over the water. It hadn't been just his dream. In the time they'd been together, it had become her dream as well.

Pen picked a daisy. *If he loves me, he will come. If he loves me not...*

He might come anyway.

The problem with such games was that they needed a statute of limitations. When the Season ended, Cassian would come home to Cornwall, but it wouldn't be because he loved her. It would be because it was simply time to come home. Her test would mean nothing then.

She tossed away the denuded flower. She was becoming a danger to daisies. Perhaps her game already meant nothing. She would have to give the game up soon and face reality. Wadesbridge was in earnest. He'd driven over with rose cuttings the day before. She was running out of reasons to resist. Why not marry him? If she couldn't have Cassian, what did it matter? At least Wadesbridge was no risk to her heart, yet that poor, shattered organ wasn't ready to give up yet. If she waited long enough, Cassian would come.

But to what end? To break her heart all over again, to make her face an unpleasant truth or to claim her as his own, to push away the last month of pain as nothing more than a misunderstanding fed out of proportion by a jealous Wilmington? She had to recognise that even if he did come, it didn't necessarily make everything magically better, it might just make it worse. She might have to find a way to live with a broken heart. But she'd never know if Cassian didn't come.

Chapter Twenty-Two

Cassian could not leave town. The Hawaiian King had the bad form to die, succumbing to the measles along with his wife, and requiring the pomp of lying in state at the Caledonian Hotel and then burial at the crypt at St Martin-in-the-Fields, a process that took the better part of a week. George IV insisted the *ton* turn out to honour their international guest, perhaps to make up in death for his poor form when they were alive. He never had received them, having put it off until the Hawaiian king had been too ill. There was no question of sneaking out of town even though the burial was temporary. The bones would be sent home eventually, but here he was, along with London's finest, respectfully laying the Hawaiian King's bones to rest.

Sitting in the pew, listening to the service, Cassian couldn't shake the irony that he was attending a funeral at the very place he'd hoped to be married. And how fitting it was. He'd felt dead since the morning he'd gone to Byerd House and found Pen gone. They were all gone, the knocker off the door and only a few servants left behind to manage closing the house. She'd left without warning, without a note, without any sort of goodbye. He couldn't blame her for it. She would be furious with him and, even if there'd been a scrap of forgiveness in her heart, she might not have had a choice. Her father held the reins, that much had been clear at White's.

He'd written, of course but his letters had been returned unopened. He had no guarantee she'd seen the letters or that the decision to return them had been hers. But there was no hope in that, only the certainty that each day that passed her anger and disappointment in him would be justified. She would think he'd simply moved on when she'd become too difficult of a prize to win.

Nothing could be further from the truth. He ached for her. He wanted to tell her about Kamehameha. She would grieve his passing: she'd genuinely liked the Hawaiian King and his wife. He wanted to tell her the stories going around about the vigilante, to share the news of the day with her. Or better yet, to walk along the shore at Karrek Sands, or sneak away to their cottage and make love all afternoon. Inigo nudged him. 'Whatever you're thinking, it's not appropriate for a funeral,' he said, half-joking. 'But,' he whispered, 'I am glad to see you smile.'

'I'm leaving for Cornwall the moment this service is over.'

'Regardless of your reception?'

'Yes. I have to know if there's any chance of winning her back.'

'And the land?' Inigo asked, earning a stern look for talking in church from Vennor on his other side.

'It doesn't matter without her. It's time to let the dream go. It's caused so many problems, it hardly seems like a dream any more.' It had changed him, and not in positive ways. He'd let himself be chained by the past. The dream had driven him, but it had not freed him. He was as captive to that dream as Redruth was to the memory of his wife. 'The only way to convince Pen, to convince her father that I court her for love, is to give the land up.' If he were to surrender any claim to it, perhaps there was a chance. That was the only plan he had. He was going to ride to Cornwall, walk into Castle Byerd and declare his suit.

'And your dream?' Inigo asked.

'It's as dead as the King. Pen's my dream now. I'll find another way to help the economy. I hope that wherever Richard Penlerick is, looking down on us, he understands the choice I had to make.'

Vennor reached across Inigo and gripped Cassian's hand. 'My father believed in love more.'

Cassian hoped Pen believed in love. He was gambling that Pen also believed in third chances. He'd chosen love, now he hoped in the end love would choose him, that it wasn't too late.

The end was near. The end of her father's patience. The end of her freedom. The end of her hope. Her game of waiting for Cassian was nearly over. She sat on the stone bench by the fountain in the walled gardens of Castle Byerd, the ever-loyal Wadesbridge beside her, birds chirping, water gurgling, her heart sinking as he sank to one knee in front of her.

No, not now. One more day, perhaps. Sometimes one more day made a difference. Although her wishes were pointless. She'd known this was coming. Her father had informed her it was time to move on. She'd had nearly a month to set aside her feelings for Cassian, to come to grips with his duplicity. He'd warned her, too, that Wadesbridge was coming today. He'd brought more rose cuttings from Trescowe and he'd been closeted away with her father most of the afternoon.

'My dearest Penrose,' he began. 'It cannot have escaped your attention that I hold you in great esteem.' No, it couldn't have. He couldn't have been more obvious. Or more caring or doting. Why couldn't she like him? He was a nice man. He was not the villain here. There was no villain unless one counted Cassian, which her father surely did. There were just people who all wanted different things. Her father wanted her safe and married. She wanted her freedom. Wadesbridge wanted to marry her, but she wanted to marry Cassian. As to what Cassian wanted, she couldn't be sure. Had he wanted only the land? Was that why he hadn't come? Or had something else detained him? Did he think she'd didn't want him now?

'Will you do me the honour of becoming my wife?' Wadesbridge had reached the critical point in his proposal, a jolting reminder of how real things were. She'd come to the point of no return. She had to make a decision. He pressed her hand. 'I won't pretend to think I'm the man you want. I'm older, quieter, I lived a more reserved life than your London beaux. But I can make a good life for you. We can have a family—I'm not so old that I don't want that as well. You will want for nothing.'

Nothing except passion, excitement, freedom. But perhaps these things were overrated. Just look what had happened when she'd embraced them. What did she have to show? A broken heart, disappointment. She had to stop living in the fantasy and *for* the fantasy. Cassian wasn't here. He had not come and she had to move on. She could do worse than Wadesbridge. If she accepted him the search would be over, her father would be pleased and in time, perhaps, she would find contentment. She did not think she'd find more than that, but perhaps it would be enough. Perhaps it would be the first necessary step in setting Cassian aside. How long could she cling to hope before it became ridiculous? Before she let go of a good man for a fiction of a romance that hadn't truly existed except in her mind. She had to accept someone. Why not Wadesbridge?

Her voice trembled. He would think it was from maidenly nerves. 'You do me a great honour. I would be pleased to accept.'

Wadesbridge smiled, relieved. 'Shall I tell your father? What would you prefer for an engagement? I was thinking of two months, with a harvest wedding in October. It will give me time to make the house presentable for a lady, or would you like to do that? Perhaps what I really mean is that it would give you time to make the house ready.' He laughed nervously, eager to please her, and she thought once more what a shame it was that she didn't love him.

'Whatever you prefer is fine with me.' Now that the decision was made, she was numb. She had no stake in this fight. There was no fight, not any longer. There was nothing to fight for.

The French doors opened on to the garden and her father strode towards them, a rare smile on his face. 'Do you have news to share?'

Wadesbridge smiled at her before addressing her father. 'We do. Penrose has consented to be my wife. I am the happiest man alive.'

Her father shook Wadesbridge's hand and hugged her, his joy over the decision evident. 'We shall celebrate tonight at dinner. There will be champagne and perhaps Cook can find something sweet for dessert. We shall make a party of it.'

Pen managed a smile. 'If you would both excuse me, I'd like to take a walk before dinner.' If she was to begin as she meant to go on, there was something she needed to do first.

'Just around the castle grounds,' her father warned with an eye to the sky. 'There's likely to be rain by supper.'

'Just around the grounds.' It was an outright lie. Pen fully meant to venture beyond Castle Byerd. She grabbed a shawl and stuffed her glass heart into a small drawstring bag. She didn't have much time.

* * *

The cottage was just as she remembered it. Even
prepared as she was to face memories, the familiar
space assaulted her senses the moment she opened the
door: the lingering scent of the lavender she'd brought
that last day, the ashes in the hearth, the thin quilt on
the bed. Every space contained a memory: eating meat
pies before the fire, watching Cassian build that fire
in the rainy days of spring, later, lying together on the
bed, whispering dreams to life. By the window stood
the table, still covered with the faded cloth, a chipped
vase holding the now-brittle sprigs of lavender. She
squinted. Something was propped against the vase.

Pen went to the table and picked it up. For a moment her heart raced. Had Cassian been here? Had he
come back? Was he trying to reach her? She unfolded
the note and scanned the letter, her hopes fading. It
had been written in April after she'd left. He wasn't
here. Not now.

Pen sat down on one of the chairs, reading slowly.
It was the only letter she had from him.

Dearest Em,

That seemed ages ago—when they were simply Em
and Matthew.

*Whoever you are, wherever you are, know that
you carry my love.*
 *I have gone to London to do my duty, but my
heart remains here with you in this cottage.*

The tears started and she let them come. She would cry one last time for all she'd lost. He had told the truth then, that first night at the ball. Matthew had loved Em. That was some consolation. Maybe Cassian had even loved Pen by extension. If so, why hadn't he come? Why hadn't he sent word? Or for that matter, why hadn't he told her of the land from the start when he'd realized who she was that first night in London? How different things might have been then. But he hadn't even tried to fight and now it was too late. She might never know. Pen left the note on the table and put her glass heart next to it. The cottage would be their shrine. She would leave her heart along with his. It was better this way, better that she leave it behind instead of torturing herself with the remembrance every day. She had to let go of them both—Matthew and Cassian. She couldn't keep one and not the other.

At the door, she paused. 'Goodbye, Matthew.' Perhaps some day when she was stronger, when there was more nostalgia than hurt associated with this time, she would come back to the cottage and remember. For now, she had to go home. She had her engagement party to attend.

He was nearly home. Cassian had ridden hard, taking advantage of dry roads and good weather all the way from London. It looked as if that was about to come to an end, though. Rain was imminent, and probably more. It appeared they were due for a summer storm. He pulled his hat tight on his head and spurred his horse forward for one last push. Hayle wasn't far, but that wasn't his final destination tonight. He would make for Redruth and Castle Byerd. He didn't want to waste another moment. Enough time had been lost. Never mind that he'd be travel sore and road weary when he arrived. There was one stop he did have to make, though. He'd pass the cottage. He wanted the note he'd left. He wanted it as proof that his heart had always been true.

At the cut-off towards the cliffs, he turned his horse from the road and jogged down the dirt path until the cottage came into sight. On the horizon, a fork of lightning split the sky far out to sea. He had time until the storm arrived in full. Inside, he strode to the table and stopped short. His note lay open and Pen's glass heart beside it. She'd been here! He picked up the heart, running his thumb over its smooth surface, wondering. Had she left it as a sign? Had she left it as goodbye? Was she trying to purge herself of their association or was she leaving him a message? He had a hundred questions, but beneath them there was hope. She'd come here because she hadn't forgotten.

His mind raced. What if she came back? He should leave a sign as well. Cassian ran outside, a fat raindrop catching him on the nose. He picked a handful of wildflowers and grabbed his canteen from his saddle. Indoors once more, he laid aside the lavender, poured fresh water into the chipped vase and arranged his wildflowers as best he could. If she came again, she'd understand. He stuffed the note and the heart into the pocket of his jacket and set off for Castle Byerd. With luck, he could return them both to her tonight.

* * *

He was soaked and dripping by the time he arrived at the Castle. The rain had begun in earnest. He tossed the reins to a groom and strode up the wide steps to the door. He thumped hard to be sure he was heard over the storm and had his foot ready when the door was answered.

'What do you want?' The footman passed a jaundiced eye over his dripping form. In the distance, thunder clapped. The storm was arriving in force. Cassian raised his voice.

'I am Lord Trevethow from Hayle. I wish to speak with the Earl of Redruth.'

'I am sorry, sir, the family is not receiving tonight.' Cassian got his foot in the door just in time.

'I don't think you heard me. I am Viscount Trevethow.'

'Let him in, but he won't be staying' came a low voice from behind the servant. The door opened wide enough to admit him, and Cassian stepped inside, unapologetically dripping water on the floor.

'Redruth, good evening.'

Redruth ignored the greeting. 'Did I not make myself plain? You will not be received here or in London.'

'Where is Pen? I have something to say to her and then, if she prefers not to receive me, I'll depart.' This was his boldest gambit yet. This would be the last chance in truth. But Pen had gone to the cottage. It had to mean something.

'She is unavailable at present.' Redruth met his gaze with a steely look of victory. 'Tonight, the family is privately celebrating her engagement to Lord Wades-bridge.'

'I want to see her.' Cassian was reeling. *Engaged?* Pen was engaged? This was not how it was supposed to happen. He'd ridden hard, she'd read the note. They were supposed to be reconciled.

The earl's smile widened without pity. 'You see, you and whatever you wished to say are too late.'

'Milord.' A voice spoke behind the earl.

'Yes?' Redruth snapped, not caring for the interruption. The maid behind him cowered nervously.

'Lady Penrose is not in her room, milord. We've looked for her everywhere. She's gone.'

'What do you mean, gone? Did she come back from her walk? She was on castle grounds. Did someone look in the gardens?' Redruth's attention was fixed on the maid, his brow creased with obvious worry. Regardless of his often abrupt manner, the man loved his children.

'Yes, milord. She came back, but when her maid went to dress her for dinner she was gone again.'

'Send for her maid,' the earl barked as thunder boomed directly overhead.

The maid recited her tale, her eyes drifting towards Cassian. 'She came back from her walk, milord, but she seemed sad. She asked for some time alone before dressing. She said she wanted to lie down. I left her for half an hour and when I came back she was gone.' Thunder rolled again and Cassian grew impatient. There was something the maid wasn't telling them.

'Was anything missing? Did she take anything from

the room?' This would indicate how 'gone' she really was.

The maid looked anxious, torn between protecting her mistress and doing her duty to her superiors. 'I don't know. Maybe.'

'That is not an answer!' Cassian growled. 'Lady Penrose may be in danger in that weather. This is no time to keep secrets. What was missing?'

The maid looked directly at him. 'A cloak and a dress she keeps for walking outdoors. Her jewellery. Her hairbrush. Just small things.'

'Thank you.' Cassian nodded. She'd gone out as Em and she'd taken portable items with her. Convertible items that could be turned into money. She didn't mean to come back. Cassian didn't wait for further instruction. He was already striding towards the door as the next thunderclap hit.

'Where do you think you're going?' the earl called after him.

'Out to find Pen. It's dark and wet out there—you'll need as many men as you can muster. This is the worst storm of the summer and the woman I love is out in it.' There was no time to lose. Cassian called for his horse, barely watered and still tacked. 'I'm sorry, old boy—' he swung up into the saddle '—but she's out there and she's going to need us.' He'd rather have his horse, tired as he was, under him in this weather than a fresh horse he didn't know. Ajax was sure-footed in the mud of Cornwall and solid. He didn't spook at thunder or lightning, and he was strong. He could carry two.

Cassian turned Ajax east and headed to the hills.

This was where he'd find her. The hills were her refuge. Hopefully, she'd found a cave for shelter. He didn't like thinking of her out in the weather, soaked to the skin, unable to see the ground. It would be too easy to turn an ankle, to fall. She could be lying in a ditch, unable to get out of the mud. He preferred to think of her in a cave sitting before a small fire, staying warm.

Cassian didn't get far. The hills proved to be almost impassable. There'd been a mudslide, the land giving way under the deluge, and piles of earthy debris made progress futile. He had to rethink his plan. If she couldn't go to the hills, where else would she turn? Surely she wouldn't have kept walking in this storm and she would not have taken refuge with other people if it could be helped. Anyone she stayed with would remember her, would tell her father she'd passed that way. It would be tantamount to giving herself up. He would not waste his time on the villages. Redruth and Wadesbridge would be searching there. It was the first place they'd look. It was possible she might be there. She might not have had a choice. But if she did have a choice, where would she go?

The cottage. She could have made it that far before the storm would have demanded she take shelter. What better shelter was there than the cottage? There was firewood, a bed and a roof that didn't leak. And it was away from the road. Cassian turned Ajax towards the sea and began to ride.

Hold on, Pen, I'm coming, was the litany that thundered in his mind. The cottage would be secure, but getting there was less so. Navigating the terrain in the dark would be difficult. he prayed she would be safe.

Pen pushed streaming hanks of hair back from her face and struggled to get her bearings. Was she still on the road? She should get off it. She'd be too easy to discover. The road and the villages were the first places her father would look once he mounted a search party. But to lose the road would risk losing her way. She had to go on. It was now or never. When she'd seen the dress laid out on the bed, the gown she'd wear to her engagement party, she'd known she couldn't go through with it. If she did, there would be no more choices. Her course would be set.

At the moment, however, that course wasn't set. She was still in charge of her fate. Pen could disappear. She could become Em one last time. Em could go any-where, be anything. Em couldn't disappoint her father, couldn't disappoint Wadesbridge. Em could roam the world. It wouldn't be easy and it wouldn't be safe. But perhaps she'd had enough of that. There was no time to plan, only to do. If she stopped to think, she might doubt and doubt would lead her back to Wadesbridge and the life that waited for her.

She wasn't sorry. Even in the pouring rain she didn't regret the decision, although she did regret the weather. She would have liked a dry sky and a lovely sunset to walk by. She was making no progress in this muck and her clothes were soaked. She needed to get dry. There was no sense escaping only to catch pneumonia her first night out. She was close to the cottage, though. She could shelter there and continue in the morning.

Pen turned off the road and cut through the meadow, not seeing the rabbit hole until she stepped in it. She went down hard with a yelp, her hands landing in mud, her ankle screaming with sudden pain.

It's not broken, it's not broken, she chanted under her breath as if the words could make it true. She pulled her foot out of the hole and gave it an experimental wiggle. It hurt, but she could move it. It was only sprained, or perhaps twisted. Still, getting off it was imperative, an imperative that was doubly difficult to satisfy now. A twisted ankle impeded her progress to the cottage significantly as she hobbled towards shelter.

By the time she reached the cottage, she was exhausted. If there was a condition beyond soaked, she was that too.

Inside the cottage, she set about the tasks of seeing to her needs. She lit the lamp and laid the fire, trying to remember how she'd seen Cassian do it. Cold, hurt and exhausted, the chores of preparing for the chore of taking care of herself seemed endless. She'd not realised how much work went into taking care of oneself.

With the fire going, Pen stripped out of her clothes and wrapped herself in the quilt from the bed. She dragged both chairs before the fire, laying her clothes over one and sitting at last in the other to see to her ankle. It was throbbing and swollen. It took enormous effort to pull her foot out of her boot. What could she do for it, though? She hadn't anything to wrap it in.

A bucket of cold rain water might help with swelling, but she didn't have a bucket. Even if she did, it would take time to fill.

She leaned her head back against the chair and closed her eyes. Her adventure was poorly planned and supplied. She had no medical supplies, no food, no spare clothes. She'd thought to buy those things once she got to Penzance, somewhere far enough away where her jewellery would not be recognised. She'd not accounted for any emergencies that might befall her before she reached her destination. Who would have thought an emergency would occur three miles from home?

It wasn't until she'd rested a bit and got her spirits back that she noticed the table. It looked different in the dim light of the cottage, or was that just the shadows playing tricks? She got up, using the chair as a make-shift crutch, and thumped her way over. She froze at what she saw. Someone had been here and not long ago. She'd just left the cottage hours before. But her glass heart was gone. The note was gone. She'd been foolish to leave them, thinking they'd be safe. The idea of a shrine had been fanciful and now her keepsakes were lost. She glanced around the room, her nerves on edge and what the missing keepsakes might mean. Had someone been watching the cottage? How would they have known to come and look around? Were they watching the cottage now?

Fear tickled her spine with a cold finger. What kind of a fight could she put up with a bad ankle and no weapon except for the poker by the fire? She supposed she could smash the vase and use a sharp shard like a knife. The vase. Her gaze went back to it. She noticed the lavender laid aside, dry and brittle. The flowers in the vase were new, fresh. Wildflowers from the meadow. Whoever had taken the keepsakes had picked the flowers.

Cassian. She breathed his name and fear released her, replaced by something more powerful: hope, ridiculous, irrational hope. Cassian had been here mere hours ago. Perhaps she had just missed him that afternoon. The question was, would he come again? Did she dare wait that long to find out? Pen trudged back to the fire with her chair crutch and sat down, eyes closed, weary with an odd sense of peace. Cassian was here, somewhere. The thought made her feel safe, safe enough to sleep.

She must have dozed. The pounding at the door woke her from her awkward sleep with a start. She gasped, half-startled, half-fearful. In her panic, she rose too quickly, forgetting about her ankle. She cried out as she fell.

'Pen! Is that you? Are you in there?' a voice hoarse from yelling called out. 'Can you raise the bolt? Can you open the door? Pen, it's me, Cassian. Let me in.'

Sweet relief swept her. Of all the people that could be on the other side of the door, that was the one she wanted. She levered herself up, grabbed her chair and made for the door. She was in his arms the moment it opened, ignoring the rain running from his clothes, ignoring the blanket that fell to the floor. She hadn't enough hands to hold him and the quilt too. Given the choice, she'd much rather hold him.

'Pen, thank goodness I found you. I was so worried. I went to the hills, but there were mudslides.' He was pressing kisses to her hair. 'You're hurt?' She stumbled against him, unable to keep her balance.

'My ankle. It's twisted.' She'd barely uttered the words before he'd swept her up in his arms and carried her to the bed.

'I like this, being met at the door by a naked woman,' he teased, setting her down and going back to retrieve the quilt.

'You should get undressed, too,' Pen said as he tucked the blanket around her.

Cassian arched his brow. 'Is that an invitation?'

Pen blushed, realising how it sounded. 'You're soaking wet. Lay your clothes by the fire. With luck, we'll both have something dry to wear by morning.'

He strode to the fire and began to strip out of his wet things. Even a perfunctory undressing was titillating when it came to Cassian. She couldn't take her eyes from him as his waterlogged coats came off and his sticky shirt was peeled from his body. But she could not let her thoughts stray in that direction, not until things were resolved. If they simply jumped back into bed with one another, nothing changed. She still wouldn't know where she stood with him. What was true? What was a game?

'Why didn't you come back sooner?' she asked the first necessary question. His hands stalled on the fall of his breeches.

'We are to play twenty questions, is that it, Pen?' It was softly said, kindly said.

'I'd rather play twenty answers, Cassian. I'm tired of having doubts about you, about us. Questions imply the existence of the unknown and there is too much of that between us.' She wanted surety, even if it hurt.

Cassian finished with his breeches and came to the bed, gloriously naked, distractingly so as he sat on the edge. He reached for her hands, the tenderness of the gesture unnerving her. It was the type of gesture one made when one had bad news to impart. She didn't want bad news. 'Then we will play the game, Pen, one last time and you can decide once and for all if I am worthy of you. First, let me tell you why I didn't come, why I couldn't come.' He paused, bracing her for his next words. 'The Hawaiian King has died, Pen, and his wife. When they sickened and there was a real possibility they wouldn't recover, it was impossible to leave the city. King George was adamant that, should it come to it, the *ton* must be on hand to give him the funeral he deserved. He was laid in state, his bones were laid in the crypt at St Martin-in-the-Fields. There was all the requisite pomp and ceremony. I couldn't leave. My father is gone from London at the moment. I had to represent the family and, as a new, close acquaintance to the Hawaiian King, George felt I should be there especially.' He sighed. 'Telling you now, it seems like such a little thing, a poor reason to leave your side, to not run to your rescue.'

Pen nodded. 'I understand.' She caressed his hands with her thumbs. It felt good to be touched by him again. She'd given up hope of feeling that touch. It would have been easy to give in to it, to let his body persuade her all was well between them. But his explanation didn't answer every question she had. She could not relent yet. 'You had your duty and we left suddenly.' If only they'd delayed their departure by a few hours, then her father, too, would have been forced to stay. She could have confronted Cassian personally. 'I'm glad you were there. He seemed like a nice man, a man interested in the world. It's too bad the world played him false.'

'His wife died first. After that, he seemed to lose the will to fight it. He had no immunity and no strength.' She felt the pressure of Cassian's grip tighten on her hands. The king's death had touched him. 'My friend, Eaton, had the measles when he was young. We almost lost him to them too. It's a powerful disease.'

'But you're here now,' Pen prompted. 'Why?'

'Can't you guess? I am here for you. I left London half an hour after the funeral and rode as hard as I could. I rode straight to Castle Byerd. I wanted to hear from your own lips that you were done with me. Your father was quick to tell me you were engaged to Wadesbridge, but it's hard to be engaged when one party has disappeared.' Cassian drew a deep breath that moved his chest. 'So, Pen, are you through with me? Will you give me a chance to explain? Or have you decided it's to be Wadesbridge?'

It was hard to think with that chest of his on such blatant display, but she had to think. This was about more than a handsome, half-naked man wanting to bed her and she him. This was about her future with a man she could trust. 'Tell me the truth, Cassian. Was it always about the land? Is that still what you're here for?' This was the only question that mattered and her heart was in her throat at the asking of it.

'You know it was not always about the land, not since the moment I saw you in London and realized you were Em.' He left her and crossed the room and retrieved his coat from the hearth. 'You saw the note I wrote.' He pulled the paper out, soggy at the edges and returned to her. 'You know I loved you before I met you in London. To see you that night at Byerd House and to know you were my beloved Em was like a miracle to me. In that one moment everything was perfect.' His knuckles skimmed her cheek. 'I should have told you sooner about the land, I was just too afraid I'd lose you. There was already so much doubt between us without that. Then, that day when you found my drawings for the park, I should have told you then, but you volunteered the land and I took the easy way out. I lost you over it. I will always wonder, if I'd told you sooner, would it have made a difference? Or would you have pushed me away? Would I have lost my chance altogether? You were not in a listening mood that night in London.'

He loved her. It had not been a lie. She could see it in the regret, in the pain, in his eyes and in the wanting, too, that was still there. How difficult their journey had been. Losing one another, then finding one another again, only to have her doubts keep them apart. He'd worked hard to overcome them, to make a space for them where he could tell her about the land without recrimination. He had almost succeeded if it had not been for Wilmington's disclosure. She was not going to be thwarted in love by a jealous man's trump.

Pen searched Cassian's face. 'Who says you've lost me?' she whispered. 'I've missed you every day since I've been back. I wondered why you didn't come. Was it that you didn't love me? That my father was right? I only said yes to Wadesbridge when I felt the best I could do was protect myself from being hurt again by putting myself beyond your reach, beyond love's reach. I said yes because I was out of hope.'

'Where there's love, Pen, there is always hope. Will you hope with me?' he whispered against her skin, pressing her back against the mattress.

'There is still my father to contend with. He was your stubborn gentleman, was he not? I figured it out when my father showed me the land company's letters.' She gave a soft laugh.

Cassian didn't chuckle. 'I am sorry for that. I would not have chosen for you to find out that way. When I thought of you hurting, of what you might be thinking, my heart broke anew. I would never choose to cause you pain in anyway, Pen.'

'It is in the past, now. All has been explained and forgiven.' She stroked his brow with a gentle hand, her own desire starting to heat, her body starting to burn. 'But my father must be considered. His resistance hasn't changed. He will not sanction the marriage. There is also still the issue of the land and the park.'

Cassian moved over her, his mouth brushing her lips. 'No, there isn't. He needs to know how much I love you, that I will do anything to have you, to be with you. The land is nothing. I will tell him tomorrow when I take you home. I will give it up for you.'

The announcement sucked the air from her. 'Cassian, I can't let you do that. You would come to hate me if I was the reason you lost your dream.'

'You are my dream now. Together, we can find another way to build the park.' He bracketed her head with his hands, his finger smoothing back her hair, his mouth kissing her softly. 'I wasn't sure I'd ever get to do this again with you, Pen.' His body moved gently, reverently against hers, letting her feel the press of his arousal. 'I had three long days on horseback to think about what I truly wanted and what I want is you, more than I want the amusement gardens, more than I've ever wanted anything in this world.'

'And I want you, Cassian. More than anything else in this world.' Enough to risk marriage, enough to risk her father's ire.

'You shall have me.' He took her then in a swift thrust of homecoming, and she gloried in it as he filled her, joined her. They were together now, their doubts set aside. As long as they stood together, it didn't matter what her father thought. She and Cassian would find a way.

Chapter Twenty-Three

The world was rosy after a night of storms, after a night of lovemaking. If only it could stay that way, Pen thought as they approached Castle Byerd. She sat before Cassian on Ajax, wrapped in Cassian's arms, held tight against his chest and between his thighs, last night's intimacy lingering. Her night had been far more pleasant than her father's. She had to remember that. While she'd been safe and dry in Cassian's embrace, her father had spent a restless, unfruitful night, searching for her. He would be worried beyond measure and reliving the horror of losing her mother all over again, thinking perhaps he'd lost her as well and under similar circumstances.

Guilt poked at her, marring the rosiness of the morning. She'd not meant to be cruel. She'd merely meant to live her own life. But she saw the cruelty in her decision now, the pain her choice would have brought him. 'My father will be angry.' She looked up at Cassian.

'He has every right to be, but we'll see it through,'

Cassian assured her. She wished she possessed his confidence. But Cassian had never seen her father mad.

In the stable yard, their appearance brought all activity to a halt. 'Someone fetch the earl!' a groom called out, issuing instructions. 'Someone help with the horse.' Hands reached up to help her down. Cassian dismounted behind her, issuing instructions of his own to take care of her ankle, which had been useless this morning. He'd carried her to the horse.

'My lady, come this way,' someone offered, but Pen refused, reaching for Cassian's arm. She didn't want to be separated from him, didn't want anyone ushering her away from the decisions that would be made. They were her decisions. She needed to be part of them, she needed to fight for them.

Her father appeared in the stable yard, drawn and pale from a sleepless night, Phin and Wadesbridge with him. Phin rushed to her and hugged her. 'I'm glad you're back.' To Cassian he said, 'Where did you find her?'

'Safe and mostly sound at the gamekeeper's cottage between Hayle and Redruth,' Cassian answered. 'She's twisted her ankle, nothing more.'

'Nothing more?' Redruth strode forward, all fuming, barely restrained anger. Pen squared her shoulders and felt Cassian's hand close around hers as the storm of her father's wrath broke. 'You're out the entire night with my daughter and you say nothing more? Step away from him, Pen. This blackguard has intentionally thought to compromise you.'

* * *

Cassian took a half step in front of Pen, just enough to shield her, not to hide her. She would not want to be hidden. She would want to be supported. 'I found her. She was in no condition to travel and the weather made travel more dangerous than staying in place. To return home would have risked our health and the horse's. Her ankle is proof enough of that. I appreciate that you spent a night in worry over her, but she is home now.'

'She is disgraced now! A night spent with a man?' Redruth sputtered.

'I fully intend to marry her, to renew the proposal I made in London.' He glanced at Wadesbridge apologetically. Wadesbridge was an innocent bystander caught up in the contretemps. 'I should think my proposal overrides any other offers on the table since I did make it first.'

Redruth scoffed. 'You were refused in London and now you think to compromise her, to give me no choice. This is exactly what you want.'

Cassian gave a dry laugh. 'I don't think this is about your choice, sir, but your daughter's. After all, I'm not proposing to you.' That brought a round of nervous laughter from the stable boys before they were glared into silence. 'Might we go inside? Perhaps more privacy would be appropriate for this discussion?' Cassian suggested. He could practically feel Pen's cheeks burning beside him and her hand was crushing his in its grip. He didn't want to make this fight harder for her than it had to be.

Redruth nodded and ushered them inside, Wadesbridge diplomatically declining to join them on the grounds that this was a family matter. It was the most minute of agreements, but it was a start. If they could agree on this, perhaps there were other things they would find agreement on. Phin poured out drinks while Cassian took up his position at the right shoulder of Pen's chair. 'My lord, we both agree we want what is best for Pen,' he said. If Redruth could realise they agreed on that, it would be a monumental step forward.

'And you think you're best for her?' Redruth was cool as he took a glass from Phin.

'I don't think that's my decision to make at all,' Cassian corrected. 'Or yours. Pen should decide what's best for her.'

'She should be guided in those decisions by the people who care for her the most.' Redruth did not back down.

'I have been,' Pen interrupted, reaching for Cassian's hand. 'Mama taught me to embrace life, not to fear it. I do not want to live my life behind walls. Last night, when I was out in the storm, I was frightened. I was soaked, I was hurt, I had no help to rely on except myself. It would have been easy to turn around. But while I was afraid of being out in the storm, I was more afraid of what would happen if I came back and committed myself to a marriage that would be lukewarm at best. Wadesbridge deserves better. I deserve better. You *and* Mama showed me that. You loved each other every day of your lives. I left because I couldn't live without that in my own marriage, nor could I live with your disappointment in me if I refused Wadesbridge.'

'Pen, you've never disappointed me. Challenged me, perhaps, but I love you. You can't disappoint me. We'll find you another husband. It doesn't have to be Wadesbridge.' It was the softest Cassian had ever seen Redruth. He squeezed Pen's hand, knowing how difficult this was for her. She had done her part, now it was time for him to do his.

'I want to be that husband. I believe Pen loves me and I love her. I would be here asking even if last night did not demand my honour required it. You know this to be true. You know I came to you in this very hall last evening to renew my proposal.' Cassian locked eyes with the earl.

'I want him, Father. He is my choice,' Pen offered in support.

Redruth shook his head. 'Any man but him, Pen. He only wants your land. That hasn't changed. He'll take that land and he'll corrupt it with his plans. I can't give my daughter to a man who only means to use her. He courted you with the intention to deceive me out of the land I'd refused him outright.'

'Then I give up the land. I renounce all claim to it and to her dowry in toto,' Cassian announced. 'I only want her.'

The interruption stymied Redruth. 'If this is a bluff, you will lose, Trevethow. I will not relent.'

'Neither will I. We'd prefer to have your blessing, but we will wed without it because that is the strength of my love for her.' There was satisfaction in seeing Redruth stunned, at a loss for words. Cassian seized the opportunity to press his case. 'With the issue of the land settled, there is no reason to reject my suit. I am a peer of the realm—I will inherit the Dukedom of Hayle in due time. My estate is not far from yours, so you will have plenty of opportunity to visit your daughter and your future grandchildren.'

Redruth's gaze went to his daughter, the last of his arguments refuted, leaving him no grounds for resistance, as Cassian had intended. 'You're sure, Pen? You have no doubts?'

'None.' Pen's single word filled the room, and Cassian's heart swelled.

'Then I suppose I cannot withhold my blessing.' It was as close as they'd get to the earl's approval. Cassian would take it. He understood a man had his pride and his limits.

'I'd like to wed as soon as possible.' Cassian knew he was pushing his luck. He'd just gained the man's permission and he was already making another demand of his father-in-law. But he'd been pushing his luck in other ways. Who knew—Redruth's grandchild might already be taking root. 'I want to marry as soon as I can get my family here and Pen can walk down the aisle.'

As soon as Pen could walk down the aisle turned out to be two weeks later in the middle of August. It might have been three weeks, if they'd chosen a larger church. But the aisle at the Castle Byerd chapel was short and Pen assured him she could manage. What she could not manage was another night without him in her bed. Cassian agreed. When a man has the rest of his life to enjoy the woman he loves in bed, he is determined to make the rest of his life start as soon as possible.

He waited impatiently for the rest of that life to start at the front of Byerd's stone chapel. The interior was cool inside, the altar simply decorated with a pristine white linen cloth and a vase of summer wildflowers. Pen had not wanted anything lavish and neither had he. In his opinion, the love between a man and a woman was a private matter for them to celebrate alone with their closest friends. To turn it into a circus cheapened it. The guest list was short but meaningful, limited to Pen's family and his. His parents sat in the front pew across from Phin and Pen's aunt. Behind his parents sat Inigo and his father, the Duke of Boscastle, followed by Eaton and his family—his wife, Eliza, and her daughter, Sophie—Eaton's father and mother with them. Behind them were Sir Jock Treleven and his wife along with their oldest daughter, Rosenwyn, her husband Cador Kitto and their new infant son born in March. Nearly all of Cassian's friends and mentors were there. Only Vennor was missing. But Cassian understood. When Ven was ready to celebrate life again, he would return to the fold.

At the corner of the altar, the five unmarried Treleven girls sat with bows poised to provide music. With a nod from the vicar, the girls began a beautiful rendition of a Vivaldi piece on their violins and cello. Cassian had chosen the piece as a remembrance of the night at the St Piran's Day fair and the Venetian glass-blower.

The heavy oak doors of the chapel opened and Cassian's heart began to pound. His bride was coming.

And she was there, standing in the doorway, framed by sunlight; an angel, a Madonna, *his*. Another perfect moment, the beginning of his life. Pen made her way down the short aisle, slow and dignified on her father's arm, dressed in her mother's wedding gown, a pale blue slip overlaid with an overskirt of white lace, a high waist like the ones worn at the turn of the century, a wide expanse of blue ribbon under her breasts, her mother's pearls at her neck, her mother's veil of old lace covering her hair. But at her wrist, tied in a blue ribbon to match, was the glass heart he'd given her that first night. Blue for truth. Blue for loyalty. She'd not worn gloves today, had insisted on it, in fact, saying she wanted to feel his hands when he held hers, skin to skin, in prelude for the night to come.

Pen reached the front, her father placed her hand in Cassian's and Cassian nodded his thanks. He knew what an effort this was for Redruth. In some ways, the earl was losing his daughter, setting her free into a world where he couldn't protect her. 'I'll take good care of her, sir,' Cassian said in low undertones as Redruth stepped away.

Eaton had told him he wouldn't remember any of the service, that it would all be a blur. Eaton was wrong. Cassian imprinted every moment of it on his mind: the way Pen looked as she took his hand, the way tears had glistened in her eyes as he'd said his vows, promising to worship her with his body, the tremulous smile on her face when he'd slipped the ring on her slender finger, the feel of her warm lips when he kissed her. He would remember all of it. Most of all, he'd remember the hope in her eyes when she looked at him. Together, they would dream new dreams, see new places and build a new world. Starting tomorrow. Tonight was to be spent in the gamekeeper's cottage and tomorrow they'd begin their honeymoon—a year-long affair of travel. He would take her to Italy, to Venice and Rome, they'd yacht the Mediterranean and see the Grand Bazaar of Istanbul and the great temples of Greece.

'This is the best day of my life,' he whispered as he led her down the aisle and out into the sunlight and the cheers of those assembled.

She laughed up at him. 'Only until the next one.' He drew her close and kissed her hard, much to the approval of the crowd. She was right. There would be other best days: the day she'd tell him she was expecting their first child, the day she had their first child, the day she told him she was expecting their second child, and their third and their fourth. There'd be every morning he woke up next to her and every night he went to bed beside her and those would be the best of days too. He had meant to show her the world, but, deep at his core, he knew that she'd been the one to show the world to him, a secret, private world of the heart.

He recalled the words she'd spoken to him that first day in the cottage. *'You are my adventure in the very best of ways.'* Yes. Every word of it was true.

Epilogue

Late summer, 1825

Cassian stood at the ship's rail, his arms wrapped about his wife as the Truro Quay came into view. They were home. Very shortly they'd be on Cornish soil after nearly a year away, a year spent on a travelling honeymoon, a year spent watching his wife's eyes light in joy at the wonders of Venice, of the Turkish bazaar. More than that, it had been a year of discovering love, a love that enabled him to forgive himself, to find peace with his brother's memory, to let go of dreams that had weighed him down instead of setting him free. He might not be building a pleasure garden, but he was more than that. He understood that now. That dream did not define him. He would find other ways to help promote economic recovery.

Pen looked up at him. 'Are you happy to be home?'

Cassian grinned. 'I've been home all year. I've been with you, haven't I? Wherever you are, that's where my home is.'

'I think it will be nice to sleep in one bed for a while.' Pen laughed. They waved to the figures on the dock, growing closer. Inigo was there, with his new bride, a veil covering her face. He'd sent word to one of the ports that he'd married. 'I wonder who she is? He was so mysterious not telling us.'

Cassian wasn't quite as interested in Inigo's new bride as he was in his wife. He was pleased to be home despite his comments. After all, he had responsibilities to see to and one could not rely on stewards for ever. But he would miss the rhythm of the road, of not having to share Pen with anyone. On the road his time was all hers. 'It was a grand adventure, though.' He nuzzled her ear with his mouth. 'We'll be unpacking our souvenirs for weeks.' His wife had proven to be an insatiable shopper and a shrewd bargainer. The hold of the ship was full of carpets and silks and gifts for everyone.

Pen turned in his arms, her smile coy. 'Some of the souvenirs might take longer than that, up to nine months even.'

It took him a moment to fully comprehend, but when he did, a broad smile took his mouth. 'You're pregnant? Are you sure?'

'Three months. I am pretty sure.' Pen smiled. 'Are you happy? It's not too soon? We won't be wandering again any time soon.'

'It's not too soon,' Cassian assured her. 'It looks like Inigo won't be the only one with a surprise to share.' He was counting backwards in his mind. Three months would mean Venice. They'd spent the spring there in a palazzo overlooking the Grand Canal.

'I think it was the night we took the gondola ride.' She laughed.

'That only narrows it down slightly. I have fond memories of many gondola rides. Too bad England doesn't have more canals.' Cassian kissed her, long and hard, as the anchor dropped. Pen had already given him so much: her love, her trust, his life back. And now, she was going to give him a child. He could want for nothing.

'I have something else for you.' Pen reached into the pocket of her travelling skirt for an envelope. 'I don't want you to be bored here at home, so I thought this might keep you busy.'

'What is it?' Cassian eyed his wife with mock suspicion as he unfolded the paper inside. His brow furrowed. It looked very legal. He read slowly, carefully, not daring to believe what his eyes saw.

'It's a deed for the land my father refused you,' she explained. He was aware of her eyes on him, of the hesitance in her voice. 'Do you like it? I thought it was what you wanted.'

'I do like it.' Cassian folded the deed and put it back in the envelope. He tucked it away with reverence, overwhelmed. She'd found a way. He was going to build his amusement garden. No, correction. *They* were going to build *their* amusement garden. He'd let that dream go willingly, and it had come back to him. 'But make no mistake, Pen. You are what I wanted always. I won't say that thirty-two acres of empty land between Redruth and Hayle doesn't excite me. But rest assured, nothing will excite me as much as my wife and thought of our child.' He took her face between his hands. 'How did you convince your father to re-lease the land?'

'Love works in mysterious ways.' Pen wrapped her arms about his waist. 'I told him you were worth it.'

'And he believed you?'

'Yes, but I think in the end it was you he believed, a man who would give up his dream for the sake of love. Your actions spoke to him far louder than any words ever could. You showed him love was worth fighting for.'

'Well, it is.' Cassian drew her close for a last kiss as the boat thumped against the pier, or maybe that was the thump of his heart. He was home and all of his dreams were within reach because one good woman was in his arms; because love had found a way.

* * * * *